Praise for *Girl Reading*

"*Girl Reading* is a vivid portrait of a timeless subject."

—*Minneapolis StarTribune*

"Fun and fleet-footed. Ms. Ward renders her settings in bright detail and shows her characters at captivating moments—the very traits that make genre interiors so appealing."

—*The Wall Street Journal*

"Hot Read: 'Seven scenes come together into one slide show . . . the best thing about this story is what's not told: silence, mystery, and what's outside the frame converge, showing that even the imagination can be—must be—limited. . . . The title is deceptive: the strength of this promising debut is not in "reading," but in "seeing."'"

—*The Daily Beast*

"Ward's sinuous language wraps around serious ideas concerning sex and love, freedom and power. . . . Throughout these stories' deceptively straightforward prose and pleasant surfaces, there's something here that reminds one of Katherine Mansfield's short fiction. It's exciting to imagine what she'll write next."

—*The Boston Globe*

"A luminously vulnerable debut novel. . . . Ward's characters are so utterly relatable that you'll feel you know them after a few sentences."

—Oprah.com

"Undoubtedly the work of a writer to watch."

—*Kirkus*

"We forget, often, that artifacts survive us, but survive they do, and that is one of the points that Katie Ward makes in her fascinating new novel, *Girl Reading*."

—*The Brooklyn Bugle*

"An exquisitely rendered celebration of women and reading in seven portraits."

—*Shelf Awareness*

"*Girl Reading*, with its intricately worked, wide-ranging scenarios, rewards the careful reader and would make a great book group selection, with plenty of latitude for discussion. It's an impressive, intelligent debut."

—*Barnes & Noble Review*

"A fascinating testament to the universal themes of art and literature and the spirit of femininity."

—*Bookpage*

"Ward's debut novel deftly weaves together seven beautifully crafted vignettes, each based on an actual painting or portrait of a girl or woman caught in the act of reading. The result is a kaleidoscopic rendering of intellectual women from the Renaissance to the present."

—*Ms. Magazine*

"One of the many astonishing things about this astonishing and novel first novel is that the author makes the reader an implicit character in the act of creation. . . . Engrossing!"

—*The Washington Independent Review of Books*

"Exquisitely written."

—*Daily Dose*, **Powell's Books blog**

"A debut of rare individuality and distinction. Katie Ward inhabits each of her seven eras with a fluent and intuitive touch, and sentence by sentence, deft and mercurial, she surpasses the reader's expectations. What is set down on the page has a rich and allusive hinterland, so that the reader's imagination has a space to work, and what is unsaid has its own fascination. The writing is alive with fresh and startling perceptions."

—**Hilary Mantel**

Girl Reading

A Novel

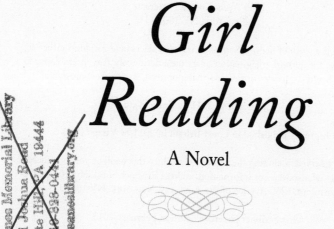

Katie Ward

Scribner

New York   London   Toronto   Sydney   New Delhi

SCRIBNER
A Division of Simon & Schuster, Inc.
1230 Avenue of the Americas
New York, NY 10020

For information about special discounts for bulk purchases,
please contact Simon & Schuster Special Sales at
1-866-506-1949 or business@simonandschuster.com.

The Simon & Schuster Speakers Bureau can bring authors to your live event. For more information or to book an event, contact the Simon & Schuster Speakers Bureau at 1-866-248-3049 or visit our website at www.simonspeakers.com.

Designed by Carla Jayne Jones

Manufactured in the United States of America

1 3 5 7 9 10 8 6 4 2

Library of Congress Control Number: 2011431843

ISBN 978-1-4516-5590-2
ISBN 978-1-4516-5732-6 (paperback)
ISBN 978-1-4516-5733-3 (ebook)

This is a book for David

Contents

Simone Martini
Annunciation, 1333
1

Pieter Janssens Elinga
Woman Reading, 1668
52

Angelica Kauffman
Portrait of a Lady, 1775
100

Featherstone of Piccadilly
Carte de Visite, 1864
146

Contents

Unknown
For Pleasure, 1916
189

Immaterialism
Reader in a Shoreditch Bar, 2008
234

Sincerity Yabuki
Sibil, 2060
290

A Note
339

Acknowledgments
341

You can never say with certainty whether what appears to be going on in the collective unconscious of a single individual is not also happening in other individuals or organisms or things or situations.

—C. G. Jung
"Synchronicity: An Acausal Connecting Principle"
(Collected Works, volume 8)

Simone Martini

Annunciation, 1333

S he arrives glowing from the effort of running, strands of red hair coming loose from her kerchief (she tucks them in), marks on her neck like bruises on fruit. A few minutes late but not enough for anyone to mention it. Is almost surprised to find herself in the wards once more amid illness and suffering (on an evening such as this). Her mind is elsewhere. She accepts a dish, a spoon, instructions to feed a patient who rasps with each breath, whose sores stink, who has for eyes one piercing brown bead and one sagging black hole. Familiar and strange, ordinary and violent.

She does not smile encouragingly at the invalid to finish her meal, does not add to the whispered hubbub of the stone halls. They labor together in silence. The crone chews and swallows slowly despite the impulse of her body to reject what it consumes; the girl holds the spoon out, withdraws it, rests it; the food on the plate scarcely diminishes. Candle flames are skittish in the draft, creating the impression of hasty movement.

The old woman speaks; the girl is roused from her private thoughts. Who are you?

My name is Laura Agnelli.

That is not what I asked.

A patient in a bed farther along screams with pain. There is a disturbance. Some run to her aid, some are disgusted and afraid to be close by.

Laura offers one last mouthful to her charge, wipes the remnants from her bluish lips. I am a daughter of Santa Maria della Scala hospital.

You are a foundling? What is your history?

I have none.

You have a name, though.

The rector himself named me Agnelli. It means "lamb." He is over there. Laura indicates, without pointing, Rettore Giovanni di Tese Tolomei, a man as wide as he is tall, his thumb tucked into his finery as he makes his inspection of the wards.

The woman swivels her eye toward him, then back to the girl. You were plucked from a crop of innocents by that man?

He showed me compassion because I was weak. He held me in his own arms and gave me his blessing, so I am told.

I am surprised he did not mistake you for a ham.

Laura frowns at the crone. He saved my life.

Did he?

And the lives of many foundlings, before and since.

But he bestowed his favor on *you*. It is not an honor I would wish for a daughter of mine.

The patient's pillow needs rearranging, the bedclothes have slipped down; Laura sets them right, noticing as she does so how cold are the limbs beneath.

The old woman winks her eye. What else do they tell you?

That it was Our Lady who inspired him. The rector heard me

2

crying, held me and foretold that I would take religious vows—and that one day, I would bring rewards to Santa Maria della Scala hospital and the whole city of Siena.

The woman raises her good eyebrow, exaggerating the unevenness of her face; Laura covers the marks on her neck, uneasy.

What do the other children make of it?

They never say.

How did you come to be called Laura? Did your mother call you this?

I know not.

Maybe when she could provide nothing else, she gave you this name—Laura—hoping you would like it?

Yes, you might be right.

She did what she thought was for the best, like all mothers who bring their babes here and turn them over to Signor Rettore. *Suffer little children to come unto me.* (The woman shuts her eye, while the other socket hangs open still.) Yes, I can see her perfectly, even though she is doing her best to hide. Her head is uncovered, she lets her hair hang about her shoulders like the fallen woman she is. Pitiful. But we should not be too harsh on her; it is only because she is using every fragment of cloth to keep the infant warm. She is giving it her blessing before she parts with it: *I hope you will be spared the pain I knew.* Is that all? Such a small request, for such a small wriggling bundle! And yet it is worth a dozen of Signor Rettore's grand pronouncements. She looks tired . . . poor thing has not slept in days. She should sleep now, I think.

Laura counts the lengthening spaces between the woman's breaths, stays by the bedside for many hours until it is over.

What pretty feet you have. Like two pigeons with their wings folded and their heads tucked in. Do you dance?

Not often. Not well. When there is music, and I am moved to.

I imagine you bouncing and bobbing like a wheat stalk in a breeze, and afterward I imagine you rosy and out of breath. What pretty knees you have too. There is no doubt about it, God intends you to be a bride. *My* bride.

You are making fun of me.

I would swear to it. Pretty legs. Where the heart goes, the body has to follow.

What did you say? What are you doing?

The magnificent cathedral is the envy of every city-state. It matches the ambitions of those who built it, and the saints themselves would nod their appreciation. The Duomo is absolutely Siena's, and Siena is absolutely the Virgin's. How they flourish under her protection.

A man stands before the high altar but he is not here for mass, and he has no awe in his heart. He is inspecting something he has seen hundreds of times before, his objectivity strained. Wealth does not impress him, for he is wealthier than most. Lavish decorations hold few surprises these days. His arms are folded across his chest like a farmer's, his gargoyle features contracted in a scowl; a short lump of a man. Were it not for the fine weave of his tunic, the opulence of its color, the ornate trim, he might be mistaken for a pilgrim or even a beggar. He senses a presence in this marvelous place (how it glitters, how it is still!) but it is no angel or deity: it is the laughing ghost of a man he knew extremely well in life.

The altarpiece is the *Maestà,* the enormous panel showing the Madonna and Child upon a throne, adored by a host of angels and saints. It is surrounded by smaller storytelling panels and drenched in gold. For the faithful, the *Maestà* is a channel to the Virgin: she sees out of those very eyes, hears their pleas through it. On the day it was installed in the Duomo, there was a procession led by the bishop, the priests and friars around the Campo, attended by the Nine, the entire Commune, the citizens of Siena. Resplendent, it passed through the crowds. Bells rang, alms were given to the poor, prayers were made to Our Lady, our advocate. It is Duccio's (old master, old rogue). Simone Martini snorts.

Simone Martini? I've heard of him! He was Duccio's pupil.

This is the best accolade he can hope for now. One wants to be trained by the greatest living artist, and then to transcend him. That will not happen.

Simone examines the icon, trying to see it as a peasant would, as a monk would, as a lord, a foreigner, a child, a dog. He tries to see it for what it seems to be and for what it is. He tries to see its multiplicity in order to see its truth, but the truth eludes him like incense. It is before him, around him, above him, but vanishes into air. He is morose.

A new commission for Siena Cathedral. Something *different.* He is getting what he wants, and he does not like it. He does not like the serpent of his vanity being provoked by a bishop's crozier.

Vescovo Donusdeo dei Malavolti glides toward the artist, extends his hooked hand for Simone to kiss the episcopal ring. The bishop has an ancient face but his frailty comes and goes. Sometimes the sharp edge of his willpower is visible, which can be dangerous; sometimes he is as meek as a kitten, which can be lethal. When the formalities are over, he extends a trembling pat of reassurance to the artist's arm and wheezes, It warms me, Maestro Simone, to see that you have begun your work. That is what I like about painters, they always have their most valuable tool on their person: their imagination. You cannot help it, can you? You are making lines and filling shapes with pigment even as we stand here. If I were a betting man, which naturally I am not, I would say you have made up your mind what the finished piece will look like. But I must reign in your impulses, though it grieves me to, for I would be intrigued to know what the farthest limits of your creativity can do. It is the Opera del Duomo, you see. You know what they are like. Some of them can be resistant to innovation. They mean well, of course, but it would be remiss of me not to repeat, for appearance's sake, the prescriptions they have made.

Prescriptions?

Prescription, guidance, what you will. You know best, and I trust you will interpret their expressed wishes suitably. They are not as brave as you and me. Were it my choice, I would say go and do your best, give to the cathedral whatever your genius can conceive of, and be as radical as you dare. They ought to listen to me, but they do not. I am too lenient with them. I sympathize, Maestro Simone, I do. Having someone restrict what you can paint must make you feel as I would feel if someone restricted my prayers.

I would not want my prayers inhibited either. What are the instructions?

Hardly worth mentioning. As I have stated already, you are to paint a functioning altarpiece that celebrates our principal protector, the Virgin, and represents an episode from her life. In due course there will be four new altars in the cathedral, each dedicated to one of Siena's auxiliary patrons, starting with Saint Ansanus—and then Saint Savinus, Saint Victor, and Saint Crescentius. Each altar will feature a moment from Our Lady's history. Yours is the first commission. I insisted to the Opera del Duomo that you should have the honor.

You flatter me, Vescovo. So far, these are reasonable specifications.

I am glad you think so. The next point is one I am sure your expert eye has already discerned: that the new altarpiece must be in harmony with Duccio's *Maestà,* and naturally in keeping with the traditions of the faith. How do you fellows say? The spatial relationship, the style, must not depart from his. There should be accord.

Simone takes some steps away from the bishop and faces the spot where his altarpiece would be installed relative to Duccio's: to the side of it; smaller in size than it; dedicated to a relatively obscure saint instead of the Virgin herself; replicating his old tutor's hand. Vescovo Donusdeo is correct; the artist had indeed guessed as much. Simone says, What if I am engaged in another commission? I am in great demand.

The bishop laughs. Who in Siena would put his own interests above the needs of the Church? Tell me the name of the man who is attempting to commandeer you, and I shall personally intervene. It must be at the preliminary stages of negotiation in any case— I spoke with your brother-in-law and know you not to be under contract at present.

Simone remains rigid and silently curses Lippo.

Besides, the patronal altars of Siena will become supremely famous. After the first has been dedicated, artists will flock from miles around to beg for the next commission. People will expect it of you, Simone, as Siena's famous son, to make a panel for the Duomo. The question is not whether you paint one, but *which one* you will paint. I suspect that you would prefer to be the pioneer, and to have the freest hand. Have I not said, moreover, that what the Opera requires of you is something quite new?

You wish me to create an icon that maintains tradition, and yet is entirely original?

I am relieved you understand. You are capable of it.

The artist gazes at Duccio's legacy.

The bishop shares his contemplation briefly and sighs. It is a remarkable object, a singular tribute to the majesty of Our Lady. Do you think I am blind as well as old, my dear Simone? Do you think bishops arrive in office fully formed? Every day I walk in the footprints of my predecessors.

Have the Nine been informed of this project?

I am sure somebody has conveyed the news. You know how easily these things get about.

Are they aware the Duomo is appropriating some of their imagery?

Their imagery . . . ? I am not sure I follow.

Well, you say there shall be four altars dedicated to Siena's patrons—and citizens will come here to the cathedral to petition the saints through prayer, and the saints in turn petition the Blessed Virgin Mary and she in her turn is their advocate to God. True? I am simply wondering if the politicians could view this arrangement as—evocative.

You amuse me. What a cynic you have become. You have such a low opinion of people, and for what reason? I am sure such a misplaced and petty notion would not occur to any of the Council of Nine. And if it did, shame would prevent them from saying it aloud. And if they said so, I would answer, the Church is staking a claim only to that which she already owns.

Simone senses the bishop's enjoyment in being able to rehearse his argument.

But let me explain something to you, in strictest confidence. I know you will appreciate the spirit of it. Siena is a beam of marble supported by three columns: the Town Hall, Siena Cathedral, and Santa Maria della Scala hospital. If one of these cracks or weakens, the other two must take more of the strain, so all is kept stable. Coincidental that you and I should visit this topic now, when I was debating it with Rettore Giovanni di Tese Tolomei just yesterday. He and I have had many productive conversations on this matter . . .

He notices how the bishop leaves the ribbon of his remark hanging in space, inviting someone to tug it. You have concerns about the Nine?

Certainly not. The oligarchs do a fine job. Legislating, scrutinizing decisions, collecting taxes, arbitrating—how shall we say?—*disputes* regarding boundaries and livestock, and so on. Custodianship of these mundane matters is, I suppose, a necessity. And yet, even the ruling classes must acknowledge that truth is to be found not in the letter of the law but in the Word of God, and that the richest currency is not vulgar struck metal but what is scored into men's hearts. You count real wealth by good deeds and by saved souls, by charity and by faith. The Council of Nine, through no fault of their own, do not understand how transient they are. Their world is unstable, fickle. When the government of fair Siena has fallen twice-twenty times, the poor will still seek respite at her hospital, and sinners will still pray for salvation at her church. *These* are permanent. *These* endure. I know it absolutely, and Signor Rettore is of the same mind. It is our moral obligation as Christians to act in accordance with what a perfect God has decreed, not with what imperfect and fallible men have frivolously decided. *Render to Caesar the things that are Caesar's, and to God the things that are God's.* (The bishop pauses, waiting for the other to concur, but Simone remains dispassionate.) I hear unsettling rumors.

Rumors are rarely of the reassuring kind.

I ought not to repeat them, because I do not believe them, they are too ridiculous. But you are a well-connected man and they will reach your ears sooner or later, so I really might as well tell you; apparently the Nine are planning an assault on the hospital and the cathedral. Not one of physical force, you understand—one of diktat. For Siena's hospital: a meticulous inventory of their assets and a regimen limiting their tax-free entitlements. For Siena's cathedral: the creation of a new "official," a secular bureaucrat who would mediate between the church and the Nine, and be ever present. Well, it is very far-fetched.

And devilish?

Must you be so glib, Maestro Simone? I do not concern myself with the little schemes Siena's government might or might not be

9

concocting, I have no time for it. But Signor Rettore and I agree that our institutions, or rather God's, could cooperate much more. We acknowledge that we can be of unique help to each other.

There. The bishop has all but told the artist he and Rettore Giovanni di Tese Tolomei have formed an alliance. No, Simone sneers inwardly, more than an alliance; they are in cahoots. He pictures the handshake: one hand gnarled and sinewy, covered in the spots of age, clasping the other, plump and pink, the jewels on their knuckles knocking together. What Vescovo Donusdeo dei Malavolti says next confirms his suspicions.

I understand you are planning a trip to Avignon, Maestro? If you manage to have a private moment with the Pope, please convey my personal greetings to him as his humble servant, admirer, and brother.

You are misinformed. I have not yet made up my mind about going to Avignon. If I make the journey, I will of course pass on your message.

I hope you will also consider putting in a good word for Santa Maria della Scala hospital. The Holy Father is able to bestow favors on the agencies performing God's works, you know.

Yes, I am aware.

I was holding a light aloft for you. Our Lady would want you to remember Siena's hospital to the Pope, I guarantee it, and I shall entreat her to speak to your better judgment.

The painter reexamines the sallow features of the bishop and wonders what precisely the rector of the hospital has offered him that has him so enthralled? Something more than mere strategic advantage. It has a filthy-dark quality to it and moves Simone to change the subject. Tell me, Vescovo, when does the Opera del Duomo expect their new altarpiece?

By the feast of Saint Ansanus, on the first day of December.

That is less than two years hence, but not inconceivable.

Considerably less than two years. They want it by this coming feast of Saint Ansanus.

Simone Martini stares at Vescovo Donusdeo but does not speak. The acquisition of materials, carpentry, and gold-beating alone would normally take at least a year.

If the bishop perceives a problem, his face does not betray him. He waits serenely for Simone's reply.

The artist's mind turns to the wife he will neglect if he accepts this commission, and intuitively he recalls her birthday and the gift he gave, her intake of breath when she saw it, the gratification to have chosen a present she adores . . . and his annoyance when she insisted on having her fortune told (it was her birthday, he could not refuse her whim). A card was turned over for him, La Papessa. He says aloud, I have a condition before I agree.

A condition? The bishop crosses himself and mutters a prayer. Maestro Simone, I am not a well man. I cannot vouch for what will happen if you presume to make demands. But you may make a request, and I shall take the matter to the Opera for discussion.

I want to do an Annunciation.

He recoils. Oh, my dear Simone. Extraordinary. I am amazed. What an idea. Oh. I am struck by your audacity. Are you sure this is what you want me to tell them?

Do you not think the Opera will approve? Did they not specifically request something new?

The bishop's serenity appears to have deserted him; he succumbs to a vicious cough.

The artist does not inquire after the bishop's health, remarks instead, Funny that you should approach me now, when I am actively considering retirement from painting—did I not mention it before?—in order to spend more time with my wife. She tells me I have made my mark on the world. I take her views very seriously.

Vescovo Donusdeo puckers his dry mouth and draws his hairy

eyebrows together, two caterpillars meeting on a leaf. Eventually he says, Can you do it?

Simone does not need to look at Duccio's *Maestà* anymore; every inch of it is committed to memory. He nods.

The bishop throws up his hand in surrender and agitation. I do not know. I shall have to make a very thoughtful argument. Some may call it controversial, but if it were done correctly, if it conveyed Our Lady's obedience and piety . . . on balance I am cautiously optimistic that the officials of the Opera del Duomo could be—how shall we say?—*persuaded* to take a risk on a talent as unique as yours. After proper consultation and prayer, of course. An Annunciation, then! Congratulations, Maestro Simone, we are thrilled to have engaged you for this commission. There is one further detail I ought to tell you, although it is of such little consequence.

Three girls, including Laura Agnelli, kneel or crouch by baskets of almonds, shelling and grinding. It is hard, repetitive work. Imelda calls it peasant work, and moans that the land laborers should do it, not the daughters of Santa Maria della Scala. The almonds they have done are paltry in number, while the almonds left to do seem hardly to have reduced in volume. They will be at this for hours, aching and numb afterward, sick of the sight and smell. The time would pass better were talking permitted. The noise of the scraping makes discreet conversation difficult; nonetheless Imelda manages to mutter some of her complaints into Gisila's ear.

When I am married I shall have servants, and if they displease me I shall not flog them but make them grind mountains of almonds, then I shall feed the almonds to the pigs.

Servants and pigs? Almonds to dispense as punishment? What a daydreamer you are, Imelda.

Why should I not? Look at what they make us do. We are no

better than slaves. As long as we are here, they own us body and soul. What have I to lose by indulging my dreams, when they take practically everything else?

We are the fortunate ones.

Are we? Do you think they love us as God's children? We embody our parents' sin. We are the offspring of harlots, beggars, and adulterers—and they treat us as such.

What happened to Guido? I thought you liked him. He certainly fancied you. Or is a boy raised at the hospital not good enough for you anymore?

I can do better than Guido. There are plenty of men outside this compound, you know. You just have to make sure you are not caught. (Laura quickens the rhythm of her labor to drown out Imelda's nattering.) Guido is immature, and his breath smells horrible. Is it too much to ask for a husband who has whiskers and a kiss that does not suffocate me? I expect at least that of a man—and that he will have a legitimate lineage and a fat inheritance coming his way.

Gisila laughs at her friend's bad temper. Then take comfort in your dreams. Think of the servants you will have one day, and how you can mistreat them, if it cheers you up. Think of your fine furs and your enormous house with a balcony, and your own mare to ride. Think of what your husband will look like, whether he will be dark or fair, whether he will be lean or broad. And think of your father-in-law, who will be elderly and who will dote on you.

I do, every day. If God loves me, he will send a rich man to save me from this hell. And when I am married, I shall definitely have a big—

Imelda stops short of naming the thing she will have, for the rector himself is visible in the passageway, speaking to a gentleman neither of them recognizes. The stranger is distinctly handsome, with black hair and brown eyes, dressed in a plaid kirtle and a red chaperon, with a buckle on his belt that gleams. Gisila cannot resist it and whispers, Your prayers have been answered, Imelda; here he comes now to take you to his mansion.

Imelda presses her attractive mouth to stifle the giggle and permits herself a look of admiration at the man in conference with the rector, surely here to make a donation and so avoid paying unwanted duties. It is the rector's method to show off the charity and industry of the hospital, to emphasize the spiritual benefits of generosity to Santa Maria, and to make people part with more than they initially intended. He is as skillful as a market pickpocket.

Then he does something surprising. He abandons his visitor momentarily in order to come over to the three girls (there is an increase in speed and purpose under his gaze). He clears his throat. Laura Agnelli, come with me, please.

Laura obediently wipes her hands on her apron, stands, follows.

Behind her back, the malign eyes of Imelda and Gisila meet, then separate. It is not unheard of that a man comes to the hospital and points to the young woman he wants as though selecting fish for the dinner table. Usually there is some semblance of paying court and an opportunity for the girl to refuse, followed by a wedding. *Usually.* However, Rettore Giovanni di Tese Tolomei is fond of saying the well-being of the hospital is more important than the well-being of any one individual—many times his actions have demonstrated the sincerity of his belief.

Imelda murmurs savagely, I thought she was going into a convent.

The rector presents Laura to the visitor, who looks her up and down and answers yes, she will do. The rector continues, Laura, you are to go with this man to his master. You are to do whatever they ask of you for as long as they have a use for you. They will give you your meals when you are there. You will be submissive, patient, meek and conduct yourself as though the Blessed Virgin were standing at your side. This is a privilege and a test, and it will be a shame upon us all, not to mention a personal offense to me, if your behavior is not immaculate. In fact, it may have serious repercussions for your future. Do you understand?

Yes, Signor Rettore.

And Laura goes with the stranger. Perhaps, she acknowledges inwardly, into danger.

They do not walk far, up and down the city slopes, through the narrow streets, the stalls and relative safety of the Campo. He does not speak. It is when they go into a house and ascend a stairway into a private room (the door locked behind her) that Laura's heart jumps and she sends silent prayers to the Virgin to protect her, and if she cannot protect her, then to limit her pain and suffering as far as possible, and if she cannot do that, then to grant Laura the strength to endure whatever is to take place.

The room is sparse though large, like a tradesman's workshop or rented storeroom, with enormous windows letting in Siena's glorious sky above and commotion beneath. It is occupied by a second man, significantly older, a hunched gnome who does not acknowledge them nor interrupt his inspection of documents. Laura looks for a bed, but there is none, just commonplace wooden furniture, scrolls, and tools—as though a great plan were being executed, a military campaign. That is Laura's impression. The ugly man is the general, the handsome one his lieutenant.

The younger man says, Maestro, will you see if you approve?

Simone Martini answers with a growl and puts down his parchment. As before, Laura's face and bearing are scrutinized, but this one pinches her chin to turn her head in profile and appears displeased with what he sees. To his subordinate he says, I have begun to think this is a terrible idea.

Signor Rettore was . . . um . . . quite *specific* that the girl ought to come every morning after Lauds and not return home before dusk, unless called for.

(Laura blinks at this news.)

We must have her here all day, every day?

Except the Sabbath.

This is unacceptable. You did not counter him, Lippo?

(Laura notices the assistant's fingers crossed behind his back.)

Well, it was not easily done.

Simone Martini is exasperated. Lippo, the keen and insecure patron will be constantly at your elbow, interfering, finding defects that do not exist. And now we have, in effect, *two*.

Lippo Memmi replies with more conviction, It is not too late to refuse the commission. I for one will not care about displeasing the bishop. We can go to Florence or to Venice, where your genius will be appreciated.

Simone grumbles indistinctly and returns to his plans, which Lippo interprets as a direction to continue.

For Laura, Lippo has further instructions, picking up the rector's refrain: You must sit in complete silence, for your very presence disturbs my master's work. You must let no one in without the master or myself being present, and ensure always this door is locked. Do you fear God? I said, do you fear God?

Yes.

Do you fear the flames of hell and the trident of Lucifer?

Yes.

I hope so, because I am about to make you swear an oath of secrecy. If anyone inquires about our panel, or asks you to report what has taken place in this room, if anyone—the rector, the bishop, anybody from the Commune, the Nine, or the Opera del Duomo— asks you what is happening or is spoken about within these walls, you will cut out your own tongue before answering them and rot in hell when you do. Do you so swear?

Laura wavers. A promise of this kind is an extremely serious matter. If what you say is true, Signore, then what answer may I make to men such as these?

You may say the master works hard, and it appears to be going well, and that what you have seen of his design is extraordinary and confounds your understanding. You will furnish any details that distract from the substance of what they seek to know—describe the shoes my master is wearing, say whether it rained on your walk here, or that you had a splinter in your finger. You will tell them *anything* that protects the panel and my master from their scrutiny. Now, do you so swear?

Laura stammers, Yes, I swear—

Good.

—but there must be a mistake.

Child, they will all seek you out; yours are the most valuable eyes and ears in Siena. But remember, you belong to us. And while you are with us, you shall not chatter nor venture unnecessary questions; in fact, you would do well to make yourself invisible. Hush now, this is serious business.

A small chair has been set aside in the corner, and Lippo gestures for Laura to sit down. Uncertain what exactly is required of her, Laura Agnelli does so tentatively.

The two men turn away to confer in lowered voices. They discuss names and plot dates, and estimate quantities and measurements and sums of money, extravagant sums of money (initially she thought she misheard), the kind of money Laura has never seen and will never see. She waits to be given another instruction, has nothing to occupy her except to sit alternating her attention between the gentlemen and the bustle outside, which, unhappily, is out of sight unless she strains in her chair to peer over the sill. The older man is agitated; his fury sinks and rises over some problem or other, some unreasonable behavior that maddens him. The assistant is unruffled by the master's shouting, suggests a solution, a different solution, then a compromise. Then he makes a note of their decision and does calculations.

At midday, a maidservant brings a basket of bread and tomatoes. Laura lets her in. The maid greets Signor Martini and Signor Memmi—this is how Laura learns their names—leaves the food, and, to Laura's dismay, departs forthwith.

Later Laura is sent home, unaccompanied.

And this is how the second day passes.

By the third day, Lippo Memmi is not present, sent away to procure materials and appoint workers. Simone Martini spends the day reading his books. The boredom makes Laura weary, but she does not complain. She has ample time to ponder how much longer she will be required to come here (a whole week? two?) and whether her role is simply to sit quietly and observe, or whether there is more to it that will be revealed later. At dusk, when Simone Martini lights a candle, she rises from her seat.

Maestro Simone, it is time for me to go, unless you have further use for me . . . ?

(This would be sarcasm if spoken by another girl, but Laura Agnelli does not mean it that way.)

The artist drags his attention from his research and appears startled to find her there. Yes, you may go.

She makes a small bow of respect.

What is your name, child?

Laura Agnelli.

Indeed, you are like a lamb, one that does not bleat. Tomorrow bring your spindle. You should not be idle.

*   *   *

Simone Martini has begun preparatory drawings; with each one his humor deteriorates further still. He sketches them out with a pen and red and black inks, bent like a monk in a scriptorium, his back giving him pain. Sometimes the *modelli* are more elaborate—he goes as far as making meticulous scale paintings. Laura watched with curiosity the first time he broke an egg into a cup, the familiar sound causing her to look up. He slithered the yolk in his fingers, pinched it, pierced the sac with a tiny blade, let the yellow liquid run out to mix with ground pigment. These are Simone's experiments in color and design, but Laura knows them only as a flourish and a blur when he casts them aside as inadequate.

In the absence of Lippo, he finds reasons to bellow at Laura—for staring at him when she drifted off into a meditative state; for her stomach groaning the day she missed breakfast; for the clatter when she dropped her spindle on the floor. She begins to dread her next misdemeanor.

At noon, Laura rises to let in the maid but instead it is an elegant young lady, hair like the feathers on a rook, slim and exquisitely dressed, carrying an armful of cut lilies and a basket. Laura withdraws to her corner.

So this is where all the yarn comes from! I did not truly believe one person could make so much in a day.

Simone Martini huffs and Laura does not reply, assumes she is not meant to. The young woman lays down the bouquet, the heady aroma of the lilies overpowering the warm space, and unpacks the basket: swaths of lavish fabric and wrapped parcels, which Simone stirs himself to sort through. He frowns. Why did you not send the maid, Giovanna?

Because Antonia is busy. And I wanted to come myself. To see you, my lord. To eat with you.

And yet you have brought no food.

Giovanna tilts her head in reproach. I thought I would bring the things you asked for first, then go to the Campo to buy some. If it is not too distracting for you, you can tell me what you would most like to eat.

Laura expects this tartness to be answered in kind, but Simone Martini's expression softens into paternal indulgence.

Figs, Giovanna, should do very well.

Figs. Then I shall bring you some. How is your work?

Simone sighs, waves the question away.

Giovanna picks up some of the studies—figures and trip-tychs—and looks them over. What is the matter with all these? Why can you not make a decision?

Do not concern yourself with it. Only one of us needs to be troubled.

Giovanna pouts, examines the sketches more closely, briefly glances at Laura, then murmurs, Not one of these Virgins is in the act of spinning.

Simone Martini takes them from her and shuffles the sheets together, grunting, I am getting to it.

My lord, the panel is within your reach. Your greatness is more than equal to this task. When it is finished, it will undoubtedly be the jewel of Siena. And yet . . . I must protest, if it is affecting your health, if the sacrifices you are making are too much for you—

Simone kisses Giovanna on the forehead and she leaves the rest unsaid. Laura senses this is a longstanding family argument, that he has mastered the girl's grievances and has gently reminded her of it.

Then I will go to the Campo for you. Would you like to come with me?

The question is not to Simone but to Laura, though he answers for her, *She* has instructions to stay.

The lady's voice has a note of weariness to it: Yes, from the rector, I know . . . but he did not mean to trap her here, to deny her sun and air every now and then! What do *you* think?

Again this question is thrown to Laura rather than Simone. Laura forms the impression Giovanna often gets her way.

The gradient of the square slopes down to the Palazzo Pubblico. People are at work on the construction of the impressive tower, specks moving on the scaffolding. Laura waits to be addressed by Giovanna, who is preoccupied with the wares and produce on display. Finally she says, This must be strange for you. I expect you ask yourself why you agreed to do it.

I did not agree to it, I was commanded.

I see. Yes, that makes more sense. I suppose you are indebted to the people who raised you?

They saved my life, and gave me everything.

No doubt you are often reminded of it. Do you like it at Santa Maria della Scala?

The hospital is all I know.

It is your home but not your family, maybe? Do they tell you anything about your parents? Do you know whether yours are alive or dead?

No, they do not, and it is for the best, otherwise people would always be running away to try to find them. We have enough problems of that sort as it is. Oh dear, perhaps I should not have said that.

You do not need to worry, I shall not betray a confidence. You have been put in a position of trust while you are with us, so we must treat you in the manner we wish to be treated. Please feel free to say whatever you like, and be assured that I for one will not abuse you, and shall prevent others from doing so if it is within my power.

Laura Agnelli raises her eyes to Giovanna properly for the first time, notices her companion is a little older than herself but not by much, and despite her cool voice has a face that is not unkind. She also perceives a personality like a set of scales, reliable and balanced, speaking the truth. Laura licks her lips and continues: I used to try to feel whether or not my parents were alive. I would shut my eyes and let my mind wander through Siena and the contado and beyond, as far as the sea. I gave up when I was nine or ten. I am now quite convinced my parents are dead, and have been for a long time. I have made peace with that, but I should like to know who they were, where they came from.

Yes, I would want to know too. Tell me, what becomes of you orphans when you are grown?

We have some tuition. When the boys are old enough they can go into a trade. And the girls are given a dowry of fifty lire to marry or enter a convent with. Some stay to live and work in the hospital their whole lives. Some want to.

Not many, I expect. And what will you do?

Laura has the sun in her eyes, so she raises her hand to shade them. It has long been my intention to take vows and dedicate my life to God.

Giovanna does not reply—she is either struck by this revelation and covers it well, or is genuinely unmoved. I guessed before today the commission was faltering. My lord cannot hide his moods from me. He is struggling with the burden of choice. When a man has a decision to make, it becomes a great and weighty matter; yet if you or I behaved the same way, we would be accused of dithering, would we not? They would say, Woman, make up your mind! Excuse me, now you think I am being disrespectful. My poor husband gives me license to say what I think, and I use his grace to make complaints. At least I am being consistent. I have spoken my honest opinions to him on many occasions.

Is your husband an artist too? The words are out of Laura's mouth even as she realizes she has made a mistake.

Giovanna is amused. No need to feel embarrassed. After all, he is older than me. You let slip an innocent remark because you know no better; others are malicious about my marriage behind my back, which is far worse. You have not offended me.

Nonetheless, I profoundly apologize. It was thoughtless.

If it pleases you. But you are curious now, are you not? You think maybe there can be no genuine affection between an attractive woman like me and an old rich man like him? That the exchange must be one of convenience, not love?

Laura's face burns.

Convenience is not the worst reason to marry. It happens every day. Tell me, are the marriages of girls leaving Santa Maria della Scala all love matches? To many men, fifty lire is a lot of money, and maybe they wish to be looked after and to have children. For that, they need a wife. And I doubt many young women would choose a nunnery or servitude at the hospital over having a home of their own. Not you, I know. You are the exception that proves the rule.

Laura presses her temples as though to absorb Giovanna's words, as though this will make them fit comfortably in her head. I am not unsympathetic. To some, matrimony is an attractive proposition. To some, it means if not freedom, then at least a preferable sort of bondage. The rule of a husband might be gentle and benevolent compared to the rule of a religious order.

That is not always true!

No . . . it is not always.

Are you all right, Laura? You look dreadful.

Yes, thank you. I am relieved to be outside for a while. It was kind of you to invite me.

Giovanna answers it is her pleasure before continuing, I suppose all the children of Santa Maria are instilled with a sense of duty—a family one, or a vocation. That is the commonality. Duty is a powerful influence on people's lives and would be a valid reason for my marriage to Simone, perhaps. So would you be scandalized if I said duty played no part in our betrothal? What if I told you that on our wedding day he gave me a generous financial gift? I am not teasing you. I am trying to show you how sometimes appearances are one thing and the truth another. And the truth is this: my brother Lippo was Simone's student, Simone came to our house on several occasions and was kind to me, and I grew to love him as though it had been written. He feared for my reputation. He said if we married, people would always gossip about us—and they do. He tried to put me off. I am extremely lucky to be his wife. If he were not wealthy and not a genius, I would still love him and I would still be extremely lucky.

Then yours is a good example to follow for those who are the marrying kind.

We are not perfect. There is an empty space in our lives, can you tell? We have no children yet, and it saddens us. I have tried various remedies and I have prayed my hardest, but so far we have not been answered. Money cannot buy everything—

Giovanna breaks off to buy the figs and some oranges.

They are over halfway around the Campo and Laura realizes her time left alone with Giovanna is probably short. When they walk on she says, There is something that has been bothering me. Your brother told Maestro Simone I was instructed to attend his studio every day by Signor Rettore. But that is not strictly true. He did say I am to be obedient and present when I am required; however, since then the rector has expressed some surprise at my being needed so very often.

Giovanna flattens her lips together. I am afraid that was my doing.

How can it be yours?

I am sorry. I admit it: I made Lippo tell my lord this tiny white lie. Please try to understand, my husband is not very good with new people. It takes him a long time to trust someone. He needs to get to know them first. He has his method when he paints, and what they have asked of him is utterly unreasonable. And he is getting very . . . this commission is the worst I have ever seen him. It is affecting his health and his inspiration . . . and it makes me so angry! I rarely meddle in his work, I assure you, but we are living in strange times. I was certain your presence would hasten the conclusion, whatever that might be, *good or ill.* In fact I was convinced of it. Yet here we are, still waiting, still unsure what will happen.

Laura shivers despite the heat, hugs her arms across her body.

Giovanna puts her hand on her hip. Tell me, Laura Agnelli: how is he when he is working?

I hardly know.

Does he exhaust himself? Does he rest? I know about the promise you made my brother, by the way, but a wife should know about her husband's welfare no matter what the oath is.

No, he never rests.

What of his temper? Is he content? Is he calm?

Laura hesitates before she replies. Generally his concentration is given over to his work. He goes for hours at a time without speaking, so I cannot comment on whether or not he is content. He is industrious, as you saw, makes many pictures. When he does speak, it is to scold me for disturbing him.

Does he shout at you?

I ought to be more careful.

You are afraid of him. I am right, he frightens you. This is very bad. (Giovanna takes an orange out of her basket and rolls it between her palms before continuing.) It does not matter how fate brought you to us; you are here now. Being afraid of someone is a terrible condemnation of his character. With Simone, you should know the dog that barks does not bite. He is a good man, and he needs your help.

I do not know what help I can possibly give.

He will need your assistance soon with the panel painting. At some point he will come to acknowledge it, and then you must be prepared. More than that, he needs you to be a friend because he does not have many. It might seem odd to you—he is so esteemed in Siena—but being admired and having friends are not the same, and even the greatest men need friends. Will you promise me that you will not judge him too harshly and, when the time comes, you will do whatever you can?

Laura is reminded of the promise she has already made to Giovanna's brother, struck by how alike the siblings are. She gives the lady her word, then ventures, Why me? Why not someone else?

Well, it was up to Signor Rettore to choose, and he chose you. He must have lots of reasons: your piousness, your gentle nature, your dedication. It is an enormous privilege, you should be pleased.

It is indeed a privilege to meet Simone Martini. But for what end?

Giovanna halts at this, then looks incredulous. To be in the . . . Wait. Tell me why you think you are made to come to the studio?

Laura shrugs. I sit while Maestro Simone works, and I spin to pass the time. I think I am his witness, or something like that. Signor Memmi said people would ask me about their progress and he was quite correct—Signor Rettore wants to hear news practically every day. Do not worry, your brother also told me how to answer, and it is basically the truth, so there you are. Today I will say I met Maestro Simone's wife and you brought us lunch from the market. This is what happened, and to say so is not a violation of my oath.

Giovanna shakes her head in disbelief. You actually do not know. Well, I did not think I should be the one to tell you, but if you are truly unaware, I feel I must. My lord and my brother Lippo have been commissioned by the Duomo to make a panel dedicated to Saint Ansanus celebrating the Annunciation. You know the story of Saint Ansanus?

Laura beams. But of course! His nurse, Saint Maxima, baptized him in secret and brought him up as a Christian. She was martyred through flagellation, but he survived and went on to convert and baptize many people here in Siena. Eventually he was martyred on the orders of Diocletian.

Yes. At the same time, the Duomo and the hospital have formed—how shall we say?—a partnership, because they are both anxious about the interference of the Nine in their affairs. The story of Ansanus is pertinent because he was raised to be a Christian and do God's work by his *nurse,* not by his own parents, who were members of the Roman ruling class. It therefore has a certain resonance. Through the altarpiece the Duomo will be, to an extent, restating its relationship with Santa Maria della Scala to show how the spiritual works of the cathedral and the charitable works of the hospital are joined, and are favored and blessed by Our Lady. Siena's citizens will look at it and be reminded of how the Virgin bestows her protection on the faithful and the charitable.

How clever, I would not have thought of it.

It will encourage people to be loyal, and generous, to both institutions. It is also a veiled message to Siena's oligarchy, who will be capable of reading it quite clearly. Do you see? Government has been left out of the picture. And just for emphasis, an orphan of the hospital has been chosen to be a part of it: *you.* The politicians would have expected a daughter of one of the noble families to be given that honor. It is a snub. The Nine will be furious when they find out, and yet it will be unseemly for them to criticize it.

Laura considers. I do not understand politics. If it is as you say, I am sure the rector and the bishop know what they are doing. But what have I done that could possibly make the Council of Nine so upset?

I am not explaining myself very well. Your *likeness* is to be in the altarpiece.

Giovanna said it plainly and sensitively, concerned about how a young girl who has led a sheltered life might react to such news.

Initially, Laura Agnelli does not respond, except for her deepening frown and narrowing eyes. Then she mumbles she is hot, feeling dizzy; she sways on her feet.

Giovanna leads Laura into some shade, makes her sit and drink from a flask of wine until she has recovered her wits.

When the incident is over, Giovanna offers to take her home, but Laura is adamant that it is not her wish.

I apologize, Laura. I honestly thought you knew.

No. No one saw fit to tell me.

And you did not guess it?

Something like that would simply never occur to me. It is too unexpected.

Laura Agnelli offers a silent prayer, feels it leaving her and flying up into the sky beyond her reach, beyond even the reach of the new tower and the stonemasons tapping the stones with their hammers and chisels, the clicks answered with echoes.

Laura returns to the hospital while most are still at vespers. Some have duties that excuse them from attending; some are sly and find ways to avoid it when it suits them. Laura rarely misses the evening prayer service, and to have been kept from it for days in succession is a trial for her. She needs these renewals even more than she did before.

In the dormitory, Laura finds Imelda and Gisila sitting on a bed, their heads close together in conference as they wind laundered cloth strips.

Imelda whispers to Gisila, whose uncontrollable giggle turns into a pig snort.

Laura almost pauses to greet them, but even as she slows her pace their laughter dies. Suddenly they are absorbed in their work.

It would not hurt Laura, not normally. She would take solace in her prayers and think about the life she will have at Santa Marta. She is finding this more difficult of late. Because she is in halves.

A word, Laura Agnelli!

The shouted demand is from Rettore Giovanni di Tese Tolomei, whose pompous girth has appeared as abruptly in the girls' quarters as if he had followed Laura there. She turns to go with him, passes by the other two but a few steps before their joke resumes. Imelda sniggers into the back of her hand. Gisila drops her head onto her friend's shoulder, limp with laughter, tears forming on her lashes.

She has had enough practice at finding her way through Siena's streets in the dark, and takes the precaution of covering her head so that her red hair does not give her away at a distance. She knows from experience which entrances will still be unlocked and, once inside, which are the quietest passageways leading back to the dormitory.

The hospital is never entirely asleep. Individual candles are kept lit in alcoves; oblates keep watch in the wards and the pilgrims' hall; voices are still audible, though fewer, muted, more urgent. Night is a dangerous time for the weak.

Laura traces her way close to walls and peers around corners before moving on. She has not been seen so far, but is not complacent either. She has tried to imagine what would happen if she met Imelda, or one of the other orphans, creeping around out of bed too . . . and done her best not to dwell on the consequences if she were caught by a sister or Signor Rettore.

She listens. Blood thuds in her ears. Footsteps ahead send her back in the direction she came from and toward a main corridor. Rather than risk it, she is compelled down a stairway and when she hears them approaching once more—whether or not her mind is playing tricks on her—goes deeper into the underbelly of the hospital. The swinging flare of a lamp sends her hurrying away.

She tries to dampen her tread as she traverses the labyrinthine passages hastens down steps behind pillars makes stealthy progress. The tunnels are twisted and unfamiliar here.

She stayed out longer than she intended; it is so late it is almost early. Fatigue and fright and frustration and the need for prayer like thirst. She stops. She leans against an archway to steady her nerves, to get her bearings, to console her heart. It is futile to feel distress, or indulge unwanted thoughts at this particular moment: getting back to the dormitory undiscovered is what matters; ignore the rest of her troubles if she can.

Laura Agnelli looks about her. She decides on reflection she has been here before, years ago, can find a route that will bring her close to the girls' quarters from beneath. Here at least is one solution.

As to the rest (Laura summons her strength), I will try again soon.

And it is when she resolves this that she realizes she has arrived almost at the door of the hospital's oratory. She lingers; turns away from it; is instinctively tugged back.

The rules are plain: the oratory is out of bounds.

Is it possible that a benevolent hand has steered her here? that a few minutes of solace and solitude will provide Laura with the guidance she needs?

She peeked within it once, when she was small, but has never been inside because she was never invited—or desperate—and remembers the ghost stories they told one another about the place, as children, for the cemetery and the charnel house are right next to it. These features made it fascinating and forbidding.

But the terrors are real enough now. And Laura Agnelli enters the oratory at last.

It is unlike any space in the sprawling warren of Santa Maria della Scala. Hewn. Enclosed. It exudes a dim glow of its own, a pulsation, a palpable intention, is ancient and potent as though the very walls had cognizance. This power presses upon Laura Agnelli, compresses her, makes her tingle. Is it evil? Is it sacred? Is this awe, or ecstasy?

The oratory is a stone vault with a simple altar, relics, bones, skulls, fragments of wood set in cases and embellished stands. A smaller doorway in the opposite wall is partially open. Beyond it, luminous and inviting warmth, an angelic figure retreating into the next chamber—its brilliance makes Laura shield her vision briefly.

Laura is lowering her head and following before the folly of disturbing the room's occupant prevents her—

She is in a narrow recess wide enough for a single person, a niche of several yards, and there at the end is a woman kneeling at a second tiny altar. A stranger. Her presence is somehow wrong, impossible, as if she does not belong here but has come for a special purpose. It is arresting.

Absorbed in her meditations, it takes minutes for the woman to perceive Laura. When she does notice, she does not speak. Instead, the lady symbolically covers her mouth . . . then makes confusing movements with her hands, as though they contained a message.

She has fire in her. Laura can see the flames in the blacks of her eyes, can feel the heat emanate.

If this is a spirit sent to warn her, or a saint sent to comfort, then Laura is unprepared for it and baffled by the whole encounter. She leaves the oratory without uttering a single word of prayer, without the answers she craves.

* * *

Dawn rays find the edges of feet suspended in midair, fingers curled and stiff, a shape like a rag draped over a branch. Dew forms on the skin like stone. There she is, surprisingly small, discovered first by the sun, then by birds to be pecked at, then by a cart, then a staring multitude. The act was done with a red cord, it becomes apparent. There is one just like it tied around a curtain in the women's chapel of the hospital.

Laura opens her eyes, wakes without so much as a sigh, the vision still vivid. In the dark, the familiar outlines of sleeping girls huddled together and the sounds of their breathing flowing like a river. A stab of panic: which one of them did she dream about? In the haze of partial sleep she forgets. As she drifts off with the swell, she remembers; it is only herself, and there is no need to warn anyone.

Out of breath, she climbs the stairwell and pauses outside the room—tries the door, squeezes it open without the hinges squeaking.

The artist is standing by the window eating olives from a small dish, the people of Siena going about their day below.

It confirms her anxiety to find him thus, because each and every day previously he has been at work with his back to the world and paid her no heed. But now he watches her secure the lock with unabashed interest. There is a moment . . . maybe while she waits for him to summon his rage, or he waits for her to volunteer an apology. He breaks the silence first.

I bought us some olives from the Campo. I had to buy some eggs to make paint because I tend to run out without Lippo around to remind me. I am very fond of olives. Are you?

Laura Agnelli nods faintly, yes, she is.

Then it is good you came when you did, or I would have eaten them all, then there would have been none left for you. Here, you had better have some.

She cautiously takes one without eating it.

Simone pops another in his mouth, making a noise of pleasure at the flavor, takes the stone out, drops it on another plate. He wipes his finger on his tunic.

You did not come yesterday. (It is a statement of fact, and he declares it that way.) I waited the whole day for you to come, but you did not. It was disconcerting. In fact, I got no work done. I was going to send someone to Santa Maria to find out why, in case you had been taken ill, you see? Giovanna talked me out of it. She said if you were indisposed, someone from the hospital would have been dispatched to tell me about it and there was probably another explanation. That made sense. I said, then Laura is surely missing, and we should raise the alarm so she can be found! I was adamant.

Laura lifts her horrified gaze.

But Giovanna said we should not do that either—that if your absence was for a different reason, I ought not to draw attention to it in case it caused you difficulties. She said you would probably turn up in your own time if we left you alone. And look . . . she was right. Giovanna knows much more about girls your age than I do.

Laura exhales, closing her eyes. I am sorry, Maestro Simone, to have caused you inconvenience.

Giovanna calls me *prickly*. She says I do not inspire confidences from the young. Huh. Eat your olives.

Simone gives Laura what is left, beckons her to take a seat, not in her usual corner but beside him for a while.

You disappeared for an entire day. I am not cross about it, but a child whose whereabouts are unknown is a cause of concern for any Christian.

Ashen, she apologizes again.

Katie Ward

At least you are here now, and your behavior has been impeccable so far. I dined with the good rector at his palace last week. He artfully conveyed to me that he has a small mouse who squeaks all the newsworthy events into his ear every evening. He has really asked you, then . . . ?

Regularly.

I thought so. What a rascal. And what an appetite, for food and for intelligence. Somehow he has heard I am considering traveling to Avignon. He is trying to persuade me to petition the Holy Father for privileges for Santa Maria della Scala. He thinks I would make a good ambassador, and he has now offered as an incentive a new commission, to paint an exterior fresco for the hospital. A grand artwork, outside, where everyone can see it and admire it all the time.

It sounds marvelous.

Bah!—Simone flicks his wrist in a noncommittal gesture—he is appealing to my vanity. The hospital, the cathedral, and the Nine are as bad as one another, what with their sumptuous art and their colossal architecture. They are all posturing schoolboys. Sometimes I think the wars we make with Florence are a blessing in disguise because if we did not fight the Florentines, we would descend into war with ourselves. However, he was vague on the details of the altarpiece, which I am pleased about, Laura, especially when he was trying to create the impression you were his informant. You have done well to resist his coercion to reveal what you know.

I have an oath in heaven. It was not difficult, anyway, as I know so little.

Are you curious to know more?

Signor Memmi said I was not to ask questions unnecessarily, so I have not.

I see. Keeping your word is important to you.

I think it is important to anybody who is God-fearing.

34

I hear you are to become a nun someday?

Yes, Signore, at the convent of Santa Marta. At least, I hope so.

Ah—Abbess Emilia Pannocchieschi d'Elci.

You know her?

A very strict woman. Very devout. Extremely kind. You are fortunate if she takes you under her wing. She thinks novices should know scripture. Do you know scripture, Laura Agnelli?

How can I answer without sounding proud? or ignorant?

Be truthful. Do you read it regularly?

Laura fidgets. Ye-es. Some, at any rate. My Latin is not good, but I can usually identify the passages I need and have committed many more to memory. I often recite. I—cannot write.

Assuredly a woman has no occasion for writing?

No, I suppose not.

But many nuns are literate. If it holds a genuine attraction for you, perhaps you will have the chance to learn reading and writing at Santa Marta? Hmm?

Laura's blush deepens.

I think the rector unwittingly did me a favor when he inflicted you upon us. My wife tells me you are troubled at the prospect of your likeness being in the painting. I did not take it seriously before. Now I have talked with you, I understand a little better. You are naturally closed like a bud. (Simone Martini brings his hands together, fingertips pointed upward as though in prayer, palms cupped as though protecting hidden contents.) I wish I could dispel some of your concerns. If you would care to look, I can show you some aspects of the panel, although you will have to use your imagination for some of it.

She frowns. Are you not worried I will betray what I see to the rector?

No. Neither should you be.

Simone retrieves some of the vellum leaves from the rest, studies of figures and objects, definite shapes and contours and pigments. I have settled upon these elements. Here.

She hesitates.

Go on, it will do us both some good. I would like to share the fruits of my creativity with someone trustworthy, for a change. Tell me what you see. Think of it as practice for when you are discussing theological questions at the convent.

Laura leans over to examine them. White lilies in an ornate gold vase.

Yes. Why?

White lilies are a symbol of purity and virginity. They are an obvious choice to represent the Blessed Virgin.

Quite right. A peasant could understand that, and it is a painting as much for him as for the bishop. They are pretty to look at as well, do you agree?

Yes. Very pleasing.

Do you have any other thoughts on the subject of lilies?

Laura says she does not.

They are a symbol of virginity, innocence, and heavenly purity, as you mentioned, but some would say that lilies are . . . naughty flowers, that they suggest illicit passion and temptation. Have you heard that before?

No. People who say that are wrong. It is a flower of Our Lady!

Not necessarily. There are examples in pagan religions of this being the case, religions older than ours. Have you really smelled a lily before, Laura? It has an intoxicating and powerful fragrance, and the shape is uniquely alluring. I can see perfectly well how other cultures have bestowed it with more dubious connotations than ours. So I, as the painter, need to consider whether the lily is truly appropriate for inclusion. And I think, on balance, it is, because through Our Lady as Theotokos, sin *is overcome*. Furthermore, lilies are used figuratively to remind us to trust in God's will and providence. *Consider the lilies of the field, how they grow: they toil not, neither do they spin.* We are told Mary was troubled and afraid when first the angel appeared, then she surrendered herself as the Lord's handmaid. These particular flowers add this wisdom to the Annunciation story.

Laura is astounded by the artist's elaborate construction.

Then he asks her about the vase.

The vase? Is it not a pot for the lilies to go in? (She chastens herself for her rudeness.) It is such a lovely pot.

I could have shown lilies planted in the ground, or cut stems being held, but I have chosen specifically a vase. Does this not strike you?

Laura shakes her head. I see only flowers in a vessel.

Aha. A *vessel*. Follow that line of thought.

I am ignorant, Signore. I have not studied these matters.

I think you are doing yourself a disservice. Do try for me . . . ?

I suppose the Virgin Mary could be called a vessel, in the sense that God chose her to give birth to Christ.

Precisely. Capital work. I can hear the abbess's praises already.

Laura feels a spark of gratification.

A vase also means "treasure" in certain traditions. And at the Annunciation, God gives us the most precious treasure of all, do you agree? The vase is a "vessel" and it is a "treasure"—but even an item as mundane as this can have more than two meanings. In alchemy, the vase is where miracles occur, as in the Virgin's womb. The mouth of this vase is open to God's divine influence.

Laura is taken by a new thought, one that would explain Maestro Simone's inclination toward layers of symbolism that are lost on her. Are you an alchemist scholar, Signore?

Ah, no. I find the toil of painting more than sufficiently fills my time without my attempting to purify the soul and turn base metals into gold. I do not mean to imply these things are impossible—who knows what can be achieved with enough study and luck?—only that it would be futile for *me* to attempt such goals. I leave that task to those who are more fit for it. Although, being able to conjure gold would be useful just at the moment. You heard me and Lippo discussing it, of course, on the first day?

A lot of it went over my head.

I have charged Lippo with a difficult mission, to procure me a large amount of gold leaf in a short period of time. It is expensive, but believe it or not, affording it is the easy part. Finding an adequate supply and the gold beaters who can make it fast enough— well, he has not let me down yet.

An altarpiece for the cathedral needs to be decorative.

This is true, and a man like Vescovo Donusdeo expects it. Nonetheless, I have the idea that I would like my Annunciation to *shimmer*. (Simone slides one of the sheets out from the sheaf and lays it on top for her to see. It is the angel kneeling to deliver his message in yellows and golds; the patterned cloak swirls and curls as though lifted by air, wings raised, mouth open midspeech.) The Angel will go on the left of the panel and face Our Lady, who will be here on the right, the figures set against a background of pure gold. I will not show a room as such, because in effect it has been swallowed up by ethereal light.

(Laura recalls her experience in the oratory—was it a dream? Aspects of it feel distant and unreliable; when she turns her mind's eye toward the memory all she can see is light.) He is bearing an olive branch for peace. And for . . . ?

Victory, among other meanings. Have you heard this . . . ?

Simone Martini lifts a book from his collection. He wants to get it word for word.

God is the Light of the heavens and the earth;
The similitude of His Light is as if there were a niche;

And within it a Lamp: the Lamp enclosed in Glass;
The glass as it were a glittering star;
Lit from a Blessed Tree;
An Olive, neither of the East nor of the West;
Whose oil is nigh luminous, though no fire has touched it;
Light upon Light; God guides to His Light whom He will.
And God strikes similitudes for men, and God has knowledge of
  everything.

Do you like it, Laura?

It is beautiful.

I was recently reminded of this passage, and I had to look it up again. The light, the star, the olive: all of it is in harmony with what I am trying to do . . . even the niche. The triptych will be a sort of niche, will it not? And the painting is itself a similitude. I like it a great deal.

Where is it from?

A book called the Koran.

Laura opens her mouth in shock. The Saracen text? That is heretical.

First, they are not Saracens, that is a name we have erroneously given to a people who do not use it themselves. Second, what is considered heretical is largely subjective, and we should be careful how we apply such an accusation. And third, you yourself just called it beautiful when you did not know its origin.

Laura bites her lip, burning at her inability to argue her point of view. He is too clever for her. Signore, I simply meant, what can that have to do with the Blessed Virgin? Theirs is a different god to ours. It seems to me you do not have time for these investigations. You should be concentrating on the commission for the cathedral, the church of our faith.

On the contrary, it has been extremely useful. I will leave aside the question of a "different" god, or we will be here all day, and simply tell you this: Our Lady is exalted in the Koran; indeed, she has a whole chapter named after her. I have learned more about her here than from the entire New Testament.

Laura is uncomfortable with this conversation and wishes to avoid more disagreement. Will the Virgin also be dressed in gold, Signore?

If she were, it would be troublesome to distinguish her at a distance on a background of the same material. No, she will be in a red gown with a night-sky blue mantle over it. I have a first-rate color especially for this purpose. Her form will recede into the brightness; the eye will be irresistibly drawn toward her.

Laura leafs through the images. There is a preparatory sketch of a tondo for God the Father, and four more circular designs for the great prophets—Isaiah, Jeremiah, Ezekiel, and Daniel—to be placed along the top of the triptych.

Simone explains that Lippo will be responsible for the side panels of two full-length saints, Saint Ansanus, to whom the altar will be dedicated, and Saint Maxima, his nurse. After Lippo's hard work, he should at least be allowed to paint something.

Laura lifts the last sheet, which is blank. Where is she . . . ?

Simone Martini laughs. You understand my problem.

But you have been working for all this time, I have watched you for hours. I thought you had made numerous pictures of her.

I have. None is satisfactory, none I can use.

The artist picks up an object wrapped in cloth, one of the items Giovanna brought. He uncovers it, a luminous codex bound in red leather, pages edged in gold leaf, thin black straps with intricate gold fastenings, the illuminated manuscript within.

This is my wife's own book of hours, which I gave to her on her last birthday.

Laura receives it, rests it carefully in her lap.

I know at least that my Virgin will be holding this, to show her as pious and wise—I knew it almost instantly when I was approached. As to the rest—the old man shrugs—how will her face be? How does one paint her receiving this strange and wonderful news? What can I paint that will be truthful?

Laura's heart aches, the guilt at her absence as fresh and sharp as a thorn; Simone's kindness in spite of it, and that he did not press her for an explanation. His need for friends precisely as Giovanna described; the position of trust in which she has been placed; a desire to do good. Laura feels these desperately.

What can I do?

It is a problem for me to worry about, young lady. I will solve it.

When? How?

Ideas are not rainbows that appear in the sky, at least not often; they can be worked on, planed like wood, improved with friction. Have I worn you out? You look quite unwell. Would you like to go home and rest?

I do not need rest. I want to be of service.

Simone taps his mottled cheek. Are you sure you want to offer your help?

Laura Agnelli insists she does.

Very well, then.

The painter gives her folded garments belonging to Giovanna and bids her put them on behind the screen. The rich fabric, blue and red, is heavy in Laura's arms, the clothes cut slightly too big for her. Simone organizes his materials: pen, brushes, ink, new parchment. Arranges chairs: one for you, and one we will pretend is the angel. He gives her the codex.

Laura is pinched by self-consciousness. How should she sit? How should she hold the book?

The man mutters for her to do whatever she thinks best.

Laura forces herself into stillness and grasps the book of hours.

It is the most fabulous object she has ever held. Maestro Simone, is there a difference between a closed book and an open book?

A vast difference. (Simone breaks an egg and separates out the yolk, neglects to tell her what the difference is.)

Laura opens the book, then closes it. Open, it ought to be open. Randomly—it is a page from the Penitential Psalms, and what Laura recognizes as *De profundis*. It used to be a favorite passage of hers. Her mouth dries. *De profundis clamavi, ad te Domine. Out of the depths have I cried unto thee, O Lord.* She sits upright, using her backbone in a pose she hopes is both modest and resolute.

Simone Martini commences a new Marian *modello*, the first he has made led by the instincts of an orphan. The novelty of the experiment reignites his enthusiasm.

They fall into a half-trance.

Time is measured for Simone by his progress, outline correction face hair feet chair blue gold. He is transfixed by the delicate doll that materializes—she has a sweetness, a primness, and a restlessness—as though the figure on the page would drop her book on the floor, stand up, walk away. His experienced eye discerns it is not exactly right for the altar (it lacks drama, narrative, presence). He did not expect immediate gratification but senses this is the closest yet he has come to his Virgin. He is on his way at last.

For Laura, it is oddly similar to sitting in private. She soon realizes the painter is consumed by his work. Though he concentrates on her appearance so intently, he is barely aware of her person as long as she does not move. She finds this easier than the hours she endured when Simone was trying to ignore her and she so frequently irritated him. It is a relief. It is an opportunity to think, to untangle some of the mess.

De profundis clamavi, ad te Domine. Domine, exaudi vocem meam.
Fiant aures tuae intendentes in vocem deprecationis meae. Out of the
depths have I cried unto thee, O Lord. Lord, hear my voice: let thine ears
be attentive to the voice of my supplications.

Laura, you are slumping.

The girl straightens, her muscles aching. Maestro Simone—her
voice cracks a little—will your wife, will Giovanna, come today?

No, she is visiting her parents.

I should like to see her again.

You had a pleasant conversation, did you? I shall ask her to
come by next week.

I should like to see her again very soon.

I am sure she would like to see you too.

Laura trembles. As soon as she can, please.

Simone Martini raises his gaze to her. Whatever is the matter?
Her skin has turned to a dreadful pallor.

The artist sets aside his tools and goes to her. He asks whether
she is sickening, and she does not deny it. Should he send back to
the hospital for a physician?

She refuses. It is true that Laura has the urge to cry, but she
does not want to shed tears on anything that does not belong to her,
least of all the precious book of hours. She rests the codex with her
thumb to mark the page (it might be important for it to look the
same when the study resumes).

I will be all right soon. I think we were doing well, Signore. We
ought to continue.

No, we will stop. There is a burden weighing upon you, Laura
Agnelli. Why not tell me what it is, and I shall see if I can help?

Laura mutely shakes her head, makes a brief and artificial
smile.

It is why you want to see Giovanna, you want to confide something in her, I think. Regrettably she is away for several days. What-

ever it is, can it wait for so long? To me, it seems not. To me, it seems you are suffering now.

It is unimportant.

Is someone hurting you? Are you in trouble? To confessor, doctor, and lawyer, do not hide the truth.

Laura wrings the folds of the fabric with her free hand but does not, now, avoid his gaze. Which are you being, Signore?

Whichever you are most in need of. Just a friend, if it pleases you. I thought we had become friends today, you and I?

We have. We have.

Then tell me what ails you. Tell your *babbo*.

Laura's reply is a whisper. I am in despair, Maestro Simone. I have been robbed.

Who has stolen from you? What have you lost?

I have been seeing a man outside the hospital, and now I am sure I am with child.

There is a flicker of astonishment in the artist's face, and a glimmer in his eye like the breaking of day, which fades as his features rearrange themselves into the mask of deep thought. Then your demeanor and your recent disappearance are finally accounted for. What can you tell me of your young man?

Laura fixes her suspicious stare on him. Why? What are you going to do?

Nothing. Not anything. Not one thing, without your express wish: you have my word.

At this, she relents. His name is Bartolomeo Pavoni. He is a citizen of Siena, I think. I had not considered marriage until I met him and he began paying me attention. He was very charming at first.

Yes. I see. Now I must be indelicate for a moment and ask a necessary question: are you absolutely certain that what you and this Pavoni did together can cause pregnancy? Because if you just held hands or merely kissed and touched each other—

Laura cuts across this speech. Yes, she knows what took place is the thing that causes pregnancy.

I had to make sure. Can you tell me the way this occurred?

We had a special place only we two knew about—

No, not that. I wish to be clear about whether or not this person physically harmed you. Did he force you?

Once again, Laura looks ill and for a minute is tongue-tied. He said he loved me. He made promises. He said I was too good for a convent, and he wanted me for his wife. I tried to reason with him, to put him off, but he was eager and impatient with me.

Was he cruel to you . . . ?

Laura covers her mouth, then composes herself. He was persistent, and I was deceived. He was kinder afterward and assured me no one would find out.

And no doubt he seemed mature to you. Did you see him again? Does he know about the pregnancy?

I did not wish to see him. I wished to break it off. I intended to do my penance and, God willing, to go to Santa Marta as I originally hoped. When I realized, I sought him out and told him. I said I accepted, I said I wanted to get married and to raise our child together. I thought he would be pleased because he had asked me often enough, but he just stopped coming. At first I thought he needed to get used to the idea, but I have since heard he has gone to Ravenna and I think it might be true because it is a city he talked about, and I have searched everywhere else I can think of. In my heart I acknowledge he does not want to be found, but I do not know what to do without him.

Do you love this fellow?

You will think badly of me if I say it was his honeyed words that affected me most, the thought that someone cared for me and found me desirable. I have lost the life I might have had for *that*. (Laura's voice cracks.) I have been trying to think precisely which of my sins has merited this treatment. I have been trying to under-stand why God is allowing this to happen to me, and yet denies you and Giovanna the child you both yearn for.

Because God is either not as benevolent as we would like to believe, or not as powerful. Or maybe he has his own reasons.

I would have married Bartolomeo even though I do not love him, even though he would have made me miserable. I would have tolerated him and made do. (Laura covers her face.) I am on my own now.

Despair is also a sin.

If I bear this child and raise it as a bastard, we will be destitute. I have no income, nor the means to make one. We will be ostracized. I will never find a man who is prepared to marry me and take care of someone else's child. Shall we live on alms from Santa Maria della Scala until we are found dead in the street? Shall I become a prostitute like my mother probably was? I know I am complicit and I could have avoided this if I had behaved better, but why must I alone be punished when two people have sinned? Is it because I am the vessel? I am remorseful, Signore, but I am also angry. You will not tell anyone . . . ?

No. But nature is going to give your secret away unless you take your destiny in your own hands, young Laura. Clearheaded-ness must prevail over desperation.

Laura rises to pace to and fro.

Simone Martini sits with his fingers linked across his belly. Would it be so terrible to entrust one more foundling to the care of the hospital that raised you? It would give both of you a chance.

A chance . . . it has not occurred to me before that my own mother might have been a daughter of Santa Maria della Scala, that I might be but a link in a chain. I always imagined I came from outside the walls, from somewhere else, was taken there out of mis-fortune. A chance? I might still go to a convent, then, perhaps not

Santa Marta, but another may still take me. If not, I suppose I could marry, although it has never held much appeal. Eventually I may even be able to have the child back. (To Simone's surprise there is amusement in Laura's face.) We call that "the lie."

What do you mean?

It is the sentimental promise made by women when they bring their babies to the hospital. They give the infants tokens and trinkets to identify them by later on: engraved coins, rings, pins, buttons, embroidery—you would be amazed at the variety. But it has never happened, not once. The objects are disposed of and the women never come back.

You could stay on at the hospital and watch your child grow.

They would not allow it. Only one of us would be permitted to stay. But then, in all likelihood, only one of us would survive.

My child, do not think such morbid thoughts.

You have not seen it, Signore. You have not seen how many women and babies are killed by childbirth. By sickness. So many horrible ways to die. When disease ravages the wards, the smallest and weakest are the first to succumb. It is accepted, which is the same as saying it is acceptable.

You have lived to adulthood. Why do you doubt your offspring would?

Maybe it will. Maybe it will be a beautiful youth. Maybe one of the hospital's benefactors will take a fancy to it. You must have heard the rumors, Signore? I expect that you would recognize one or two men from your social circle who are regular donors. Quid pro quo—

A hooked hand springs to Simone's mind; it repulses him momentarily, he forces it away.

I have been spared. If anyone's eye fell upon me, the rector steered him away because it was assumed I would be a nun and should be kept chaste. But some are too pretty for their own good.

And stubborn. They draw attention to themselves. But I can see perfectly well why women who bring the children they cannot keep to the hospital believe it is for the best, for the slim chance you speak of.

What is in your prayers, young Laura?

That God will take this thing away. I know it is awful, but I would count it a blessing.

It is a risky strategy, simply to hope. Have you considered fully all your choices, or are you going to be a victim of fate?

She darkens, catching his meaning. I cannot undo one sin with another.

Not "undo," but potentially limit the damage. It sounds to me that you are in a position where you must pick the lesser evil.

It would be wicked. I would be excommunicated if I were found out.

I am old now, but I was young once. Ought I to believe the thought has not occurred to you? Are these accidents new or unusual? There is nothing new under the sun. You are not the first young woman to be in this predicament, and you shall not be the last.

But to harm an unborn—

Tell me where in the Bible it says that a woman shall not end a pregnancy if it appears the least harmful course of action?

Thou shalt not kill.

Simone Martini nods. Yes, it does say that. I cannot deny it.

The artist gets to his feet and turns his attention back to the plate of olives. He takes one and offers them to her, which she refuses once more. He eats the olive and spits the stone back into the palm of his hand and holds it there.

Whenever I eat an olive I discard the stone. When you eat an olive, what do you do with the stone?

I discard it too.

Yes. It would be strange indeed if everybody attempted to plant the seed from every single olive fruit and grow a tree from it. The olive tree is sacred, you know. Myth has it that a goddess called Athena quarreled with the god Poseidon and won a competition against him to be the patron of a Greek city by giving its people the first olive tree. I like the idea of another great city with a powerful protectress like ours. Even if it is not true, it is a good story. It would be extremely destructive to cut down a fully grown olive tree without good reason.

It would be wrong . . .

Quite wrong.

But Signore, we are not talking about seeds and trees. We are talking about immortal souls. Your analogy does not hold.

I admit I do not have the flair of a bard, but I want to know whether you genuinely believe the cutting down of a tree and the discarding of a stone are of *equal* severity. Are they?

A simile is not reality.

But you agree that a grown tree and a dormant seed are not the same as each other? If you believe they are the same, have the courage to say so. *I* do not think they are. I think that one is life fulfilled, and one has the potential for life requiring soil, water, sunlight, time to grow and be actualized. That is my opinion. And I say these things to you because you have suffered much in isolation, because you have already been misled, because you have no parents to guide you. And a student of scripture really ought to know that on this specific matter, the Bible is silent. Why? Well, that is anyone's guess. Perhaps the authors do not pronounce judgment because they believe it to be a private matter, or a matter for society to decide. The Bible tells us *thou shalt not kill,* and yet we do, when there are sufficient reasons. Rather often, as it happens. What about defending one's city in war? What about the execution of a guilty man? Our *church,* on the other hand—the one that you and I are members of—is indeed vocal and would call it a crime. But that is not the same.

Your words are hurtful.

I am sorry for that, Laura Agnelli. You ask God, why has this happened to you? I ask myself, why did God ensure you and I met? I believed at first it was for the painting, but now I am not sure. Be wary, Laura Agnelli, of anyone who claims to know what is in God's mind and what God wants us to do. *For my thoughts are not your thoughts, neither are your ways my ways, saith the Lord. For as the heavens are higher than the earth, so are my ways higher than your ways, and my thoughts than your thoughts.* Whatever you decide, young Laura, is up to you, because it is you who will have to reconcile your conscience and live with the consequences of your actions.

Laura murmurs, Graves are filled with after-the-fact wisdom.

Simone throws up his hands. Giovanna says that all the time; it is her favorite expression. My wife is a know-it-all.

Poor lamb. What shall we do with you?

Laura lays her head on Giovanna's lap. Giovanna rubs Laura's shoulder, pulls back the strands of Laura's hair so they do not fall into her face, tucks them behind her ear.

You know what I want most is a baby son or daughter, given to me by Simone. I still have hope that God will provide us with one.

Laura closes her eyes.

But I believe we can help you. We have connections.

If the Blessed Virgin gave but a moment of her attention to the prayers of the citizens of Siena, what might she hear?

A voice as thin and as sharp as a needle: Thank you for the new altarpiece. Let it bring to the Duomo many worshippers, regardless of its controversial design. Please do not be too displeased with it. Artists are wayward and unpredictable, and need your leniency . . .

A voice guttural and well fed: Ensure successful representations in Avignon on behalf of your beauteous hospital, and the privileges to guarantee its continuance and prosperity . . .

(These entreaties, and thousands more besides.)

A lady who renews her request every month: I know my life is rich, but give me this one blessing more and I shall never ask for anything else . . .

A girl whose pretty face is wrinkled with effort: Please bring me a husband who will take me away from here! Let him be talented in music so he can write me songs, and wealthy so he can buy me presents. Most of all, let him come quickly! I do not even mind if his breath smells . . .

(Not all requests shall be granted.)

Bless the new novice who has come to us, who seems troubled, who reminds me of myself . . .

Help me to be worthy to live here for the rest of my life . . .

What of the numerous pleas that are made without words, and to no one in particular? Does the Blessed Virgin distinguish between eloquent prayer and an infant's caterwauling? Would her eye fall, fleetingly, on a humble cot? Does she know one undersized baby from another? Recalling its history, is she moved to extend her protection to this one? Would a whisper from her to a flawed human heart be enough to save its life?

Many details go unrecorded.

Pieter Janssens Elinga

Woman Reading, 1668

They are friends, the two children. Children have a talent for making friends. They have not yet learned the inhibitions of grown-ups. The friendship between a woman and a man can be fraught with complexities, expectancy; but a girl and a boy may be friends and play together. Yes, let's play. What shall we play?

The girl is bossy. Girls are. They can be precocious and have fixed ideas. Girls like to think and feel, boys like to do. This girl is no exception: it shall be a game of dragons and swords—it is decided, she has decided it. Green dragons (the very worst dragons are always green) and golden swords with jewels in the hilt. We will use stinging nettles for dragons and sticks for swords. I shall be a knight and you can be my page. Or horse: you choose.

Boys can be ignorant, and here is a potential barrier to their friendship . . . he does not understand.

Patiently, Esther explains again. She is the knight, he is the

page—or the horse—those nettles covering that bank are the dragons. And we are going to slay them.

Hugo responds to her instructions with bewilderment. She
repeats herself once more, but his attention wanders. Rules and
crafted stories are wasted on him. She resorts to pantomime, to dragging him by the arm to her chosen place, to exaggerated pointing.

Over *here*, Hugo—and this is your sword.

She forces a stick into his fist and picks up her own; hers is longer and straighter. He inspects their tools. His would make a useful
walking cane and he tries it out.

This is the way we kill them.

She swishes her stick into the foliage and lacerates the leaves.
Fleshy specks fly.

Boys are predisposed to destructiveness, so this game appeals
to little Hugo. He has no idea of the romantic saga constructed
around them; rather, he copies Esther (bossy girl) and their friendship strengthens—out of mutual hatred for nettles, out of shared
enjoyment for smiting them. Heads of leaves chopped off, torn up,
never to harm anyone again. *Swish smack,* for all the bumps and
rashes, for terrorizing the villagers with fire, for eating maidens. The
children are ruthless in their work. The stems snap, excreting sticky
resin—dragon's blood. Slice, poke, stab. Two small bodies doubled
over like farmers, heads bobbing with effort, their sticks could be
sickles harvesting the overgrowth.

A villager, unaware she has been liberated by the brave
adventurers, approaches. It is Hugo's mother, her clogs kicking
up dirt with each step. The knight and her attendant, the nettle-
vanquishers, punish their prey without pause until she interrupts
them.

Hugo's mother moves her lips. Hugo moves his lips. She moves
hers again and Hugo stares at his toes.

Esther cannot fathom it.

The woman flares her nostrils at the little girl, her expression uglier than before. More lip movement.

Hugo, as though pulled on a string, waves good-bye to Esther and goes home.

Esther watches them leave and a familiar loneliness descends on her. Whenever she thinks of a good game, whenever she finds someone her own age to share it with . . .

She seeks solace in her task with more violence than before, but the spirit of Saint George deserts her. The dragons fade; the malevolent weeds take their place and counterattack with invisible teeth, biting the backs of her fists, her bare legs, making her skin sore and scratchy. She bashes them down, *desist, surrender,* but they are winning. Without her friend, the battle is futile.

It is not fair. It is not fair.

And there is something else that hurts her horribly: how can Hugo—who is slow and unimaginative and needs commands and leadership—do this remarkable trick that Esther cannot?

Geertje is making pastry, sleeves rolled to her elbows, hands deep in the mixing bowl. She rubs the fat and flour together, lifts it up, lets it fall. This is the delicate process her mother showed her and she has shown Esther—who comes home. Her daughter's skirt has new stains on it, her hands and ankles are red and patchy, she is on the verge of crying. Geertje brushes off her fingers, wipes them on the cloth so she can sit with Esther, troubled child.

Now tell me what is wrong? I am sure I can make it better.

Esther recounts what has happened, leaving out some parts, but Mother can guess them.

Like this? Mother stills her hands and opens and closes her mouth like a trout.

Yes, exactly.

Then Geertje explains. You and I, we talk differently to other people. It is nothing to be sad about. God has simply decided that some people will talk using actions . . . and some people will talk with mouths. However, it often causes confusion. When we cannot understand each other's words, it can be very irritating. So we have to be tolerant, you see? We learn to manage and make the best of it. That is all we can do.

Does God not want everyone to talk to each other?

Yes, he certainly does. Yes, he would like that very much—which is why he made your father, who is especially talented and can do both kinds of talking.

Esther does not understand; she does not feel different from other people.

You are, my love.

The girl must check this with Father.

Christiaan is in the smithy, hammering a glowing bar with controlled force on the anvil, sparks escaping. It complies with his modulated strength, the blows softer, harder, softer, responsive and accurate. Esther stands clear as she has been taught her whole life to do, the wall of savage heat keeping her at bay. Christiaan slides the worked metal back into the furnace, a blade sunk deep into hellish, fiery jaws.

Am I different?

The little girl implores the blacksmith to correct the mistake, to flatten it out, to reshape it. Yet if Mother is wrong about this, it will be the first time in Esther's life she has been wrong about anything. Geertje is commonsensical. Her ability to master the mysterious and fearful was one of the main reasons Christiaan married her.

Black. In her dreams, Esther sees a figure arriving at their village carrying a rake. It shuffles along passing the church, passing the well, passing the mill and the modest houses. It is not a man and it is not a woman. It is a creature. Old and covered, crossing an erratic path, touching walls and doorframes, windows and cradles, hearths and pillows. It touches what we touch and is guided by moonshine. Its robes are miasmic, seeping into cracks and crevices. It blows poisonous breath into lungs, on the napes of necks, under armpits and dissolves stout hearts into nothing. It hears neither prayers nor argument. It sways with each step; it is bent, it is evil, the most efficient killer with the lightest caress. It leaves behind black footprints.

And Esther dreams of a land populated with skeletons. Skeletons that trip over fields, ride in wagons, crouch in boats, climb trees. They chase and hide and tumble. Bonfires are set alight in their names. They clatter their bones, they gnash their teeth. How quickly their abominable numbers swell, doubling doubling doubling.

All are equal, are leveled.

The blacksmith's forge is cold. Only one kind of work to be done: the ghoulish business of digging ditches and filling them in. Christiaan's arm is strong; he shoulders his spade and joins the volunteers. They improvise masks, communicate in single-word sentences. Here. More. Stop. Mounds appear beyond the boundaries of consecrated ground. Whole families laid waste, including Hugo's. People say, perhaps the whole village . . . ?

Geertje cannot hide the lumps under her arms and in her groin for long—she is bedridden in hours and dead within days. The brightest and kindest are as susceptible as any, and returned to the earth in a putrid heap.

The visions and smells and sounds penetrate Christiaan's mind, attractive to the demons that Geertje's strength had kept at a distance. He recognizes their advancing shadows and approaching tread. Their warnings.

Miraculously some do survive. Life grows back, gradually, like ivy, clinging on, breaking through. The peculiar blacksmith and his deaf daughter are long gone.

Where are we going?

Church.

You always say that. We passed a church this morning. We passed two yesterday. Churches abound. Do you really know where we are going? If you have lost your way, you ought to admit it and not be so proud.

Keep up.

I think we should go home.

We cannot.

Yes, we can. Mother would want us to.

No. She would want you to have a future.

We can go back to the smithy and I will take care of you.

She would want you to have a husband and a family.

Maybe I will, one day. But if that happens, I will still be your daughter and look after you. We can turn around and go home, right now, if we want to. I could even find work.

Not safe there.

Safer than on the road. Safer than having nowhere to go.

We are going to church.

And what if the same thing happens when we get there? It might. It could. Who knows, it might even be worse.

Be quiet.

Do you have the pain?

No.

Are you sure? You promised to tell me when it comes. You made a promise.

No pain, and this is the way.

It must be some church, if we are going to all this trouble.

57

*   *   *

They arrive in Amsterdam. Suddenly they are walking along canals and through side streets and by the IJ Bay itself. Esther is in awe of the assault on her senses.

Here are the whalers, the shipbuilders, the sugar merchants, the fishermen, the customs officials, the innumerable networks of contracts and dealings, the constant braying and barking of beast and hawker. Here are ropes, crates, and kegs slung with force from deck, to slipway, to cart, from man to man. Faces and arms cracked and browned from exposure to sun and salt.

Chinese porcelain held up and admired for its decoration and translucence; silk from Bengal; tea from Ceylon; Japanese gold and silver; cinnamon, mace, nutmeg, precious pepper from the Moluccas, the Banda Islands, Malabar, and Sumatra; coffee and rice and opium and camphor: jealously guarded treasure. Even souls are bought and sold, written up in a numbered column by the slave traders.

The glitter of currency counted out of the port and immense wealth counted back in. Warehouses filled and emptied and refilled. A signature. Hefty mariners straining with physical work, men in expensive robes surveying progress, barefoot children chasing and climbing in dangerous places, prostitutes competing for trade. Boisterous inns. The rowing boats pass, and the shouting and the whistling, farewells and greetings. The pong of decomposition on the breeze. Flick of sails and twirl of smoke. Here in the grime, in the dipping and rising of vessels on the tide, in the maps of secret routes across the oceans, in the firm handshakes, in the bureaucratic structures, *here* is the most powerful agency in the world at work.

When they find the right church, it is on a shabby lane and indistinguishable on the outside from other Amsterdam houses. Hidden, as it were.

Esther will never know for certain whether this was Father's last action as a sane man or the first action of a madman. But she will always be thankful for the day he brought her to a room noisy with conversations she could understand; will cherish the discovery that a place existed where people use their hands instead of their tongues for speech.

She tells him he is the cleverest of all fathers, he has got them here and now he can rest. But he is withdrawing into himself before her eyes, turns away from her entreaties, folds into a crouch on the floor.

Excuse me, lass, is your father all right? Would you like some help? You bring that chair over, we will pick him up.

Christiaan's imagination burns hot yellow and red; the iron of his personality is smelted. What is left is scorched and brittle: debris, the rubbish. His wife protected him when she was alive but now, after he has buried her in unconsecrated soil, the fiends are coming for him in hordes. It is Sunday again and they are here—the grotesques have come to stare at him and torment him (they demand their entertainment, they have paid their entrance fee). They wear civilized clothes and speak in refined voices but are plotting all the while, and will eventually drag him into a hole that is at once dark and aflame, smelling of rot, slithering with worms that will crawl over his flesh, eat him alive. He can feel them on him, in him.

His distress is amusing for the visitors. They find it hilarious when he makes funny gestures, waves his distracted hands in the air. What is he doing? Pumping pretend bellows? Carving with a pretend chisel? Striking a pretend nail on its pretend head? They believe he is miming the smithy he fantasizes about. They do not know he is trying to communicate with the daughter he pines for.

The mute maid who has been taking care of Jurina's stepson must go and that is final. There was a period of grace following the wedding—Jurina Bos is no tyrant. But that was almost a year ago and her baby is due any day. It is, she thinks, unseemly for a lady of her quality to have servants without the requisite skills and abilities. She has been charitable thus far, gracious in her acknowledgment of the maid's diligence and cleanliness, and yet the time has come—

Pieter Janssens Elinga, the painter and the husband, acquiesces. His adolescent moneyed bride shall have her way. He is beholden to her. The arrangement was supposed to be temporary anyhow, following the death of his first wife, Beatrix van der Mijlen (whom they do not talk about). Esther, barely more than a child herself, was cheap to employ and all he could afford. An investment that enabled him to woo and remarry, for he was disadvantaged as a suitor: poor, widowed, a young son to look after. All he offered Jurina Bos was the prospect, the hint of a prospect, that his talent might be recognized in Amsterdam one day and prestige would follow. Will it do? Then he will give her as many children as she wishes to have, one or twenty or none, it is up to you. Is it enough for you, my sweet? He was artistic and persuasive.

More than enough. For Jurina this is a love match, and she is glad to share her wealth with him. With *him* and *their* children, in the home of *her* making, with servants of *her* choosing. She is a diplomat, has waited tactfully for the appropriate occasion. To be clear: the birth of her first child is the appropriate occasion.

Notice has been given to the girl despite Young Pieter's tantrums (that Elinga's son sometimes prefers sign language to speaking normally has grown tiresome). She is a benevolent mistress, intends to help Esther secure a post in a different household, a household more suitable for her.

That is all there is to it. Let it be done, let the matter be closed. For goodness' sake!

The labor starts.

The venerable doctor (handpicked by Jurina on account of his position within the surgeon's guild) does not hurry when called for. In this, at least, he turns out to be right. It is difficult, protracted; two nights go by and the baby does not arrive. Jurina has no choice but to be attended to by the silent, inexperienced maid, who blends into the background. The lady sinks in and out of consciousness, barely feels the flutters of attentiveness, licks the water drops on her dry lips, has her hair pushed back from her forehead, squeezes the skinny hand holding hers. Unbearable. Agony. Exhausted, Jurina starts to pray. Not the prayers of the past nine months (let it be a son, let it be a strong, bouncing son, let him be tall and gifted and rich). Those prayers no longer matter. A new prayer entirely erases all the old utterances: Please, God, if you have any mercy, let it be over.

Does God answer? What, or who, will be his instrument?

Maybe it is the mercurial doctor who announces it is dead. It is worse than any of them thought; the baby is dead and in order to save the mother the legs and arms must be amputated inside the womb. He is taking the implements from his bag, reverently lays them out; eyes and blades glint with fascinating light.

Jurina screams, the mere sight of them sending her into histrionics.

It is normal to be apprehensive under the circumstances, but let me reassure you—

Elinga is beside himself. Helplessly he paces back and forth, nerves in tatters, allows bloody thoughts to overwhelm him.

A quack. Sheer quackery. At best the man is deluded; at worst he is a rogue. Yet it is this devil to whom they defer, his perverted expertise, his distorted sensibilities. Lack of sleep and food, anxiety, mortal pain . . . all have taken a terrible toll. Rationality is defeated.

Fortunately, amid turmoil, a vibration of good judgment can

prevail. The shock is wearing off and Jurina succumbs again to her body, disorientated, drowsy, making the surgeon's job easier so he thinks. But he is dismissed by the deaf-mute maidservant.

Absurd. He is insulted.

She cares not a whit for his indignation. Her gestures are unmistakable: Go! It is done before the master and mistress are truly aware of it.

A warm, nutritious broth rouses the lady, carrots and beetroot and chicken and herbs, with Esther at the bedside gently feeding her. It is accepted gratefully, humbly. Two women from a neighboring house answer the appeal for help (you should have come to us sooner) and the labor is resumed.

They deliver Baby Lucas, whole and perfect. For a time, Jurina will brook no discussion about Esther leaving.

Esther and Young Pieter sit by the Singel, feet dangling over the edge, shoes removed and laid beside them so they do not drop into the canal. They are playing their game, which involves pointing at what they can see. They take turns to be the teacher. Esther shows Pieter the sign and Pieter shows Esther the mouth shape. Practice and repetition help the lessons to stick.

Rope. Reflection. (Esther's hands form each one and Pieter copies.) Green. Fat. Wet. Canal.

And they make up phrases to test themselves. Pieter's goes like this: I saw a fat man wearing a green hat and he made a reflection in the canal. If I pushed you in, you would be wet and I would need a rope to pull you out.

I would like to see you try.

I would like to see you fall in. Basket. Old. Gray. Apron. Window. (Pieter says each word aloud and Esther studies his lips.) Flying. Fighting. Bone.

Esther's story is: I carried a bone in my basket to give to the old gray dog. People were fighting in the street and I looked out of my window, then I put on my apron and went flying over the houses.

Pieter exclaims, No you did not, that is nonsense.

I do fly, I do it when you are not looking.

It is a lie!

Esther assures him it is the truth and then gives him some words to do: Bricks. Woman. Fish. Parsnip. Short and . . . Esther.

If the short woman who smells of fish sent Esther away, I would put bricks in her bed and I would never eat another parsnip.

The boy gazes at the maid loyally, unashamedly.

Esther reminds him he must treat his parents with respect.

Lucas, all of nine years and nearly ten, has an instinct for other people's crises. His knack for smelling the truth is so much a part of his nature he is barely aware of it . . . and there is a new scent on the air. Not the ludicrous number of departing servants; anyone can see them for what they are, unimportant, uninteresting, unappealing. But what about the change in Esther? Stupid, dumb Esther who prefers Young Pieter—of all people—to handsome, clever, lovable Lucas. Who but a man with his father's weaknesses and a child as intelligent as he could detect a difference so subtle? Who in the household but canny, perceptive, astute Lucas could anticipate the chaos that will follow in its wake?

He sits alone deep in contemplation of the eddying currents at work in the family home.

Probably Esther is cleaning. Probably Father is drunk. Mother is out.

Then he is climbing the winding stairs before he thinks to do it.

Esther is a tall woman (taller than her mistress), adept at her role, has outlasted all the staff introduced above her. She sweeps dust into a pan in one of the bedrooms, oblivious to her master, Pieter Janssens Elinga. Her head is bowed over her broom and her white lappet cap obscures her peripheral vision. She is concentrating on her work, and why would anyone have cause to stand and watch her without declaring himself?

The artist, his back to the wall, tightening throat—what does he look at?

Her profile. The veins showing through her transparent wrist. The slope of her back under her jacket. A tiny scar where she once burned herself on a pan. Her poise, her purpose, her motion: he looks at that. The folds of her skirts, the hem moving to and fro. She goes into and back out of a corner, sweep sweep turn sweep; the floorboards will be spotless when she is done. That she pauses to scratch her nose, that she continues where she left off, it is endearing, has resonance. She is methodical and pretty in her way, and he cannot help himself.

Being alone in her presence fills him up. He feels it. He has experienced this sensation before, tastes the familiarity of it. He craves her body (he tells himself), to uncover her, to reveal her, to be in her. Yes, he wants her, but no, not quite, not exactly.

Of course he would—if she ever came to him, he would. Though she is somewhat older and shapelier than he prefers, he would probably risk everything for her. He has imagined it often, imagined them together, imagined plenty of obscene details when he is fathering the children promised to his wife. Esther's face, Esther's skin, Esther's tongue, Esther's hips, on him, beneath him, bent in front of him. What prevents him then from having what he wants? If he has managed it before without compromising his reputation, made the arrangements before, found replacements, honed the techniques to make it discreet, enjoyable, and perfectly possible from start to end?

She picks up a thread from the floor, displaying her angular ankle, and puts it in her pocket. She slips her hand under her cap to adjust the hair beneath. Upturned eyelashes.

He watches because he likes her spirit. He wants to be acquainted with it, intimate with it. He likes her for herself. He likes . . . her.

If she came to him, only if she came to him, only if *she* came to *him*. Even her silence is alluring—nothing to remonstrate or criticize or nag with—merely patience, admiration, empathy, the splendid qualities he attributes to her passivity. Regal and untouchable. He comprehends, finally, it would not be like the other maidservants, not a bit, and the feeling is familiar because it is the same as *Beatrix*.

Unlucky Pieter Janssens Elinga. Wretch. It has taken him more than ten years to discover this truth and when it happens, he is devastated, hardly anything left of a man. Your body tremors, Pieter Janssens Elinga.

At last the maid sees him, eyes vivid. Should she reproach him? A scowl?

He crosses the room, is too close to her too fast for her to believe it. All these years he has never shown any interest in—

Despite his high-minded sentiments and pure motives, he reaches out to twist her hair, is touching her cheek, is drawing a line along her jaw with his thumbnail, construes her astonishment as curiosity, her reluctance as shyness. Would have her after all. This is part of the dream he has woven: their telepathy, their connection, the round, pink open mouth that lacks a kiss—

She does not find it charming. That he has caught her off guard has contributed to her predicament, but composure is returning. How to repel him without turning him against her? She tries to pull away but Elinga tightens his grip, making indentations on her pale throat.

The absence of sweeping is most suspicious to Lucas. And he

did not hear Father go to his studio at the top of the house, his sanctuary from his family. He wants to know what the grown-ups are doing, peers within rooms, finds them at last.

And what does Lucas see? Father holding Esther near to him; and the maid's hand reaching up to reciprocate, to clasp his, pressing her face into his palm like a cat.

Lucas's intake of breath alerts his father. Elinga stares at his treacherous son and while his guard is lowered, Esther peels away from him, dips down to pick up the dustpan and broom, and escapes, strides directly for the doorway, straight at Lucas.

He squeaks (would Esther beat him with her broomstick for what he has seen?) and flees, hastening down, down the awkward staircase, running the whole way to the yard, heart pounding pounding out into the sunlight—

His little sister and baby brother are hunched on the ground, playing with wooden clothes pegs. Anna does well to occupy Allart. The pegs are his toy army; she lets him give the orders in his burbled speech, sending them into war to be victorious, or killed, as he chooses.

Lucas crosses the yard to the opposite wall, presses his head to it with his arms around his face, as though counting for hide-and-seek, stays there a while. Then he appears to stop counting (did he reach his goal of one hundred?) and kicks the wall instead, once, twice, repeatedly, rams his fist against it as if he would knock it down. Allart pays him no attention; Anna pretends not to.

Lucas is not crying. Lucas never cries.

Then he stops and immediately assumes authority—he is the captain now and the captain musters his rabble crew (the smaller children) for inspection. They are for him and with him, willing and impressionable, deserting the wooden army on the battlefield in favor of stronger leadership and a better game. Get them moving seems the best plan, get them busy busier busiest. Lucas resolves that his brother and sister will run around in a large circle with himself in the middle of it. He shouts his instructions.

Anna is seven (bonny and moonfaced); she screeches with delight, relishes the attentions of her admired older brother.

Faster if you can, lazy dog, chants Lucas.

Anna obediently tears about the yard. Waf-waf! Waf-waf! If she is the dog, Lucas must be the human.

Run, run, lazy dog. Catch the rabbit. Lucas encourages or reproves their progress.

Anna fizzes with excitement and chases Allart, who has been consigned to the role of prey.

Allart, too little to care about becoming someone's dinner, is enjoying the game. He nods his blond head repetitively, as though in agreement with every command and insult Lucas throws at him, while Anna still shrieks with pleasure. If Allart trips over, he hauls himself up again on his chubby legs, bottom first, body following. Anna overtakes him more than once, doubles back when it pleases her.

In the yard (or is it a forest?), the dog captures the rabbit. The rabbit wriggles free but with further incitement from the human is apprehended again, giggling and hot.

Anna growls at Allart because she is thoughtful and knows how to inhabit a role.

Good dog. (Lucas pats her on the head.) Bad rabbit for trying to get away. (He wags his finger at Allart, and the rabbit laughs harder in response.) And now it is time to skin the rabbit.

Yes! Yes! Skin the rabbit! Skin the rabbit!

Anna says, But how can we when we have got no knife?

Simple, we will tickle him until his skin falls off. And then we will eat rabbit stew and I will have a new pair of gloves for the winter.

Lucas and Anna set to work. Allart is rolled on his back and transforms into quite a different animal, from a rabbit to a tortoise stuck on its upturned shell—he chuckles merrily and enjoys being the center of attention. The laughter is shared by the three children, who have a pitch and pattern similar to one another. Anyone hearing them, like three bells ringing together, would think it delightful. Good fun and easy to join in with (at least at first). They grow louder, exhilarated, hysterical.

Eventually Anna feels the joke wear off, tires of it. As the only girl she has to be sensible. Her tickles have subsided, become less vigorous, less frequent, and then are finished. That is enough now.

Lucas does not agree; he is just getting started.

Allart's face glows and tears form in his eyes and still he laughs his helpless laughter, squeals belting out.

I think it is time to stop.

He likes it!

Allart is short of breath, gulps from the back of his throat, bursts of noise indistinguishable from cries. He is too small to fight back. Lucas tickles him all the more—some of the tickles resemble pokes, some are barely concealed pinches.

Lucas, I think you're hurting him—

But Lucas is determined.

Anna backs away. It is not fun anymore, has turned quite nasty. (Why does Lucas have to spoil it?) She does not like being an accomplice and is now confronted with a horrid decision: to watch, to tell, or to run away. She frowns at the cruelty of men while she considers her choices but is spared the anguish of committing to one—Esther is upon them in a trice, grabs both brothers, separates them, halts the attack.

Esther stands Allart up, loosens his buttons, rubs his back, checks him for bruises and lumps, dries his eyes. He recovers quickly but is gasping, bewildered, and flushed. Odd laughing sounds still escape him, as though, already shaken loose, they must all come out until he is empty.

The maid beckons Anna, puts her in charge of Allart. Anna will take him inside, splash cold water on his face, clean him up, calm him down. Anna does so without complaint because she reckons she has got off lightly.

Then Esther straightens to her full height, folds her arms, glares down at Lucas.

Normally Lucas would launch into his defense: they were only playing—it was an accident—it was someone else. Ah, but this is not a normal day . . .

Between them is the incident that took place upstairs, what was seen, what was perceived, what might be said or left unsaid, what consequences will follow.

Lucas looks back at her intensely, as though she has injured him, then he flings his arms around the maid, hugs her tight at the waist—too tight; he is strong for his age.

It is his turn to be patted on the head . . .

This child is difficult. He has long spells of moodiness and bad behavior. When he is not having tantrums he is often serious and solitary. He has emulated his mother's dislike of Esther, is unafraid of showing it. Teasing, derision, spitefulness are his ways. Not neediness, not the offering of affection—it is atypical and uncomfortable.

Esther disentangles herself from his embrace. She would like to get away from him but he is disheveled from his rough game, has mud on his knees, broken skin on his knuckles; his clothes are askew. And after all he is just a boy. She tends to the marks, brushes them off, dabs them with a hanky, straightens his collar and his garments in a matronly manner. She will not show him fear. She will not behave as if she has done anything wrong.

Something else he never does: he never signs to Esther but always makes her read his lips. The only member of the family willing and able to converse fluently in her language is Young Pieter.

But Lucas is signing a sentence now, deliberately and correctly. I . . . want . . . to . . . lie . . . on . . . top . . . of . . . you.

Lucas has seen the private activities of his father, watched with fascination and revulsion from inside a closet and through a keyhole. It is the secret adults keep from children.

He waits.

For a moment, nothing. And with a flourish, abruptly, suddenly, making Lucas flinch at her speed, Esther turns on her heel and marches back inside.

Lucas is left alone again. He does not smile. He does not sneer. Of course he does not cry either.

He has a coin in his purse—one single coin. He does not yet know its full buying power but is certain he can spend it only once. The question is where to spend it, and on what? Where will it bring the most personal benefit? Or where will it cause the most damage?

It is sure to make her sister envious. In the lesser reception room, Jurina composes letters sitting upright at the desk, working with a quill pen. The bulge of pregnancy shows beneath her gown.

Her veracity has been tested of late. She has described in loving detail the accomplishment of Elinga's most recent still lifes . . . and omitted that his productivity has become erratic, the gaps between completed works wider. She has gushed about expectations for the new baby's health and possible names . . . but failed to mention the acute financial pressure an extra child will bring. Meditations on the exquisiteness of tasteful Delftware purchases have been replaced with inane chatter about coughs and colds. She has written herself into a corner. By naming their important guests, she will draw attention to the length of time since the last sale of a painting. Tricky. But, oh, Jurina wants to tell the witch about it, she will hate it!

Restraint, Jurina. Dignity. Best to stick to women's matters.

The baby has been moving and I wonder which sex it will be. It would be nice for Allart to have a brother near his own age to play with. And I think it might be good for Lucas to have two brothers.

She intends to write that another daughter would be an equally welcome addition when she realizes her error. Not too late to save it—*it might be good for Lucas to have two brothers, to look up to him.* There.

Allart is a bright and perfectly adorable child. If I can produce another little boy to match him, it would be an achievement indeed. Too much, even if it is true. Her sister will find a snide remark to make about it, unfavorably comparing Jurina's modest brood to her own unruly flock.

(I know you agree that hyperbole is a mother's prerogative!) & a girl would be a welcome addition, so I find I do not mind.

The lady stretches in her chair, her back aching, perspires from the discomfort, massages it to bring some relief. Jurina could never have believed she would grow sick of pregnancy this quickly—how has her sister endured it eight times?

Carrying this child gives me more pleasure day by day. I shall be almost sorry when he finally arrives in the world and I shall have to return to my former self. By the way, please thank my brother-in-law again for the reference he wrote. My stepson and I are extremely grateful and will let you know of any developments.

Unusually, Jurina would like to write further about Young Pieter: that she thinks he may have left home by the time the new baby arrives; that without him Esther's employment will be untenable. She inhales a big breath at the prospect. Inside her womb her next child kicks. Despite herself, she continues—

It turns out Young Pieter is not as obtuse as he appears. He came back from a market a week ago with a stuffed lizard. Quite the ugliest and strangest object you ever saw. & said we should make a gift of it to Rembrandt van Rijn—no need to put "the painter," Rembrandt is a rare enough name—*because the old bankrupt had to sell his collection of artifacts. He (Young Pieter) said Rembrandt still has valuable contacts in Amsterdam and at the Guild, and if Pieter Janssens gave him this thing as a present, he would make some introductions with a view to arranging a sale or a commission. Here then is the surprising news. Not only did Rembrandt accept the gift eagerly, he & the prestigious art dealer Johannes de Renialme are coming to a viewing appointment at our home today. Who would have thought my stepson to have an aptitude for business and influencing people? Pieter Janssens insists that I be there, that he cannot do it without me.*

Jurina rereads it, visualizes her sister seething. So what if she guesses there has been a drought? It will be worth it. *Suffice to say, I find the whole thing an ordeal and would prefer a quiet afternoon with the children. How lucky you are not to have these burdens, and only the house and family to be concerned with.*

Esther enters, and Jurina is compelled to turn the letter over. She has brought a bowl of fruit and a cushion. The maid has noticed how her mistress neglects to eat and drink for several hours at a stretch when she is anxious; the meeting with the art dealer is clearly playing on her mind. The dish and a sharp knife are set down, and Jurina alters her posture so the cushion can be placed at her back. These kindnesses are infuriating.

Allart appears, rosy and dimpled, staggers into the room; Lucas lurks at a distance. Allart wants to be on Mother's lap so she lifts him up. Beloved Allart, darling prince; she kisses his temple.

Lucas, are you idle because you have finished all your lessons?

Lucas does not confirm or deny it but withdraws from his mother's sight.

Then she gives Allart back to Esther; the child whimpers as he is led out of the room.

Jurina attempts to pick up where she left off but the flow has deserted her. Instead, she takes a pear, quarters it, eats it.

The mistress of the house has considered the matter in detail and her logic is infallible. She will argue it has become too much for her to cope with, that a lady of her status with four children requires a certain standard of help. And, she will say to her husband, if our situation means we can afford only one maid, then we must make a decision. Society has expectations for the wife and children of Pieter Janssens Elinga. Jurina's parents have expectations.

Jurina does not hate Young Pieter or Esther; that would be rather strong. It is more that they are anomalous in the life to which she aspires. Pieter is to join the East India Company, the VOC, like many of his class—they are not all bumpkins and street rats. Esther? Esther? Esther will have to accept what is what and find a new position. Nothing unusual about that. The girl has benefited from long service, twice and three times longer than normal. The obligation did diminish. Eventually. The maid can take no credit for the smooth pregnancies and faultless labors that followed Lucas, not one miscarried or stillborn. Jurina has grown hard-hearted about this, waited ten years, occasionally demeaned herself by resorting to petty tactics. The maid will be gone and a different, carefully chosen servant appointed instead. No more reprieves. No more dewy-eyed willows. And no more panting bitches. This time it shall be done properly.

She thinks of another topic to put in her letter. Her sister can be relied upon to relish complaints about the help. *Another flunky has left us. (A relief but obviously the Old Irritation persists.) I should like a mature maidservant to replace her, one with years of experience. Lots of years. I want her when my new son is born or soonest after to give me the support I need ~ what do you think, a single solution to two problems? I know you know what I mean.*

Jurina turns a blind eye, for her husband's and children's sakes. It grieves her, yes, but if it is not flaunted, if she is not humiliated—

Her pen nib hovers over the page. Were Elinga to turn his

attentions to Esther for a short while, were Jurina to have evidence of it, however flimsy, then she could send the packhorse away immediately. She cannot confide this thought, though her sister would certainly have sympathy for it.

I have realized I do not know where the Irritation attends church. Not ours. I mention this because Lucas says It regularly visits the Jewish quarter these days. But we would know if It was a Jewess by now! Such a thing could not stay hidden for all these years! (Where does Lucas get his information from? If he is making up lies, it would not be the first time.) No, I am not worried about that. However, I have grown concerned that we could be inadvertently harboring a Catholic. This is much more plausible. If I discovered that It goes to a clandestine church of the old faith ~ in your opinion would that be legitimate grounds for dismissal? Do write back and advise; you are good at these knots.

When the two gentlemen are welcomed by the host and hostess, their presence fills the entire house. Johannes de Renialme is the more loquacious, a tall, serious man with a crisp white collar, his clothes and broad hat expensively dyed black. Rembrandt is dressed hardly better than an innkeeper, gray locks and sprouts of whiskers, jowly and paunchy; he says little and has a grumpy expression. Yet Jurina knows a fraternity when it arrives in her home. They shake Elinga by the hand, pay him respect as almost an equal, compliment him on his tasteful decor, his elegant wife—expecting a fourth, are you? Jurina is prim by nature but loves to be admired for her voluptuous belly. Esther is instructed to fetch the good wine.

De Renialme surprises the party by accurately describing a domestic genre painting of Elinga's, which he saw in a client's home, of a maid sweeping. It was very pleasing. Have you got any more of those?

Not at the present time.

Elinga explains he has been concentrating on the medium of

the vanitas still life recently—and the distinguished men are shown to the main room, where the paintings are hanging. There are two, displayed as pendants though conceived separately. Expertly done, remarkable, the objects look real enough to hold. One shows a perfectly formed wineglass half-filled, arranged with lemons in stages of decay upon a silver platter (even the reflections are perfect, *perfect*). The second is of a jug and some smoking materials. A pipe lies waiting to be picked up, the coal gutters in a cracked pot, and the tobacco has been carelessly abandoned by the absent smoker.

Elinga asks the art dealer, How do you find them?

Maudlin.

Thrown, the painter starts to justify his choices. The fruit is bitter and disintegrates before our eyes; the smoke vanishes into the very air, as do we ourselves suffer and are ephemeral beings, mortals on the cusp of death.

Yes, yes, but will people like it? Do they wish to look at moldy lemons every day while they are having their breakfast? (De Renialme has grown insensitive to artists.)

Rembrandt tries to defuse the situation by praising Elinga's skill and observation, but this irks his colleague further.

If you like them, Rembrandt, why don't you sell them in your own gallery, hmm? No, I thought not—and if this is how you repay a good turn, I shall remember it. Elinga, have you tried offering them to the Lottery? They might take them for runner-up prizes.

Jurina turns defensive. Are they not good? Since when did *liefhebbers,* rich and knowledgeable connoisseurs, cease to appreciate superb Dutch painting?

The dealer explains the connoisseurs are as potty for fine art as ever they were, but there are phases, cycles, you might say—

Fashions? The same as for hairstyles and dresses? For paintings? It is news to her. She thought fine art was timeless.

So it is, madam; *prices* of art, on the other hand, are a different animal and can fluctuate dramatically.

This is a blow to Elinga and his wife.

But Johannes de Renialme has not quite finished. His rudeness softens. One or two people come to mind who might be interested in your work, and a handful more will find the investment potential appealing. I think I can find someone to purchase your canvases, though if you take my advice and hold on to them, their value will appreciate.

The couple have discussed this beforehand. We cannot wait. We will accept reasonable offers.

Then—it is agreed, the arrangements follow, the tension dissipates. And, on time, the maid brings in a tray of wine and goblets, sets it down, pours. Johannes de Renialme notices her.

Are you sure you cannot muster the enthusiasm for some genre interiors, Elinga? Plenty of Amsterdam art dealers would have no problem whatsoever selling those. Pretty girls taking music lessons, pretty girls mopping floors, pretty girls cuddling pups—demand is ludicrously high. (He mentions some prices, depending on size and quality, of course.) Based on what I have seen, Elinga, yours are rather good.

Esther offers drinks to De Renialme and then to Rembrandt, then her mistress and master.

Would you sit for your master, for example?

The dealer directs the question to the back of Esther's head.

She cannot hear you, Elinga explains, and signals to the maid that one of their visitors addressed her.

Jurina bristles. Do not embarrass the girl.

Johannes de Renialme sips his drink, decides not to pursue it, is confident that if Elinga's family is as hard up as he thinks, the artist will soon come round.

The mistress dismisses her, and Esther takes the empty tray away (annoyed because they were talking about her).

To Jurina's consternation, Rembrandt van Rijn follows the maid, his feet flapping on the tiles all the way to the kitchen.

Esther knows who he is, folds her hands demurely at this breach of etiquette.

Rembrandt stands respectfully in front of the woman. In low tones he asks, Can you understand me, miss?

She nods.

Rembrandt smiles, a wrinkly, mild, jocular smile that unmasks his severity, makes her smile back. I am very fond of faces, and I like yours. If ever you wish to be painted by me, if your mistress can spare you, come and see me.

The artist doffs his hat.

Esther beams.

Bodies crammed together surge into the East India House courtyard. On the threshold of ambition and uncertainty the men and boys thrust themselves forward, a crush of folk, the strongest climbing over the weakest. From slums, villages, orphanages, and foreign countries—brought here by poverty, bankruptcy, aspiration, and pimps. Waves of meat. The crowd bottlenecks at the archway, regroups, and scrabbles to the entrance steps of the VOC headquarters, where marshals struggle to hold the mob back so they can be seen individually within. The gang vents its frustration by jostling and grumbling at the front, by pushing and yelling at the back, where they strain to see what is happening. They press onward. Desperation and conviction swell the throng, each applicant eager to catch the eye of the Committee, impatient to be signed up. Advance, advance, stand out from the masses. Be fearless. Many will be turned away.

The son of a painter, more timid than most, huddles down and presses between the shoulders and torsos of his rivals. He is kicked

Katie Ward

and punched. The new suit of clothes his parents gave him marks him out as middle class, may get torn before he is seen. His nose may get bloodied or his teeth knocked out. If he stumbles, they will trample him. He pushes toward the front of the multitude. He digs deep.

At the same time, elsewhere in the city, a maid works vigorously through the rooms of a house, brushing, scrubbing, shaking out. When she has finished a job, she slaps the furniture or object, admonishing it for becoming dirty. Now she makes the beds, *smack* for being slept in. Now she empties a dustpan, *bang* for getting dusty. She picks up her mistress's shoes and drops them, *thud, thud,* find your own way back. It is only when she is standing on a chair forcefully rubbing at the windowpanes that her energy subsides, the glass gleaming, the latticed sunlight streaming in. She has expended some of her anger.

Esther can only be this way when she is on her own. Is it really the best use of her solitude? Closing the widows gently and stepping down from the chair, she looks about to see what is left to do in the lady's bedroom. Cushions to be set straight, jewelry to be put away, the mirror on the wall needs a polish. It is too early to move the cradle in, but perhaps time to sort out baby clothes from the storage trunks. She wipes her hands down her apron, tries not to think of Young Pieter.

Certain there are some in a chest here, she opens it and examines the contents. Jurina's dresses and petticoats are at the top; these Esther sets aside in neat piles. Beneath are the shifts, bootees, and bonnets each of the children has outgrown; blankets, swaddling, a christening gown. Jurina should choose. Carefully Esther excavates the layers and separates this from that. A few family documents and letters and sheet music are kept here. Milk teeth in a jar. A perfume bottle from the Orient. Spare leather. Embroidery thread. And books. Only three, all unwanted gifts. The maid knows these. Jurina's books, literature, are neglected. She prefers her Calvinist Bible.

78

At this moment—when temptation invites, when it hurts no one and discovery is unlikely—a pause. Esther covets this. Not wealth, not the station of her mistress, not the person of her master. She covets *this,* the liberty to sit, to choose. A suspension. The awareness of an indistinct version of herself who comes into focus, who steps into the light.

The beautiful story of the knight Malegis, who won the famous horse Baiart and undertook many wonderful adventures.

The rhythms of the story fill her up.

Esther does not have the disposition to dwell on who deserves what, and why she should be born to one class and not another, for reality is reality. She is concerned with her own spiritual well-being and goes to church for that. She is good at her job, for if she has to work, she will work well. But who is this other Esther, stirred into life when she is permitted to read stories? She remembers her from childhood—the girl who picked wildflowers for their magical properties, who had imaginary friends, who would stare at the fireplace alive with dancing, wicked goblins. This is the Esther to whom her parents would tell and retell parables and folk tales, and she would sit and listen without interrupting while their hands made dancing shadows.

The romance she is engrossed in has made etchings in her mind's eye; she retraces them easily. The wind that convulses trees, the coolness of a spring, the snort of hot breath from Baiart's nostrils, his stamping hoof, an outline of a castle on a hill. Esther's heart is with Malegis at each test of strength and virtue: do not drink from the poisoned chalice—hold fast—fight back. She fears for his safety and wills him to win. They travel for miles together. Parts she has forgotten she rediscovers; the imprints of favorite passages burn bright with renewed color and feeling. If she reads on, the horse will reveal his fabulous qualities and save Malegis's life.

It is time to stop at the end of this paragraph this page this chapter. She reminds herself she can return to a given point in the knight's journey another day. Malegis will not leave without her.

The shadow of Esther, the twin, the companion, has a stubborn streak. She wants more and has elaborate ways of keeping the world at bay—as he rides the hero looks over his shoulder and has the face of a man outside the Portuguese synagogue.

The maid chides herself for her idleness. She cannot indulge in this any further; it is dangerous. Only in bed, in private, may she permit foolish thoughts. The practical Esther, her mother's daughter, is roused into action. She shuts the book. Still, a niggling, a reluctance. Rather than returning it, perhaps she could hide it in the kitchen under her pillow for a while? No, that is risky. It would not matter that the book is never read, that its absence has gone unnoticed. Were one of the children to discover it, were Esther to be accused of stealing . . .

Esther stands. Book, contents, lid, chair must be put back immediately and it is done. Cushions are beaten into shape. Garnet brooch and diamond necklace dropped into their cases. Cleaning rags pocketed, the shoes she almost falls over reunited. She will take the baby garments downstairs for Jurina when she has given the mirror a quick clean. Esther wipes the looking glass and sees behind her Pieter Janssens Elinga, watching.

This is the first time she has been on her own with him since he compromised her, and it strikes her hard. She does not wait to see what he will do next, does not consider how long he has been there or ponder his intention (good or bad). Practical Esther is in charge. She snatches up the baby clothes and hurries away, knocking past his open, insulting hand.

At the company's headquarters Young Pieter signs a bond, takes possession of two months' wages in advance and an appointment to the VOC ship *Prosperous.*

Jurina wants Esther. To sew a button for Lucas, to buy some cloves because Allart might have a toothache, to lift a heavy object for her. Has she gone out? She must have done, and Jurina's bile gives her pain.

The lady has only herself to blame. Esther is doing what was asked of her, cleaning and tidying Elinga's studio while he keeps an appointment at Johannes de Renialme's office. Cups and plates have been discarded up there, some of his clothes have been draped and abandoned. Jurina said it offhandedly, Do the studio today, will you? Remember, the composition and the materials must not be disturbed.

Elinga is consumed by painting once again, has a project he is executing quickly, zestfully. It fulfills him and calms his mind, and he suspects the picture will fetch a decent price when finished. Jurina wants to encourage the optimum conditions for his creativity and yet has forgotten her instruction, or rather has fixated on the notion that the maid has gone out without permission.

Esther has felt the change in the atmosphere. Esther—who thinks always of self-preservation, who fears being blamed for accidents, who avoids going into her master's private space unless explicitly directed—is wary. She feels a threat from what she might see in there.

Jurina hastens from room to room in search of the maid. It is ludicrous that she cannot call her but must go and get her. She navigates the narrow stairs, up, up as far as the second floor, no farther, then down, down back where she started, her pulse and breath increased. She will confront the maid about this.

Esther can carry out her task without necessarily seeing the work in progress. The easel, camera obscura, and an arrangement of furniture are at one end of the studio, and by averting her eyes she need not discover the true content. Collecting the dishes, a cursory dab of the duster, and laying the stockings and undershirts over her arm, she can circumvent the working area completely if she desires. But she does not quite desire. She prefers to know.

A knock at the front door, a figure visible through the window—and Jurina must answer it herself. No, she will not. She makes Lucas do it, adds this to the list of Esther's mistakes. Female voice. Lucas comes back to his mother, fiddles his fingers coyly. Well? (Lucas grins without answering.) You are the least helpful sort of child. Jurina—impatient with her son, with her servant, with everything—goes to meet the unwanted person so she can send her away again.

Esther sets down her master's forsaken garments to inspect the scene unencumbered. From here, viewing the arranged furniture without proper sight of the canvas, what she can see is essentially a vacant interior. Two frames and a mirror hung up, a chair pulled near to the window at a peculiar angle, two more set either side of a closed chest with a cloth cover by the wall. There is a fruit bowl pertinently left on the upholstery (strange choice), a cushion and a pair of lady's shoes on the floor. She knew that Elinga had gone back to genres but from here, without a model and an activity to complete it, she cannot tell what the composition is doing. There is no musical instrument, no writing desk, no needle and thread, no foot warmer, no basket of linens, no clue about the story being told. Every picture contains a story, be it history, fiction, legend, or myth.

In the hallway, there she is, with her back to Jurina, the back of her white cap, the looped bow of her apron down the back of her skirt. Jurina knows better than to bother saying her name. She strides up behind Esther and taps her hard on the shoulder. The maid turns but it is not Esther. Jurina has never seen her before.

At last, Esther steps in front of the easel, and it becomes clear. Though unfinished, the components slip into place like marbles dropping into holes. The artist's model, Margaretha, is being a maid reading a book. Jurina's book. (Esther throws her glance to her master's bench—there it is among his effects, waiting to resume its place in context.) Yes, it is, the moment when Pieter Janssens Elinga caught her in the act of reading her mistress's book. But it is not the same, not exactly. The artist has changed it, cleaned it, emptied it of domestic clutter. The sorted baby clothes and familial belongings have evaporated; the room is a fictitious one, not Jurina's. The eye is drawn to the patch of sunlight glowing on the floor, giving a sense of the personal and serene. Crucially, it is not Esther. She exhales with relief. She rests her hands on her hips.

In her haste, Jurina must not have looked at the woman properly. The woman has a similar height and build to Esther, but the cap is new cambric, the jacket a deep red. She has a spotty complexion and is not so attractive. When asked her name, she haltingly replies that she is Margaretha, working for the master in the studio. The model? Yes, he did say he was using a model this time. Jurina has not met her; she is always shown straight through.

No, not Esther. There is nothing in this painting to betray her. Nothing that puts her employment at risk.

(Lucas covers his mouth. He guesses this is not a coincidence but a street conjurer's trick—and his mother is the dupe.)

Esther looks again, properly. Not her; not Margaretha either. The woman in the painting has her back to the viewer, estranged and unidentifiable, her face and hair obscured totally by her white cap. It might be anybody.

Jurina berates herself for her lack of composure. The master is out on business. (What does this mean?)

What does this mean? Esther folds her arms. Could someone construe the subject to be her?

Lucas, go and see to your brother.

He scurries away.

Well . . . ?

Madam?

(Madam thinks, Silly bitch.) I said, the master is not here. Come back in an hour.

Margaretha shows herself out.

Jurina leans against the wall. What does it mean? She tries to assemble her thoughts and calm her body for the sake of her child. What, exactly, does it mean? Maybe nothing.

Esther wonders: Could anyone have grounds to demand to know whether it is her or not? Then her future would rest on how Pieter Janssens Elinga chose to answer. He would surely reply that it is only Margaretha, a poor girl who sat for him playing the part of a negligent maid. He would surely explain it is a typical genre painting that panders to the tastes of the modern Dutch family.

Jurina decides that the girl has only a passing resemblance to Esther, the same resemblance most maids have to each other from behind when their heads are covered, their bodies hidden in frumpy clothes. She strokes her bump for comfort.

But he knows, and Esther knows. It is she. He has gone to some lengths to disguise the fact, but not far enough. What if Jurina should ask outright?

Esther, did you cause my husband to paint you by sitting on one of my chairs and reading one of my books when you ought to have been doing your duties? Did you allow him to stare at you, to memorize your posture and shape, to watch you indulging your lascivious fantasies? Did you ensnare him? Did you flaunt yourself? Did you mean to seduce him?

The honest answer is no. Esther imagines herself denying it, but Jurina is capable of twisting this into something terrible.

Then why has my husband admitted that you are the subject of this painting? Why does he dwell on your image in this way? What have you done to captivate him?

Subject, madam, *subject*. Not *object*. I am not, nor have I ever been, his object. (The distinction will be immaterial.)

Is it a pious scene? Are you reading the Gospels so intently? No. It is voyeuristic. It is fetish.

Esther will implore her to see reason—

Jurina will develop a mental block, conveniently forgetting any sign language she once knew so that she can override the maid's protests and play her trump card. *Lucas has seen you and my husband making love. He has seen it. Do you deny that something has occurred between you?*

Evidence of a physical relationship—evidence of emotional entanglement. Enough to send her packing twice over. When Young Pieter has left, there will be no reason to retain her at all. Esther shakes her head at the treacherous painting. It will not matter that she has never encouraged Elinga. That he has all the power and has behaved improperly. That she is the victim.

She will get rid of me.

Downstairs, Jurina's temper has cooled and cold logic reigns once more. Whatever has gone wrong here, the leverage of this new baby will set it right.

I will get rid of her.

Lucas toys with his imaginary coin. He senses that its value is not fixed, that if he waits too long it will turn out to be worthless. And there is another question he has been considering in his brilliant mind: Who will be the most eager to sell their wares? Who has the weakest disposition and will therefore put up the least resistance? Which transaction will give the highest yield for the lowest risk? The answer is obvious!

Lucas has decided what he wants—Young Pieter's bedroom. New shoes with buckles. A globe. His very own sword. And a pony.

He is going to ask Father. No need to say why he wants them or what will happen if he does not have them. He will simply say, Father, I am too grown to share a room with the babies. I need my own room and a pony to ride. And seeing as the new baby will be showered with presents, I think I ought to have some presents because I am the older brother and have many responsibilities. Please?

After the farewell dinner will be the best time. Father will be drunk and suggestible.

Lucas is glad Young Pieter is leaving; anyone can see his half brother does not really fit in. He also likes special occasions, because they have a way of making people less discreet. But it is in Lucas's interests not to be difficult tonight, so he has thought of some appropriate words to say: My dear brother, I will miss you deeply. Without you as my guiding compass, what path shall I follow into manhood? I will pray for your safe return every day.

He wants the family to hear his speech. After Young Pieter is gone, Lucas will be the eldest child, with all the rights and obligations that entails. Being held in higher esteem by his father and mother, for example. And perhaps . . . a bit more tenderness from Esther (if she survives).

The meal is in Young Pieter's honor. The youth sits tensely, endures his stepmother's performance.

Let me toast our son.

The family obediently raises their glasses, apart from Allart, who picks through his food with his fingers.

I drink to you, Pieter. You will see wonderful sights, foreign horizons; I don't doubt you will return wealthier for it in every respect. If I could wish for anything, it would not be to keep you here, rather that we were all able to go with you and share in your adventure.

The children mutter their agreement, the supporting cast in

Jurina's play, sip solemnly from their wine. Lucas has to admire their mother's flair. Elinga drains his glass and waves Esther forward to refill it and remove his plate. She steps out to the kitchen.

When Young Pieter does not make a reply, Jurina addresses her husband instead, and conversation turns to the buyers who have already expressed an interest in the genre piece without having seen it. Johannes de Renialme is running a whispering campaign and attracting a few nibbles. Jurina pouts—I knew it was only a matter of time—and flatters her husband relentlessly, going as far as biting his finger under the guise of a kiss. You must show it to me before it is taken away. She feels powerful. Is satisfied to count the hours until her stepson's departure, to count the days until her baby is due, and then—

(She leans over to cut up Allart's food and prompts Anna to eat what they have provided for her.)

Jurina resolves to plant the seed with her husband this very night while they are in bed, her hands around his hard cock. It needs to have the appearance of being encouraging but contain the underlying point: I am so relieved good fortune is *finally* smiling on us, my love. I have put off searching for *qualified* help to raise our four children because—oh, now I can do so *confidently*.

And tomorrow, after Young Pieter has gone, it will be: My love, the baby is arriving imminently, it is time for us to prepare the house.

The day after, Jurina will initiate her husband's favorite sexual act but she will find herself distracted, weeping, putting off his moment of climax because what if they cannot afford to pay two salaries . . . ?

Young Pieter's voice breaks over the hushed table, clear, unexpected: I will not see it.

The lady pushes a ringlet of hair from her face. Pieter, what do you mean?

I will not see my new sibling, it will be born after I have left. I will miss the first two years of his life, I will not be a part of the home he knows.

Jurina hesitates, putting her anxieties aside. My dear son, blessings on you, you are a credit to us. (She reaches over to briefly take his hand in hers.) Do you hear that, Pieter Janssens? Your eldest son would forgo his own future happiness in order to meet his baby brother.

Or sister!

Anna is the one who has chimed in. Mother soothes her only daughter's displeasure. Esther brings in grapes and cheeses, sets them down. Lucas indicates his own plate for Esther to take away.

Jurina thinks this would be a good time to reaffirm her generosity, asks Young Pieter if there is anything else he needs for the voyage, reiterates he must have whatever he wants from the house, that if there is anything left to buy, Esther can be sent for it in the morning. She sounds firm, as though to mask her own pain. A loving mother putting on a brave face at her first child's departure.

He answers, Thank you, madam.

Jurina finds she has an appetite.

Father has advice to dispense: You must stay healthy, avoid contact with the sick whenever you can, avoid altercations.

The youth hangs his head. Yes, sir.

Anna declares, I promise I will talk about you to the baby so she will know who you are and know you are coming back one day. Then when you do come back, she will recognize you and, and, we will look at maps of where you are. And I promise only to say nice things, I swear it by Jesus in the Manger.

Jurina tweaks her daughter's cheek. What a perfect idea! Anna will remind the baby of its big brother every single day.

Elinga Senior manages his first smile of the evening. Perhaps you can do the same for me, Anna?

For his part, Elinga Junior nods in gratitude at the person who, apart from Esther, has been his kindest friend.

Anna does not notice Lucas glowering at her and adds, We can write letters and save them for you. Would you like that, Pieter?

Lucas, not to be outdone: Or put messages in bottles and throw them in the sea so they float all the way to Asia.

He replies that news will be difficult to come by and he should like to know, one way or another, what has been happening at home.

Anna asks, Ought I to come to wave you off from Silly Jack?

Jurina resumes her leadership. Partings are difficult, Anna, and best not done in public. You would not want Pieter worrying about you when he should be concentrating on the journey ahead and making a good impression on his first day. No, of course not, and you are a big girl for understanding. We can say our good-byes here at home.

The child contains her feelings; the reality is taking hold.

And do call things by their proper names, Anna. It is the Montelbaans Tower; only ignorant people call it Silly Jack.

Lucas senses his moment has come. I have something to say to Pieter too.

Indulgently, Jurina focuses on his earnest face. What is it, my pet?

Lucas sits up in his chair and his expression becomes grave. My dear brother, I will miss you deeply. Without you as my guiding compass, what path shall I follow—?

What is wrong with Allart? Anna is the first to have spotted his contorted face. He seems pinkish and confused . . . something unexpected is happening to him.

Is he breathing? Lucas's tone is curious.

Jurina's heart constricts, and inside her, the baby squirms. Allart makes a tiny gurgle.

Katie Ward

Father announces, Yes, he is fine, it is only wind.

Is it? Jurina, shrill. Are you sure?

In truth, he is not sure. Allart's face reddens further. The little boy mutely suffocates under the diners' gazes. Esther comes back to the awful tableau at the dinner table. She drops the ceramic jug—it smashes on the tiles, breaking the hypnotic spell. Jurina tries to move from her chair (she insisted they buy these huge carved chairs, she insisted upon it), hindered by heavy gown and cumbersome body.

Lucas wonders whether he is about to watch someone die.

The small body is jerked into the air by strong arms and struck on the back with controlled blows, *thump, thump,* for choking, *thump,* for not breathing. *Thump.*

Allart spits out a piece of maimed meat. The silence lasts a second more, then lifts as he wails his distress and the family give way to their own startled reactions. Jurina overcomes her enormous bulge at last, lifts Allart from Esther's grasp as though she were the real danger and this were the real rescue. There, there, my darling one, there, there. She coos and purrs, comforting him, coddling him. Allart bellows with all his might.

Father is pale and shiny. Young Pieter trembles. Anna tries to come to terms with what she has just witnessed by attending to her meal as she was urged to do before.

Esther sees she is no longer required, goes to fetch a bucket and a mop. (There on the floor a whole jug of the second-best wine, shards of pottery, chewed food, and a mouthful of vomit.)

And Lucas . . . Lucas's mind races, clicking like the beads of an abacus, and arrives at several conclusions in rapid succession, confirmed by the way Mother fusses over Allart and Father wordlessly leaves the room. First, Lucas has missed his chance to gain from what he saw and what he suspects; second, Father does not love Jurina's children the way he loves Pieter; and finally—

Allart whimpers, rocked back and forth by Mother.

Lucas leans close to Jurina and whispers it: Now you will never get rid of her.

Please come in, Esther.

The maid lingers in the doorway of the studio.

Pieter Janssens Elinga beckons her, Do not be afraid, come in.

She hesitates then obeys, standing before him.

He sits by his workbench strewn with brushes, linseed oil jars, powders, and paper. At the far end of the room, the painting, virtually completed, rests on the easel, drying.

I thought it was time for us to have a talk. Do you understand what I am—?

She nods.

For a time he does not speak. Perhaps this is the conversation that has been waiting to happen since she was first employed by him. Heaven knows it was not meant to last this long.

Remind me, I have forgotten, where is your mother?

She signs it and when he does not understand, fingerspells it instead.

Forgive me, I am out of practice.

He indicates for her to sit down opposite and take up a pen, which she does, reluctantly. He repeats his question.

paradise

And your father?

asylum

The one at Kloveniersburgwal?

She signs, Yes.

Elinga thinks this over. You visit him sometimes.

Yes.

He asks how her father is but she declines to respond, so he asks if she sends him money regularly.

Yes.

You always have?

A pause. Haughty, Esther raises her chin to him. Yes.

It must be hard seeing Pieter leave home. It is hard for me too.

The flash of rage in her does not go unnoticed.

You think I should have intervened by now, that I have sent him into the abyss. You think he is leaving because Jurina is making him go and because he does not want to disappoint me, that Pieter could be my apprentice or I could find him a trade if I tried. You think I have not done enough by him. Is that so?

Esther does not disabuse him of it. He leans on his hand and she notices how old her master has come to look.

If you do think that, then you do not appreciate the extent to which we all rely on Jurina's income. (The master sighs, picks up a stained rag, and wipes his palms.) Despite any bad opinion you have of her, Jurina has not been ungracious to Pieter. She is a tolerant lady, virtuous, constant, a devoted mother. She has the well-being of her own children to consider. Their futures. And despite what you might think of me, I do care what becomes of my son. However, I have made errors—and my wife keeps fastidious accounts.

Esther picks up the pen. *not too late*

I am afraid it is.

She shifts on her seat and flattens her apron, then signs a complex sentence. Some years ago her master would have understood her meaning. She dips the nib into the inkpot. *you are not the man you were. what has happened?*

I am the same man, but I am worn down by the world.

She turns the paper over. *you have lost already one wife one son yet you risk losing much more. i say this as your servant & your friend.*

Esther, are we still friends?

She barely nods. She could comfort him, in the past would have done. But always, now, she is thinking of self-preservation.

Girl Reading

Elinga says, I do not want Pieter to go on his own tomorrow.

She signs that she is going with him. Then adjusts her apron, again unhappy at the way he watches her.

I meant to say, your idea to make a gift of that lizard to Rembrandt—

Esther jumps in her chair. No, not I.

It was your idea, I knew it straightaway. Pieter would never have thought of it on his own.

Esther folds her arms.

You have given much to this family. And perhaps you have guessed already that you have inspired me to paint genres again.

No, not I. (It is quick, assertive.)

Elinga ponders for a moment, then indicates the painting. Tell me, do you like it, Esther?

Yes. It is beautiful.

No one says that anymore. In the art world it is "sentimental," "romanticized." Beauty is out of fashion.

The maid shrugs her shoulders.

It is an old idea from my studies in Italy that I finally got around to. (He subdues his heart.) An old idea I stole from an altar. I just wanted you to know that.

She exhales and makes a simple sign that she knows he can understand.

Esther, have you never been inclined to find another job in another house?

She fingerspells deliberately, p, i, e, t, e, r.

Yes.

She touches both her ears in a mime.

But I am positive another family would appreciate you just the same. And if one of your employers or one of their children was deaf, well, your ability to communicate would be an asset.

My father.

His son used to address him using that sign, so it is fixed in Elinga's memory. It was hard to make him stop. The two of you depend on your salary? I see. Do you not wish to marry someday and have children of your own?

Esther explains: On Sundays and holy days, people go to look at the lunatics. For amusement. If the inmates' families can pay enough, they are given privacy and are not exhibited. The ones who rely on charity or whose families cannot afford the rates are exploited. I think it makes him worse.

Elinga glazes over until he speaks again, matter-of-factly. I remember all your kindnesses to this family, the grace you have shown us.

(Esther thinks he confuses grace with powerlessness.)

It is important at his age that your father is comfortable, that he has sustenance and medical treatment, whatever he needs. I propose making a charitable donation to ensure this is the case. And your years of unwavering service mean that you will be employed here for as long as you choose to remain. Your mistress and I are both extremely grateful to you.

Esther does not immediately react. She holds his offer in her mind and examines it for flaws. Is it tainted with additional expectations? Can Jurina be persuaded to honor it? Will it crack at the first test of its strength? She concludes it is the best commitment her master is able to make her and thanks him for it.

After the interview, the maid returns to the kitchen, and Elinga is left alone in his studio. Prior to this evening, it would have been simple to send her away. He was merely waiting for his wife to bring it up. He tears up Esther's handwritten notes so his duplicitous son never finds them. It will be a painful promise for him to keep. His guilt. Fear of his own selfishness. He hates that Esther knows him so well.

He must quell his lust, or find more suitable outlets for it.

He must quell his heart and allow its object to be free, to stay or go as she chooses.

There is a festival atmosphere around the Montelbaans Tower by the Oudeschans canal. Some people joke that Silly Jack will randomly peal its bells in honor of the occasion. This is an orderly version of the events at East India House—these are comrades for the time being, sharing empathy and excitement, brothers to look out for you. Some lads are cocky and unruly, sizing up their potential rivals, showing off. Rumors are passed on, blessings and superstitions are swapped.

The parents demonstrate their affection and grief. Embraces, kisses, pledging their prayers, their love, Godspeed. Wishes and presents are exchanged. Bystanders stop to marvel and celebrate or to pity them, the third who will not come back.

The company officers administer and direct the crowd from their ledgers. To the cutter do not dally we are racing the tide. Next soldier come forward.

As the small vessel fills with recruits, another cutter returns from the *Prosperous* having delivered the most eager, mast leaning to the tower, fat sails deflating, colors flickering, oars engaged, coming about. The full boat is pushed away to make room, the people cheer and whoop, family and strangers waving them off, hats and spirits lift when the boys aboard energetically wave back. Dozens of youths with nothing to lose but their lives. One starts to sing and the rest join in, sending their voices to those they have left behind. Children run alongside to the end of the jetty— They have gone out to the bay, are out of reach.

The empty craft is secured in its place; the boarding process is beginning again.

Esther is vulnerable, caught between shifting groups. Sunlight sears off the imposing form of an observer: it dazzles and disorients her (the highly polished breastplate and helmet of a pikeman, it must be), and she collides with another youth who could easily be a woman dressed as a boy, striking features, comely mouth; Esther bobs in apology to the prepossessing delinquent, finds Young Pieter's arm, and links hers through it for security.

They hold back; there is no need to hurry.

Pieter has something on his mind, and this is his last chance to ask it. If there is an opportunity not to come back, should I stay forever?

You mean permanent settlement at the Cape of Good Hope, or Batavia, or another VOC base?

Yes. Make a new life for myself. If I can, should I?

Esther does not answer immediately. You may find you want to come back. You may find you are homesick, you miss your family, the climate does not suit you. You may long to return to Amsterdam, marry a Dutch woman, and have children with her. Life in a foreign country may be harder than it is here.

However?

However, if I were in your place and there was advancement or love for me on the other side of the world, nothing would induce me to return. Not even you.

Do you mean that?

Esther knows it hurts his feelings but adds, I would not give you a second thought.

Pieter does not respond. Instead, he checks his bag, his document. Esther rubs a smudge from his cheek. She used to be able to pick him up; now he is a full head taller than she.

Pieter marks the accent of secrecy in her eyes, realizes there is something else to ask, something important that he should have asked much sooner, but he has been insufficiently sensitive until now. Esther, are you in love?

She is stunned by his insolence. On any other day, at any other time, she would have denied it. Yes.

What is his name?

I do not know. We have never actually met.

Who is he, then?

I think he is a student of medicine. Furthermore he is—Pieter does not know the sign so she has to fingerspell it—a Sephardic Jew. I am ashamed to admit that when I first noticed him, I followed him. He led me right into the Jewish quarter.

Pieter gazes at Esther in astonishment.

She says she has seen him several times since, always looks for him near the synagogue—would not dare go in, in case she caused offense. She describes the Jews she sometimes sees him with, chatting and sharing a joke; they seem like nice people.

Eventually, uncertainly, he says it does not matter.

Stop it.

But it does not. You have to meet him. Someone at your church can interpret for you. I would have done, if you had only asked me.

I insist you stop it.

Pieter is frightened by her sadness but persists. Esther, why should you not tell him how you feel, if he is your heart's desire?

Because.

She hides her face. Pieter puts his arm around her while some tears come, the way she used to comfort him when he cut his knee or banged his head. In a crowd of separations they do not stand out, and stay this way until her shuddering has ceased.

It is not only that I cannot speak to him. Even if I could, I have nothing to offer. He is well born and I am in service. He would prefer a woman of his own race and of his own faith, I am sure of it. The obstacles are too big and too many to overcome.

But how can you live like this? My father loved my mother,

Beatrix. They were happy and they had such a difficult time. I wish you had seen them. You would have liked my mother.

She smiles at his innocence. Yes. My parents loved each other too. Yet I can live like this, and I must. Besides, this way he remains perfect, this way I can never be betrayed or disappointed by him. He is just exactly what I hope and wish for.

To Pieter it seems tragic. He asks after her father.

Esther shakes her head. I do not think he knows who I am anymore. Sometimes he acts as though he is pleased to see me, but I think it is the food I bring him that he is truly glad about.

Esther, are you going to marry one day?

One day I will be too old.

You there! The VOC official is summoning stragglers.

Me, sir?

Say good-bye to your sister and get a move on. We need to fill all the spaces.

Pieter and Esther hug briefly. She kisses him on the cheek and finds a way to be pleased for him.

He presents himself to the company officer, gives his name, Pieter Janssens Elinga, the son of the painter.

Not anymore, you are the company's son now.

Details are confirmed, the clerk makes a record. The young man boards the cutter and finds a gap where he can still see her. Other families can only shout or wave. Pieter and Esther continue their conversation.

Pieter, be careful.

I will. You too. Take care of Anna for me, she was upset.

I will look after her. She will be all right.

Will you promise not to tell anyone what we discussed?

Not a word, I swear it.

Commands and warnings as the cutter casts off. Friends and relatives bid farewell, handkerchiefs fluttering. Inspired by the example of the previous boat, a chorus strikes up of a different song, louder and ruder than the first. The Montelbaans bells ring out but it is only to announce the hour; Silly Jack is disappointingly punctual today.

Get a move on time is against us come forward. Next soldier!

Thank you.

What for?

I will miss you.

I will miss you too.

I love you.

Good luck.

Good-bye.

Good-bye.

Angelica Kauffman

Portrait of a Lady, 1775

I looked everywhere for you, Frances!

But Frances does not appear to hear. She laughs, is running into the garden, following colored lanterns down to the fountain, a bottle of champagne in her hand. They are at a wedding party; music drifts from open doors, intoxicated revelers.

Frances, I looked for you.

Come on.

Maria runs after her.

Come on!

Frances pauses, turns around, beckons. It is almost morning. She waves the bottle like a prize, mocking Maria.

Maria redoubles her efforts, lifts her dress in two handfuls to run faster. Frances slows to a walk, and with renewed optimism—she will surely catch her now—Maria sprints to her. But it is not right, as though she were underwater, as though her feet were floating several inches above the ground.

Coming, I am coming.

Drunk, Frances ignores Maria. She twirls on the spot; the lanterns blur, pink and blue and yellow, too fast, dangerously fast.

I wrote a poem for you, she is saying far away as she spins and spins.

New Year's Eve. They go to the masquerade as highwaymen, arm in arm, Maria holding her tight, feeling her solid warmth, the pair flashing their pistols, robbing ladies of their tokens. They wear breeches and stockings, the shapes of their legs revealed to the delight of the gentlemen, to the disapproval of the spinsters and chaperones.

Stand and deliver, Your Grace, we have taken a fancy to that decoration in your hair.

The duchess plays along, clutches her breast.

Villainous! What if I will not give it?

Then I will take your life, though it grieves me to deprive the world of such a beauty as yours (and Maria makes a bow to the excited onlookers' amusement).

Frances declares, Do not listen to him, Your Grace, he is a rogue. I will protect you and be satisfied to steal a kiss instead.

Her lips skim the back of the lady's hand to more shrieks and applause. Many allow themselves to be stolen from several times over—kisses trifles jewelry coin surrendered for the fun of it. The pair are sensational.

Did I tell you I wrote you a poem?

Did you? Is it in the bag?

Maria searches for it amid their booty; it is not there, and Frances is gone again, at the other end of the room, enthralled by the attentions of a gaudy matron dripping in frills and filigree. The woman's thick form almost bursts from her dress and she chuckles exuberantly as she pretends to read Frances's palm.

Maria's ferocious daggers of jealousy. She remembers this incident, it happened just as it is happening now: the other woman offers Frances a drink that looks like milk but gives off a nefarious green tinge. Maria wills Frances to refuse it, but she does not.

Mesmerized, they toast each other like lovers, and Frances tastes the mysterious liquid with the trepidation of a child taking an adult's medicine. Whatever is in that glass, it causes Frances to lean toward the wench and whisper into her ear. They share a secret moment of understanding, a connection.

Maria is helpless, watches them, horrified. What a row there was afterward.

Did you see the lady made of light?

Is it part of the poem you wrote?

Oh, here it is.

Oh, there you are. I have been looking for you.

Maria has found her, is glad.

Now Frances is in the library bay window at home, her writing board on her knees, has been here the entire morning.

I am writing a poem for you.

Maria suspected as much but is nonetheless flattered. It is June; the smell of cut grass tells her so.

Please may I see it?

Frances holds out the paper and Maria attempts to take it once, twice; she cannot, it dissolves at the touch.

Here it is. It says everything.

Maria tries again carefully but the sheet eludes her—a wisp.

Frances is radiant. Like a lady made of light.

Maybe Maria can make out the words from here? No. The words slip over one another, little black fish swimming about.

What does it say? (It is her poem, Frances has written it for her.)

Everything I ever wanted to tell you.

Maria feels the edges of the world beginning to break apart and she guesses, or remembers, why it is imperative—

She is pleading with Frances to read it to her but her voice is muffled, will not be summoned. Everything is in it, she said. The room becomes as broad as a valley, the bookcases as tall as a forest; they are being swallowed by the sun. If only Frances would read it aloud, then she could memorize it, take it with her. Her begging is inaudible even to herself.

You read it, Maria.

I cannot. The words are moving. The paper does not like to be held.

And she tries once more, grabbing at space. The sun is getting brighter, draining the room of lines and depth. She is trying to shout, but the sounds take no form. She thinks, *I must not frighten Frances, she seems to have forgotten she is dead, and I ought not remind her.*

Read me some of it, Frances, because . . . because—

Frances is puzzled: Maria is rejecting it, something is amiss. Her face is impossible to see as the daylight blazes in.

Now—you might not have the chance again!

Maria reaches for her, has the parting perception that Frances is annoyed with her.

Just a few lines, Frances.

She is thinking it only, mentally imploring the fading vision.

Mrs. Plett draws back the curtains and opens the shutters, the window, then another, and another, letting in fresh air.

My Lady?

The countess is deep in the middle of the mattress, a mess of bedding and auburn hair, asleep. Coward also, curled at the end.

Mrs. Plett moves closer to her; firmly, My Lady?

Her breathing is regular, undisturbed.

Making no progress with the sleeping woman, Mrs. Plett shoos off the black pug instead, who sneezes at the indignity.

My Lady?

The housekeeper cannot suffer it. She picks up one of the hard pillows and wallops it back down.

Maria!

Maria stirs not immediately, is groggy.

What is it, Mrs. Plett?

She is here.

Maria knows that if she ignores her housekeeper, she will tire soon and leave her alone. Failed efforts to make her get up have become integral to their routine. The maidservants do not have the willpower to challenge the countess; only the housekeeper has enough authority to bully her for her own good. Already the tendrils of dreams ensnare Maria, pulling her back down (can still find out what is in that poem) but something Mrs. Plett said peals like a bell.

Who is?

The Paintress.

Oh, nonsense.

You can tell her so yourself, My Lady.

Maria finds she is awake, narrows her eyes against the daylight, leans on one elbow.

Why would she turn up so early in the morning, unannounced?

The housekeeper stands to her full height, reaches the limit of her patience.

My Lady, it is almost three o'clock in the afternoon, and I would hardly describe the visit as impromptu.

The countess heaves herself up, gathers her thoughts.

Shall I bring tea to the drawing room and send Rachel to dress you?

The younger woman nods, and when Mrs. Plett has left, she steels herself to resist the comfort of her bed, rises. She finds she can remember her dreams most clearly in the dim seconds between sleeping and waking, can carry the figments with her by clinging fast, repeating them in her mind . . . occasionally they survive the scorch of day and it is as though Frances has just left the room. And sometimes the images collapse like sandcastles.

Maria pours cold water from a jug into a basin, splashes her face. The Paintress is here, is she, Coward? And after Maria had given up hope. The dog watches his mistress with expressive eyes. Yet she finds she is not pleased, not pleased at all. She splashes again and dries herself with a towel. The glass tells her she is aging.

While she waits, Angelica Kauffman examines the paintings in the drawing room. Antiquities, mediocrities, noticeably nothing contemporary (someone told her once the earl keeps the best for himself). The room is clean, elegant, fine, but old-fashioned and smallish. The Turkish carpet is beautiful but in need of repair, the furniture shabby, the stucco embellishments could do with touch-ups—opulence gone to seed.

The countess is dressed and wigged, though her bearing is slug-gish, crumpled, unmade, shawl trailing, cameo askew. Coward fol-lows, her little soldier. She sees the luggage as she passes through the hallway, greets the guest with a loose handshake, invites her to take tea.

Angelica is a beauty. Her hair is up in a turban of sorts, her mantua has sashes and accents of the pseudo-oriental in white and green. She is brown-eyed and slender, and her English retains hints of her European roots.

Your Ladyship looks well.

Thank you, Miss Kauffman, that is generous of you. Maria serves her, asks about her journey.

Long, Your Ladyship. I have come straight from London.

So far? You must have left early.

I did, it was still dark.

Maria lifts her own teacup and sips. She is nauseous, at sea, and this exotic creature perturbs her. She asks, Do you have business in the area, Miss Kauffman?

No, Your Ladyship.

Have you turned into the itinerant artist? Perchance this is a midway point on a longer journey up-country?

No, Your Ladyship. Angelica frowns.

Then, Miss Kauffman, may I ask what has brought you here?

I came to see you, Your Ladyship.

Maria chinks the cup into the saucer. How sick she has become of society; how long it has been since she had visitors. She wonders if she will ever find it appealing again. Already this encounter is draining her.

Very conscientious of you, Miss Kauffman. And were the roads agreeable?

Dry.

Good. Wet roads are inconvenient.

The countess rises, a glance out at the garden, flattens her wig absentmindedly. The artist, hungry after traveling, takes dainty bites from her biscuit. Coward, the spoiled baby, snuffles for scraps.

What is the news in London, Miss Kauffman?

One topic dominates the rest: the American colonies are saying they want independence. From what I understand, the Loyalists are greatly outnumbered by the Patriots, who would declare the colonies a republic—are prepared to go to war for it against their king. They would risk mob rule, and even make alliances with France and Spain to shore up their cause.

How boring . . . To underline the point, Maria yawns and then adds, Do the Americans know that France and Spain are still monarchies?

I should not think it has escaped their attention, Your Ladyship.

Maria can see the delicate spine of the artist revealed by the sunken neckline at the back of her outfit, reminding her of a bird.

What is your view, Miss Kauffman? Ought the king to surrender the colonies to the American people, and save everyone a costly war?

Angelica sighs and answers, I have no interest in politics. One cannot be both an artistic and a political being—not the kind of artistic being I am, anyway.

She eats the meager offering, while the countess circles the room and asks if she has had enough.

Angelica replies she has eaten plenty . . . and hopes she did not arrive at an inopportune time.

When I get headaches I sleep most of the day.

I am sorry to hear you are unwell, Your Ladyship.

Maria riffles through her correspondence, opens two letters with an ivory blade, scans them, ignores the rest. She leans back in her chair, head in hand, lifts her feet onto the ottoman, and closes her eyes for a few minutes. Eventually she rouses herself: Miss Kauffman, may I ask how long you intend to be with us? Naturally, you are welcome to stay as long as you like.

Though I came at your urging, I do not wish to impose, Your Ladyship. I will remain only for as long as is necessary.

One month? Two?

No, not nearly so long. A few days at most. I have commitments in London.

Of course you do. While you are here, you must make yourself at home. You will want to settle in, explore the house and grounds, recover your strength. I will send a message when I need you.

Mrs. Plett enters at just the right moment, announces the blue room is ready.

Maria, anxious to go back to bed, gives her instructions briskly.

Mrs. Plett, the day has been tiring for Miss Kauffman. Would you please show her there now? And arrange for the item to be taken out of storage and brought to her?

Yes, My Lady.

I shall leave it in your capable hands.

The countess bids Angelica good afternoon and stalks away.

Angelica follows Mrs. Plett through the house, up the expanse of staircase, allowing her hand to follow the curve of the banister, to the other wing and a beautiful guestroom in cerulean and gold brocade. The housekeeper leaves momentarily, returning with a footman carrying a canvas wrapped in gauze. She directs him to place it on the rosewood table and to leave.

Mrs. Plett lifts the canvas easily, removes the cover, and gives the unfinished painting to the artist.

I took the greatest care of it, Miss Kauffman. I had to hide it.

Angelica examines the portrait, holds it toward the light.

The face has some resemblance to the sitter (oval, aquiline nose, high forehead), though more work is required to bring it to life. The outline of the body is in place (flat and formless neoclassical garb), and some color has been blocked into the background while other areas remain bare. Hardly more than a beginning of a painting—a false start. Angelica thought she had made more progress than this; recalls a portrait on the verge of completion, is disappointed by its feebleness. Then again, she is often disappointed by her own work. What is conceived of as sublime, an ideal, loses much in its execution and is eroded further still by criticism from her colleagues until at the end, the work can seem trite, trivial, even to herself.

Miss Kauffman, may I be permitted to speak in confidence?

Angelica inclines her head.

It was unfortunate, what happened. Believe me when I say Her Ladyship has suffered terribly since and has many regrets.

Each of us is human and deficient, Mrs. Plett. I have not come to settle a score.

Your consenting to come at all is appreciated. I know you have many demands on your time.

As we are speaking in confidence, I am emboldened to say Her Ladyship is melancholy.

Yes, she is.

Then she is lucky to have you, Mrs. Plett. We need our friends most when we are bereft.

Angelica Kauffman is in a residence that reminds her of a mausoleum, and she imagines herself its roaming ghost. She wanders from room to remote room, initially to discover its paintings, taking a lit candelabrum with her as the end of the day closes in. Ancestral portraits; other mismatched or uncared-for pieces bought but never appreciated; a handful of jewels from the Flemish and Dutch schools (her experienced eye picks out the ones made by copyists). She chooses one or two she might make sketches of, includes a composition of a maid sitting alone in a room with her back to the viewer. No face. But why?

She finds she is drawn to the vacancy, the stillness, the decrepitude of the place, the sounds of her heels reverberating along corridors. The ballroom, the dining room, the impressive library where Angelica lingers, running her finger along the spines; her gaze meanders along the titles. Unoccupied spaces. Haunted by sadness. It is a grand building, but Angelica has been in grander, and it is the absence of society, of comings and goings, that makes it feel enormous as a cavern, serious as a church. Her artistic mind responds to the atmosphere, gives fictional accounts for it—this is a palace, a forest of briars surrounding it, its occupants put to sleep by an evil spell. When she passes a servant on a wooden step straining to collect the cobwebs with her duster, these fancies blow away.

She strolls through the grounds during the late-afternoon sun, then sunset, then twilight, around the rose garden and an orchard. It occurs to her that she may not be dining with the countess. It occurs to her that she should not have come, that she would like to return to London.

But they do have supper together by the drawing room fire, leftovers with port, Coward snoozing on the carpet, Maria being cordial—

And did you look around, Miss Kauffman?

Yes, Your Ladyship. I particularly admire your library. I should like to spend some time in there, if I may. For research.

By all means. I do not expect you to work during your entire stay, indeed I hope you shall not.

Your Ladyship . . . ?

I mean, I want to hear all about the ton and their exploits! I have had no gossip for simply ages. You must tell me everything.

Angelica, having access to the fashionable ladies and gentlemen of London, is able to answer many of the questions Maria has about their mutual acquaintances, and shares some stories about the absurd height of ostrich feathers and the ridiculous width of panniers currently seen around town.

Suddenly the countess interrupts the artist: Actually there is no need for that.

For what, Your Ladyship?

That . . . or "My Lady." Just plain Maria will do, if you do not mind the familiarity?

It would be my pleasure.

And I prefer to call you Angelica, if you will indulge me?

Of course.

Or I can call you Miss Angel, like Sir Joshua Reynolds does.

The artist smiles at the mention of her friend, at the affectionate joke.

Angelica . . . You are more accommodating than our Mrs. Plett. I have known her my whole life, and still she will not call me by my first name, unless she is across with me.

I should be afraid if your housekeeper were angry at me.

With good reason! And Maria smiles, yes, this is the way it was supposed to be, the way it had been. She goes on, Anyway, it is a convention that I do not see the need for in intimate company, and were we not on intimate terms once?

We were. We are. That is why I came here.

The ladies find this concession to each other makes a pause in their dialogue, the chink of cutlery on china, the gleam of candles in crystal, until Maria continues: I was thinking that you should use the orangery. It is warm and has the best light, very conducive to creativity. No one will disturb you.

For research?

For your work.

No. The orangery will not be necessary.

It was only a suggestion; you must work where you feel most at ease, wherever you like.

Maria, I think there has been a misunderstanding. I am not here to finish the painting.

You are not?

No. I am sorry if I gave you that impression.

But you turned up without sending a message. What else was I to think?

Angelica feels the sting of their previous encounter renewed, testing her compassion. You said it did not matter anymore. You said other things were more important.

It most certainly matters. Besides, it is polite to state your intentions in advance, to say if and when and why you are paying a visit to someone. You do not just appear one day and expect to be accommodated and entertained.

111

With respect, you wrote me sheets of letters imploring me to come.

Yes, to finish the painting.

You did not always say so. You would say one thing, and then something else. Some of your letters did not even sound like you. You seemed muddled.

I was upset. I was angry, and then . . .

Yes, I understand, but by the end I did not know exactly what you wanted from me, whether you would even see me. I came here expecting to be turned away.

Well, Miss Kauffman, I am telling you now, plainly: I want you to finish the painting of Frances.

That is not going to be possible.

Why not?

And the artist says it as gently as she can: Because you cannot afford to pay me, Maria.

The countess is thrown. Of course I can.

The whole world knows you cannot. If your creditors called in all your debts, you would not own even the gown you are wearing. It is only through the intervention of your husband that you have your home, your servants, your pin money.

The countess stands and turns away. I am sure we can come to an arrangement. I could pay in installments. You can name your own terms for as much and for as long as you like.

You confuse me with someone else.

All right. You have refined sensibilities, I acknowledge that. You admire some of the artwork here? We have many interesting pieces. Why not choose a couple as payment in kind? That is a fair exchange, more than fair.

I have no desire to pillage your property, and I live in a tiny town house with barely enough room for the possessions I have.

Then what do you want? You are negotiating hard; you must have a price in mind.

No, I have not. I want nothing from you.

Miss Kauffman, my circumstances notwithstanding—though, by the way, I am appalled you presume to know about my private affairs, much less taunt me about them—I am still a person of influence. I have the ear of some of the richest and most powerful men and women in the country. I can help you. I can do wonderful things for your career.

Please stop this.

I can do terrible things too, if I want.

Angelica takes a moment to weigh these words, to be sure she has understood. She sighs. Maria, I am a woman of immense wealth in my own right. I am a founding Royal Academician. I have among my friends and colleagues Benjamin West, Francesco Bartolozzi, Thomas Gainsborough, and Joshua Reynolds. My patrons include Johann Joachim Winckelmann, David Garrick, the king's sister, and Queen Charlotte herself. Paintings, engravings, lady's fans, *teapots* for goodness' sake. They say I am one of the most famous artists alive; they say the whole world has gone *Angelicamad*. I do not need your patronage, Your Ladyship. I do not need your endorsement. A smear campaign would not hurt me. In reality, it would probably exclude you from society forever.

An ugly silence follows. The fire spits and cracks. The countess's shallow breathing is audible, and then she speaks again: That was awful of me to attempt to threaten you, Miss Kauffman. I never used to be like this. If you did not come here to finish the portrait, then pray tell me, why did you come?

Out of friendship.

Then, out of friendship, go home in the morning. Good-bye, Miss Kauffman.

The countess picks up a candlestick to light her way.

*　　*　　*

She turns over, sits up; it is the morning, and last night is vivid in her memory. Coward, alert as a hunter, barks, wags the knot of his tail. Maria is wide awake and putting a robe on over her shift, hair unbrushed and uncovered, running down the great staircase to stop the carriage, but there is no sign of it. She checks the drawing room, the dining room.

We are too late, Coward (as though this were for his benefit).

She feels the nip of despair, loneliness digging into her ribs. She wishes she could escape her own company, if only temporarily; respite from this wickedness and sorrow. Damnable. Idiotic. Perverse. The frustration is a compressed spring inside her. The pressure chokes her.

Though it is unseemly and the morning is chill, she goes for a walk in the grounds in her nightgown and slippers with the pug, for the sake of movement, for the expenditure of the fidgets, for Angelica, who was perfectly correct: Maria is a countess in name only. Because she might as well, as not.

This is Maria. This body, this mind, these emotions. This is what there is to Maria, and the sum of what she will ever be. She has had the best of her life: her youth, her marriage, her wealth, her children, her great love. The fabric has unraveled, only the filaments are left.

She breathes in the cool air—it is replenishing—thinks how they used to love being outside. Picnics and walks and sunrises and swims and snowmen and drinking under the stars. It is a whole other person who was loved by Frances.

If you could see me now. If you saw me.

Maria's toes are wet from the dew. She moves fast, walks through the herb garden to smell the lavender and the rosemary, and then to the rose arch to sit on their stone bench, tapping the energy away. In the midst of her anguish it occurs to her how well Duncan, the gardener, has maintained the grounds practically single-handed.

It is on her way back that Maria is jolted into the present, like the glimpse of a fox between the trees.

In the orangery, Angelica is at work on the portrait.

She pauses when Maria enters.

My apologies. I do not mean to disturb you.

You are not. There is still some tea.

The artist points to the tray with the end of the brush.

Maria rests on the chaise longue, lifts the little dog (arthritic from the damp), enfolds herself in a blanket, speaks not another word.

Angelica Kauffman paints seated at her easel and has a talent for not spilling liquids or marking surfaces, putting the colors only where she wishes them to go. She is disciplined, methodical, with a strong work ethic. True, she was dissatisfied with her past efforts, but it is the way of creative temperaments that they find energy to turn around weak work, to view it as a stage in the development of better work—an optimism that is just short of delusion, persistence that is just short of obsession, self-belief that is just short of vanity. If this were a love affair, Art would be a brute, offering hope, making false promises; Artist would be a wronged and resilient victim, making excuses and accepting blame, always prepared to reconcile and try again.

Painting the face of a sitter from memory is tricky. At least she did the basics from life, has her preliminary sketches as a prompt. When a receptive mind observes and considers the minutiae of a face in order to draw it, the outlines and proportions stick. Angelica can remember what Frances looked like; that is not the problem. It is the soul that is absent, because that would have come later. The soul is the true likeness. The motion, the quickening, the particular expression of an individual caught off guard. That is what Angelica paints, that is her specialty. That is why she gets to know her subjects, uses her placid nature, her charm, puts them at their ease. Making people be themselves long enough for it to show through and yes, she gets it, holds it, and, incredibly, records it (or something rather like it)—this is Angelica's gift. And she did not manage to capture Frances's essence before they parted.

Angelica has not mentioned this to Maria. The outcome will be inferior, is unlikely to meet Maria's fragile expectations.

Angelica Kauffman has decided not to accept payment. She makes this gesture out of friendship. And as she is a friend giving a gift, the picture has taken on more significance than a regular commission.

So she sets aside her worries, for now, and works on the parts she can do: the table with lion's legs, the Greco-Roman pillar, the chiton the figure is wearing. It takes time to give cloth a sheen and make it drape convincingly (Angelica has decided to make it the cerulean of the room where she sleeps). Even a lady's hands joined at rest, one elbow on the back of the chair, can be done generically. But this is not yet a portrait of Frances; it is a portrait of someone who resembles Frances. How to finish it without resorting to a map of features?

Coward likes Angelica. She gives him tidbits, tickles his tummy, and the orangery is a warm place to lie. Switching his affection to another is not beneath him. When Angelica looks into his enormous eyes she can see a reflection of herself.

Angelica Kauffman is here, Frances, and I still make concessions to you. After what you have done! We made peace, so you have got what you wanted; she is finishing the painting, so I have got what I wanted.

I pace up and down for an entire morning, pace pace pace, deliberating over my apology, for now it must be done. One difficulty (I am ashamed of it) is recalling accurately what I actually said and did, and what was merely in my imagination. I remember distinctly coming into the room during the sittings—you posing, she daubing—and being possessed by the notion that you had ceased speaking that very instant, as if you were keeping secrets from me. This happened once, and I let it go. This happened again . . . and I felt a terrible heat in my chest.

We fought a lot around that time, did we not? Rather, I fought. You would wait for the torrent to subside, keeping your power dry in order to wound me with a single shot. I could only make you cry by crying myself.

I caught Angelica holding your face, and you allowing it to be held. It looked just like a seduction. It looked like you were giving to her something of yourself that you held back from me.

You defended her, saying that she is an artist and artists must look closely at the faces of their subjects.

You would say that!

Then you accused me of drinking gin, as if it made any difference.

This much is clear, but emotion blurs the rest.

Did I call her names, or accuse her of attempting to steal you? Did I, in fact, threaten to strike her, or did I daydream it? Did I shout and pick up a pitcher and hurl it against the wall? (Is that how it broke, in the end? Is that where the stain came from?) Or was my rage contained in the simple instruction for her to leave immediately, uncompensated?

I remember being ill afterward, and you still furious. I remember you saying it was not the jealousy that was intolerable but that

117

Angelica was one of the few real friends we had together, who knew us both as we really are, who accepted us. And I chased her away.

My skin puckers with shame, even now.

I do apologize to her. I try to.

The lady brooks not a word, soothes me, promises it was forgiven long ago. And, without my asking, assures me you were always loyal, and that doubting you was my worst offense. Confesses (if it be a confession) I caused you both to worry, and this was the only subject of your private conversations, the only concealment.

I am glad it is Angelica. I cannot think of anyone else, apart from Muriel, whom I could tolerate just now.

She works for as long as the light is good. I need not see her unless I wish to. We eat together, pass the evenings. These are surprisingly bearable. For all her elaborate tastes, she is understated as a companion, content to sit in quietude. I embroider, she sketches or reads. She asks bluntly if I will always be this way, and what will become of me? She senses no one can go on like this. *I will fade and die*—I do not say it but I think it. Then she says, And what would Frances want?

Indeed, what *would* you want? Your opinions and ideas have become a mystery to me, you who had so many. I look through your notes again and they seem so delicate, dropped leaves. I like the unfinished poems best because it feels as though you have been interrupted momentarily, called away to make a decision about the horses or the baking, will be back shortly to shine them up. I did not appreciate your calling enough. I am sorry for all the times I was flippant about it, or worse, tried to make you publish against your will. I am no poet, but I can at least keep them safe for you.

I have such black days. Whole hours are blotted out—what did I do? where did I go? was I alone? My nerves are in shreds.

I fear that before long I shall lose the ability to recall your voice and your smell and your advice. You have left a Frances-shaped hole. Everything familiar is falling through it.

Angelica wants to know how Coward came to be named, and if he was always mine or originally yours. I tell her I gave him to you as an anniversary present, that you called him Howard, that he constantly trembled, et cetera.

I like her. She is imaginative, thoughtful, like Muriel, like you (are these the qualities I value in women because I do not have them myself?). I like the way she asks about you, probing without being vulgar. But I cannot wait for her to leave.

The housekeeper fumes. She wants someone to read to her, My Lady, while she paints. You said we were to give her whatever she wanted . . . ?

Maria does not see the issue but is certain Mrs. Plett will spell it out; she does enjoy a good gripe.

Miss Kauffman works in the orangery for hours at a time, I do not have time to sit and read to her.

Of course not. You are far too busy.

Mrs. Plett is mollified: What ought to be done?

Make one of the others do it. Or are they unable?

William has no more time to spare than I do. And to have Rachel reading out loud would be cruelty to all concerned.

You will think of something. Is there not one task that could wait? For not even a single day?

Suppose Miss Kauffman requires to be read to tomorrow and the day after? Suppose she wants to be sung to next?

I have heard your singing voice in church; it is adorable. Maybe I will ask you to sing for me while I do my needlework? (Maria is glared at for that.) Did Angelica ask specifically to be read to?

Yes, My Lady.

Then I realize our situation is not ideal, but we must give Angelica whatever she requires. It is a small request, considering what she is doing for me. I am sure you will manage beautifully.

Mrs. Plett presses her mouth into a tight line.

What does she want to hear?

Poetry, My Lady—

Mrs. Plett anticipates the effect of this detail on Maria. She pats her on the wrist . . . and when Maria's eyes remain unfocused, she lifts Maria's chin, encouraging her to stand the way a countess does. Maria will take the matter seriously now.

Yes, yes. I will look into it. Thank you, Mrs. Plett.

So Maria must go to the library. She balances on the step, stretches to her full height to reach the shelves, turns books over, sorts them into piles, and replaces them. New books and old books, books she has never seen before. Flicks and fans through pages. What would Angelica want to hear? What is Maria prepared to read?

Frances's favorite piece of furniture was a raspberry-red fainting couch. Maria had it moved into the library so Frances could be comfortable there. And she loved the door that looked like a bookcase, found it humorous and decadent. All the poetry books Frances either bought herself or claimed as her own by virtue of her love for them.

You did not care for shoes and hairstyles and fashion. You said that your mind required decoration.

The memory tugs at Maria's heart. She selects some volumes haphazardly (this and that, and this Maria recognizes and takes, and that she does not and rejects), feels as though she is invading her lover's privacy, carries them in her arms like babies.

Angelica does not stop painting or even look up when Maria enters the orangery but says, I think I annoyed Mrs. Plett earlier, and she was exactly as fierce as I feared.

Not at all. She likes you, and I have brought you the poets.

Angelica sighs with satisfaction: Whom did you bring?

Alexander Pope, *The Rape of the Lock*. Milton, *Paradise Lost. Paradise Regained*. Shakespeare's sonnets. *The Iliad* and *The Odyssey*.

Do you have anything modern? Anything by Friedrich Gottlieb Klopstock?

Yes, but my German is so poor you might wish it was something else. I have a poetess called Phillis Wheatley: *Poems on Various Subjects, Religious and Moral*. She is fairly new.

I have not heard of her.

She is an African.

Do you mean she is a slave?

Yes. In America.

Angelica pauses, brush in midair: A woman and an African and a slave and a poet? And you have her book right there in your hand?

Yes. There is a picture of her on the frontispiece.

Let me see it.

And Maria shows Angelica the etching titled *Phillis Wheatley, Negro Servant to Mr. John Wheatley, of Boston*.

How did you come by such a book?

Frances acquired it. Poetry was a particular interest of hers.

Angelica lowers her voice: Did Frances ever write any poems herself?

Maria answers with a sting in hers: Occasionally.

The painter suppresses the urge to ask more, senses she must choose the proper moment. Instead, she says, And is Miss Wheatley very good?

I have not read her before.

Well, we must find out, mustn't we?

Angelica, would you not prefer to have a respite from your work?

Hearing Miss Wheatley's poems will be respite enough.

And Angelica says nothing else, resumes painting, lets the silence run on until Maria settles on the chaise longue and begins.

She starts with a poem about virtue . . . then one to the king. Poems about recollection, imagination, humanity, and a composition, "To a Lady on her remarkable Preservation in an Hurricane in North-Carolina." Several are written following the deaths of children or loved ones, and after the awkward experience of reading one out she eschews these. But the poet has reinterpreted Niobe, from Ovid's *Metamorphoses*. And it says here, "from a view of the painting of Mr. Richard Wilson," which sparks Angelica's interest.

Familiar now with the poet's lyric style and meter, Maria comments: It seems Miss Wheatley is partial to artists; this one is "To S.M., a young African Painter, on seeing his Works" . . .

Here are two short poems like siblings, "An Hymn to the Morning," and "An Hymn to the Evening" . . .

When Maria has read these, she realizes Angelica is no longer painting but sitting at rest at her easel, listening.

Maria, reread me the last part of "Evening"? From "placid slumbers."

> *Let placid slumbers sooth each weary mind,*
> *At morn to wake more heav'nly, more refin'd,*
> *So shall the labours of the day begin*
> *More pure, more guarded from the snares of sin.*
> *Night's leaden sceptre seals my drowsy eyes,*
> *Then cease, my song, till fair Aurora rise.*

The artist sighs: Then you could read "Morning," "Evening," "Morning," "Evening," an infinite number of times in a cycle, inhaling and exhaling. Do you like her, Maria?

She is edifying. Do you?

I was just thinking of my glib assertion that one cannot be both an artistic and a political being.

You have fought some battles, no doubt. It is late, we should have some dinner.

Maria tidies the books, leaves them in the orangery for when Angelica wants them next.

Angelica slots her brushes into a pot, straightens her materials, stretches, and then goes to her friend.

I meant to say it sooner, my condolences for your terrible loss.

Maria's grief grips her anew, sore and penetrating, yet she finds she is able to reply, Thank you; that is very kind.

You were half right about my debts, Angelica. When my husband intervenes in my affairs, he does so using money that was mine in the first place. He took it. My money, to pay off my debts—and yet I am supposed to be obliged to him? In a way . . . in a way I am, actually. He could set conditions or make demands, make me beg for his help. He does not. If he gets angry, he does not show it. When I see what other people have for husbands, I conclude he is not a bad sort entirely. Oh, he has plenty of faults, and I can happily enumerate them: he is a dullard and a glutton and sanctimonious, and he looks like a pig walking on its hind legs. But he is not cruel, and I have plenty of faults of my own. We have reached an understanding. He has his mistress, I am sure you know, but perhaps you did not know that he has had the same mistress since before we were married, installed with their children at Carsington. Her name is Dorothy, and she must be fifteen or twenty years older than I am and is apparently very fat. Then again, so is my husband. She lives in my place, sleeps in my bed, squanders my money on her chubby children. Copulating must be difficult, though at their age perhaps it is no longer an issue. My husband is going to die one day, and I know how she dreads that because my eldest son will inherit and the cuckoo will be out of the nest. I have two sons, Georgie and Augustus, the heir and the spare, and I thank God for them every day not only because I love them but also because, after three years of a dire marriage, they bought me my freedom. At least, a degree of freedom. My husband gave me this house, the least valued of the family's estates, and an allowance. Said they were mine to do with as I wished. Plenty of women would exchange their lot for mine, I know it. I used to be enraptured with the ton—the parties, the operas, the intrigue, the gambling. Cards can undo a person; faro was the ruin of me. But even when we are in decline, we deal another hand and dress like parrots and drink like fishes because we know no better, because society is disparaging of the alternatives, because it is reinforced that if you do not do this or have this or behave in this way, you are deemed inferior.

What are the alternatives, Maria?

Finding harmony in one's domestic life. Investigating the inner world. Sharing it with someone who makes a restrained existence feel like a mountain range of possibilities. Frances was never seduced by the perfume and the lace. Oh, she could blend in, could even make herself the center of attention—she had the wit and the manners for it. But she found it unsatisfactory, and dare I say a hardship. No matter how grand the occasion and how fashionable the company, she said, given the choice, she would prefer an evening at home with me. She would go only because I wanted to. Oh, we had such sport for a few years! We were invited simply everywhere. Our entrance was always anticipated. People were curious to see if we would arrive dressed identically, if one or both of us would be in the garb of a gentleman, whether we would bring a monkey with us and pretend it was our child, or a goat and pretend it was our lawyer. We spent hours devising and preparing our novelties. She was my comic heroine, my Viola, my Portia, my Rosalind. For a while we had them eating out of our hands. But a beast, if it is wild, if it is savage, will regress to its nature however tame it seems. You know what happened.

I have heard reports, but I was not there. And you do not have to repeat it for my sake.

Then I will tell you for mine. It was February, the coldest and blackest of nights, no moon, and the London fog thicker than I have known it. These were contributory, as if the scoundrel had arranged them. The cold meant that my coachman did not wait the whole night with the carriage; the dark meant that the deed went undiscovered until lights had been brought out and there was a crowd to behold his handiwork. We were in town for one of Lady Thetford's card parties, a genial and modest gathering by her standards. A number of us kept playing until the marquis entreated us to leave—we teased him for being an old man with no stamina. We assembled in the vestibule to wait for the carriages. Mine pulled up, the servants shone their lamps upon it—and Frances saw the offense before I did and bade me avert my eyes. I pushed her aside, I had to see for myself what was provoking such horrified gasps among our group, and attracting more eager witnesses from within the house to stare in fascination and amusement and disgust. I was merry, quite inebriated, until I laid eyes on the message left for us.

I am afraid to hear it.

Along the side in white paint was the word *TRIBADES*.

Angelica catches her breath, then mutters, An enemy?

I suspected one of my creditors. In a single stroke we became pariahs. We were shunned.

You and Frances were the victims of a crime!

You do not know these people as I do. It gave them a reason to turn on us. It gave legitimacy to the disgusting and salacious thoughts they had kept hidden. We were lepers, we were the most obscene kind of joke. They relished in our downfall. *My* downfall.

Apparently, in England's brothels it became a fashion for a while to make two women perform *The Countess and Her Companion.* Even my husband, aware some scandal had occurred, was obliged to visit me. He said, *Maria, can you please explain why I am receiving notes from anonymous well-wishers telling me Sappho is in my bedchamber?* (Maria manages to laugh.) Remarkably, he did not get angry. I gave him my theory, that I believed it was to do with money, and he said, *With you, my wife, it is always to do with money.* He was thoroughly decent about it, settled my accounts, and advised for the sake of appearances and for my well-being to give up Frances or to avoid society—one or the other. Interestingly, he refrained from explicitly forbidding me anything. And then he went away again. That was that. My porky, useless husband. Frances offered to leave if it would set me free . . . or to stay and live in disgrace. Whatever would bring me happiness, she was prepared to give.

And she did stay—

—and we did live! For a short time. Do you know what I realized in the end? They envied us, because by their standards we had no right to be happy. Because for them, happiness requires pomades and powders and ruffles and diamonds and concertos. And we required a roof, and a dog and a paper and pen, a candle at night and sometimes a sip of wine or port, and we were more than satisfied. They must have begrudged it so much. Why else would they desire to poison something harmless and beautiful?

They love each other, His Lordship and this Dorothy?

Yes, I think they probably do.

Then it likely follows that your situation, and His Lordship's tolerance of it, would have required at least her blessing.

Funny, she wrote to me once.

What did she say?

But Maria is done with this subject, so Angelica introduces another: I was not completely honest with you before, Maria, when

I described the extent of my influence as an artist. I oversimplified it. (Coward raises his head and Angelica scratches his ears.) I endure a stream of commentary and pronouncements from my contemporaries. My portraits *do not bear a likeness*—there is one I have heard time after time—because I exaggerate the best features of my sitters, because I tend to flatter them. Well, show me a portraitist who depicts his patrons accurately and I will show you one in poverty who does not paint at all. We artists use some license to ennoble our patrons . . . at least I try to get beneath the skin of a person, to reflect back what is true about them. So, I ask myself, why am I disproportionately criticized for it? Why am I singled out? My portraits of men are *feminine,* they say—as though feminity were exclusively the reserve of females, and not a character trait shared to a greater or lesser extent by both sexes; as though the men of today's society were not a muster of peacocks, posing and prancing. They say the heroes in my history paintings look at best like androgynous youths and at worst like women wearing beards. They say, constantly, that I cannot draw the human body, that I have no knowledge of anatomy, and for this reason my work will always be inferior. Do you know why I have no knowledge of anatomy? Because, being a woman, I am not allowed to attend life-drawing classes. They deny me the opportunity to learn the techniques I need, then insult me for not having them. I have to make do with working from sculpture or other drawings and paintings, seeing the physical body through someone else's eyes, their bias, the limitations of their talent. Maybe the art of the ancients reached a summit of aesthetic beauty, but I can tell you it is a poor substitute for flesh and bones, for the work of God's own hand. Yet I want success and I play up to my strengths—color and romance—and so I become guilty of the very defects of which I am accused. I always thank these experts for their insight because I know belligerence encourages them to repeat themselves, more loudly and with greater conviction. But if I am gracious, maybe they will be inclined toward generosity and one day the history books will say: *Miss Kauffman was a painter of middling accomplishment but delightful in conversation.* That is how I shall be remembered, as a dilettante and a moll. They whisper that I have got this far only because I use womanly wiles to advance myself, that I did not work for, and do not deserve, what I have achieved. Always eyes are upon me looking for fuel to add to that particular fire. I cannot form a friendship with a male colleague, however distinguished, without setting tongues wagging. Am I to form relationships only with lady painters? Must we, all three of us, sit in a room by ourselves? And now they do more than merely whisper it out of my hearing. Earlier this year, one of them made a painting that included a nude figure of me, flaunting myself, and exhibited it at the Royal Academy.

Did the members not act?

Joshua was incensed, and one or two of the others spoke up for me, but I suspect many of them found it satirical. It was a slur on my reputation and hurt my pride more than I can tell you, and yes, it was removed when I wrote to them. After several days.

They are galled by your fame. You will be remembered. Your art is unparalleled, exalted. Your work—and that of Miss Wheatley—will survive. Your legacy means that artists in future eras will flourish, and they will thank you for it.

Is that why I endure such humiliation, Maria?

Why you both do, Angelica.

I almost became a musician, you know. I wonder what life would have been like if I had chosen that path.

You picked art over music?

Easier, perhaps. It was a dilemma, but art was the more urgent calling of the two. I fear that Miss Wheatley has picked the most difficult art form in which to thrive. And the barriers she has to overcome are manifold.

Frances said that many of life's skills can be taught—oratory, carpentry, agriculture, drawing too, by the sounds of it. But she was convinced that poets are born. So you may be right when you describe poetry as the more difficult art form, but you are probably wrong that Miss Wheatley knowingly chose it.

Angelica lies awake in the dark, her arm curved above her head. Her instincts prickle. Does she hear anything amiss, or is it only the sounds of the night scraping and rustling outside? Stepping into her shoes and wrapping a blanket about her shoulders, she feels no fear, only the ache of fatigue when one cannot sleep, the relief of giving up the attempt.

On the landing the moon casts rectangles. The furniture becomes stone, the picture frames are as dark as tunnels, eyes peering out of them. Blood rushes in her ears as loud as the wind. The house holds its breath. Nothing dangerous—just unsettling, vexing, a puzzle to be solved. Angelica leans over the balustrade and stares down into a space as impenetrable as an underground lake. She hears a disturbance coming from Maria's room.

She does not knock, lets herself into the chamber, is unsurprised by the sobbing woman. Coward is also awake: restless, grumpy. She does not talk, except to hush and hush the tired body buried in the pillows. With a confident embrace she encircles Maria, who responds with stillness, tears leaking down her face into her hair. Sheets and covers are pulled around, tucked in against the night, and Coward is the first to find repose. Then Maria, grateful for Angelica's company, feeling nonetheless alone in the world, sleeps with this pain like a pin in her chest.

Angelica lies awake, listens to their breathing, dozes for a few hours until the morning, when the shadows are banished and the heartbeat of the estate increases in tempo once more.

* * *

It is consuming me. I feel nothing but this grief all the time. I find a wardrobe filled with gowns, and I think they must have been yours once, but they are mine. I had forgotten them because I have forgotten myself—literally the Maria I was. She is a foreigner. How did she do it—those parties, concerts, assemblies at court—when I cannot stand even to leave the house? I am afraid of the world, of its faces and jagged edges, of its venom. The thought of a journey brings on the terrors. I never want to leave here. I never want to make false conversation for as long as I live, or be judged by people I detest. I want to build a wall. I am falling so far, so deep, but I have yet to hit the ground. I could have killed you yesterday, for doing this.

The portrait is surprising. She is adding the bronze Minerva from the ballroom. A trick of composition to stop the eye trailing off the edge, she says. I almost collapse when I realize: of all the objects d'art she could have chosen . . . ?

You sent it back to me. You sent it back, saying I had misunderstood your motive but I made you accept it, because you had misunderstood mine. I was not attempting to buy your body, or your silence. Honestly. I just wanted you to have something I knew you would like. I fully expected not to see you again.

I betray myself to Angelica but will not be drawn out. And something else, though I do not know if you would approve.

Is it too late to make a change? to have a symbol to show—

My head hurts. Everything hurts.

I ask. I ask Angelica if she can show that you were a person who wrote.

I expect her to be annoyed. She is not, has anticipated my request, has already made a drawing of the hands in the painting adapted to hold a scroll and a pen. I remark that the scroll is rolled up, and she says she could include a whole legible stanza if I—

No, I like it that way, in the drawing.

I sense her disappointment; she wants me to share that aspect of you. I do not. The change is agreed.

Mrs. Plett is suspicious. She has taken to ambushing me in the morning, flings petticoats and hats on me, hides things away. Of course I find them again.

All of it stays inside me, hissing and biting. I cannot, physically, sustain my anger at you, but if I stop, there will be nothing left, just a void. I do not believe I shall be free of you in this life. Extraordinary—I can almost hear what you would say to that, an echo of it, a chime. You are wrong. Besides, you went away, so what you think no longer counts.

They picnic on the knoll overlooking the village, Angelica in a cream shalwar kameez trimmed with burnished red, Maria in a white dress with a royal-blue hat and sash. The excursion has been forced on them by Mrs. Plett, a means of restoring order, Maria explains. The potted meat is rich, the honey is sweet, the salad is sharp, the bread is wholesome. The sun radiates warmth until it is covered by a cloud turning the air fresh, then the cloud passes, the sun returns. Coward rolls on his back in the grass, plays like a puppy, investigates.

Maria complains aloud, She should be here. Why is she not here? As though Frances is running late.

She is here.

And Maria shields her eyes to see her companion.

Do you believe in it when you say things like that?

I believe that when someone loves someone it leaves an impression after one of them has gone.

Have you ever been in love, Angelica?

What makes you ask that?

Because you speak knowingly.

Cannot a heart believe in something it has yet to encounter? (And Angelica turns toward the steeple of the church, the roofs of the houses, the hills.)

How have you formed such notions of love without experience?—Maria narrows her eyes, not only because of the glare— Were you married?

I am married to my work.

And to a man, I think.

Angelica rises, brushes crumbs and grass from her trousers, steps away.

To a blackguard, then. And yet you still keep faith that love is unbreakable, conquering, enduring.

The Paintress folds her arms, gazes at the view around them, does not reply.

I had the best that love can offer, and look what it has done to me. You, I think, have had the worst. Somehow it becomes you, you have mastered it, turned it into a resource for your creativity. No wonder you are prolific.

I was prolific anyway. The only man who deserves any credit for my work is my father.

Ah, fathers. There is a different muddy puddle.

Who is that?

Climbing toward them is a blonde young woman raising her hand in greeting.

She is too far away to shout, yet she does, her hello scattered by the wind.

Maria stands.

It is Muriel! My goddaughter—she probably heard you are here.

Maria trips and strides down the slope, meets the breathless girl partway, takes both hands in hers. Angelica watches them. The young lady is laughing, perhaps at her aborted attempt to run up the hillside, is explaining a complicated story to Maria, who clasps her around the shoulders, links arms with her. Both smiles are radiant.

And this is Angelica Kauffman, the renowned artist and my good friend.

The girl exclaims, Can it be? Miss Kauffman, I am so delighted to make your acquaintance. Muriel Wyndham, but I should like it if you called me Muriel.

Thank you. You must call me Angelica.

What a wonderful costume, Angelica. Is that trousers? I never can keep up with what society is wearing from one week to the next. They look very comfortable, as if one could play in them all day, then go to bed without changing out of them. Hello, Coward, you smelly animal.

She picks up the dog and fusses him. Maria leads the party back to the picnic.

Muriel talks fluidly: her parents in the village, a problem she had with her stocking this morning, a story from her childhood about getting stuck in a hayloft, and then, This honey is delicious, Maria (finally going quiet as she eats some).

And how are you, Muriel? I feel as though we have not talked for an age.

She nods emphatically, mouth full. I am so glad you have a visitor, Maria, and such a famous one at that. Were you going to tell me?

No need to tell you anything, you seem to find it all out on your own.

That is true. I have my spies. For example, Angelica is here to work on the painting of Frances, I believe. Is it finished yet?

Angelica says there is still work left to do.

I am desperate to see it!

This topic sets Muriel's mind alight with questions about Angelica's art. Where does she get her ideas from? What does she like to paint best? Who in society has she made portraits of? What is her favorite color? I wish I could see every canvas you have ever touched!

If you are so enthusiastic, you must come to London and visit me at my studio.

Oh, may I?

But of course. Perhaps Maria can be persuaded to bring you? I shall show you around the Royal Academy.

Muriel turns to Maria, presses her lips together in supplication, urges with her eyes.

Maria murmurs, We shall see.

The younger woman kisses her in gratitude, as though it were settled.

Then Maria announces she has to speak to Mrs. Plett, asks whether Muriel and Angelica would mind amusing themselves until she comes back.

As Maria heads to the house, Muriel becomes more reflective.

It was good of you to come; I was starting to worry. She seems better for it. She has not seen anyone since—you know—not even her sons.

They are estranged?

Not exactly. I think they have always belonged to their father. She has grown so very tired of society, become reclusive, exists with hardly any human contact. Poor Maria, and poor Frances, and praise God for the indomitable Mrs. Plett. You must be especially dear to my mama.

Your . . . ?

It is a silly pet name, she asked me to call her it once. Maybe the others will follow now, and she will have a semblance of her old life back.

134

Angelica does not contradict the girl, so youthful and determined.

May I be candid with you? In the days that followed, Maria was completely devastated. It was dreadful to watch, and I . . . I had very bad thoughts. I stayed with her for a while because of it, because I could not shake the suspicions I had. She is my godmother and we are close, but still, it was presumptuous of me. I was overcome by these fears, overwhelmed by them, and I think Mrs. Plett thought the same, although she did not say so. I told myself I would only stay until her friends or relatives came. I ended up staying with her for a long time. No one came.

How did your parents feel?

My mother and father are simple people. They said the countess had shown me many kindnesses. They said I had a duty to help, if I was able to comfort a soul in need.

You shared her burden. That was kind of you.

That was when the portrait of Frances became important to her again. It became an obsession.

It is human nature to want ways of remembering the people we love.

What Muriel says next is hastily thought, hastily shared: Do you think likenesses of departed loved ones possess a special power?

I would have to say yes.

Like heathen idols? When the physical resemblance has been locked in paint or stone, is some aspect of the unique spirit also fixed, also sealed? Is the soul drawn to its image in life like a beacon on the shore?

What makes you ask these questions?

Muriel checks over her shoulder. Because I think, for Maria, the picture has an element of the occult. I think she has some plan for it when it is finished.

Angelica Kauffman decides it would be wise not to dwell on these ideas and leads the conversation away: Did you know Frances well, Muriel?

Yes. And at first I did not like her. Rather, I wanted not to like her. It looked too much to her advantage. With hindsight, I now hold the opinion it was the other way around. Frances tolerated a lot. Maria can be demanding.

Angelica just smiles at this.

Maria may have been the countess, but Frances was definitely the adult. She was a force. Never bitter or resentful, always gentle, always sensitive. Maria seemed, what is the word . . . ? Besotted? No, *smitten*.

What made you change your mind about Frances?

She visited me at home, arrived at the doorstep with some strawberries for my parents and one of your engravings for me. In a way, I was smitten as well, because I could see they were the right fit. You will never tell Maria any of this? I would be mortified if she ever found out.

No, I swear it.

I knew you would not be shocked. As an artist, you must be good at reading people. Creativity and perceptiveness are linked, I think. Both require one to see clearly with the mind.

Angelica is surprised by this creature, watches her pick at salad leaves without self-consciousness. What are your passions, Muriel?

Gardens. I like flowers and fruit trees and insects and earth and birds. The way it is all interconnected, a balancing act. I like the way everything gives something back. Maria's garden is wonderful. I spent a lot of time in it as a child. I shall have my own garden one day; it is what I require from a prospective husband.

You cannot be thinking of marriage already?

Muriel shrugs. Perhaps you will introduce me to a wealthy bachelor when I come to London?

There are plenty. Not all are desirable mates, and competition for the best prizes is fierce.

I do not need a prize for a spouse, only a man who is sensible and friendly and has a simply enormous garden that is mine to do whatever I like with. That is not too much to ask, is it?

Are you prepared to leave your home?

I shall have to one day.

The wind quickens, making both women shiver.

Muriel points: Look at that! Coward is dragging a stick in his mouth that is obviously too big for him. Enjoy it while you can, because you are not taking it back with you. Silly beast. Shall we pack this away?

I might get some work done, if we go back.

Do you know if Mrs. Plett has made a cake today? I think I will ask.

Muriel carries the rug over her shoulder and they each take a handle of the basket.

We called this "Jack and Jill" when I was little. (Muriel recites the nursery rhyme, which Angelica has not heard before, and makes Angelica do one in the German dialect of her childhood.) It was Penelope, by the way. The print Frances gave me. *Penelope at the Loom.* I look at it every day.

What am I doing, Frances? Caught up in the moment, giddy and—this is awful. No one will come, or if they do it will be out of morbid curiosity. I have forgotten how, what to do and say.

The way Muriel gasps at the suggestion, the reaction, yes, it makes me melt. Seeing the glow of pleasure. Giving her a reason to stay several nights with us, helping to plan it. That is why, I know it, of course.

I say that I can send someone with a message to her father's house requesting his permission and to collect anything she needs.

Katie Ward

She exclaims, Oh, let the theme be *Angelicamad*!

Angelica is mortified, but accepts gracefully. Then Muriel runs to find Mrs. Plett, hungry for cake.

When we are alone, Angelica asks me, Does she know? That you are her mother?

I reply that Muriel is an innocent. Or maybe I do not say it aloud.

Muriel opened my eyes. You showed me the sky.

The ballroom is lit by tiny lights and swathed with curtains. Statues, objects, and plinths are arranged like a set for a play—Roman ruins, or Atlantis to Muriel's fertile mind. Pagan gods gleam and cast shadows.

But the incomplete portrait of Frances will not be displayed.

To avoid the expense of entertaining society and the inevitable flurry of refusals, guests have been chosen for their youth or for previous kindnesses or because they are admirers of the arts, and, in a few rare cases, because they were once friends of both Maria and Frances together. They mostly accept. Maria is still a countess, after all; Muriel has a knack for galvanizing the mannered young people of their parish; and the draw of Angelica's fame certainly swells the numbers. Assistance comes from Maria's uncle in the form of carriages and servants, gifts of sugared sweets arrive that supplement the repast. Muriel and Duncan gather peonies, gladioli, lilies, carnations, roses, poppies to make delicate and glorious arrangements, as though the garden has come indoors smelling delicious and wet. Maria finds she has little to do, with Mrs. Plett attending to the practicalities, and Muriel and Angelica taking care of the aesthetics. Her idleness compounds her anxiety. Your job is to thank people, Angelica reminds her.

The musicians strike up. The guests mingle, greet and compli-

138

ment one another, dashing praises for healthful complexions and ingenious ensembles. The spectacle of the fancy dress. Some have gone to great lengths: crowns, masks, flora, instruments, weapons, and puppets. The company in the ballroom includes Mark Antony in a bedsheet toga, Cleopatra with a crepe-paper asp, Queen Eleanor, Cordelia, Prospero in emerald robes, carrying a carved staff, Socrates in a horsehair beard, Troilus and Cressida, Ulysses, the Muses and allegories, a bevy of nymphs. A minority have resisted the impulse, dress conventionally or incorporate a single salient detail denoting their character. A woman who has brought an apple with her explains she is Aphrodite after the judgment of Paris; a priggish gentleman is dressed as "a lord," one of Miss Kauffman's many portraits, he says, though is vague about which one. Muriel is most pleased with her costume, for she has come as a self-portrait, Angelica lending her one of her own exotic outfits; she proudly carries a palette and brush.

Among the gathering are Maria's second son, Augustus, and her daughter-in-law, Harriet.

It is wonderful to see you both.

He kisses her hand.

How well you look, Mother.

Thank you. How are my grandchildren?

Harriet replies, A handful. They have sent you their love, and these letters and tokens . . . She gives a little bundle tied in pink ribbons to Maria.

There is a pause. Harriet raises her brows at her husband. He coughs.

Mother, it occurs to me you have not seen the girls for some time, and how nice it would be if you deigned to stay with us . . . (That appears to be his whole speech: either he has not prepared or cannot remember the rest.)

The daughter-in-law takes the initiative: The children would be very pleased, you would be welcome to come whenever you liked, either to the country or to town. If you had other appointments to keep in London, then a visit might be of particular benefit?

Maria wavers, promises to give it some consideration.

The rhythms and swirls of conversations, the swish and ruffle of gowns, the fragrance of hairstyles and snap of fans, the pounding of feet and the shower of clapping at the end of each dance. Muriel leads a game of Bluff—the blindfold is tied on her first, and she is turned and turned, hands outstretched, giggles and jibes until she catches a young man (he does not try hard to evade her), then he is It and the game goes on.

Muriel flops next to her godmother, catches her breath from laughing hard, her hands over the twinges.

Is this what you wanted, my girl?

You have not called me that in a long time. Yes, it is splendid, perfect. Do you like it?

Maria kisses the young woman, uplifted to have given her something she enjoys, thankful there is at least this much beauty in the world. And so the party continues, peaks, and peters out— warm-blooded jolly tipsy noisy fatigued. The chatter fades, the mood dims, the music concludes; they bid good night, the candles are snuffed out.

Angelica is to be found in the orangery early.

I wanted to finish this.

Maria is disheveled and bleary, stands behind the artist to inspect the picture.

You have put a book on the table. One of these? She picks up a poet.

Writers are readers.

* * *

Initially Angelica refuses Miss Wheatley's book.

I said I would accept no payment.

A gift then, from one friend to another, as you have done for me, Miss Angel.

Angelica is uneasy about leaving, repeats her invitation for both Maria and Muriel to visit her in London. They embrace.

Maria waves at the departing carriage; Angelica's hand is visible waving back until the horses turn down the lane.

Maria pulls her tippet around her against the morning, walks to keep warm, follows Coward between the flower beds and high hedges, his tail disappearing through the rose arch. Sitting on the bench within is Frances in her red and black riding habit, a writing board and pen in her lap.

I am sorry. I do not mean to disturb you.

Frances sets the tools down by her feet, scoops the dog into her lap: You are not.

Maria sits by her, tears sliding down her face; how easily they fall: Why did you not come before?

I came when you called me. You waited for Angelica and Muriel to go home, you waited for Mrs. Plett's sister to get ill so she went to her bedside, you waited until you and I would be entirely alone.

I am so glad to see you.

Yet you did not ask for me until now.

Where have you been?

Here. Nearby. Nowhere.

You are angry with me? You *are* angry with me! Why are you angry with me? This is your doing. You have done this to us, it is your fault.

Stop it, Maria.

Look at me—look at what you have done. I am a wreck, an invalid, I am broken into pieces.

You know I never chose this, so why do you insist that I did? What is it about being abandoned that pleases you? I treasured every second we had. I would not willingly have given you up. I fought to stay alive, and it is hateful to imply that I did not. Sometimes love is not enough to bind us to the world. What is beautiful may also be finite. It is written: *The Lord gave, and the Lord hath taken away.*

Well, *you* were the one who was taken away, not the one who was left behind! Maria gasps, hardly composes herself . . . I changed everything for you, Frances.

Yes, you did.

You did not have to beg me or argue with me. I did it because I wanted to.

Yes, you did.

It is mortally unfair that what we had, what we made, was ripped from us.

Yes, it is.

You were the strong one, Frances, I was never made for this.

Then pray tell me, what were you made for, Maria?

To spend my youth and fulfill my duties, and after I met you my purpose was to love you.

Is that your purpose still?

More than ever.

A ladybird lands on Frances's skirt. She lets it crawl onto the tip of her gloved finger and fly away.

I know that you hide my writings in your bedroom with a loaded pistol and a bottle of gin. Were you waiting for the portrait to be completed so my face would be the last sight you saw in this life?

And the first in the next.

Is this how you love me, Maria? Forlornly and destructively?

I have this pain, Frances, or I have nothing. I have told you enough times.

Does the painting resemble me, I wonder?

It is at once a pale reflection and speaks the truth.

Frances presses her temple, thinks. Maria, I shall speak the truth to you now. I shall tell you what I would have done if it had been the other way around. I would have mourned you desperately. I would have grown sick, I would tear my hair out and not sleep, I would weep and wail and despair and long for death and lament that it had been this way and not different, and scream until the ceiling fell in. I would break every glass within reach and knock over furniture and throw objects just to watch them smash. I would rage, I would blame you for leaving me, I would consider diving into a swift river or drinking poison. I would be shattered, I would be defeated, I would be mad, I would be the undead. And then, then—*the following day*, I would look into the glass and begin the process of healing. I would . . . devise a tour with Muriel, yes, that is what I would do, to London to begin with, and the friends and relatives who will have us. She is a young woman who deserves the advantages that being introduced into society can give, and per-haps under my guidance I can help find a suitable path for her. Share what small seeds of wisdom I have acquired. Bath next, then Europe. It would enrich her.

How would you afford it?

You will have made provision for Muriel and, though it does not match the wealth of the ton, I have my own income. Also, I did not squander all of your gifts. I worried that one day I might have to take care of you. Did you not know that already? I left the papers in your desk.

Maria pictures a mess of documents she has not yet faced.

Muriel's foster parents should be consulted. Although she is not actually theirs, they love her just the same. It occurs to me, you would be a better tutor in the ways of society; how much more gratifying and extraordinary the world would seem to Muriel when viewed in your reflected light. Still, I would do my best. I would keep Mrs. Plett with us. She has spent her life in service to you, saving you from yourself. What else is she to do? I would let her take charge of Muriel, and me, as a consolation. And I would visit your sons, if they would receive me, and your grandchildren.

Why would you visit my grandchildren?

Because they are yours. Because I would want to be an aunt or a friend to them. Whatever help I could give, they would have it—and who knows when they will need a listening ear or a sanctuary? A real grandparent would be better, but I would do my best.

I see what you are doing, Frances, and it is wasted.

Is it? And if he will hear me out, I would try to persuade Georgie to make provision for Dorothy in the event that His Lordship dies first.

She has no right—

That is why I would raise it sooner rather than later. His Lordship's estate is enormous. It would not harm the legitimate heirs, it could prevent an embarrassing scandal, and she will not need a pension for long, anyway. It is the clever and the moral course of action. That your son fears offending you is probably part of his motive for procrastinating. I would at least try to resolve it. And then I would never think of it again.

Why did you not say any of this before?

Because I was alive and—distracted.

Frances . . . I did not make any provision for you.

Then it is a mercy I died first.

Maria's tears swell childishly.

Oh, Maria, it is only a joke! I would have survived, I would have made do. It would not have inhibited me, nor would I have been angry with you. Put it out of your mind.

Frances puts her arm around Maria's neck; Maria rests her head on her shoulder. A kiss.

Maria whispers, What else would you do?

I would honor your memory by living my life. I would explore whatever we would have explored together. I would regret **deeply** that you were not with me to share it, but I would let the pain go because I would be grateful each day that I had loved you and been loved by you. I would laugh at your wit whenever I recalled it. I would be steered by your precious influence. I would not even reject love if it crossed my path again.

Frances's voice becomes as indistinct as the breeze, her shoulder becomes Maria's own palm, the caress on her arm is only Coward's rough tongue, his black body warm at her side. A ladybird is on her knee, opens its shiny case to reveal transparent wings, flies away.

Featherstone of Piccadilly

Carte de Visite, 1864

Florence and Rosemary, the Gault twins—Flossie and Rosie to each other and their mother—dark-haired and green-eyed, are playing among the graves.

The little girls skip between the headstones, pausing to inspect the worn inscriptions, to pick at the lichen, to place twigs and leaves in mysterious shapes on the dirt of the dead. They commune with the sleepers, listen for the shriek of the magpie, the damp air making their frocks cling, the soles of their feet black. Their nails are clogged with filth.

Florence is the elder by a few minutes, considers herself to be wiser in the ways of the world for this reason, to have forever an advantage over Rosemary. Rosie is fortunate to have an example to follow. They are bony and pale, but not miserable children. This churchyard is one of their "best places." They natter, they crouch, they chase and hide, they are identical guardians of the crypts.

One says to her twin, Let's do Our Secret. She likes to do that because the physical world warps into patterns, and the flow of sisterly understanding between them is powerful but *not at all* terrifying. Her sister does not want to, is content to be, runs along the row of mounds instead. They play and explore until their mother comes to fetch them.

Mrs. Harry Gault—Isabella—the wan woman, sickly bearer of seven surviving children, five of them strapping boys destined for the Lancashire textile factories and coal pits. Her youngest are the twin girls who she had hoped would take up her mantle, for in her youth Isabella was both a great beauty and a brilliant dramatic soprano. Letters and gifts from enamored princes, the whole of Europe her wardrobe and dining table and boudoir. The nectar of immortality was within her grasp, until a jealous rival (in love or in opera?) attacked her with a straight razor, leaving her face and career in tatters.

Isabella has known destitution, and in the end she could do no better than Harry Gault. The scarring is permanent and deep.

It was disappointing to find that her girls, though they can learn a song and some harmonies if they are repeated, have no special aptitude or inclination for music. And there is a houseful of boys and men to attend to anyway, chores to do, the permanent threat of pregnancy—

Mrs. Isabella Gault, wrapped against the weather in gray wool, makes her way toward the cemetery. She calls to her girls in her melodious voice.

One waves. She can see it is Florence (only Isabella could tell them apart at this distance). Rosemary is out of sight. The church spire points to a pale sky where starlings flock, swarming cloud shapes, pulsing presentiment, their mass contracting and expanding in collective consciousness. Isabella stops to watch the evening delight. Florence looks, then disappears from view farther behind the graves.

Isabella climbs the hill, makes her way to her daughters, Flossie elevated on a grassy mound, Rosie huddled by a wall.

What have you been doing?

Flossie replies, We were talking to the beggar; he said the night was death.

Where is he now?

Flossie shrugs. Gone to heaven, I expect. You saw him too, didn't you? She addresses her twin.

Rosie turns, disconcerted.

Flossie scowls. Well . . . ?

Yes, I saw him. He had white hair and a staff. He had traveled far.

At first Isabella fears a criminal in their midst, then: Tell me, where was this man?

Standing there—Flossie points to the vacant threshold of the church where the thick oak door is shut fast. He was in pain. For a while. Then he left.

When was he here?

A moment before you.

Which way did he go?

Flossie looks to her sister to supply more details, but Rosie frowns. Flossie shrugs: Gone whence he came.

Isabella looks about her in case the stranger is nearby. He is not. She walks the perimeter of the building, determined to see in each direction so she can swear on the Bible she searched with her own eyes and found nobody. She has already begun to create the legend. She knows that twelve years ago an elderly man who had wandered for many miles seeking shelter in the depths of winter, finding the church locked and bolted, died of exposure on that very spot, his body frozen solid, his face locked in the grimace of pleas unanswered.

Florence goes to her twin. She and Rosemary whisper together.

*   *   *

Isabella Gault knows about the nurture of talent. She knows that finesse comes with rehearsal, that effortlessness requires effort.

The lamps are extinguished because the medium, Mrs. Mortimer Solomon-Black, is giving a demonstration. She is an American, though her transatlantic tones merge with the furrows of another dialect. The participants at the séance hold hands around the table to ensure the authenticity of the experiment, the room so dark they cannot see their neighbors or the person opposite, or the lady herself. Listening to their own breath. They wait. Two of their number are avid spiritualists, thrilled to be in the presence of one of the most famous and proven mediums of the day. One man is an ardent skeptic, has come to figure out the trickery, deride the folly, denounce it as charlatanism. One attendee is bereaved, and three more are here for diversion, as though this were the music hall or a game of whist.

Mrs. Solomon-Black is going into her trance: We are here as friends. Is there a spirit who desires to make contact with the living this evening?

The silence is painful. The members of the party attempt to repress the rustle of clothing, the whistling from one gentleman's hairy nose, the creak of the chairs they occupy. They grip one another's fingers tighter.

A clear, loud rap.

They react, shared relief and achievement. It came from above or beneath them somehow, from no discernible source in the room (which was examined in advance).

Two more raps.

Mrs. Solomon-Black translates: Three for yes, we have broken through. May I remind you at this critical juncture not to break the circle. If the person sitting next to you lets go, you must draw attention to him immediately so that there can be no tampering or interference, and what happens here remains spontaneous and honest.

A man of city finance (and also the bereft son) asks whether it is his mother.

Mrs. Solomon-Black puts the question to the spirit: Are you Hilda Merryweather? For there is someone here who wishes to contact Hilda Merryweather.

One rap. One rap for no. Then one more, then a third—it is she, after all.

Hilda, your son, Phillip, is here. He longs to speak with you.

Phillip Merryweather can hardly contain himself and exclaims into the darkness, Mama! I am so happy. I have been lonely without you. But Mrs. Solomon-Black, how do I know for certain it is she?

The medium agrees: We must make sure. Hilda, appear to me. Let me hear you. Let me bear witness. Show your love for your son by showing yourself.

The piquancy of the anticipation is heightened. Assuredly if the spirit is genuine, it will not deny her son solace? Assuredly if the medium is a fraud, she will expose herself now?

Aha. I see a most elegant lady, adorned in pearls, with white hair that used to be red. She holds a posy of thistles and has been reunited with a white cat she is very fond of.

Phillip squeaks with emotion because this is an accurate description of his beloved mother.

She is giving me some names. She is saying Victoria and Albert. But that does not make any sense, Mr. Merryweather; why should she be naming the Queen and her consort?

Because Victoria was her middle name, and Bert was the cat she loved and lost. It is Mama's way of letting me know it is indeed she. (Some of the group murmur in amazement.) What is she saying now?

She is anxious about her pepper pot.

Oh, dear. I gave it to Mrs. Middleton after Mama died. Was I not supposed to? Does she want me to get it back?

It has some special significance.

I cannot think what.

And she is worried, fretful, about an unpaid bill to the butcher.

He raises his voice as though addressing someone across the road.

We have settled your accounts, Mama, including the butcher's. He was saddened to hear the news and gave us a ham for the wake.

The medium listens intently.

I see. Was your mother one to accept charity in life?

Phillip Merryweather does not reply, senses disapproving eyes on him in the blackness.

I think your mother wants you to settle the outstanding payment.

Of course. How foolish of me. Mama, I am sorry, I was distraught. It never occurred to me—

She is saying that is no excuse. However, she is saying you were a good son to her, and she is proud of you. And she is saying a wonderful opportunity has recently come your way that you should take advantage of, with a Scottish connection.

Phillip Merryweather thinks instantly of his planned investment in a shipbuilding contract in Clydebank. The engineer's drawings were magnificent, the business model as tight as a drum, the potential returns fabulous. Uncanny!

She means Edward McClancy's proposal, of course. I am glad of her approval, for I intend to sign the papers tomorrow.

A single resolute knock.

Not McClancy's ship, Mama . . . ?

He considers.

Hmm. She cannot mean the loan Nicholas Nash asked me for, for his geological survey? (The cost of the project was enormous. Merryweather had laughed the man out of his office—it was a fool's errand, a lot of old rocks and marine fossils and glacial drifts and no money to be made whatsoever.)

Three distinct knocks. Yes.

Mama? Are you positive that Nash is the man I should be financing, not McClancy?

Hilda . . . ? The medium strains in her chair. She is being called away. She is leaving us.

Phillip Merryweather is peeved, but the two experienced spiritualists, Miss Langdon and Miss Mellor, can be heard twittering with excitement, for Mrs. Solomon-Black is thoroughly convincing and there is still more to come.

This is most unusual. I see a bold spirit-light taking on the form of a maiden, an Amazon princess made of white spirit-energy . . . wait . . . it is making a pathway for someone else, it recedes and is replaced by another female—I see her with total clarity—she comes forward with intention. She is drawn, disheveled, she has lost her good looks but has determination and an exceptional mind. She is adorned with a single precious stone that resembles the deep sea . . . and it is as if she is falling into it; the blueness swells up, it covers her head. She has turned her back on love. Poor, fragile lady, what a frightful waste.

No one present claims ownership of this woman.

Mrs. Solomon-Black persists. This vision is vivid. Will nobody speak up for it? There is nothing to be ashamed of.

When no reply is forthcoming, the medium suggests to the ghost that she allow a soul with a more urgent message to come forward . . . and concentrates.

A different spirit is attempting to communicate, a gentleman called G, wearing a fetching waistcoat in bright colors, carrying a carved-bone-topped cane, and with him is— What is this? An exotic bird, if I am not mistaken.

The gasp of recognition comes from Mr. Thomas Hubbard, the cynic, here to pooh-pooh, here to call it all bunkum.

The medium senses a conquest.

Do not furnish any details, Mr. Hubbard, allow me: the G stands for Godwin, am I right? And in life, he was a great intellect, a distinguished man of letters. He may even have worked in the law, for I see justice and fairness are imperative to him.

Good gracious. Thomas Hubbard perspires in the darkness, unable to mop the moisture away without breaking the séance circle.

And so on. The spirits are willing and talkative, until all in the party but one have made contact with a friend or relative who has passed over—Miss Langdon fails to reach her late aunt Mildred but does not mind, as she spoke to her only last week.

Mrs. Solomon-Black's style of clairvoyance is calm. Her job is, she says, to foster peace by aiding the spirits in their communiqués so they may be restful, and to reassure the living that they might live. Toward the end of the demonstration, she briefly loses control and the séance gets out of hand: the table levitates and turns, the participants feel spectral fingers on their faces, scratches, jabs in the ribs, tweaked knees, and yanked hair. An object flies from one side of the room to the other and smashes. (My poor shepherdess, says the hostess who has arranged the entertainment.) The medium is angry at the disruptiveness of those spirits who are trying to sabotage their civilized meeting; one enters her body and begins speaking through her to someone present: I know you, I know what you have done. You think you have covered your tracks, but I shall unmask you and ruin you, monster, fiend, wretch—

There is bedlam, during which the person who thinks this

warning applies to him is stricken with fear, relieved his peers cannot see his horror at being found out.

Mrs. Solomon-Black fights back, sends the wicked spirits away, is shaking with exhaustion afterward, and apologizes: When unfriendly spirits upset proceedings it is very draining, and even if my mind is able, my body is weak. I shall have to bring this evening to a close. I do hope you understand.

Her clients do not feel shortchanged; on the contrary, the excitement of the malevolent spirits has added flavor to the experience. All present are persuaded of Mrs. Mortimer Solomon-Black's authenticity, all (apart from one) are extolling her extraordinary abilities for weeks afterward to any who will listen.

In the photographer's studio, all must be done at the critical moment while the glass is dripping wet with light-sensitive chemicals. Not one of the steps can be blundered or missed. The paper print with which the client is presented, at which they exclaim out of pleasure and fascination, that is the easy part—the very last part, the sprint to the end. One can make dozens, hundreds of reprints with barely any skill. But the innumerable difficulties that arise before them, the inordinate potential for things to go wrong—being heavy-handed or hurried or less than systematic or simply unlucky—and behold: blemishes, ridging, specks, or possibly nothing whatever where the portrait should be. And when the entire intricate process has been conducted flawlessly to make an image that is as naturally near to perfection as possible, and the sitter *moves* during the exposure, it is enough to send one into a fit.

In the cramped darkroom, the photographer can do little more than arrange the bottles in order of use, labels outward, and lay the equipment in readiness so it can be accessed by the dimness of a single orange windowpane.

Not all photographers are as meticulous. The sheer number of studios in the towns and countryside suggests that virtually anyone is capable of making a photograph, that there is no mystery to discover, no alchemy to master, no craft. Some call it sneeringly "a trade." But see also how inferior their pictures are? Nasty. No doubt they employ a tout to browbeat passing customers, especially on Sundays, when people are dressed for church and should be observing the Sabbath. Let them part with their guinea, and may it bring them luck.

Featherstone of Piccadilly is a superior establishment. Mr. Amos Featherstone, a schooled painter, accomplished, gentle, genteel, maker of fine photographic portraits, was also the most amiable of companions to the end. On his deathbed he whispered to his wife, I deeply regret it is time for me to go. I wish I didn't have to.

Amos Featherstone's widow checks the workbench where her son has prepared some plates; he has smoothed the edges with the sharpening stone and polished the surfaces with tripoli. Jem has done it thoroughly, but each will need to be cleaned again with a soft brush, because any dust particles whatsoever will show as spots on the final image. Jem has been busy mounting albumen prints for collection in the morning, and has replenished the stock of collodion solution that will ripen next week. He is a good boy.

She hesitates, places her hand upon her breastbone. Heaviness, that dratted heaviness. The tightness of a vise. Pain in her shoulders and neck. In minutes it subsides.

Mrs. Amos Featherstone did not imagine having to take on the studio at this age—at any age. She was her husband's helpmeet. Her role was at home raising their children. The moral paradigm, the pillar of virtue, the protectress of domestic order. Two sons and two daughters grew into adulthood, the girls safely married off.

It had been intended that their eldest boy, Robert, would run his father's business, though his heart was never truly in it, though he longed to join the British Army, though he was clumsy and made errors and spilled and damaged. But it was a moot point because Robert was lost to cholera. This left Jem, whose delicate disposition was perhaps better suited to photography . . . but who did not have long enough with his father to learn the art, whose nervousness with the public and naïveté as regards money meant it would have been irresponsible to give him full control just yet. Therefore Mrs. Featherstone became the custodian of Featherstone of Piccadilly. It felt like a failure on her part. Her daughters believed as much; indeed, she has raised them to.

A lady of mature years, the decades have added bulk to her body. The wearing of a corset and crinolette provides a more fashionable silhouette, and her gowns are of the plainest, black or gray, and spattered with chemicals. Amos's pocket watch on a chain pinned at her waist is entirely practical, for the timing of exposures and so on. Her hair, mainly still dark, has a straight parting at the front and is gathered in a net snood at the nape. By the end of the day wisps of it escape, reminding her when she looks in the mirror that she is not a dowager but a woman who must work. She has fat cheeks, a severe mouth, hooded eyes. Which episodes in her life have done this?

She could have sold the business as a going concern. It would be worth a small fortune, for the premises alone are ideal and neatly formed. On the ground floor is their shop, where clients may browse a gallery of glossy brown-reddish, brown-purplish portraits of ladies, gentlemen, children, families, couples—a testament to the quality of the company and the satisfaction of the clientele. The shop displays some of the choices on offer: the range of poses, the size of prints, the design of mounts. Here is the counter where the first consultation and final transaction are conducted. There is also a selection of royalty, nobility, and celebrity *cartes* that can be added to a private album for a shilling apiece (the Prince of Wales and Princess Alexandra are doing exceedingly well, as is Mr. Charles Dickens). The first floor is the archive—some of it, at any rate—for the studio retains the negative for at least a year from last use; miscellany storage. The photographic studio itself is on the top floor, has a northern aspect and a roof the length and breadth of which are windows windows windows, the light modulated by curtains and blinds on a matrix of pulleys. And, as in a theater, there are backdrops and props: tables, potted plants, a section of a banister, a faux mantelpiece, chairs, a rocking horse, and so forth, used for creating the scene. These are muddled with the backstage equipment and tools, the various chemical jars and beakers, the posing stands, the wet-plate multiplying camera—a box of wood and brass with bellows for focusing affixed on a tripod, its various lenses and appendages—and the sectioned-off darkroom is here too. Amos spent years accumulating and perfecting this. Selling was never an option.

Neither was installing a man to run it, not only because the halcyon days might be coming to an end, but because Amos wanted Featherstone always to mean Featherstone. Wanted it this way. He was a good father and provider, and so his wishes have been respected.

Jem is in his waistcoat and loosely knotted necktie, his sleeves rolled up like a grocer's, his hair untidy as though he has just risen from bed. Humble by nature. Aware of what his mother is doing for him. Honored that one day he shall be Featherstone of Piccadilly, having believed for most of his life that it would be Robert. He asks if there is anything she needs.

Mrs. Featherstone has made a list. As it is quiet, he can run these errands for her, and she will see him at home for dinner. She can hold the fort for the last hour or so. As Jem puts on his jacket and derby, she tells him he has been a help today.

He then ventures, Mama, perhaps we can take a walk to Regent's Park and visit the zoo? We might enjoy the aquarium and the hippopotamuses. What do you think?

Jem has made a suggestion for an outing nearly every week since his father died. Parks, museums, exhibitions, strolls to take in landmarks and monuments. Initially it irritated her; initially she rejected these trivial distractions from her duties and adjustment. Then she remembered how young he still was, took pity on him, thought she would humor him once, because he was in mourning as she was.

The lecture on electromagnetism was followed by an evening at the Haymarket to hear a comedy, an omnibus to Richmond for lunch, a day in Greenwich. She came to understand why he had persisted, came to acknowledge the wisdom of these trips, to see how they helped them both and restored normality of a kind.

When he had suggested taking the train to Brighton and staying overnight, his mother simply said what she is saying now: We will not know what it is like until we find out for ourselves. They had walked arm in arm along the esplanade, taking in the views. The sea air was cleansing after the effluvia and fetid vapors of London. Mrs. Featherstone found the illustrations exhibited at the Royal Pavilion especially diverting, charming, quaint. She bought a souvenir print very cheaply, telling Jem the figure in it was probably an allegory of poetry.

Hippos in Regent's Park? She can manage them with ease.

Jem touches the brim of his hat to her and goes to his tasks, the shop bell ringing on his way out.

After watching him disappear down the road into the crowds and smog, she turns the sign over to read CLOSED and sits at the counter to peruse the *Morning Post* until—

The shop bell rings again, and a lady enters. She is dressed grandly, dramatically, in violet and black with stripes on the bodice, crimped trimming, and a velvet coat. The voluminous silk ties of her bonnet make an enormous bow. She is adorned with jewelry in a way some would find vulgar: an enormous locket, lengths of beads over her bosom, earrings that glitter. Two spots of rouge make her look like a painted doll.

And she is, in every physical detail, the exact replica of the lady at the counter.

Hello, Flossie, says Mrs. Amos Featherstone.

Hello, Rosie, says Mrs. Mortimer Solomon-Black. You do not seem very surprised to see me.

The *Morning Post* announced you were in London. I expected you to drop by.

Really? Do go on.

Your profession means you still keep late hours and were therefore bound to visit in the afternoon. And I read that this evening you are to give a demonstration at rooms in the White Hart, which is close by. I said to myself, Flossie will come today.

Florence shakes her head in disbelief—her sister can tell what she is thinking.

The twins regard each other. It has been eleven years since they last spoke, an interval of four years before that, and an ocean between them. Yet it may as well be eleven hours. In a moment they have become the Gaults of Lancashire again, their relationship with each other longer and deeper than with anyone else—parents, husbands, children. Each was her twin's first experience, what she first saw, knew, and understood about the world, a copy of herself.

Florence takes in the displays of photographs, turns a page or two of a made album, says, I am sorry about Amos and about Robert. How sad.

Thank you, and thank you for your kind letter. You are married *again*, aren't you . . . ?

Yes. No need for that tone, little sister. I have been divorced only the once, don't you know.

You did not keep your name.

Mortimer's name carries weight in its own right. He is with me here, in London. We always travel together. You can meet him if you like.

Is America still making you happy?

It is home, even with its faults.

You are not in any danger, I hope . . . ?

Oh no, we will be all right. What a thoroughly despicable war! This is a nice shop, Rosie, it rather suits you.

This does not please Rosemary Featherstone; she does not respond.

And Jem—it is Jem?—how is he working out?

He has a natural eye and a steady hand.

No magnetism, though . . . ? Perhaps it skips a generation—or it is simply that none of the Gault menfolk has it. Have you heard from any of our kin? (Florence pauses long enough to realize Rosemary will not rise to that.) Come on, Rosie, don't look sad. If you are sad, no good will come of it, except perhaps that people will be able to tell us apart.

Rosemary smiles at the truth of it, at the innumerable mix-ups and misunderstandings of the past. As girls, they encouraged the confusion, dressed the same, wore their hair the same, lied frequently to cover for the other.

I have also come to bring you business—don't panic, not the kind you dislike. I have been in England for only five minutes, and people are swamping me with their *cartes de visite*, but I cannot reciprocate. So I wondered if you would oblige? I do not require a special rate, just whatever you would normally charge, but I will need several dozen, maybe a hundred or more if I am inundated. Would it be possible?

It is possible to oblige immediately, and Rosemary leads Florence up to the studio and hangs her bonnet and coat on the hat stand, revealing her twin's black hair tightly braided and styled with oil.

The visiting sister takes in the room. What a marvelous place. What a pretty view of the city. If I were you, I should live here just to be able to see it.

I practically do.

Rosemary has Florence try out some poses in front of the camera. Initially Florence wants full-length standing portraits, but Rosemary can see that even with the aid of a posing stand under her skirt or a prop to lean on, her sister is too much of a fidget, so they agree upon a three-quarter-length seated pose. The Featherstone studio makes eight images of standard size to a plate. Florence is keen to experiment; Rosemary persuades her just two poses of four each will be sufficient variety. She makes Flossie practice, first sitting in the mode of reading a book for the duration of one exposure, fifty seconds at this time of day and in this weather—

Mrs. Beeton . . . ? Really, Rosie!

Don't move, please, Flossie.

Florence holds her tongue and herself while Rosemary explains her lady customers are usually happy to be photographed with it, though the title on the spine will not actually be visible.

And then the switch to resting her elbow on the table and looking over her shoulder for the same length of time, for a second exposure. Rosemary angles some mirrors so Florence can see and maintain her facial expression.

Well done, Flossie, but I am afraid that was only the rehearsal. Are you ready for the real thing?

Without waiting for a response, Rosemary takes up the glass plate by one corner in her white gloved hand, pours some collodion into the center—yellow like castor oil—and begins flowing the plate by gently tilting to cover it evenly in the liquid.

The photographer says, You will have to bear with me, as I am doing this without assistance.

You haven't changed.

Rosemary goes into the darkroom and places the plate upright in a bath of silver nitrate. She then brings the pocket watch up to her ear and starts counting. A few minutes later—

Rosie, what are you doing?

Prepare, please.

Florence gives herself a stretch, then opens Mrs. Beeton's *Household Management,* affecting interest.

Rosemary comes out of the darkroom with the sensitized plate inside a wooden holder to protect it from light. Some of the solution leaks out of it. She slots the wooden plate holder into the back of the camera and pulls out the slide, saying she is about to make the exposure. Taking her twin's silence and stillness for assent, she removes the lens cap and times it, counting down aloud. Florence breathes shallowly, does not blink, does not read a word of the page but stares quite through it. She could be mistaken for a waxwork. Then Rosemary replaces the cap, directs Florence to alter her posture, and adjusts the wet plate. The second exposure is taken. Florence has proved to be a good subject after all.

In the darkroom once more, Rosemary gently pours developer on the glass plate to make the image appear—silver and grainy. When her eyes were stronger she was able to discern the image materializing, halt it at the optimum second; now she must rely on her experience. Water stops the development of the negative, and at last Rosemary can take it out of the darkroom and submerge it in the bath of sodium thiosulphate fixer. She waits while the eight images become clear and vivid. They are not unsatisfactory thus far.

Rosie, we ought to go to Mama's grave together while I am in London. You and I haven't done that since we buried her.

Will your engagements permit it?

Will yours?

Rosemary gives the plate a wash in water and lays it out. The negative is extremely delicate. She lights the paraffin lamp for warmth.

Rosie, have you been to Mama's grave since she died?

Rosemary's face is hidden. She busies herself at the workbench.

You must stop being mad with her. She was doing what she knew, what she thought was best for us.

Mama was doing what pleased her most. If we had been born joined at the hip, she would have put us in a circus.

Florence cannot deny this. Didn't you enjoy any of it? At times it seemed you did.

Rosemary sighs, pauses her activity, sits on the just-for-pretense sofa. It is not a part of my life I think about anymore, and I have forgotten a lot of it. I look at a city on the globe and realize I cannot remember if I have been there or not. Cities, and even whole countries, have merged together in my memory. Maybe it was because there were so many, and maybe it is because I do not revise them in my mind's eye—and maybe it is just because one's faculties tend to diminish. Anyway, it is history to me. Why should I dwell on my past when there is Jem's future to consider? I really do not think on it.

You must know if you enjoyed it. Can you not recall a single minute of pleasure?

I don't remember. I know that I did not enjoy the limelight as much as you.

I adore it. I mean the work, not the attention. Mama did right by at least one of us.

Then who am I to criticize? (Rosemary picks up the plate, practically dry, and gently warms it over the lamp flame.)

Her twin says, However, if I had to identify something I disliked about it—

Heats the bottle of varnish next until it is blood warm.

—It would have to be that it emphasized what was different about us.

I don't know what you mean, Flossie.

Yes, you do. I liked it when we were as identical as two people can be, when we looked the same and spoke the same. I liked it when we were following the same road and having the same adventures and thinking the same thoughts. I loved sharing it with you as much as anything else, as much as the novelties and the trappings. You made me secure about my place in the world. I am very happy you got the family you wanted and the home you deserved. It turned out wonderfully for me, so I can't complain. But it was a blow to find out we were not as alike as I thought we were—that one of us was fulfilled and one of us was not.

Rosemary holds the glass by the same corner, pours the tepid varnish—yellow like urine—into the middle, and flows the plate as before to coat the negative. She finally lets it rest.

You are putting on quite a show over there. Maybe it is not such a different vocation as you would have me believe . . . ?

This is not my vocation.

If you are doing it for Jem, which you are, then it is. You thought it was beneath you, didn't you, Rosie? You thought it was degrading.

Public exhibitionism and parlor tricks are degrading. Affectation, performance, and insincere speech are demeaning for a lady.

The medium shrugs: And yet you have given a performance every day since, as a spouse and a mother. Isn't that demeaning also? To pretend to be less than what you are?

Less?

Florence continues, Was our mother more than, or less than, what she once was after she married our father? It was not the attack that broke her spirit; it was what it reduced her to. Anyone can marry. Anyone can bring children into the world. But you are unique, and you gave it up for the sake of dreary convention.

Rosemary stares at her twin. Florence has done exactly what Rosemary expected: found a way to spite her.

Well, Flossie, what you see as sacrifice, I see as freedom. What you call convention, I call stability. My greatest achievements are being obedient to my husband and setting a good example to my sons and daughters.

Florence is nonplussed. But you admit it is all for show? It is not what you really are. I do not mean to cause offense, Rosie, just to speak the truth. Being "mistress of a house" requires putting on an act, does it not? And dressing in costume. And speaking lines. And doing what is expected.

You would say that, Florence, because you have never had a family.

On the contrary, I have had a family. I have had more than one. I have never had any *children;* is that what you are referring to? I was merely pointing out that you have exchanged one role for another.

You disapprove.

No more than you disapprove of me.

I have never given you reason to think such a thing. (The photographer removes her gloves, businesslike.) I am afraid I cannot make you any prints until tomorrow because the negative is wet. And it will be better to do duplicates in stronger sunlight.

I am grateful.

Would you like me to have Jem deliver them?

No need, I will send someone to collect them. By the bye, where is my nephew?

Doing errands for me.

The spiritualist replies, Strange . . . you guessed I was coming today . . . and when I arrive, he is out running errands.

Life does go on, Flossie.

I tell my clients exactly the same, Rosie.

The carriage of Mr. and Mrs. Lennox, a young couple, pulls up outside Featherstone of Piccadilly, and Jones the valet enters the shop, presents Mr. Lennox's card, and speaks to Jem. His employers require some *cartes de visite* of their daughter, Edna, as a matter of urgency. They are waiting to be received.

Jem smothers his nerves, affirms it can be done this instant, and while Jones returns to his master to convey the acceptance of the commission, Jem calls to his mother.

Rosemary Featherstone greets Mr. and Mrs. Lennox, both pinched and dressed head to foot in refined black tailoring. Mrs. Lennox, a blonde, watery woman, wears crêpe and an exquisite jet brooch. Mr. Lennox carries his top hat, occasionally touches his moustache as he speaks. This type of portrait is always problematic. The photographer assesses the couple, and it is as she fears—he is exacting, suspicious, has expectations, is enumerating them.

Mrs. Lennox is mute until she spies a portion of the display set discreetly in one corner. Mrs. Featherstone, you have done child *cartes* of this kind before? These are they?

Mrs. Featherstone replies, Yes, Mrs. Lennox, we have plenty of experience and testimonials from parents pleased with the outcome. A photograph of a child is a highly cherished possession.

Mr. Lennox examines the pictures himself, nods.

Jones loiters outside, awaiting instructions, and Rosemary sends Jem to assist.

The sofa and a selection of satin cushions are chosen for the little girl to rest on. Edna turns out to be blonde like her mother, dressed in white, piously holding a crucifix in her fragile ivory hand. A pale cherub. But it is not an easy photograph, not nearly as easy as it ought to be. The parents are anxious, determined to supervise, obstructive. Jem has yet to acquire the skill of diverting unwanted onlookers and keeping them at a distance; his attempts to assist Mrs. Featherstone are a hindrance. Jones the valet serves no purpose, none, gets in the way. And the child herself . . .

It is down to Rosemary Featherstone to manage the situation tactfully without making any errors. It will be disastrous if she has to take the portrait a second time. She must patiently accommodate the patrons' needs, lead assertively and diplomatically, trust in her abilities, ignore the distractions.

Tiny footsteps across the floorboards—investigative fingers—a shrill giggle.

Rosemary prepares the wet plate, laments not for the last time how many things can go wrong.

When the picture has been taken, the Lennox party leaves. Mr. Lennox carries Edna in his arms.

An hour later, and Rosemary is able to make the proof in solitude. She puts the glass negative into the printing frame in contact with the albumen paper and exposes it to sunlight. The eight identical pictures emerge; she watches it to arrest the exposure and fix the print. Here, then, is the first proper sight of the Lennox child's *carte*. She looks carefully. It seems to be all right.

She will have Jem make the duplicates. No need for her to do it herself. But—

She takes out her magnifying glass because she does not trust her weakening vision and examines the paper proof again, each eighth, carefully, looking not at the girl on the sofa but around her, in the background, on the curtain, for imperfections, for—

Edna Lennox, you naughty child.

Rosemary scrutinizes now the plate negative. She sighs with exasperation, puts the magnifying glass down with a clunk. She cannot face having them back in the studio for a second attempt, and even if she wanted to, it is probably too late. It will just have to be retouched.

Amos Featherstone was a purist, outwardly opposed to retouching. But in private he, like the majority of his colleagues, would paint out unwanted spots and markings that detracted from the finished result (but, unlike some of the less scrupulous studios, he stopped short of improving the sitter's personal appearance). Amos, a trained artist, used watercolors or India ink on the negative. Rosemary uses instead a soft lead pencil. She makes the corrections using the magnifier, bends over her task; her hand trembles with concentration.

Jem appears at her elbow. He is grinning.

What are you so happy about?

He shakes his head. 'Stonishing.

Apparently he does not mean the proof, he means the lady standing in the studio.

Rosemary, startled: Why are you here? You said you would send someone.

I sent myself. Are you glad?

Yes, I am rather.

Jem looks at the two women, shakes his head again.

Rosie, we have not been formally introduced . . . ?

Flossie, may I present my youngest, Jem. Jemmy, this is my sister, your aunt, Mrs. Mortimer Solomon-Black.

He dips in a bow. How d'you do?

Florence says, What a handsome man you have grown into. You were a baby when I last saw you. Now look at you.

He blushes at this—and coming from such a lady in jewels and polka dots—he finds the resemblance intriguing. Would you like some tea, Mrs. Solomon-Black?

That would be very nice. (Jem goes to boil the water, Florence follows him out with her eyes.)

You have made a beautiful boy. He looks exactly like her—does he sound like her too?

He would be horrified at the very notion of singing on a stage. Thankfully none of my children was that way inclined. He likes this—Rosemary gestures about her.

I am surprised you told him about me.

Well, why shouldn't I?

What about the girls? Do they know about me? about us? about *you*?

Rosemary is nettled. They know what they need to, which is more than they care for. If you try to see them, of course I would not presume to prevent you. On the other hand, you oughtn't take it to heart if you find they are not at home.

They would turn me away . . . ?

I doubt it would be their decision. One is married to a lawyer, the other to a man of industry. They are directed by their husbands, as they were brought up to be, and have reputations to maintain. Mary read that you were coming to London. She hopes your trip is a success, but said it was a shame that your public engagements would keep you from visiting her.

Florence wonders how Rosemary could have permitted this, yet her sister is unrepentant. Rather than forcing the issue, Florence says, I have brought you and your son an invitation to dine. (Gives her sister the short letter in a looping script.) If you decline, I shall not question it.

Mr. and Mrs. Mortimer Solomon-Black present their compliments to Mrs. Amos Featherstone and Mr. James Featherstone, and request the honor of their company to dinner on Thursday, et cetera.

Rosemary notes the venue, replies quietly, The gesture is extremely kind.

It was Mortimer's idea. For some reason he wants to meet you before we leave.

I intended to invite you both to our home.

You did not mention it yesterday.

No, I suppose I did not get to it. Your *cartes* are printed. Rosemary lays the letter down, shows Florence a finished picture mounted on a card from a boxful.

Florence opens her tortoiseshell lorgnette. Superb. This is much better than what I have been using.

Rosemary offers to send a bill, but Florence wishes to make payment now. The transaction is done. Rosemary wraps the box in paper.

It is while she is doing this and counting out change that Florence notices the Lennox proof and examines it through her spectacles, remarks, This photograph is postmortem. She looks as though she is sleeping peacefully.

Rosemary represses the urge to take it back. That is our job, sometimes.

My God.

Florence gazes hard at it. The recognition is twofold; what is on the proof and what Rosemary is now doing to the negative. You are unbelievable.

It is just a mistake on the film.

It is not. If it were, it would appear only in one place, but it is identical on each image. Do you know what you have got here?

Give it to me, please, Florence.

Do you know how many fakes are out there? Photographers making double exposures, painting in figures on the plate, lurkers in bedsheets coming out from behind curtains when the subject's head is in a posing apparatus and he cannot see what is going on behind him. And yet, here you are—

Rosemary snatches the print away at last.

Let me buy it from you. You can name your price.

No.

You have a responsibility.

No such responsibility exists. She is someone's child, the parents are grieving. It would be indecent.

Are you going to show it to them? They have the right to know.

Rosemary does not answer.

I assume this has happened before. How many times, Rosie? Rosie, how many times?

I have said it is a mistake on the film, and I have said no. I am sorry, you will have to do without.

Florence sighs, knows she cannot change her twin's mind, collects her package. As you wish. Let me know about Thursday, will you?

As she turns to go, Jem returns with the tea tray. Are you leaving already, Mrs. Solomon-Black? I was looking forward to hearing about your life in the United States. It does sound a fascinating place.

Florence and Rosemary exchange glances.

I was looking forward to telling you about it. Regrettably, I have more engagements.

The shop bell rings downstairs. Jem, unable to hide his disappointment, says, I should see to that anyhow.

His mother intercedes. I shall see to it. My sister has a few minutes to spare for some refreshment before her next appointment. You two can stay—

Rosemary takes the proof with her, out of temptation's reach.

Mortimer Solomon-Black shuffles off his frock coat, undoes his floppy cravat, discards it, groans as he pulls off his shoes. He takes off his waistcoat, undoes the studs on his stiff collar and some more on his shirt. He has muttonchop whiskers and a resonant New Yorker's diction.

Fire is going out. I'll do it. Got to do something—so damnably damp in this country.

He rebuilds it with coal and a poker while his wife, sixteen years his senior, begins to undress—peeling off her outer layers, stepping out of the dress, out of the crinoline, plucking hairpins from her hair—remains in her corset and undergarments. The fire grows lively, warming the room.

Mortimer admires his wife, her shapely body, her hair long and loose. You were a marvel tonight. There wasn't an empty seat in the house.

That was your doing.

Your doing. They were captivated.

Florence settles on one of the chairs, rests her feet on a stool. Without being asked, Mortimer kneels down to remove her boots. He kisses one of her ankles and begins to massage her tired foot. They stay this way for a while, Florence growling with pleasure, the tension dissipating. Perhaps Mortimer does not want to chat, wants to go straight to bed . . . ?

Mortimer would like that very much. But he is the kind of man who likes to have his mental faculties as well as his physical senses stimulated. His wife was sensational this evening, note-perfect, saw off an attempted sabotage by a heckler, hit each target first time, every time, like a sharpshooter. The audience was spellbound. He loves how they admire her, the stirrings of awe, the way doors open for her and people jostle to be near. All the same, he loves to have her for himself and when they are touring these hours become rare and precious. He will make love to her, but first they will have this—their conversation, when they share or spar or pontificate. Mortimer shows her an emerald bottle—she smiles, removes her earrings—then pours an ounce of absinthe, dragonfly green, into the bulbous reservoirs of two glass goblets. The scent of the holy trinity, aniseed, grande wormwood, and fennel, escapes. He balances a perforated spoon on the rim of each vessel, and on the spoon a lump of sugar. Slowly, hardly more than a drop at a time, he pours iced water from a carafe over the sugar, which begins to dissolve, the white solution dripping into the absinthe at the bottom, swirling and merging as the liquids meet like living creatures. He does this for her, this ceremony; they are forced to wait until the transparent green spirit is absorbed by white cloudy water. When the last trace of liquor is gone, the process is not yet complete, for three more parts of water must be added, gradually, until the drink is a fluid fog with a faint green tint.

To us.

They sip.

He says, I have begun to wonder whether it is time to phase out the smaller venues. No more parlors and tea parties, except for patrons of quality who can be a help to us. We can do private demonstrations at the beginning of a tour, find a scientist or conjuror who wants to test you, to generate some publicity, but that is it. Focus on larger venues—800 seats minimum—1,500 seats should be the norm, not the exception. You can do it. You outshine anything to be seen onstage in Britain or the United States. No intimate gatherings anymore, unless we can have who we want and charge what we like. We need you to conserve your energy. Do bigger shows, better shows, fewer of them.

Florence visualizes it in the mist of her glass.

He continues: I wonder if it is time to revisit the idea of a bill of acts, with you at the top?

I have been doing this on my own for a long time now. I don't need anyone else.

That's fine by me, if it's what you want. But it will be hard to grow if we don't make some changes.

Look at me, Mortimer. How much more growing do you think I have left to do?

He sneers at the implied suggestion. You are svelte-like, and young and beautiful. You also have a special talent, and you owe it to the world. You can become the most famous spiritualist who ever lived if you want to. Nonetheless, I think we should talk about touring with other psychics. Lesser-knowns, up-and-comings. They provide the support act—they will be inferior to you, of course—they will do it to make their own names and to learn from the best.

Florence shakes her head. She says, If we put other mediums up there, we run the risk of being undermined. They will overreach, crack under pressure, especially in front of large audiences. At the very least they will steal my best marks from the front three rows before intermission, and then I will have to work twice as hard. We are as likely as not to get some magician's apprentice trying to make a name for himself by disproving me, like that fellow tonight.

You handled him splendidly.

I don't care for it.

As you please. No other spiritualists, then: they are your rivals, they are unreliable or they are frauds. There is not anyone we can trust enough. So be it. (Mortimer drinks from his absinthe.) You have not told me how the second encounter with your sister went?

Ha. Florence feels the absinthe filling her, tingling. Unbelievable.

Why so?

She looks at her husband over the rim of her glass, perceives something in his attitude, makes a decision. My nieces are prigs, is all. I have been waved off. She practically forbade me from trying to contact them while we are here. She said they will not be at home to me.

Preposterous. Shun you? You are the toast of the town. I'm astounded.

It is not important. Her son is a decent sort, anyway.

Did you give her the invitation after that?

Yes.

Will she come?

Who knows? I think she is lonely, I sense that from her.

Mortimer begins to feel the absinthe taking effect. It makes him bold. He ventures, I did have another thought about the act.

Florence leans her head on her hand to listen.

What if the Gault twins were to make a comeback . . . ? Eighteen months in the United States, starting in the small towns and backwaters to correct any teething problems, then Canada, nine months in Europe and then Australia. Then we'll take six months off for a vacation and to perfect a new routine, followed by a second tour of just the very finest venues in the finest cities of the world, and the odd audience with royalty thrown in for good measure. In four years, maybe less, we'll all be millionaires. What do you think?

To his chagrin, Florence bursts into laughter. When she comes to herself again she says, That's it? That's the big idea?

Is it so absurd?

I'm afraid it is, Mortimer. My sister would be appalled. (She drinks more absinthe.) You should ask her at dinner, though, then I can sell tickets for people to watch that.

I was only trying to help.

You are a help, I could not do it without you (she reaches forward to tweak his chin, pouting her lips at him). And if Rosie says no, you can always go back to catching bullets and pulling doves out of your sleeves.

Mortimer Solomon-Black sulks. Well, there's no need for sarcasm.

Poor old Rosie. You know, she is still cross with our mother. Florence dips her finger into her glass and sucks the end of it.

He answers, It can be hard on a child from a theater family. You are either center stage, a part of the act, or you are in the wings of your parents' lives.

Like my brothers were. Like my father.

My folks made me perform practically from the day I could stand up. I whistled tunes and took the cap around the saloon while they did the songs and skits.

How old?

Four? Honestly, I don't know.

I bet you were darling.

Difficult to leave it behind, though. Incredible she managed it after all those years—such success, such an ingrained way of life. She must have hated it.

She did. It was why she left, but not why she got so angry. I thought so at the time, but now . . .

Mortimer frowns. What else happened?

Rosemary broke Isabella's heart . . . and then Isabella died. I have come to realize my twin hates her even more for that.

Guilt is a sickness, it can kill you. What about you? You could have given up this game years ago, enjoyed comfort and respectability.

There is wickedness as Florence makes her answer. But I settled for you, didn't I?

Florence's first marriage was adequate in many aspects, except for her husband's habit of beating her. After this experience she resisted overtures from a number of bachelors and spurned two proposals. Then it dawned on her that Mortimer Solomon-Black, her trusted business associate, was also pursuing her. He did not press the matter—or rather, pressed it lightly, indirectly, deferred his own gratification. She kept him at arm's length for several years, insisting she would never remarry, while always keeping him near at hand. Out of pity maybe, out of grace for his tortured heart, and somewhat against her better judgment, the wedding came to pass, in a green haze like the one surrounding them now. How startling to discover marriage to Mortimer had an unexpected recreational quality.

In bed they bounce and bound, uninhibited, at liberty, manifestly themselves. The mattress squeaks like a wheelbarrow, the headboard bangs against the wall like a locomotive, their exclamations and moans audible to the landlady passing in the hallway.

Obaysch dozes in the afternoon sun, what muted beams there are. He lies in squalor, fat and dense, his skin shining and hot breath exhaling from his nostrils, bristly muzzle. It causes a ripple of amusement to see him yawn. A hint of personality. His teeth yellow, protruding, the enormous mouth pale and textured compared to his smooth, thick hide. Dormant fellow he is. Nonchalant. Ignores his admirers. No further action until one of his ears twitches and then is at rest. He is as broad and as gray and as motionless as a boulder. Tame, not wild. He has a wife, Adhela, who wallows in the pool. The onlookers are dismayed when she submerges for minutes at a time, gleeful when her facial features appear on the surface in another spot, and she sinks again. Bigness, solidness, laziness. Popular with the children, who like to ascribe to them human characteristics (he is taking a nap because he has had a busy morning and a large lunch; she is going underwater because she is shy and having her bath).

The girls, boys, and nannies lean on the railing to watch them, the hippopotamus enclosure out of their grasp, compounding the wish to be able to touch or feed one.

Rosemary and Jem have seen. Stroll on. Families and friends promenade in their finery, hats, umbrellas on show like flamingos.

He says, Do you think it would be a notion to make photographs of zoo animals? The hippo or camel or quagga?

What do you think, Jem? What would be the virtues?

He licks his lips with thought. That they would make nice pictures. People might like to buy them for their albums.

What do you think the Zoological Society would have to say about it?

Jem considers. You would have to ask. They might want good photographs of their animals for posterity and science and such. They might want to sell prints themselves. And other people, ordinary folk, may want photographs made of their pets and livestock, horses and cattle, not just cats and dogs.

What would be the disadvantages?

Jem swallows and does not answer.

Rosemary persists firmly, When you are in charge one day, you will need to think of ways to make Featherstone prosper. The suggestion of taking photographs of animals has some merit. Examining ideas for faults and problems to solve is an important skill, don't you know.

Right you are, Mama. Well, animals would be difficult subjects, wouldn't they? Making them lie still, or getting close enough, and that. Developing the plate would be tricky too. You would need a portable darkroom, like the itinerants have. And then there is the cost of it.

She tries not to show her relief. Rosemary has been drilling Jem with the need to consider expense and economize when possible.

He presses on. If it were affordable, you could do both. Featherstone of Piccadilly could do studio portraits and sort of itinerant photography in London. Then you would be able to do other pictures of, of anything, really. Shops, carriages, people standing outside their shops, houses—anything.

What should you do first?

Find out whether people want it . . . ?

Yes, I think that would be a good starting point.

His confidence deteriorates. Maybe not, though? Maybe people only like their *cartes de visite*. No point going to so much trouble if no one likes it.

Maybe so. And maybe tastes will change someday? And people will want to try something new? And you shall be a pioneer?

It does not sound like him, he thinks. Sounds like it would go wrong before it started. He hangs his head, discouraged, unaware how he has pleased his mother.

In fact, she intends to tell him that it is precisely this kind of thinking that will benefit the business in the long run and ensure its continuation—

But she cannot. For the sensation has come back: a weight, a strain, a constraint. It is hurting. It causes her to sweat and struggle for breath.

Jem supports her under one arm. A gentleman on an outing, somewhat unwilling to manhandle a widow, is prompted to help by his wife (right you are, m'dear). Together they lead Mrs. Featherstone to a bench where she can compose herself until the distress has passed. Jem thanks the Samaritans, assures them he will be able to take care of her. Mother and son sit in silence.

Rosemary blames it on indigestion, feels better, expresses her enthusiasm for visiting the reptile house.

Jem grips his knees and knits his brow. He would like to see the snakes himself (serpents move infrequently, and space in the building could be used temporarily for a make-do darkroom) but decides they should take a hansom cab home instead, decides not to seek approval from his mother first in case she overrides him, which she is more than capable of doing.

Turtle soup is set before them. Jem has not eaten turtle before, has not seen the interior of the Café de l'Europe until this evening. Thus far, his most formal experience of dining out was Dolly's Chophouse in St. Paul's Churchyard. And apart from in correspondence, no one ever called him James until he met his uncle.

It is a delicacy, James. Exquisite.

Jem observes Mortimer sucking a spoonful of meat and gravy, some of it sticking to his moustache, humming with appreciation. Jem tries his. The meat is dark and chewy, reminds him of offal. It is not unpalatable, though overpriced in his private opinion.

What do you think? Come now, be honest, James.

The women also pause to hear what Jem will say.

Very tasty.

They murmur their agreement. Mortimer beams. Wait until you try the oysters, they are the food of kings.

The effect of the twins' similarity on Jem has begun to wear off. Although they sit to his left and right, facing each other like a mirror image, he can discern differences not only in their apparel (one elaborate, one modest), not only in their accents. There is something altogether contrasting, even opposite, about the sisters that is almost visible—in his mother's case beneath the eyes, in his aunt's case at the corners of hers. Two carriage wheels, weathered differently. He eats the soup fearing for his constitution, which is unused to rich foods.

Today Jem paid visits to his two older sisters, Mary and Winifred, to inform them that their famous aunt was in town, and to ask would they not like to see her? Was it not an occasion for the whole family to celebrate?

Mary flummoxed him by explaining that as much as she would like to, she was occupied with a string of entertaining commitments with her husband's partners and clients, and it was vital she not let them down; and no doubt Mr. and Mrs. Solomon-Black would be sympathetic to her plight because they were busy people themselves.

Winifred blanched at the suggestion, before explaining that she and her children had been ill of late, were not quite recovered—indeed, she felt the chills coming on once again and gave a cough—she would not want to risk her aunt and uncle's health unnecessarily.

These reasons seemed fair and frank in their own right, but taken together even Jem, ignorant in the ways of society, harbored the discomfiture of suspicion. Curious, he cannot fathom why Mary and Winifred would choose to distance themselves from such a friendly and interesting lady.

Mortimer kisses his wife on the wrist, then leans to whisper something in her ear. She sniggers.

Jem assumes this must be what all Americans are like, that the United States must be a jolly country if you are free to marry whoever wins your heart and to express your affection in public. He cannot recall meeting an English couple like them—concludes he would be most satisfied with a wife who is kind and wise and jovial like his aunt.

Mortimer is telling Jem about a demonstration he saw the Gault sisters give when he was a young man, younger than Jem is now, before he had the privilege of making Florence's acquaintance. Rosemary politely listens as though the story relates to someone else entirely.

It was at the Walnut in Philadelphia, Pennsylvania. Have you heard of it, James? It is a fine theater—we have fine theaters in Manhattan too, of course, but the Walnut is historic. I was just beginning to establish a reputation as an illusionist. I come from a family of variety singers and comedians, knew how to work hard and rough it with a volatile crowd, but, seriously, I have an inferior singing voice, and telling jokes is not my forte. Conjuring, however, can be practiced and perfected and has all the finesse and excitement of professional gambling, except you are not playing for money, it is pride that is at stake: the audience's pride that they are intelligent, observant people who cannot be fooled; your pride as a performer that you can deceive and entertain them. An impresario on the circuit, a man I respected, advised me to go see the Gault twins from England, who were in Philadelphia at the time doing the best stage magic he had laid eyes on, packing houses, he said. Part of the job of an entertainer is to monitor the competition— what has he got in his act that you should have in yours? How can you steal it from him and make it better? I went along just to see what the fuss was about. There they were as alike as two people can be. Feminine but still authoritative, in control. I can even remember what they were wearing. Very beautiful, very strange to see and hear. All manner of peculiar occurrences—furniture tipping over right there in front of you, people in the balcony complaining of being touched by invisible hands. For me, though, it was the amount of detail, the specifics, that were incredible to hear, the reactions extraordinary to behold. The number of people moved to tears, ladies weeping, and even uptight old men sniffing into their handkerchiefs. When a medium picks you out of a crowd, when she accurately describes someone you have loved dearly and lost, when she tells you about yourself using words and phrases only you would recognize, well . . . (Mortimer lets his point trail away.) I don't know what that fellow was talking about because I have been to literally hundreds of shows, seen thousands of performers, and that was definitely not regular stage magic. That was something entirely *other*. James, there are two obstacles that prevent spiritualism from becoming acceptable to society. The first is the amount of fakers. If they are hearing voices at all, which is questionable, it is due to a disturbed mind and not discarnate spirits. While they persist in muddying the reputation of spiritualism, real mediums will never gain the respect they deserve. Second, this era is uncomfortable with a movement where the individual emotional experience is so pervasive—not to mention the consequences for science and religion as we understand them in the modern world. Society is far from ready to embrace spiritualism. But I don't worry. Revolutions happen. And when someone comes along with a gift, like your aunt Florence here, it is incumbent upon all of us to help her do what she was put on the earth to do.

Jem observes Florence Solomon-Black squeezing her husband's hand, her face shining with admiration. Jem observes Rosemary Featherstone adjusting the napkin on her lap as though she did not hear all of it, as though weary—bored, even.

If this is the opportune moment for Mortimer to broach with his sister-in-law a business proposition—to make the argument for her to join them on a world tour that would make her wealthy and independent, bring guidance and relief to the bereaved and hapless, and, for a great number more, enjoyment and entertainment—Mortimer does not take it but lets his chance slide quietly by.

Jem has thought of some questions to ask about photography in his aunt and uncle's homeland. The soup bowls are replaced with a platter of oysters.

Two rooms in different London boroughs. Two women—at a casual glance the same woman. Alone.

The first, bothered by an old problem that makes her tut and flap her hands to herself.

The second has busy thoughts, mundane trivialities about the following day, when she discerns a coaxing voice, male, whispering humane words. She sighs on hearing it. Flinches.

The first, her twin, stands in a room with her arms open, takes deep breaths, looks within, appeals to the darkness for answers.

The second hears his benevolence and love. He emerges. Wants to converse. He is thankful for his life, reluctant to let go, to depart. She tells him, You must.

The first banishes her doubt, her previous disappointments, the last traces of envy rubbed away—will come to this as new, refreshed, and yes, receptive this time, feels her heart beat lower, and the distant echoes of the ages that are beyond her touch draw near.

The other: You were always so thoughtful and considerate; you shall do me this one last kindness and go. Do go. Please go.

While the first is saying: Come, come. I urge you. Alight. Enlighten me. Show me.

He is sad. The other replies, I am sad too, but we will soon see each other again, and I have such a lot to do until then. Really now, this is the last time, the very last.

The lady's palms are moist from effort, she knows her own weakness, despair saps her conviction. Why not? Why always this way? Why do you never come when I ask? It is the unfairness of it—the unfairness!

The lady's familiar pressure in her chest. Worse. It hurts her arm. Can you guess what I am going to do? I am going to see a doctor. That's right. You know how I abhor doctors. He recedes for the last time, she hopes. It has become too much like being tested. She is needed, has work to do.

The first knows there is only emptiness here. Here and everywhere, and each and every time. True silence. Ordinary silence. It has never worked for her. Not once.

Highgate Cemetery, draped with vegetation, bitten with early frost, cloaked with grief. The stone angels cower and cry over their charges, the obelisks strike heavenward, the imperial mausoleums stand firm with the strength of centuries marking the entrances to eternity. A hewn gray scene of Gothic ornament. A shroud of fog disguising and revealing. Symbols clamor to be understood and indelible writings to honor, to make sense of loss, to endure. Steps and footpaths and shrubs and trees. Last destination, a home for the deceased, and a refuge for smaller lives, for foxes, birds, creepy-crawlies, flowers waiting to grow in the spring. Names and dates carved upon headstones, sarcophagi, and the hearts of mourners. Cold. Souls flitting and compressed and dispersed. Thoroughfares for the dead and pilgrimage for the living. Mineral and organic matters coalesce. All of its jaggedness, hallowedness, drama, and transition. Sanctuary, but not from oneself.

Here rests Isabella Gault.

By it, one of her daughters—a lady in a hat, coat, and gloves. Which twin?

It does not matter, for the other arrives presently.

Each brings a tussie-mussie—one of harebells and one of heartsease (subtle blue, bold purple, presumptuous yellow)—and the tokens are placed on their mother's grave. Fallen leaves rotting and crumbling underfoot. The women link arms as they walk.

Will this be the last time we see each other? It is Florence who asks. Their voices make mist.

No. There will be others.

I thought it might be the last.

Because Amos is gone, and spouses of a certain age follow suit? Not I. Nor you, if you were in my shoes.

Why did you marry him, Rosie? It is one of life's puzzles.

There you go again, divining a mystery where there is none. I liked him for being unassuming and sensitive. I married him because he asked me so sweetly, and because I knew he would never let me down. And he never did.

Bull's-eye, as always. Not like the mess I made the first time around. I have never got anything quite so wrong as I did that day—

Hush. None of it was your fault.

Florence ruffled: You warned me about him. You said he was selfish and unpredictable, you said he was trouble.

Rosemary gives her sister a severe glare. It was not your fault, it was his.

Still, I ought not to have married him in the first place.

You did your best. And what does it matter now? Mortimer is not like that.

No.

He cares for you.

Yes, he does.

You do dishonor to him and to yourself by fretting over what cannot be undone.

What else do you think of him?

Well. He is garrulous. He is adventurous. He is dashing.

Admit it, the age difference shocked you.

Rosemary raises her eyebrows. I anticipate the phantom of a scandal is always nearby when you are around, Flossie. I cease to be shocked, for I do not have many shocks left.

Stop talking like that. Remember we are the same age, you and I.

Au contraire: you have the distinction of being the older sister.

Florence smirks at this, pulls closer to her twin.

I hurt you, didn't I? Rosemary drops the question like a pebble into a pond.

I don't know what you mean.

You do. You never let on because you were protecting Mama, carrying on without me. All the same, I put myself first, and you felt I had betrayed you.

Florence is impassive. I was surprised. It was a change. And it was very long ago.

Nonetheless, I want to make amends, for both our sakes. I want you to have the postmortem photograph. Truly. Flossie, I am giving it to you.

No thank you, I have no need for it. You were right in the first place, I will do without and be content.

Please take it. It will be evidence. It could be good publicity.

Florence sighs. On consideration, it is of limited use to me. It does not quite look authentic enough. I would be ridiculed. I choose my battles and have done very well so far. Your offer is generous, but I decline it.

Then, how may I serve you?

Florence can see her sister is in earnest. Very well. I shall forgive you for leaving to make a life of your own—if you will forgive our mother for whatever wrongs you continue to blame her for. And that is the last favor I am going to ask of you.

For once, Rosemary is surprised by her twin. I have.

Good. Then there is nothing left for any of us to feel pained by.

A blackbird hides among the naked twigs of a tree, his feathers bristling, the vivid orange of his beak and eye contrasting with the sobriety of his surroundings.

Florence announces, We are setting off for the West Country tomorrow.

Rosemary answers, Give one of your *cartes* to Jem before you leave, will you? He would enjoy that.

I shall write a message on it for him.

Flossie, do you remember Our Secret?

Oh . . . She hangs her head and smiles. Yes . . .

Rosemary strips off one glove, holds up her hand in the crisp air.

Florence is cautious—is frightened it will not work, is frightened that it might. She takes off her own glove and touches her fingertips—little, ring, middle, index, thumb—to her twin's.

They can see Isabella binding the wrist of one of their brothers after an accident at the factory; can see their father carving a cockerel in wood; can see the outline of the church at the top of the hill at sunset and themselves eating gooseberries, juice running down their chins. They are in the halls and parlors and clubs and theaters and filled rooms once more. Isabella is stepping out to introduce them. They are on the steamship, catching their first sight of America on the horizon, in their dressing room that smells strongly of mildew, befuddling the invited skeptics from an empirical science society and drinking coffee in pink cups—

Rosemary can see Flossie shopping for hats to match a checkered dress; can see her reading the *Illustrated Lady's Companion* in a train compartment; can see her removing her makeup at the end of the night. She is choosing wallpaper and throwing her wedding ring off a bridge and opening a letter from a desperate young woman and singing along with a group of friends around a piano and eating the flesh of a pomegranate with a silver spoon and making a donation to a children's charity and having a sleepless night in the height of summer and listening to a Mozart horn concerto and walking through New York with the man she will eventually marry—

Florence can see Rosie admiring Amos's first portrait taken at the new shop, realizing she is pregnant again and crying, opening a present of lace from her daughter Winifred, having a cramp in her left foot, decorating a Christmas tree with her four children, being persuaded to join her daughter Mary and her soon-to-be son-in-law in a boat on the Serpentine. She is saying a prayer for her twin on their birthday and stepping off an omnibus in the snow and meeting a solicitor to make a will and consoling Amos when Robert died and dancing a polka with Jem and asking the price of some crockery in Brighton and pruning roses and weighing tea and tying a key on a ribbon for safekeeping and—

This is how the years dividing them shrink away, how their empathy is elevated.

It does not seem fair. You wanted it, I didn't. If it had been possible to swap . . .

But we could not, which is probably for the best.

Their arms linked, they draw closer to each other against the cold and walk farther on.

Unknown

For Pleasure, 1916

I vy clings to Arnault. Not Arnault Lodge or Arnault House, just Arnault, according to the plaque. Occasionally in conversation, Old Arnault. And once, Monsieur Arnault, but thankfully that did not stick. The house has been so named since before Cynthia Everard's childhood summers and is now hers. Arnault has seen Cynthia at her happiest. Seen her leaving wet footprints across the floor after a dip in the Lagoon (not really a lagoon), has seen the owl pellets and snails and pinecones and wildflowers collected and displayed on this very table for—for whatever purpose was in her mind on that particular day. Seen Cynthia in new hats. Heard her recite poetry, complain of stomachache, lie about how she lost five bob she was given as a present, cry when she was stung by a wasp. Is the Cynthia Everard of today recognizable as the same girl?

Cynthia the intellectual. Cynthia the drab academic. Cynthia Everard, editor of Professor Norman Creegan's *Selected Writings* (a work in progress), and, if his son, Charles, has his way, Creegan's biographer. The son argues that no one else living understands his father's works better than she does. She agrees. And that nobody within his professional sphere was as liked by him as Cynthia. Entirely probable. And if she does not consent to do it, there shall never be a definitive biography. On this Cynthia is noncommittal but suspects it to be the truth.

Let me work on his legacy first, Charles, she said, postponing the day when she will have to refuse, ensuring for the present she has access to her mentor's essays lecture notes letters scribbles. The son cannot be accused of withholding. No. She is grateful for that. But the message about not commencing the biography has not been listened to, and she must have in her kitchen every paper and publication Professor Creegan ever owned in his eighty-eight years of life. Piles of it. Towers of it. Work and life, life and work mixed together. By teasing out the components of one, she will necessarily tease out the components of the other. It is a tactic and it may be working, for Cynthia finds herself drawn into travel journals, lists, theater programs, appointment diaries, correspondence with his mistress; even the guides to angling and rambling hold some fascination because she only saw him indoors at the college—imagine the old man with a fishing rod or a walking stick! There was more to him then than mere philosophy, and that alone would fill twenty volumes. But why must he cram every space with his ideas? Why whole paragraphs written in the margins of a letter from the bank? Why whole synopses written across the sky in *Pleasant Highland Walks: A Guide for the Adventurous Gentleman*? Why is she starting to see coded notations in his diaries that suggest he was considering amending, if not reversing, one of his most renowned theories? The tantalizing glimpse of an unpublished essay developed over not less than nine years—she is convinced she has found four and a half pages of it with more surely to be discovered.

Whether or not she does the biography, the selected writings must take precedence. The labor, then, of deciphering a life's work, of separating what should be included from what should be left out, of deciding somehow upon a reading order, of hundreds of annotations to write.

Cynthia. Unmarried. Badly dressed. Her skirt crumpled and her silk blouse faded. Her crocheted shawl. Fair-haired (it is tied back with a scrap of fabric). Long neck, long limbs. Heavy shoes—hideous. Yet she bothers to wear rose lipstick, a gold pendant, a sapphire ring. Perhaps the child Cynthia is not so far away. Here she is, scruffy and oblivious.

What boxes and what files. What mess. It will take weeks longer than she allowed for it—and she is not displeased. The responsibility is worthy of her. The work is to her liking. Today is one of the good days, and she must make the most of these. She is invigorated. She has the edge from feelings of superiority, an impatience to succeed; her thoughts are sharp. Creegan's materials bestow their favors, disclose their content, drop their nuances before her like dogs fetching sticks. She is making progress. Yesterday is yesterday, it has gone. Today, and a clutch of similar days—though numerically fewer than the ones of slog, tedium, cross-referencing, indexing, weighing, disregarding—are the hours of inspiration that imbue a project with permanent light. It shall be a principal work. Students will have this open on their desks for hundreds of years to come. Arnault is the scene for this event. Reading matter spreads like the petals of a flower with Cynthia at the center—on the kitchen floor and dresser and draining board. Food is less important than work. Comfort is less important than food.

If this forward motion continues, she will almost lament the arrival of Alec Worsham. Dear Alec . . . but she cannot pause long for him when the work is flowing. You will have the others to entertain you if I am busy.

As though summoned by the thought, one of them interrupts

her now but she is only passing through and does not bother to speak. Gwen. Cynthia does not lift her eyes from the pages until Gwen is on her way out again, striding elastically, her boyish form illuminated through her cotton dress by the sun, her head covered with a summer hat, the cloth bag she is never seen without slung across her body as though she is going fruit picking. Whatever foolishness Gwen is embarking upon this morning, Cynthia has no time for it and reasserts her concentration.

Gwen steps into the garden and breathes the luxurious air. It is filled with pollen and makes her sneeze, *choo*. She grips the brim of her hat to prevent it from falling off, checks that no one saw. No one did.

A day for love. No, for seduction, why deny it? Why be afraid of naming it truthfully? Her conquest does not know it yet, does not know today is the beginning of their affair. They will induct each other into the mysteries of heart and flesh. She is giving him permission to court her as of *now*. He said, pointedly, he would be alone near the pond, so she goes there in a hurry, pauses—ought not to seem eager or uncouth. A lady, how does a lady behave? A lady would not hike to her beau and appear to him perspiring and out of breath. Gwen will walk serenely. Beautifully. It will be the most elegant of gaits. A sway of the hips, which will wake within him ecstasies of passion. Unrealized passion. Hitherto unknown passion. Layers and layers of passion.

Oh, Venus, we are bringing you the gift of ourselves.

Of course—and here Gwen flattens some of the jumble in her head like a drawer of knickers—he may already have some acquaintance with the mechanics of male and female: as he is a man and ten years older than she, it would be unusual if he had not. Gwen has reconciled with this. It is a relief, a man ought to have more experience than a woman. Ten years may sound long, but (she does a calculation) in five years, four really, when she has reached twenty he will still only be thirty. When she comes of age he will be but thirty-one. Who can call that gap significant? This thought pleases her. And—building on her theme—do not people say, interminably, how mature Gwen is for her age? She will soon catch him up. Her logic fires her enthusiasm.

She trips along the path, pushing aside low-hanging boughs fat with foliage until the trees thin and a space opens, revealing the pond (Cynthia has a childish name for it). It is shaded by bending and swaying perennials that repeat upside down in the pool, hidden from view to one side by coppice and obscured by a woodland incline to the other, away from local thoroughfares. The water probably deep. It is secluded and has drunk centuries of rain. It is made of the fresh greens and earth browns of nature's England, and its sounds are the staccato chiffchaffs and excitable wrens, the hum of damselflies and the plop of invisible fish kicking the surface with their tails. Leaves answer with hushed applause.

Gwen sees him. Visualizes her appearance in this place like the entrance of Titania.

Laurence Fern is painting the scene with intensity, like sickness, holding a stub of cigarette in his mouth. He attacks the canvas with his brush and palette knife, works quickly, the strokes going on in thick globules, raises his glance briefly to confirm some detail, and attacks again. It is the stippling of the Impressionists, but with less regard for form and an arbitrary use of color. "Expressive." He works with speed and can make a picture in a day or two.

Gwen had never seen anything like it until he showed her. At first she thought it infantile, but having it explained to her so richly, so fiercely, has come to the conclusion that Laurence might—just *might*—be a genius. He does not look like a genius, to be sure, if geniuses are hoary, wrinkled men grown pale with obsession, grown withered with deep thought. Virility usually precludes talent; attractiveness is the compensation of a mediocre mind. Yet here is

Laurence, with creativity and the physique of a boxer, a man who combines artistic sensibility with latent brute force. That Laurence is unaware of his attributes makes him more charming. That he paints with personal disregard, that he gives his art to the world selflessly . . . rapture.

He does not look like a conscientious objector either (the first and only one she has knowingly met). Gwen had preconceived ideas of how they ought to look: pallid little boys, trembling weaklings. Not this. Not a specimen like him. It had not been easy to accept but accept it she did, although she still does not fully understand it.

It definitely has something to do with some men being too good to fight in wars (she likes the sound of that, even if she cannot make up her mind what it means). Perhaps, when you are touched by enlightenment, you have to take a contrary and lonely road. It is the lot of the tragically gifted, and all part of Laurence Fern's mystery. And would it not make—she thinks to herself as she steps down to the edge and nearly falls in—would it not make their journey together, as two halves of the same being, one of mutual discovery and therefore the sweeter for it? As long as Gwen is able to know him and his thoughts in the end, however complex they are, however long it takes, every one.

Good morning, Laurence.

Miss Watts.

Miss Watts? I think it is time for you to call me Gwen, like everyone else.

Laurence does not reply.

I often come to this spot to read my book. You don't mind, do you? (This is not exactly true; Gwen has never read here before but resolves to do so frequently from now on.) It's *Emma* by Jane Austen. (This is important to say aloud, so she does.)

She takes his silence for consent. Laurence works on mutely.

Can I see it, please, even though it is not finished?

194

If you like.

She steps behind and announces, It is your best, Laurence, your very best. Really it is.

I am most dissatisfied. It is average. It is repetitive; I have done it all before. I have not the inspiration today.

Oh, but you do. I love it.

Laurence Fern makes an expression that Gwen interprets as pleased embarrassment. He paints on.

Gwen finds a seat where she can watch. She takes off her hat so the sunshine can play on her hair and tries to find her book absorbing. Indeed, Austen usually moves her and induces sighs of admiration, but today she reads it barely at all, only the same lines over and over, never coming to the end of a paragraph or needing to turn the page because there is some sound or movement to take her interest, some stone digging into her rear that makes her rearrange. The game of predicting when Laurence will speak next is as distracting as thinking of things to say that he might find fascinating or witty.

She pipes up, You know, people tell me that I am the best at drawing in my class.

He does not seem to hear. No matter. She is certain they will have plenty to talk about when they have found the words. She must be patient with him whenever he is working, and while their relationship is new and tender. She shall be no shrew.

The heat is overpowering. She leans back on her elbows, for thinking can be work. She tilts her face to the sun.

Like a daisy; I am a daisy basking in the warmth of the sun.

Gwen reminisces about herself as a child pretending to be a bride. That is too bourgeois for us, she now concludes; I will simply live with Laurence as his mistress and there will be a terrific scandal.

She raises herself, shields her eyes. Is there anything you would like? I can go back and fetch it for you.

Not right now.

She frowns.

He wipes his hands on a rag, screws it up, then takes a new cigarette out of a silver case and mutters, It is not working, I am going to have to—I don't know, maybe try to salvage it, maybe abandon it.

Gwen sits up, worried. It isn't my fault, is it?

Why should it be?

No reason. (She senses this as an opportunity to show her worth.) Don't abandon it, that would be dreadful. Perhaps just take a break? Do something else this afternoon? Have some fun and try again tomorrow. It's like when you're stuck on an algebra problem: best to leave it for a while, and then when you come back to it, you have it figured out.

Laurence sticks out his chin as though impertinence will shame the picture into shape. You could be right there.

You have been working nonstop. There ought to be a balance.

Ought to be, but there isn't. Who knows how long the weather will hold? If the light is different tomorrow—you have heard the phrase striking while the iron is hot, Miss Watts?

Gwen has heard it. It is a sign of their growing intimacy that she empathizes with his frustration. To leave a painting incomplete would be torture for him. He must finish it.

He adds, Anyway, I have to meet Sinclair from the train station tomorrow.

Who?

Sinclair.

Yes, she remembers him now. Laurence has already mentioned it. Another guest at Arnault; another conchie that Cynthia is giving asylum to; another artist, perchance. I could go? She offers without thinking.

Could you?

Gwen would like nothing better than to do a favor for him, but she shrugs as though she does not care.

I would appreciate it. In fact, that would make it easier. Thanks. He smiles a small, odd, delicious smile like a sip of wine.

But you must do a good turn for me and call me Gwen. No more Miss Watts, it is too fusty. Sinclair should call me Gwen too. We are all friends here, aren't we?

Yes, I suppose we are. Laurence begins to dismantle his equipment. At Gwen's insistence he gives her the easel to carry back.

Gwen runs. She runs fast. She is good at running, can outrun most boys her own age. She runs from the station, avoiding pedestrians, crosses a road and down the lane. She runs past the Cross Keys and St. Peter's Church—hair, hat, and skirt streaming behind her like she is being chased by wolves, bag swinging at her side. Her blood rushes, she rushes—the exertion like a lashing for some transgression or a reward for the endurance of some trial. It feels good to expend the tension, the energy, to be doing this instead of thinking. She runs away from the image. Runs the shortcut to Arnault, will get there first. Knows she will, without having tried it before. The house is in sight.

Within Arnault, Cynthia bowed over the table. She acknowledges it is not the way it was yesterday. What had seemed clear is now muddy. What had seemed obvious is now uncertain. And the thoughts, the unwelcome thoughts have come back. The wavering between existence and nothing. The mental vertigo. Whirling. Dizziness. When life and silence smear into one. It makes her irritable.

The hefty thump of approaching feet up the path—it is Gwen.

What are you doing here? I thought you went to the station to meet Laurence's friend.

I did.

Then where is he?

Gwen pants for breath.

Did something happen? Was the train canceled?

There is something you should know about Sinclair . . . he's a woman.

Cynthia opens her mouth, partially. I can't help that.

Gwen leans against the wall, feeling her exhaustion—and because this is a disaster and one makes such a pose during disasters.

You didn't just leave her there . . . ?

Gwen rolls her head over one shoulder, then the other. She'll be all right, she'll find a taxi.

She thinks someone's going to meet her.

Gwen has an answer for this but knows it is unbecoming, so she whispers it to herself: Tough toads.

Cynthia has never known the agony or elation or perils of love, cares only for her studies and was to be pitied until this morning . . . now Gwen envies Cynthia her ignorance, her frumpiness, her dreary life isolated from the politics and pitfalls of human relations. Cynthia has never had a rival and, if she did, would faint at a rival like Sinclair.

Gwen has spent her life willing her hair to grow into luscious locks, has fought battles with her mother over it, thought it a badge of femininity. Her hair is longer than most but insipid; she is still waiting for the swishing tresses of her imagination. It would have been hurtful to find a woman who was Laurence's friend and had such a gloriously long curtain of hair, but Sinclair is worse than that, for she is a crop-head. The first feature that struck Gwen about Sinclair as she stepped off the train carriage and onto the platform was her short, androgynous haircut, and that she wears it with the unmistakable air of sex. The woman is divine, simply too divine, and predatory. The clip of her heels, the insolence of her red lips, her nipped-in waist. Detestable. The vacant face, oh, how empty of serious thought. Her nose and forehead powdered. Wearing dark blue as though it were autumn, not the height of summer. Gruesome. A piece of heavy luggage and a man in uniform assisting her with it gave Gwen the opportunity to abandon this monstrosity unobserved—if it cannot make its own way to the house, then what exactly is its purpose?

Gwen wants Cynthia to hate Sinclair as much as she does, for them to be allies, but already Cynthia has lost interest and gone back to her work. Her drudgery.

What of Laurence? He cannot mean to like this interloper, this miscreant? Gwen shoves away the thought. No, he will certainly see through it—the tailoring, the cosmetics, the reek of fragrance—it shall not impress him, it shall not penetrate. He will find it for what it is: labored, common, obvious. Laurence is a man of substance, his taste is more refined, his mind on higher matters. Gwen ought not to be afraid of Sinclair; Gwen can still win.

She sniffs her fingers. They have the smells of bacon fat and pencil sharpenings on them, have cuts healing, the nails and cuticles bitten down. Sinclair's will be graceful, as pale and even as milk, have buffed nails with tinted polish, the scent and slipperiness of lotion. Even Gwen realizes, through her agitation, that Laurence may prefer those pampered hands on him to her own. Can it be that bad?

Laurence has returned to Arnault to meet Sinclair; Gwen realizes he may be annoyed at her for breaking her promise.

He is not annoyed, though, because he has forgotten it, has expunged the gesture from his memory—does not notice Gwen hiding in the parlor and peeking out of the window, notices instead the unflustered outline of Sinclair paying the cab driver. He goes to her with a secretive smile and, here is perhaps the worst, kisses her full on the mouth—greedy kiss, public kiss—and Sinclair is almost bent in half backward from the pressure of it, then rebukes him with a tap. To apologize—flippantly, ironically—he opens his cigarette case and offers it to Sinclair (he has never offered it to Gwen before), lights it for her. Sinclair smokes it smugly.

This is terrible.

Gwen slides to the floor in a heap, for there is nowhere on the ample furniture to rest a spirit as battered as hers. Armchairs are too good for her. She must feel the woe and discomfort in her whole body, even in her knees. She must assume the position of melancholy. She is suffering, her heart is in shreds. Laurence Fern, behold your greatest work.

Is she overreacting?

Gwen carries a basket of eggs from Mr. Bolingbroke's back to Arnault (all her eggs in one basket; if she drops it, it will be some sort of poetic warning).

Perhaps it can be explained. Perhaps Sinclair has a hold over Laurence that he resents, for Gwen detected some contrivance on his part. A stiffness. A definite strain. Indifference, even. Or is he playing a game with Gwen's affections by testing her fidelity, knew somehow that she was watching? Will she be unreasonable? Possessive? Will she give in to her tantrum? Will she show her disgust at the trespasser, at her shoddy treatment, at the injustice of it? No, that is not Gwen.

Be as carefree as he is, is the key. She will twitch lightly on the line for fear of it breaking. Actually, she should behave no differently from the way she did before Sinclair got here; he said himself they were all friends. It is Sinclair who will have to fit in. She does not know their ways, their rituals, has missed days of conversation and shared experiences. Gwen has got a head start and shall simply act as if nothing has changed. (What a relief.)

Laurence has picked some tomatoes from the vines and put them in a pottery dish to paint as a still life. Some of them are green, while others are bright red and beginning to split.

Men like to be taken care of; therefore, Gwen has offered to make omelettes for lunch. She makes splendid omelettes, fluffy, golden on the outside, runny in the middle.

Laurence, what would you like me to put in your omelette?

I don't really mind.

Shall I give you some choices? You can have potatoes and cabbage from last night, or salad onions or ham, or have it plain. Unfortunately we don't have any mushrooms, but I can go out and buy some if you want them desperately. I do like mushrooms myself. Eating them makes me feel quite pagan— Gwen laughs at her own imagery and flicks her hair, which has become a trophy once again (it took simply ages to grow). I suppose one could put whatever one wanted into an omelette, pickles or broad beans. What about jam? We could invent the world's first sweet omelette, wouldn't that be exciting?

Whatever the others say shall do for me.

Gwen did not intend to ask each person staying at Arnault what they wanted in their omelettes, only Laurence; otherwise she will be making four separate dishes.

Laurence takes out his cigarette case and slots one between his lips.

I should like to—have one. (Gwen prevents the words "try one" from coming out.)

I didn't know you smoked.

Occasionally. Mummy doesn't know.

Laurence appears to like this admission, extends them toward her. She fumbles, then holds one up between two fingers like she has seen other people doing, her wrist open. When Laurence clicks his lighter she puts the fag in her mouth and enjoys the seconds of close proximity with him while the flame takes. He comes nearer than the action necessitates and this, or the concoction of tobacco, makes her warm, makes her tingle. She drags a little, swallows the urge to cough, and remembers to smile in thanks. If he watches for signs of unfamiliarity she does not betray any. Quite ordinary.

She resumes: I hate to be the one to tell you, but you are working much too hard. Isn't this your third picture this week? You will wear yourself out.

He drops a brush into a cup of several, clatters them around, subtracts another, inspects the bristles, applies it.

Gwen admires the painting. Oh, but it is rather good, so edible looking, so round and ripe. How I should like to gorge myself on your tomatoes, Laurence, and consign the real ones to the rubbish. I bet yours taste delicious. (Gwen paces absently, taking a puff or two.) I do worry about you. Do you understand? I think you do— what it is like to worry about the welfare of a friend, someone you care for and think highly of. It is human nature to have sympathy for one's fellows. Our sympathy sets us apart from the animals. Come to think of it . . . we once had a small dog that was quite good at reading emotions. If you were crying, or even if you weren't, if you were just sad about something and keeping it to yourself, he would scamper in and put his head in your lap as though he were trying to speak. Isn't that funny? He ran away, of course. (Gwen compares the painting to the subject and sucks some more on her smoke, finds it has grown easier, tastier.) I declare you work harder than Cynthia, and that is saying something. She rather neglects herself. Mummy says Cynthia will never marry. She looks so ghastly all the time. For what, precisely? Some crusty old university scholar who no one has heard of and who is now dead. At least you are sharing of yourself through your art. You are reaching out. I think it's noble. But it can't be all work, can it? You ought to enjoy yourself sometimes. Part of me thinks I should do you a kindness and cook these tomatoes so you can't paint them anymore—

And Gwen has been pacing the room while she speaks—

Emboldened by the success of the cigarette and its stimulating effects, she playfully lifts one of the fruits from the bowl.

What the hell are you doing?

Gwen stops at the voice, at the venom in it.

Put it back. Now.

She does so, wounded, mortified.

I am trying to finish this, will you leave me alone?

That would have been bad enough, but as she goes she hears him mumble behind her—

Fucking pest.

Gwen finishes the rest of her cigarette outside, drawing some comfort from it. Indeed, they are perfectly habit forming. She is in full view of Cynthia, who is in the kitchen, standing, reading, separating one folio from another. But if Cynthia sees, she does not rebuke her.

You are an oddment, Cynthia Everard, Gwen murmurs to the vision through the gray windows and interior gloom. I wonder whether it would occur to you to spill the beans to Mummy about anything here? You must miss out on so much. Poor Bluestocking.

Sinclair materializes at the other side of Arnault, heads in the opposite direction away from Gwen and toward town. She minces down the path, does not shut the gate after her.

Gwen narrows her eyes.

As it happens, Cynthia has *not* paid any attention to Gwen. She has shooting pains down the back of her neck and the start of a headache. She berates herself because she cannot spare a day lying on her bed with the curtains closed and a moist cloth over her eyes. It has gone wrong wrong wrong.

This is how it was when she was an undergraduate. The despair of knowing—literally—nothing. Of feeling that her presence is subversive, that her calling is nonsense, that she must be grateful for her place. Fed up with being beaten by concepts that are bigger and cleverer than she is, let alone by small, revolting men with flaccid penises. If only it were a case of learning it the way one learns the date of the Battle of Waterloo or the lines of a sonnet. Why must one's ineptness be laid bare? Why must one's limitations be exposed? And what exactly does one, *Cynthia,* want?

Cynthia slams a book on top of another.

She might as well rearrange and tidy the work of a mind better than her own, consolidate it to ensure its survival, and that can be her contribution, not an inconsiderable one—and then write a biography that will sell in reasonable quantities. If what she wants is universal acceptance in her own right, she shall never get it.

Gwen's straggly shadow appears in the doorway.

Are you actually going to help me at all? Cynthia is referring to the original intention of Gwen's stay, to assist her at least some of the time with her research.

What do you want me to do?

A space is cleared and Cynthia puts two unopened boxes in front of her.

Put these in date order. Separate out publications from private writing. If you find any loose pages, match them with the documents they belong to and make a note of anything that is incomplete or missing.

Gwen finds they are almost entirely loose pages, some of them unnumbered or constituting the middle of a longer paper that could belong to more than one source. The handwriting is appalling, and all of it is *very* boring. Nonetheless, she makes an effort because Cynthia has been a good sport, has given Gwen the liberty to do as she pleases until now.

Cynthia is writing, underlining a word, marking a paragraph with an asterisk, clipping corners together. Is tired. They work this way for over an hour and a half.

Gwen finds in one of her boxes the dead man's scrapbook (all sorts in here). She turns through it, looking for fragments of letters among the miscellany. She wants to ask Cynthia, who is ancient and must be able to remember, whether everyone in the previous century was as po-faced as the trollop on this calling card?

By the time she comes to the end of the album she has lost interest, instead makes the announcement that will rattle even Cynthia's poise: I fear I have fallen in love with Laurence Fern.

Who hasn't?

Gwen is quietly scandalized. What makes you say so, Cynthia? Everyone falls in love with Laurence; he requires it of them.

She states it. Detached. Matter-of-fact. Gwen grips the side of her own face as if she has been struck and exclaims, How savage you are! Just because you have given up on love, why spoil it for the rest of us? You are such a baggage.

Running off to cry in private seems like the appropriate gesture to go with this speech, so Gwen does.

Sinclair reclines in the shade. She is as glamorous as the film star on the cover of her magazine, which she prefers to the newspaper (folded, ignored) and its reports of war. It is, if possible, hotter today than yesterday, but the heat does not affect Sinclair like it does other people; she does not shine, she does not burn. Her nerveless face is without expression. Her body is still and enveloped by a printed silk kimono. Her movements—a yawn—when they do happen are slow, like she is on display. If she is surprised to find herself no longer alone, she hides it with perfect nonchalance.

It's you.

I brought you some cider. Gwen balances the two glasses on a tray, lowers it like a servant so Sinclair can take one and place it on the table beside her.

How thoughtful.

May I join you?

Sinclair flexes one eyebrow but replies, Of course you may.

Gwen sits, does not remove her bag, rests it on her lap. She pats it because her large notebook is inside (plain pages, with a useful line guide made of card to insert between them). She intended to take notes; now fears this may inhibit their conversation, it being the first on their own. Gwen has come to make a scientific study of Sinclair, to find out:

    i.   *Whether S is romantically involved with L.*

    ii.   *Whether S would like to be romantically involved with L.*

    iii. *What S's Christian name is & why she goes by just her sur-name.*

    iv. *What S's weaknesses are & how to use them against her.*

    v.   *Whether S has any redeeming features whatsoever.*

It is harsh but necessary. The list had only been four items last night, but this morning Gwen added a fifth to show anyone, in the future, who might find it by accident and think badly of her, that she really is (or rather was) a very good person. On paper at least, Sinclair has the benefit of the doubt. Sinclair has withdrawn into her magazine, and Gwen struggles with how to begin gleaning the required information. Neither speaks, and Gwen boils inside— This is terribly rude of you, especially when I have brought you some cider and come over to make friends. Well, not to make friends, but you aren't to know that; you should be being nice to me.

Sinclair turns a page and rests a single finger on her cheek.

This is too much for Gwen—how false! She is surely pretending to read it, is probably only looking at the pictures. The longer their mutual silence endures, the more awkward it will be to break. Gwen dives in: I thought it would be nice to get to know each other. Us girls have to stick together. You don't know anyone, apart from Laurence Fern, of course . . . you don't know us, Cynthia and me, or the local area. I thought I could help out, answer any questions you may have. Do you have any questions?

Sinclair genuinely appears to give it some thought, then shakes her head.

Plus, I don't know anything about you; where you are from? your background?

There is not much to tell. I am originally from Oxfordshire and was glad to leave it. I live in London. I am what you can see.

Gwen tilts her head interestedly. Oxfordshire. London. Remarkable. What do you do there?

Do . . . ?

Gwen can almost hear Mummy's reproaches and backtracks. Some people are volunteering, given the state of current affairs, and some people have plans for after the war and whatnot. I wondered if you were like that, if you had any plans, or hobbies?

Sinclair smirks. I let biology take its course. I plan to be looked after when I am married, and to get my own way quite as often as I get it now. When does the charlady come?

Oh (a question). Tuesday, Friday, and Saturday. Her name is Agnes Rumford, but you must call her Mrs. Rumford; Cynthia is quite particular about that, because she is ancient and has taken care of Arnault simply forever.

I have some clothes I need her to press for me.

Mrs. Rumford is excellent at ironing; makes the straightest, sharpest creases you have ever seen.

I will settle for her getting rid of the squiggling creases I don't wish to see.

Gwen's brain jars and grinds, then she realizes a corner of Sinclair's red mouth is elevated and it was supposed to be some sort of joke, and a response was expected. Too late, Sinclair is elaborating—

I shall commandeer Mrs. Rumford in the morning.

If you want to get in her good books, she does love boiled sweets, especially lemon and lime flavor.

That is useful to know; I shall acquire some before I speak to her. Thank you for the suggestion, Gwen.

And though it annoys her, Gwen is almost pleased to have been able to help. She makes a mental note: *S; maybe not all bad?* (She will write it up properly later.) In fact, this helps Gwen relax slightly, and she sips her cider with gusto.

Sinclair drinks too. Mm, reminds me of holidays. Funny the way a smell or a taste can do that to you, drop you in the middle of a memory.

I have the same with cigar smoke. The smell makes me think of Daddy's cigar on Christmas Eve. He always lets me take a puff before bed.

My Christmas smell is the paste we use to make paper chains.

Is it . . . ? I can picture it exactly. Aren't we funny, talking about Christmas in this weather? It's all topsy-turvy.

Rather. (And though they do not laugh as such, there is at least mutual pleasure.)

So . . . tell me how you know Laurence . . . *Mr. Fern.* Did you meet in London?

More collided than met.

Have you known him very long?

Sinclair sighs as though the topic is dull to her. No. Though I don't think one needs to know Laurence for long to get the measure of him. He picked me, you see.

Picked?

Yes. Laurence chose me out of a group of sisters, girlfriends, and cousins of mine. Not because I am the greatest prize, although I am, but because I am the hardest to crack.

To . . . marry?

Sinclair laughs a silvery, tinkling laugh. Goodness no, he hasn't any money. Poor boy is a fourth son, which is virtually the same as being born on the wrong side of the blanket, if you ask me. If he proposed, he knows I'd turn him down flat. No. He is charming, very charming, and of good breeding, which can carry you pretty far, but those are not necessarily good qualities without an income to match. Laurence picked me the way you would pick a plum from a plum tree. He wants to have me and, while it amuses me, I shall permit myself to be had.

Gwen is uncertain what this means but does not wish to show her ignorance. If Laurence, Mr. Fern, did have pots of money, would you want to marry him then?

Darling, if you had pots of money, I would want to marry you. I say. How shocking.

Sinclair smiles impishly. One likes to be able to shock now and then. You don't know how lucky you are, Gwen.

Am I lucky?

Why, yes. You have lots of blissful years ahead of you without all that cant about love and marriage, which is just too boring for words. "What the heart desires," "what fate has written," birds tweeting, and all that bosh . . . *Jesus*, it never ends. Men can be so bloody pompous. I admit I am exquisitely jealous of you.

Right. I suppose.

Cigarette? Sinclair offers a slim, feminine case, beautifully engraved.

Yes, please.

Shall I light it for you?

Gwen says she will do it, Sinclair lends her the lighter, and she takes a couple of snaps to make it burn. Gwen finds even Sinclair's fags to have a perfumed taste. *Thanks.* Gosh, I don't know how to say it, but I have been wondering, just now and then since you arrived . . . Do you mind my asking what your first name is? I assume Sinclair is your family name.

It is. I utterly loathe my given name. Loathe it. Can't bear to be called it or to hear it said out loud. It grieves me even to write it down.

Can't be that bad.

Ha. Sinclair sucks in and exhales the smoke like a sailor.

You don't have to tell if you don't want to.

See if you can guess it. If you were me, what would be the most rotten name someone could give you?

You promise you'll say if I'm right?

Sinclair promises.

Well, I suppose Claire Sinclair would be pretty bad, or Clara.

Nope.

No, I didn't think so. Then, something twee. Eudora? Or Philomena? Then you might want a good nickname of your own. (Gwen tries not to appear uncomfortable discussing it.)

No, nothing like that.

Um. One of the virtues, perhaps. Hope? Joy? Faith? Chastity?

Sinclair shakes her head at each of these.

My last guess would be a name that you thought of as dismal, a dismal sort of name. What about Maud?

It's Joanna.

Joanna . . . ? But Joanna is a perfectly lovely name.

Sinclair pretends to shiver. Yuck. I despise it.

To call Gwen disappointed would be an understatement. She would swap her Gwendolen for Sinclair's Joanna any day. She once had a doll called Joanna (has still got a doll called Joanna, but decides at this moment to give her away to a needy child), had considered naming one of her daughters with Laurence Joanna Jane. Sinclair is not to know this, has retreated back into the gossip columns of her magazine. If Gwen had, during the course of their encounter, altered her opinion of Sinclair, this has reverted it back. Sinclair is haughty, grasping, pretentious, and vain.

Gwen retrieves her notebook and a pencil, writes in it surreptitiously.

i. *Whether S is romantically involved with L.—"romantic" is wrong word; what is right word? Not "picked"!*

ii. *Whether S would like to be romantically involved with L.—no because S is haughty and grasping &c.*

iii. *What S's Christian name is & why she goes by just her surname.—Joanna / because S is stupid.*

iv. *What S's weaknesses are & how to use them against her.— numerous faults, why has no one noticed?/?*

v. *Whether S has any redeeming features whatsoever.—none (honest) but I do like her Chinese robe.*

Seems reasonable. Yes, and balanced. She checks that Sinclair cannot see.

Cynthia jabs at the typewriter. It is a cumbersome machine with letter keys that stick. Nonetheless, Cynthia is fond of it and perseveres. If inanimate objects have personalities, then this typewriter is an old friend, loyal, clumsy, prone to getting into a pickle like an elderly woman trying to untangle her knitting. Kind. It is a kindly typewriter. You tell me what to put, and I will type it out for you . . . it has a helpful temperament, and Cynthia cannot blame it for the defects of age.

It is my typing that is at fault, she tells herself, rather than facing the prospect of replacing it. She uses a pen to release some of the character bars that have snarled together.

Gwen stands before her, mouth an O, seems to expect her attention.

Cynthia tinkers. What's wrong?

The girl shakes her head and closes her eyes. I might just faint, Cynthia, I really might. I think fainting must feel a lot like this.

There is a snap, and the typewriter is mended once more. What has happened now?

I don't think I can tell you. Although I was not exactly sworn to secrecy. Rather the opposite, actually; they didn't seem to care who saw them.

Who didn't?

Laurence and *her*.

Ah. Them again.

Yes, and under your roof. I think it is very disrespectful to you to be carrying on like that when they are your guests. If I were you, I would put a stop to it immediately.

Cynthia stares longingly at her papers, spreads one hand on them to reassure herself they are real. Real and hers. Her thoughts and her work. She has such a lot to do and prefers work infinitely to—

It's her more than him; I'm sure she leads him astray. I just . . . I just wanted to show him something. I thought Sinclair had gone out for the morning because she usually does. Dipsomaniac, I expect. Anyway, I went looking for Laurence because he hadn't told me where he was working today, and I found him in the music room. (Gwen's mouth goes dry.)

And . . . ? He was there with Sinclair?

The girl turns paler. If you went right now, you would see—

Gwen, I shall do nothing so undignified.

It is sinful. If it is not sinful, it certainly isn't decent.

Were they making love?

Gwen blanches. No! (How can Cynthia do it? How can she be so phlegmatic?) He was painting her. She was being his model. His *nude* model. Right by *your* piano. Someone might see it in the painting and say, "That there is Cynthia Everard's piano, and she allows naked people to parade around in front of it."

Is that all? Cynthia turns back to her typewriter and clatter-clacks out her exasperation.

Aren't you going to do anything?

And what precisely would you have me do?

(The pointed nipples, the exposed armpit, the belly button like a dimple, the triangle of dark hair . . .) Someone must do something. She wasn't wearing a stitch! Naked people at Arnault, Cynthia! What if someone else sees? What if Mrs. Rumford sees? The poor dear would probably keel over and die.

Gwen, has it occurred to you that you're the one at fault? That perhaps it would be better to get past this infatuation of yours? Why not develop some interests of your own while you are staying here—make some friends of your own age? What will I tell your mother if I return you to her in this state?

Gwen concentrates on these words. Then, as though the scales are falling from her eyes, she whispers, Do you mean Laurence has a touch of lavender?

This makes Cynthia pause in her typing and look hard at her. Gwendolen, you do say the most ghastly things—

And that is that.

Then Cynthia tells Gwen she has one of her headaches coming on and had better leave her alone. Which means Gwen is powerless to prevent it—whatever it is—and were Cynthia to trouble herself, she would probably be powerless too.

Gwen can hear her typing from the garden over the sound of her heart being trampled on. So she runs farther on, down the road toward the village—

—and almost into a man carrying a suitcase.

I beg your pardon, young lady. I'm looking for the house called Arnault, is it near here . . . ?

Alec, it's you! And Gwen hugs him hard.

Alec Worsham permits it awkwardly, pats her on the back.

213

She pulls away. It's Gwen Watts, do you remember? I'm Bill and Betty's daughter.

Of course I remember, how are you?

Oh I'm . . . I'm just . . . I'm so glad to see a friendly face.

Has something happened? Is Cynthia all right?

No, she's in a foul temper.

I say, that is too bad. Should we check on her?

No, no, I don't think that's a good idea. (Gwen cannot endure the thought of Alec seeing Sinclair's nakedness.) She's fine, very busy. We had a bit of a spat.

Ah. Is Laurence there?

Yes, but I can't go back, not now. I will. I just need some time.

I see.

I say, Alec, would you take me out to luncheon?

Alec has a warm heart and cannot tolerate Bill and Betty's girl in distress. He agrees.

They lunch outside the pub, Alec drinking stout with his sandwiches and Gwen drinking ginger beer with her pie. Gwen does most of the talking, as Alec is recently back from Punjab and wants to hear about his friends. He asks after her parents.

Mummy is well, still making quilts and playing the clarinet, badly. Daddy lost a leg, you know.

Yes, I heard. It's too bad.

But he's alive, and we're ever so thankful for that. Mummy wanted to nurse him at home and Taid knows someone at the War Office, so he arranged it.

Taid . . . ?

Granddad on Mummy's side.

Is that why you are staying with Cynthia?

Gwen squints into the sun. Mummy thought it would be better. Give him space to heal without too many hens clucking. I bet they'd both love to see you before you leave, though; do you think you could manage it?

I will try. And how is Cynthia?

Oh, she's fine.

Alec leans over his pint pot. Really?

Gwen screws up her face while she tries to think objectively: She works frantically. She seems to like it. It's to do with that professor of hers who died.

Norman Creegan.

Yes, him. She is doing some kind of book. Honestly, I don't think even she knows what it's about. There's an absolute mountain of paper. I tried to help out, but I don't have the . . . you know.

Aptitude.

I was going to say brain cells. She plugs away at it all day, then drinks and smokes all night; and sometimes she is in a good mood, and sometimes she is horrid to be around. I entertain myself, mostly. There's only us, Laurence, and the harlot.

I say, that's a bit strong.

She's called . . . Joanna. But you ought to be careful, you are just the sort she would go for—that's some friendly advice for you. She has already got her claws into Laurence.

Alec nods confidentially. How is Cynthia in herself?

Well, she still gets those headaches, but that's nothing new.

Does she ever mention me?

Gwen smirks.

Or any of us from the old days?

No-o. No, sorry. I didn't even know you were coming. But she never tells me anything, probably because I'd get the wrong end of the stick . . . Gwen looks meaningfully at Alec, who in turn finds something of interest to look at by the post office.

He asks, Are you having a nice stay?

I was. Gwen pushes away her almost empty plate. If it weren't for love.

Aren't you a bit young to be having trouble with the opposite sex?

I'm really not.

Is it serious?

Not to him. To him I'm a joke. And he's right, I am a joke.

Don't be despondent. Love makes fools out of all of us.

Which is not very encouraging. Have you been made a fool of by love?

Plenty of times.

That's absurd, no one falls in love more than once.

No one falls in love *for the first time* more than once.

But I want the first time to be the only time. You aren't very good at this shoulder-to-cry-on business, Alec Worsham.

Don't I know it? He sips his stout and searches in his pockets for cigarettes and matches.

Alec, do you think—do *you* think—that some people require everyone around them to fall in love with them?

What a heavy question for a bright afternoon.

But is it true? Are some people that . . . selfish?

Alec strikes a match and takes his time to light his fag. When it burns he shakes the match to extinguish it. I didn't offer you one . . . ?

No thanks, I'm not keen.

He dwells upon it, then answers, Yes. Some people are in love with being loved.

Does that make them bad through and through?

Alec smokes and considers. It can be bad for those around them, but what a man does to himself is nobody else's concern.

But they can be changed, if the right woman tried to change them?

He laughs. What is this about?

Nothing in particular.

Laurence got to you, has he?

Gwen could scream and stamp her foot—instead hangs her head in defeat. Am I so bloody transparent?

Language. (He intones it.) I guessed.

If one wanted to make an impression on someone such as Laurence Fern, how might one do it?

One could pretend he doesn't exist, I bet no one has tried that before—

Gwen huffs and puffs (Mummy would call me The Wolf).

Alec goes on: I have to admit, I have no idea whether or not Laurence can change, but I will say this: in the years since I have known him and his brother Michael and your parents and Cynthia and everyone else in our old set, all of us have changed for better or worse, except Laurence, who has stayed exactly the same.

Therefore he is likely to stay the same?

The empirical evidence seems to support it. You, on the other hand—what a fascinating project we could make of you, recording your journey and how you change over the years ahead.

Gwen blushes at this. What about you? I haven't even asked you where you've been and what you've been up to. Or can't you tell me, is it secret?

Alec withdraws at the mention of his work, grows stern before her.

Is it secret? Because if it is, you're probably better off not telling me about it, I'd just let the cat out of the bag. I would be a hopeless spy. I can't help myself. If a shady character tried to recruit me on a park bench for King and Country I'd have to say, "Sorry, mister, I'm just here to feed the pigeons." *Are* you a spy?

No.

You would have to say that, even if you were.

I'm not.

You would have to say that too, wouldn't you? Is it hot in Punjab? Hotter than it is here at the moment?

Very.

And can you tell me vaguely what you do there, without endangering anyone's life?

I make promises I can't keep.

Gosh. How unhappy.

It is, for everyone concerned. But that is there and we are here.

Alec, you're in favor of women's suffrage, aren't you?

Alec feigns ambivalence but does a poor job.

I knew it. So am I!

How can you tell?

Because you just *would*. I say, Alec, what do you think about conchies?

We're talking about Laurence again?

Not necessarily.

You don't approve of conscientious objection?

Don't know. It does seem unfair that some people risk their lives while others benefit from it but sit on their hands. It seems a bit cowardly.

Many pacifists undertake difficult or dangerous work; they farm the land, or they serve as noncombatants.

Laurence doesn't. If I was allowed to, I would fight.

That's very brave of you. But you should know there are different kinds of bravery in the world. Tell me, Gwen, have you ever held a minority view?

She rolls her eyes. Every day of my life.

I mean, an opinion where you were truly in the minority? One that the rest of your peers mocked you and hated you for? One that could create problems for your family and could potentially put you in prison?

That rather depends on whether someone considered my opinion powerful or important. Would anyone ever take a view *I* held that seriously?

It's a fair point. But if it were just a matter of cowardice and courage, don't you think the army has enough ways to scare men into service?

You're probably right but I don't know enough about it, Alec. There is no debate I can possibly have with you that I could win.

He pauses before he responds. I did not realize one of us had to win and one of us had to lose; I thought we were just having a conversation. I don't know precisely why Laurence has chosen to do what he has, but I can assure you it must have been extremely difficult for him. If you are so curious about it, maybe you should just ask?

Maybe I will. But you didn't answer my question before: What do you think about conscientious objectors?

I think the world is imperfect. I think wars have many victims, not just the obvious ones. I think pacifism has the ring of sanity about it. And we need them. We need the minority view, if only to remind the rest of us why we believe in what we believe in, and because sometimes the minority view is the right view but its time hasn't come yet.

Like women's suffrage.

Indeed.

Gosh. You are surprising. And when you say something clever you turn all grave and handsome.

He flusters at this. Miss Watts, is that entirely appropriate?

But it's all right to say it to you, isn't it? Are you going to be prime minister one day?

Goodness no, I can think of several professions I would have to fail in first. What about going back now? Assuming that you are ready to face the displeasure of Miss Everard.

I am ready. Thanks awfully for being a brick.

* * *

Candle stubs sit in glass jars and melt onto saucers, along the wall, and on tables in the garden. It is a mild enough evening to cover bare arms with thin sleeves—the dancing and the whiskey provide extra warmth, when needed. Gwen has some, her first taste, and finds after the revulsion has subsided that it is quite as nice as vinegar, which she has always liked though never considered drinking on its own. The men savor it, so do the women; therefore Gwen will if only in small sips. So this is what getting tight feels like.

She wants to crank the handle and change the records on the gramophone, realizes too late that this is a liability that impedes her chances to speak or dance with Laurence, who is partnered with Sinclair (typical). Alec is dancing with Cynthia and seems disinclined to switch. Nevertheless, it is fun.

The recordings and the insects click and hiss.

Perhaps it is the drink or the stars appearing or the strains of songs, which have to be replayed or replaced when they come to an end. Perhaps it is the war, and that the night is precious because the world beyond Arnault is fluxing. Perhaps it is because they have spent hours talking through the people they know fighting or contributing to the effort. Gwen loses count of how many, their names and their backgrounds and their ages, who has already bought it and who is still alive. It makes Gwen feel vulnerable. Her body, still in so many ways a mystery of itself, seems to shrink at the mention of death—so it ceases to be Gwen Watts and becomes instead just organs and meat, the way Daddy's leg must have looked in a bucket. It is the presence of Alec that has reintroduced discussion of the war to the house, for he seems to know a great deal about it, is subtle in his observations and careful in his reports. Cynthia agrees with Alec on many points; Sinclair disputes a few hotly. When Alec uses phrases such as "the moral imperative" and "collective responsibility" Gwen becomes anxious on Laurence's behalf, despite Alec's remarks this afternoon.

Gwen knows she is ignorant. For example, she has to ask Alec which side the Indians are on.

Alec Worsham's expression turns somber before he confirms that many thousands of Indian soldiers are fighting alongside our troops.

How super, she answers.

Not exactly—Alec explains that they want independence in return, and she finds the melancholy in his manner unsettling.

Gwen thinks hard about it, willing her useless mind to trundle to its conclusion. It does seem a fair and straightforward exchange to me.

Yes, Alec replies. Yes, it is more than fair, but I am afraid it is not remotely straightforward.

Then three words materialize in Gwen's consciousness, the definitions of which huddle close together in her head and play tricks on her. Enormity. It is the enormity of the war that she cannot fathom, that there are corpses and destruction and family grief in unknowable numbers, and travesties of justice. Enormousness. It is the enormousness of the war that overwhelms her, the way it spans the globe, and she cannot visualize the edges of it because they have disappeared into countries she has barely heard of. Intricacy. It is the intricacy of the war that is baffling, the invisible threads of purpose and consequence crisscrossing in multiplicity over oceans and continents, so that a quiver on one alters life and death at the end of another. Because of the enormity, the enormousness, and the intricacy, Gwen will never understand it, never. If she lives to be a hundred, the war will still be there as a blemish of uncertainty on whatever fabric of knowledge and experience she acquires in life.

I will jolly well enjoy this whiskey, despite the way it burns my throat. I will jolly well enjoy playing records, despite my not having a dance partner.

After a random approach to the music collection, Gwen becomes more selective, picking out the best titles, repeating her favorites. "Dreaming"; "Somewhere a Voice Is Calling"; "I Don't Suppose"; "I Lost My Heart in Honolulu"; "In the Glory of the Moonlight"; and then "Dreaming" because she liked it so much the first time around; and then "I Lost My Heart in Honolulu" again.

Laurence holds Sinclair close, sways with her in and out of shadows. Her teeth are straight, white; she shows them when she shows her amusement at being spun or dipped or at some remark he whispers into her ear that pleases her. They pause to replenish their glasses and make a private toast, then resume.

Alec dances more formally with Cynthia, and they giggle less. They have an ease, they match like a saucepan and its lid. Alec wants to know about Cynthia, puts a question to her on this or that; she answers, using more description than normal.

Gwen tries not to stare at the two couples, and at Sinclair least of all. Tries not to think of Sinclair as graceful, as stylish, as refined. Sinclair leans into Laurence, rests her head on him, would purr if she were a cat.

Gwen pretends to study a label on a shellac disc. If Sinclair had not come, Laurence would be dancing with *her* right now. If Sinclair picked up the scent of a richer man, she would drop Laurence in a beat. If Sinclair suddenly left, Laurence would be devastated . . .

And if he was devastated, he would need to be comforted . . .

By the woman whom he has been aware of as a gentle and stable presence, the woman a part of him has silently worshipped from a distance since they first met. Emotions that he has suppressed out of respect might suddenly burst forth. Maybe he is simply waiting to be a free man again, and for the right occasion to present itself—

Sinclair breaks away from Laurence. I rather want a go of the gramophone myself. I'm sure I can find some music that isn't so soppy. (She flicks through some records, then notices Gwen.) We've had rather a lot of the same, don't you think? I say, Laurence, why don't you dance with Gwen for a bit? It's hardly fair that Cynthia and I have been hogging the men. Is there any ragtime?

Gwen can hardly control the sensation of plummeting, from the moment when Laurence extends his invitation to her until the moment she is on her feet in front of him. She wobbles, has managed more of the whiskey than she thought. This is it, she thinks. This is actually it.

Laurence has never been closer to her than he is now, apart from the day when he lit her cigarette.

He smiles. Have you danced before, Gwen?

Plenty of times, but usually I'm the boy because I'm taller than the other girls.

Would you like to lead? (He is teasing her, and she finds it attractive.)

Oh, no. You can lead.

The music starts again. Gwen realizes that Laurence has put his hand around her waist, his finger hitching some of the flimsy material of her dress; that he is holding her hand and she is touching, *squeezing,* one of his shoulders. It is a strapping shoulder that wants to be squeezed. He is breathing on her and gazing into her eyes. She can smell his sweat, see the freckles on his face. There is no gap between them; their noses almost meet. They dance.

Gwen fights to stay upright, tries not to avert her eyes or allow her cheeks to flame. She hears the music as though it is far away; is aware of Cynthia, Alec, and even Sinclair as shapes behind frosted glass. They are harmless, they cannot interfere, they do not matter. The war does not matter. What Mummy would say matters least of the things that do not matter. Only this matters.

You and I have discovered what lovers through the ages already know, that in times of chaos and decay, truth is a constant and truth is beauty. What is truer than two halves making one whole? What is more beautiful than fulfillment? Being in love *definitely* feels like this.

She remembers to chat and to laugh along with Laurence in a natural way—the words come easily. It is all easy. Gwen belongs here. She wishes they could live inside this song and dance up to the sky, beyond it, be lights among the spheres. The candles are like stars.

The short hours of darkness will soon dissolve into dawn, and Cynthia takes one of her walks. She does not know where it will lead; perhaps to the end of the road, perhaps to the end of her life. For if, one day, she gives in to the temptation, she will not have planned it nor written a good-bye letter nor settled her affairs. She will do it when it seems to her a good idea and the opportunity presents itself. Were the opportunity to present itself within the next mile, she may be inclined, for it is night and she is alone and she is only a quarter deep into her research after all, and the drinking has given her courage. And this will have been a pleasing last evening. She follows a lane, a path, the fingernail moon. She follows her thoughts, which sink and rise in waves, which ascend and dart like birds; some of them settle on Alec.

She has got lost on her walks, found the way back several hours later or stayed out all night until daybreak, when people appeared she could ask directions of and signposts became visible. She has taken a train to the seaside wearing the clothes she left the house in, and had just enough money left over to buy a cup of tea. She has been molested. She has awoken in the doorway of a shop. She has been stalked by the disembodied phantom of the future, pale and iridescent, in the guise of a naked girl. She has been asked whether she was in need of assistance by a lady of color, as it happens, smartly dressed, warm, human, in contrast to Cynthia's presentiment before—she scrutinized Cynthia's face, touched her forehead with the back of her hand, pressed money into Cynthia's palm, and dashed away as if late for an appointment.

More often than not she simply takes a stroll, goes back home, sleeps in her own bed. These walks are the inkblot patterns where random and unconnected ideas merge into solid concepts, into theories worthy of being written, into structures that can withstand force.

Alec is in her net, and what ought she to do with him? The trouble is, he thinks he is a liberal, is attracted to the bohemian life, but in reality he would not cope. He would grow to resent Cynthia because she would hold him to his promises. He has been artful in his approach, she has to give him that. Stating and offering nothing specific, is handling her the way he handles his diplomatic work. All hints implications possibilities. All of it can be denied or reinterpreted, if the outcome is against him. Dear Alec, you think you are being modern.

Cynthia comes to a bridge and stops halfway across to look over the side.

Dear Alec . . . it would destroy you.

A fling, then? He alluded to it. Cynthia is not averse to the idea, but she senses danger comes with it. Alec is the sort of man who could not take a mistress without trying to save her, and she would quickly tire of his good intentions. He kept mentioning a year, but he did not call it that. He called it "twelve months." Twelve months is "short," twelve months "soon goes by." Oh yes, I see it now, you would have us make a commitment for this length of time and no hurt feelings at the end . . . ? I know you, Alec, and I know myself, and in one year you think you could change my mind for me, and in one year we would be farther apart than we already are.

These are good arguments against, but she can refute it entirely with a mere statement of fact: I am not prepared to share. There are aspects of my life that you may not be a part of; I shall not allow it. And I am not leaving Arnault. Arnault is mine, and there is nowhere I would rather be. This clinches it.

She hums a little to herself. Pinpricks of yellow light are visible in buildings across the fields.

Alec's hypothesis is flawed, and it took Cynthia only half an hour to prove it. Now she must devise a method of conveying her conclusions.

She has gone past the need for sleep and is feeling adventurous. She could walk through the night, has some money in her pocket for a train or a bus back. Cynthia should get a bicycle. What a good idea, why has she never thought of it before? Yes, she will definitely look into buying one, and this decision makes her sure she will not kill herself tonight. A walk will suffice, to a place that is unfamiliar, but she will definitely come back for breakfast.

Cynthia.

She is being called—she has been followed. She does not reply because it annoys her to have her privacy invaded and he is coming over to her anyway, clasping her body through her clothes, is kissing her.

Thirsty and hot. Gwen kicks off the covers. It is early, the sun has risen with the amber glow of arid morning. There is no water by her bed; she will have to go to the kitchen to get some. Her head throbs. She slips her dress over her and attempts the buttons with sleepy fingertips. She pushes her feet into shoes without stockings, and because it is habit, because she is not thinking about what makes sense, only about the dryness that needs to be quenched, because the kitchen seems at this moment miles not yards away, she hangs her faithful bag across her the way she does on any expedition.

Arnault is still asleep. She tries to avoid the squeaking parts of the landing, which will be audible to people in their bedrooms. She takes the stairs one at a time, step-stop, step-stop, cautious of tumbling. At the kitchen sink she forces the tap and swallows a whole glass of water without rest, wipes her mouth, forces the tap again to refill it. This is worse than having the flu.

She is quite awake now, even though it is some two hours before she would normally get up. Like a present. Gwen, here you are with two extra hours in the day, what are you going to do with them? Nice, really. She could go out, would be curious to see how different the world looks at this time of day. She drinks the rest of the water, then pauses at a sound—

—or was it? Does Arnault make different noises while its occupants are in bed?

She ignores it, then hears it again, or one similar. It is like nothing, like a bird trapped in a room. Sound, no sound.

Gwen leaves the glass on the draining board and retraces her steps with care. The disturbance, a flutter, draws her through the house toward the music room, where instinct makes her hesitate outside the door. (If it is a burglar, she will shout.) It is open a fraction, and human rustling emanates through it. She peers in.

It is a pile of cushions, rugs, hair—Cynthia's hair, Cynthia's arm, Cynthia's hand wearing Cynthia's sapphire ring. She is sleeping here on the floor, among the fabric textures, her head tucked into her elbow. She stirs, brings her other arm up to her chin, and a third embraces her, the arm of the man she is with, and Gwen discerns two separate breathing rhythms, a male and a female, the signal to her sensitive ears that something unexpected has occurred. Their intimacy is mammalian, their entwined limbs have not the curves of poetry but the angles of prose. Gwen decides she must leave, and in the time it takes for this conclusion to form, he moves protectively toward Cynthia in his sleep and shows his face.

It is shame making, creeping away, hoping not to be discovered—but for the best. Gwen goes out into the garden, turns toward the sky, inhales the air sweet with pollen, and sneezes.

She has a handkerchief in her bag and dabs her eyes out of formality because one does so when one is brokenhearted, and this is betrayal, if ever Woman was betrayed. The life she pictured them sharing has been stolen by a rogue to whom she gave the flower of her regard. Yes, here are the shoots of her anger, they are pale and weak but they will grow and spread and harden into resentment. (Won't they?)

Surprisingly, this is not how she imagined it would feel. Where is the misery? Where is the despair? Where is the crying out of his name, and the beating of her breast? Gwen does not feel them. She is *miffed*. She is thoroughly *put out*. Apparently, a love spurned feels about as painful as finding out Emily Dibner has been named hockey captain. Pretty bad, but not too bad.

And *Cynthia* . . .

Cynthia is different. Gwen cannot be mad with Cynthia in the same way she is mad at Laurence (and Emily Bloody Dibner). Cynthia is not a rival in love, but practically family. Gwen has known her all her life. Cynthia is a spinster . . . who has cut herself a peculiar existence and is not undeserving of companionship when she finds it. Cynthia got to Laurence first, plain and simple.

Tough toads on me.

Gwen grasps her handkerchief in case she sheds her tears—the grass surrounding her rustles and she sneezes loudly, abruptly, blows her nose like a bugle.

Bless you. Alec is beside her, groomed and dressed.

From behind her mask of hand and hanky Gwen stares at him, certain he must have seen what she saw, yet his dapper demeanor suggests not: neat, genial, *untroubled*. You're up early, Alec.

Always am.

Er, is anyone else about?

I expect they're still in bed, nursing their hangovers. We got tight last night, didn't we? (He seems to mean it, seems at ease.) Something the matter?

Gwen falters, fights the instinct to blurt what she knows because this is what she would normally do. She grows aware of a new pressure, the urge to protect, to stand in front of a human heart and spare it suffering. The subtle navigation of human relations. Gwen has been aggrieved, but it would be much the worse for Alec if he knew. Why does she think this? Yes, for his attentions upon Cynthia, for their dancing and because he found reasons to be close to her, for the journey to Arnault, which is out of his way, and which his schedule of work does not strictly permit. That he wants continually to know about Cynthia's welfare and finds the driest details of her research riveting, that he tries in his way to intrigue and impress her. And Laurence . . . ? There is history between Alec and Laurence, even Gwen knows that.

She swallows the unfairness, as bitter as it is, and says, You won't tell Mummy I got squiffy, will you?

Alec laughs and assures Gwen her secret is safe.

She thanks him profusely, telling him he is a good man—and adds in a flash of inspiration. Does the bakery open early, I wonder?

I'm sure I don't know.

Shall we find out? We can bring back a loaf for the others, and I could really do with a cream cake.

At this hour?

Yes!

If you say so. I'll fetch my wallet.

No, let me buy it, I would very much like to.

That wouldn't be proper of me.

I *insist*. (I hate it when I sound like Mummy!) I'm sure I've got my purse with me, at least I thought I did. Hold these, will you? She takes a hairbrush out of her bag and some yarn and her notebook with pages curled back over the spine and some hair slides . . . roots around for her purse at the bottom.

I say, that's rather good. It's Cynthia reading, isn't it?

What is . . . ? Oh, that. (Alec is referring to a drawing on the top page.) Supposed to be. I made it to show Laurence but I never got around to it.

I like the title.

It's a sort of joke and a sort of wish for her. I don't know. It's silly.

It's terrific. May I buy it from you?

No need to buy it; you can have it if you want, not that I understand why you would.

Because it will remind me of Cynthia, and of my stay here, and of you.

Then it's yours, and I'm glad. Look, here it is (Gwen holds up the purse). I say, it's such a beautiful morning, why don't we go *this* way.

So Gwen leads Alec away from Arnault, and any risk of discovering that the people he loves best have done him wrong.

A shouting woman, like a murder is happening, and a man shouting back.

Alec and Gwen can hear it before they see Arnault. They stop by the gate and he murmurs, Trouble in paradise.

It is Laurence and Sinclair.

Laurence: It's all in your mind, Joanna.

Sinclair: It is not in my fucking mind.

You're just upset.

Yes, I am fucking upset. Get out of my way, you fucking dandy.

Sinclair appears with her case and dumps it on the path.

Laurence comes after her: Just stay for an hour or two and let me explain . . . ?

She about-faces and marches back in, though not because he wants her to.

He follows after her. Joanna? Joanna?

More shouting within, then Sinclair comes back out with her handbag, coat slung over her arm, scarf draped about her shoulders, carrying her hat.

Laurence appears at the doorway, hands at the back of his head like a man watching his house on fire.

Sinclair strains to lift her luggage.

Please, Joanna . . . ?

She sways with the weight and the momentum of her rage. I hope your bollocks drop off. And don't call me Joanna!

Sinclair spins with the suitcase and trots past Gwen and Alec without acknowledgment, away from Arnault and out of their lives.

Laurence watches the space she has left behind, gazes heavenward in disbelief.

Gwen and Alec do not look at each other. Not even when Gwen says, I'm going to eat Sinclair's cherry tart.

Of course, Alec had no intention of remaining at Arnault for long. Before he goes he spends an afternoon alone with Laurence, and whatever transpires between them makes Laurence decide to leave too. Cynthia is unperturbed by their departure, relieved to have Arnault almost back to herself. She types pages of her book with a pencil between her teeth, has taken to wearing a pair of men's pince-nez, which she found in one of her professor's boxes.

Keep working, keep thinking, keep being—

Cynthia's ghosts. She never shares them, they are hers to tame or to be consumed by. Her life is her mind, it is the superior part of her, the best and the most fragile.

To Gwen, she has become quite as dull as before, leaving the girl to puzzle over whether the incident in the music room was an anomaly or had been taking place constantly beneath the surface. She cannot ask without revealing how she knows. It frustrates her, God how it frustrates her. Not because Gwen once loved Laurence, although she did, and not because Cynthia misled her, although she has. It is a separate problem that needs to be solved: the way Cynthia is blasé about love, the way she isolates herself from the warmth of intimacy, rejects the stirrings and urges (surely within her) as juvenile and superfluous.

Gwen follows the route to the Lagoon, mulling it over.

Indeed, Cynthia chose Laurence and not Alec because Laurence is expendable. Laurence is a physical being, which does not count for much to Cynthia. And she would fight any deep feelings she had for Alec because he is more her equal; because she would have a responsibility toward him, toward herself; because it might be more than just *intercourse,* and to Cynthia that detracts from—

From what, Cynthia? From work? From loneliness?

Gwen decides it makes no sense at all, and it will not be good enough for her.

My man will be an Alec *and* a Laurence; he will have the best attributes of both, and nothing shall keep me from him.

She arrives at the pond and watches the flecks of sun on the surface.

Even if he is not . . . if he is a safe and regular soul, I demand that he loves me passionately and treat me like a queen . . . or at the very least, I want him to be a kind and entertaining fellow—then we shall be one of those couples who are still laughing into old age and die within a month of each other . . . but if he turns out to be a tormented genius, I will cure him of his demons . . . unless he is mature and wise and lavishes me with affection, then he can care for me and cure me of *my* manias instead . . . or he could be an honest, decent man with big, strong hands who is content to work all day and to sit with me by our fire at night. I think he is in a trench at this very moment planning our life together, the prospect of it carrying him through, I hope. Yes, I know he must be somewhere, but I don't know exactly where or how I shall find him or who he is.

She picks up a pebble and lobs it in—*ker-splash*. She watches the ripples expand in circles, repeat, dissipate.

Then she lifts her bag off her shoulder and drops it on the ground, twists her feet out of her shoes, undoes her buttons, and pulls her dress off until she is wearing only her white slip. She takes some steps backward, inhales a breath, runs, and jumps in—the water a fantastic shock to her body. She comes up for a gasp of air, to see how far she went, and dives into the depths again, where it is cool and shadowy. Weeds and creatures tickle her and retract their tentacles. Beams of light are filtered and split apart. Algae bacteria invertebrates fish mollusks. There is a world under here, and Gwen never knew it. There is a world under here, and it is completely different from how she dreamed it.

Immaterialism

Reader in a Shoreditch Bar, 2008

Britain's Jeannine Okoro steps onto the ice to compete in her first Winter Olympic Games. *Deafening applause.* At eight years old, she is Britain's youngest ever figure-skating champion. She was spotted at the tender age of six by Torvill and Dean when she came to this very rink for Big Sister's birthday party (obviously). The rest, they say, is history. Now she's the favorite for an Olympic gold medal. She waves and smiles to the crowd, especially to her dad, who is sitting by the drinks vending machine with a cup of chicken soup.

She glides and performs the perfect twizzle.

Dad, watch me.

She does two more in rapid succession, twizzle, twizzle. The judges are thrilled.

Jeannine is wearing a fetching Betty Boop sweater and her new ice-skating skirt—bright green with polka dots, it twirls and flutters with each and every swish and turn—and her bestest leg warmers. She has also borrowed a pair of Big Sister's gloves because hers had tea spilled on them and are in the wash.

Now she's going for the toe loop jump. Can she do it? She builds up speed, bends her knee, launches from her toe pick, brings in her arms, and lands—finishing with a sweeping gesture to acknowledge the cheers from the stands.

Dad, did you see that?

She glides. She gliiides. Another brilliant toe loop jump. The judges are in awe.

And she's going for the parallel spin. She spirals into the center of the arena and extends her torso and leg into a T, hands thrust back, she spins faster, faster. She's doing it. She grabs the blade behind her and brings her foot up toward the back of her head in a Biellmann spin—making it look easy—releases it into an upright spin—this girl is amazing . . . and out. No wonder the judges are on their feet.

Dad, I span. Dad, I'm gonna do a Salchow. I said a Salchow. *Sal-chow.* You watching?

Jeannine Okoro circles the rink, her arms spread like wings. She zooms. Six, three, nine is all she has to remember. She does another twizzle, just to warm up. Six o'clock, three o'clock, nine o'clock with her free leg and her body will do the rest. She skates. She skaaates. Her leg comes up behind her at *six o'clock,* then right, *three o'clock,* swings over to *nine o'clock* and she jumps turns lands wobbles . . . *oh no,* the judges won't like that. If she still wants the gold, she'll have to pull out her star move.

Sorry, Dad, that was rubbish. I'm gonna do an Axel instead. *Axel.*

The Axel is the most difficultest jump in figure skating. You take off going forward, *which is mad,* making one and a half rotations in the air; the trick is timing—don't twist too early. All the limbs have to work together to get you there. One arm early, or late, messes it up completely. Will the years of practice pay off? Jeannine looks calm as she skates past the fans, who have traveled all the way to north London to support her. She needs to jump *out* with arms stretched *out*, then pull 'em *in*. But whatever you do, Jeannine, don't pull into the jump too soon.

The crowd holds its breath.

She's moving. She's going. She's going to do it. Backward then *forward* to make the leap . . . gets scared . . .

She has only managed it once in training, when she had help; doubts whether she can make it. Her instincts anticipate the unnaturalness of the jump; she knows she is bringing her arms in quicker than she should and by then the whole move is already lost.

Twisting early taking off late sends Jeannine down *hard*. She feels the disappointment before she feels the physical pain as her body makes contact with the ice; automatically she pushes out one hand to break her fall, remembering to tuck her fingers in so they don't get sliced off by someone else's skates. *Bang* like an explosion. She is winded by the impact. She is hot and cold, doubled in two; the sound of the crash buzzes in her ears. She shakes her head at her own stupidity, at the shock.

Dad saw it all, is up out of his seat, flat against the transparent barrier still clutching the vending-machine chicken soup. Jeannine, are you all right?

Jeannine can't bear to look at him. She doesn't care that other people saw her but why did she have to fall in front of him? She wanted to show how much she'd improved, how the money spent on lessons and kit wasn't wasted. Jeannine hardly ever falls, and certainly never hurts herself. She's good at skating, she knows she is, practically ready for local competitions, according to her coach.

She spends several minutes slumped over in the middle of the ice, her knees and buttocks wet. Skaters zip around her, dodge past, dangerously near. Plenty of people fall over when the rink is this busy. Little girls should learn not to show off.

Are—you—all—right?

Yes, Dad, I'm fine.

Now a supervisor is helping Jeannine up and her wrist is killing her. Ow ow ow. It *kills*. She holds it to her chest with her uninjured hand.

Please let it be a sprain. If it's broken, Mum will never let her skate again.

Saturday night, light pollution bounces off wet pavements and coats the buildings in orange fur. A couple walks through Clifton hands and arms entwined, around his waist, around her shoulders; they stop to kiss. Hurry on.

Not a couple, though: two individuals who met in a hectic nightclub the music rumbling the walls vibrating an assault of beats and bass. She likes a sweet man. If she didn't, she would be out of his reach.

Leaning on the bar, he smiles weakly, persuades himself she is a lost cause, someone has put her up to it; until she is linking her fingers through the loops of his jeans, until she is pressing his earlobe in her divine mouth; he can't really believe the overtures are genuine. Why is she showing him her key ring, a large letter *J* made of sparkles? She isn't. She is showing him a set of house keys, that they have somewhere private to go, and is now leading him through the dirty streets, clearly expert in these matters. It is captured on CCTV.

At a terraced house she struggles with the front door, works the lock back and forth like she is unfamiliar with it. Shared accommodation, she explains, and takes him upstairs past the potted plant, the tangled phone, the smell of curry, and strewn junk mail.

The bedroom is a female student's, filled with cosmetics, CDs, ring binders, handbags, floppy discs, and a boxy computer with wires trailing from it. Several issues of *Fields of Science* magazine have been left in a heap on the carpet. One is open to a feature about natural language processing: *NLP-based information access technologies will continue to be a major area of research and development in the new millennium, but will computers ever accomplish human-like language processing?* (An illustration of a stern reader absorbed in her book belies such a thing is possible or desirable.) The notice board is cluttered . . . handwritten notes and eclectic leaflets, a two-for-one restaurant offer (expired). Slotted into the frame is a snapshot of a girl in a spangled outfit clutching a tiny trophy in the shape of an ice dancer in midflight.

Is this you?

Oh . . . a very long time ago. Don't look at it.

I think it's adorable.

She takes it from him, turns it over, and reattaches it blank side out. There's Absolut and some shot glasses on the windowsill.

It is an instruction. He finds these and pours two.

Lip-glossy grin— She sinks her vodka in a single swallow, then takes off her shoes and stretches on the bed, revealing a jeweled piercing at her navel.

The textbooks are about computer science, and one detail from their hasty half-conversation rattles in his skull; he thought she was doing a politics degree; in fact, he was certain of it.

No one's coming home unexpectedly, are they?

It's my sister's place. She's away for the weekend. Lets me stay whenever I need to.

You need to now because . . . ?

She kneels up on the bed and gives him kisses where he is standing.

His hand strays to the bare gap between her vest and her trou-

sers and the peep of a pretty thong, but the caresses he places there
are lukewarm.

She sighs, What's the matter?

Nothing.

Something is. Do you have a race problem?

No.

Some men do. Sometimes I get the signals wrong.

Not me. I think you're stunning.

What is it, then?

Usually I do this with a girlfriend. Not with someone I just met.
You've nothing to be afraid of . . . She kisses him again.

What if we just chilled tonight, spent the day together tomorrow?
Don't you want me?

Ye-es. But we could get to know each other first, maybe, do this
another night. You can tell me all about your course and your family
and your dreams and . . . your name.

There isn't going to be another night.

Right. I see.

She takes one of his hands, gently, pulls back his sleeve to reveal
a distorted plastic wristband. What's this?

Glastonbury.

It's *filthy.* You must have been wearing it for weeks.

He picks up a pair of scissors from the desk and snips it off.

I didn't ask you to do that.

I could see it was annoying you.

Despite his good intentions, he gives in to her mouth and her
inviting breaths and runs his hands over her body. As his confidence swells, he whispers a little question into her ear: Is there anything you would like me to do? (It was never important enough to
ask before.)

Actually, now you come to mention it . . .

He is surprisingly good at this, her sounds, her shaking, she arches her back, one hand caressing her own breasts, the other gripping the bed frame. He is good at this.

But there is a moment that subdues the mood between them. She assumes control, becomes businesslike. His pride is stung by the implied criticism—

I'm not like that, I can take care of you.

Let me take care of myself. (There will be no careless mistakes.)

Then it is done. They pass over the awkwardness and fall back into their rhythm.

She does not let him cuddle long afterward, does not allow him to settle for the whole night, can't stand his compliments or sentimental murmurs; these gestures are unwelcome. Has put her top and panties back on, becomes brusque and impatient.

I like you.

She laughs. You don't like me. You don't know me.

I want to. Do you live in Bristol?

Nope. Neither do you, Essex Boy.

I had a friend's stag night. Not really a friend, we went to the same school. What brought you here, anyway?

A bad breakup.

I didn't know you were breaking up with someone. I thought you were single.

I am single.

How bad was it?

She licks her lips, then smiles. Does it matter?

Do you want to talk about it?

I've got absolutely nothing to say. She picks up his clothes from the floor, chucks them at him without making eye contact.

He puts on his T-shirt under duress. I'd like to phone you sometime.

No. Thanks.

Then let me leave you my number?

I'll throw it away, you know I will. Don't look offended; I didn't make any promises.

I know. I think you should have told me, though.

She frowns. About?

Your ex.

It's none of your business.

True, but now I can't help wondering if you're still vulnerable. What if I've taken advantage of you?

How thoughtful . . . and yet how patronizing.

I didn't mean it like that.

Do I look upset to you? Do I look like I need rescuing?

He flattens his hair and decides to try a different strategy. Spend the day with me.

I'm sorry, I can't.

Nothing serious, just a bit of fun.

She appears to consider but replies, Stop being ridiculous.

You're going back to him, aren't you?

I'd like you to leave now.

Please? Just one day together? It'll be great. We'll do whatever you want.

Make sure you're quiet on your way out, other people are sleeping.

He finishes getting dressed.

She ignores him, picks up a compact mirror, reapplies her lip gloss, snaps it shut. Her parting kiss is chaste, almost maternal; she pats his bum.

He's all wrong for you. You should be with me.

She should feel insulted. Instead, she has the urge to giggle. *Go away, Essex Boy.*

The member of parliament for Bexhall South decides this applicant will fill the post. He reclines in his chair, occasionally fingers his tie, rubs his chin stubble as he listens. The young male opposite is wearing a pink shirt and a whiff of Hugo Boss, has spiked hair and pitted skin from acne during adolescence. Went to a top university. Is polite and talkative, right of center and a believer in the green agenda, confident, has a *keen* interest in journalism and PR, which will be useful . . . his main weakness is that he has not been a member of the party for long, appears to have had no specific involvement in politics until five months ago.

And why is that?

I always wanted to join, of course. However, when I was pursuing my career in journalism I was advised by someone, who I'm sure was entirely well meaning, that I shouldn't join any political party, as it could cast a shadow on my impartiality. Then when I realized it was more honorable to become (he mimes the quote marks in the air) "part of the solution" instead of just being a critic, I felt it was time to "come out of the closet," so to speak. On reflection, I regret I did not become a card-carrying member sooner.

If the politician has another worry, it is that this metrosexual man presents too well. His slick speech has the squeaky timbre of rehearsal. This chap likes to impress, but if he is as good as he says he is, if he is even half as good—

The last interviewee is shown in, extends a slim hand adorned with nail extensions and nail art, wears a flattering pencil skirt and fitted jacket, a vintage brooch on her lapel.

He is moved to cover their handshake reassuringly, be avuncular with her. Don't be nervous. Make yourself comfortable. You are Jeannine Okoro? Did I say it right?

Yes, fine.

I'm Jonathan Ewan. It's good to meet you. Have you been to Parliament before?

I've protested nearby.

Excellent, that's what we like to hear. Talk to me about your own political outlook.

I'm a Thatcherite.

That's not an especially popular thing to be. Would you care to elaborate?

I believe in a light touch by government, first and foremost, and for that reason I am a Euroskeptic. I believe in personal freedoms and personal responsibilities. I believe in free markets and the power of strong economies to have positive effects in communities. I think ours is the natural political party for entrepreneurs and working families, and we should be here for those people, advocating their needs, making them feel safe at night. I believe completely that aspiration and choice are intrinsically linked. I am in favor of letting people decide how to spend their own money as far as is sensible, only to tax what is necessary and not a penny more. Government exists to help people in need, and when people are doing fine for themselves, government should back off.

You have not mentioned schools and hospitals.

I like schools and hospitals. Actually no, I don't like hospitals.

You will be aware that education and health are cornerstones of public debate: these issues dominate.

Certainly.

I suppose my question to you is how do you think we, as the opposition, should be setting ourselves apart from the government on public services?

As I said, by backing off. Public services are groaning under the weight of targets and monitoring. Ask any nurse, teacher, or police officer and they will tell you they did not sign up for an admin job.

You think we should reduce bureaucracy. Haven't we been saying that for ages now?

Ye-es. But I am talking about more than mere red tape. The

current level of interference can be characterized as paranoia. The legacy of this government is one of spin and megalomania, and I personally have a problem with it. Confident leadership means delegating responsibility farther down the chain. You need to trust people because they're the professionals, you should give them space to do their jobs. That is what we should say in debate, and that is what we should do when we get in.

Anything else?

Jeannine thinks. I'm in favor of blocking up the Channel Tunnel.

Tell me more.

We simply have to stop the influx of immigrants and refugees because the way I see it, it's a free-for-all.

The politician's mouth convulses as though he is going to snigger or make an objection painfully obvious to him. The party has run on that sort of message before, haven't we? We got clobbered.

We sounded hysterical. And racist. We didn't make the proper arguments. We didn't say, "Look, the Immigration and Nationality Directorate isn't fit for purpose, and you have had a decade to improve it, why haven't you?" Or that minister for immigration is a job nobody wants, that no one does properly or stays in for any length of time. We come across as unsympathetic, but the irony is it's even more inhumane to string people along with unresolved status, sometimes for years and years. If a case doesn't stand up, then send them back to their own countries immediately. Don't ask them nicely to leave and then be surprised when they resurface eighteen months later cleaning cars for a pittance, sleeping in a squalid bedroom with six other people, and having a nervous breakdown. I'm not saying foreign nationals have an easy life here—actually it's a huge mistake on our part to suggest they do—but the added pressure on housing, on health care, on the public purse . . . voters are dismayed by the sheer numbers, and government is complicit in a black market of cheap labor, exploitation, and trafficking. We ought to be ashamed. Retaking control of our borders would be a start. Then fix the system that allowed it to happen in the first place.

Ewan taps one of his teeth while he scrutinizes the letter it took her an entire weekend to write. Let's talk about your previous experience—

Jeannine describes her first job at a local authority and her current job at the chamber of commerce.

It strikes me that, for a fan of capitalism, you didn't go into business yourself?

I still might if I don't get this job. Jeannine adds a smile.

What sort of business?

I'm not sure, but it's going to have a fantastic website. She shrugs. I am more suited to this.

What do you think of our leader, then?

Jeannine exhales. I think he came along at the right time.

Do you like him?

I've never met him.

You have a vote, though. Voters have to reach a conclusion one way or the other about people standing for office, usually without the benefit of meeting them. You're entitled to your views. Based on what you have seen and heard, I ask again, what do you think of him?

For the first time during the interview, Jeannine hesitates. Jonathan Ewan presses his fingertips together and waits. She says, He has good qualities. He is articulate, engaging, enthusiastic, appealing . . . the party has been in opposition for a while; we need a leader who is appealing in order to win back a majority and he fits the bill.

But . . . ?

He reminds me of a manager at the Carphone Warehouse. I see him on the news and I think yes, I could definitely buy a mobile-phone upgrade from you.

Jonathan makes a noise that sounds like *huh* and he turns his attention back to her CV.

Jeannine senses she should have been more circumspect, wonders if it is too late to walk it back. Her strategy was to be truthful, to speak with conviction, to be unafraid of showing her cards—it was slightly reckless. The MP has moved on to her activism at university and volunteering locally, a chance to redeem herself: On the doorstep obviously, I've been a teller a couple of times because they struggle to make up numbers. I've done a bit for some newsletters, things like that. I like going to events, so I do try to stay in touch even when I'm busy.

Jonathan describes some likely scenarios the role would bring to gauge her reactions. Finally he says, Today I have to make a decision on who I wish to employ, and I will do so based on these interviews and relevant skills and experience. Out of interest, was there any special reason why you applied to work for me? I'm asking all the candidates. (This is a lie; he thought of it just now.)

Because of your private member's bill. You were trying to help small businesses.

That was two years ago.

I think you'll find it was three years ago.

And it wasn't successful.

I know. But you tried.

The meeting ends. Jonathan likes the sound of it: My assistant, Jeannine, will take care of it; ask for my assistant, Jeannine Okoro; let me spell it for you . . . Yes, it looks good too. She went to a former polytechnic, though. Oh, pish, he mutters to himself. He has made the right choice.

Erica! He shouts for the parliamentary assistant of his colleague.

Erica Twycross, today in a houndstooth suit, comes in and gives a withering look at the MP, who is young enough to be her son.

Sorry, are you on the phone?

Not this very second, Jonathan.

Good. I wanted to thank you for your help today. Seeing as you will be sharing an office with my new assistant, any thoughts? Anyone strike you?

Erica has outlasted numerous elected members and parliamentary staff, cannot be fazed, answers, The black woman.

You mean the last candidate?

Yes, Jonathan, the last candidate (the only candidate who was a woman and black).

Why her particularly?

She was the best.

Did you talk to her? Do you know her from somewhere else?

We spoke a little. No, I don't know her.

He shifts in his chair, uncomfortable at the thought of challenging Erica on how she has come to her conclusion. What about this one? He proffers the CV of his favorite.

Erica speed-reads the pages. At one point her eyes flick up, then resume their progress. Have you checked these dates for accuracy?

Jonathan does not reply; they both know he has not.

She gives the sheets back. Anything else I can do for you?

No thank you, Erica.

It is the next working day when Jonathan Ewan comes into the office, greets Erica at her desk, says yes, Jeannine was the right applicant, has accepted the job, is starting in three weeks. He has not yet taken advantage of Erica's connections, but he may wish to one day. Until then he is building up his credit, demonstrating how he values her opinion, affording her respect. He does not mention that the boy wanted more money, that despite his assertions during the interview he dithered when he was offered it, then turned it down. That Jeannine was content with commencing at the bottom of the pay scale.

*　　*　　*

Jeannine Okoro wakes to the radio news report about the Wen-chuan earthquake. Coffee first, toast with Marmite, and deciding what to wear—gray trouser suit and pink blouse with ruffles, gold hoop earrings and DKNY bag. And suddenly the day has a shape, details, accessories. During this, an item about SATs and whether these are bogging down the curriculum; the interviewee points out they were introduced under the previous administration. Then business news.

She showers during stories about selling British nuclear-power stations to a French company and possible candidates for a European Council president; apparently there is only one contender (she smiles splashily, rolls her eyes at the name), though this assumes the Lisbon Treaty is ratified by member states. *Never going to happen,* she answers from behind the shower curtain.

Jeannine perches in front of the full-length mirror to style her hair with the GHD straighteners and do her makeup. Good days, favorite days, start with this part going well—when it goes badly, inevitably a stressful or mismanaged day follows. The presenters are describing the newspaper headlines now, and her interest is sparked by more concern on the declining economy, increases in energy prices, decreases in house prices. *Not low enough for me yet,* and she drinks what is left of the coffee gone cold.

The inevitable update on the US election; voters in West Virginia are saying many Americans will not vote for a black presidential candidate. But Jeannine thinks Obama is running a good campaign, that Obama has kismet. McCain will look unimpressive when they are standing together, debating together, will have to work hard to earn it. The visuals of a black first family. The symbol. It is better reality television than *The Apprentice,* a better political fight than Boris and Ken— She is dressed, a dab of perfume. These shoes match her outfit, though they let in the rain, but the weather report assures her it will be dry and fine and she is going to risk it. Has her purse, her mobile, her Oyster, her pass, her keys, her—

Down into Old Street station, touches in; London is going to work. On the escalator she checks her mobile; Liam has texted her.

Morning baby. Luv u. Cant wait to see u l8r. XO

Jeannine glows. Then she takes out *Never Let Me Go,* which she will finish today on the Northern or the Jubilee line. She is a Londoner, and skillful at reading standing up on public transport during peak hours. And later, in a random act of kindness, she will BookCross it for someone else in the women's changing rooms or in one of London's green squares. Commuters shake open their newspapers magazines bend back thrillers nod along to their iPods.

At Westminster station she separates from the flow of footfall to swipe into Portcullis House through the underground entrance, and crosses the atrium where assistants and politicians, police and public, are loitering and assembling, grabbing coffee to take away, chatting, lost en route to one of hundreds of rooms. A former home secretary draws the gaze of some newbies—Jeannine disdains them for it, strides past with purpose.

In the office bay, Erica's computer is on but she is away from her desk. The member Erica works for can be heard making a call in his office. As ever, the light on Jeannine's desk phone indicates waiting voice mail. She starts her computer before taking her jacket off, begins sorting the wedge of letters and memos. There are forty-four new e-mails in the inbox since she left the office late yesterday evening, of which ten are marked high importance, and more pinging in all the time.

Erica, are you getting much traffic on the Human Fertilization and Embryology Bill?

Erica's rapid typing is uninterrupted. Bit. On various aspects. Why?

We are. Jeannine casts a glance at the mustard cardigan and gray updo. She would have preferred to share an office with someone nearer her own age. Still, Erica is okay, has worked for politicians since the eighties, is the embodiment of those who know but don't tell. But sometimes, sometimes—

Her colleague rotates the chair and looks over her spectacles at Jeannine, schoolmarmish. What is it, Jeannine?

Has Terry given any indication to you . . . ?

Erica takes the glasses off and lets them hang from her neck on a string of beads. I put things on his desk, he gives them back . . . God knows what goes on between the ears. These issues (the lady dismisses invisible insects from the air), they come around every so often, and suddenly it feels like we are in an elaborate and well-funded debating society, not a place of serious work. And then it dies down. You and I are here to help them.

Yeah. Are you going to the seminar today?

Which one?

Community Responsibility for Social Something-or-Other. I've got the e-mail somewhere. (Erica never bothers but Jeannine always asks, makes an effort to be friendly.)

You should go. Erica turns back to her screen, slides her specs on, resumes her wicked-fast typing.

Hazel sips her mineral water, twists the cap on the bottle.

They are at the venue, both clip their event ID badges on their Palace of Westminster lanyards. Jeannine has yet to find out why Hazel is so thin. If she has a medical condition, she has not talked about it, no oblique references to clinics or appointments with doctors; does not mention a strict diet or a regime of exercise, either.

Jeannine Okoro goes to the gym at least twice a week (and eats what she likes) but has never seen Hazel there. Allergic to dairy or to gluten, maybe?

Hazel's hair is short, adding to her boyish appearance, is talking about her sister again: I always have to phone her. I don't get angry anymore, I just accept it. And she's always all, Hey, how are you? What have you been doing? Keen to chat. Sometimes I can hear her almost . . . I don't know what. She never calls me, never texts. I say, Didn't you get my message? and she says, No, it's not working, or, Yes, but she couldn't get back to me for some reason, or she tried to and I didn't answer. But I check, and there's no missed call on my phone or anything. I don't know. She doesn't even e-mail anymore.

Did anything happen?

I've asked, and she swears it's nothing. We used to go to the cinema every week, just to watch whatever was on, or go for a bottle of wine at the pub. I think she's punishing me, only fuck knows what I've done.

Jeannine takes a tissue out of her handbag, gives it to Hazel. Have you told her how this is making you feel?

Hazel blows her nose, shakes her head simultaneously. Would you?

Yes, I would tell my sister to get her act together. Jeannine has a forthright relationship with her older sibling; as children, this manifested as screaming and pushing and occasional hair pulling.

I don't want to be needy, but it's as if she doesn't like me anymore. It's what you do to someone when you're trying to get rid of them. I know sometimes sisters and brothers are estranged, but I never thought Lucy and me would . . .

Hazel sips her water again.

The delegates are networking over tea and coffee cups after speeches and questions. Business cards are exchanged. Groupies of both sexes congregate around a frontbencher and a newspaper columnist. There are tables with displays and literature, freebies. Political conversations are conducted in raised, brassy voices. Someone makes a beeline for the two women, introduces himself.

Hazel has met him before, remembers him from another function, gives him air kisses like they are in show business.

He describes an online project where they need people to make video clips—would Hazel and Jeannine be interested in taking part? They agree, give him their e-mail addresses and extension numbers.

Hazel says, Do you need to go back to the office?

Just to check Jonathan's messages.

I need to check Maureen's. Are you free to do something after? Go shopping? A few people are meeting for drinks later. I didn't fancy it before, but it will be good if you come—unless you have plans with Liam? Is he training tonight? Sorry, you hardly get to see him, do you? Don't feel like you have to.

Hazel's pleading is blatant, the offer not to go forced out unwillingly. Jeannine replies, Yes, I'd like to. I'll phone him, he won't mind. It's nice to go out on a school night.

In the high-street bookshop, Jeannine takes a deep breath. The booky smell. New books smell good; secondhand books smell better. She peruses literature and fiction while Hazel looks for power-reading about China, buys *The Poisonwood Bible*.

In a department store, Hazel heads for the changing rooms to try on boho dresses and tight-fitting jeans. Jeannine lingers in the shoe section. It would be useful to buy some flats, smart shoes for work and to do her commute in. Some people wear sneakers for the journey, leave office shoes under their desks or carry them in a bag. Jeannine won't, for several reasons. She picks up a high-heel in red, turns the elegant design over in her hands, eighty pounds. A satin pair in taupe has a bow strap detail, is cheaper at fifty-nine pounds but Jeannine suspects the material will scuff and age quickly. Then a black zipped ankle boot with a wedge.

At the till a customer is returning a purchase, wanting her money refunded. Clothes hangers are pushed back and forth, squeaking like old bikes, a tweed jacket with oversized buttons is pulled out by another shopper: That's nice, I like that, bet they haven't got my size. The angular white mannequin posed on a pedestal garishly lit like a science fiction prop; there is a surge in power, a technical fault, which causes Jeannine several seconds of blindness and an illusion of motion.

A floor assistant, a girl wearing a cat design top and a store headset, offers Jeannine help. She declines (spots fading from her vision); she's just browsing really, keeps looking along the shoe shelves, picks out some styles and then replaces them. Jeannine glances back at her, casually, is her heritage Japanese? Thai, maybe? Indian? Jeannine can't tell, and for some reason would like to know. She is a teenager with a youthful complexion, anyway—too pretty to be believed—and Jeannine Okoro goes in search of solace among the belts and clutch bags, though she does not need these.

We are for all of Britain: for communities, for families, and for individuals. It is time to celebrate what I have always known in my heart, that we are members of an inclusive party. Our values are Britain's values—

He paused for applause. Jeannine also applauded.

Common sense and vigilance, a shared sense of responsibility and fairness, these are the qualities that British people possess and are the components that will make our streets safer for all of us—

He praised the residents' groups, the have-a-go heroes, the parents who set clear boundaries and good examples to follow (what about a cinch belt? Jeannine has confident taste, could she carry it off?), the numerous young people not reported in the news who reject gang and knife culture. Then, there was no doubt about it, the speaker was advocating stop-and-search.

Jeannine catches her image in a store mirror. Then she catches

253

herself in the driver's mirror of her dad's Ford Cortina. Her legs are not even long enough for her feet to touch the floor, and she has her special ice-skating bag on the seat next to her. She waits until he gets back into the car and has revved the engine.

Dad, what did that policeman want?

His grave eyes answer her reflection. Nothing, he was just checking we're both okay, and I told him we were fine. I told him, thanks for asking.

She pouts and dares not contradict him, won't say there is a funny feeling in her tummy and she might need to stop for a wee on the way home if she can't hold it in.

Then Dad turns around and snarls over his shoulder as though she is being argumentative: He's just doing his job, Jeannine. You have to respect the law, it's one of the things we do. Understand?

She nods yes. Though she doesn't.

She takes out her lip gloss, reapplies it. (Would Keith say the same to Yasmin? I wonder.) Better.

And afterward, being approached by the young man with the retreating hairline, his forehead gleaming in earnest, to take part in—what did he call it?—an engagement tool for the YouTube generation. There was a whole roomful of people to ask.

Hazel pulled a face but said she didn't mind helping out.

Great, I promise you won't regret it, and he switched his focus to Jeannine because it was Jeannine he most wanted. He was polite and ingratiating, but there was an element of greediness, a twinge of desperation.

I don't mind either. And she sincerely meant it, but Jeannine is not naive.

She tries calling Liam; it goes to voice mail.

Me again, in case you didn't get my message. I'm going out with Hazel for a few hours, but I won't be late and I can't drink much because of work tomorrow. Anyway, just wanted to check you didn't mind, and you're okay. And to tell you I love you, I really do. Ring me, it will be nice to hear your voice. Bye.

In the shoe section once more, Jeannine finds a design in indigo suede with a stub toe and a metallic pointed heel, 110 pounds. She loves it immediately. When she tries on the pair she feels queenly and they will go with everything—not "with," not "everything," but they are exactly her style, would match what they would match, would be striking when they intentionally clash. She puts them on her credit card.

The assistant, the same girl, folds them in tissue paper, fits the lid on the box, puts them in a rigid store bag. There you are, madam.

Madam. Seething silently, Jeannine slips it over the crook of her arm, but the new purchase high has had the shine taken off it.

Hazel says her friends have called, have named a meeting place. About time.

As they go, Jeannine turns back. The shop assistant thanks her once again and bids her a guileless good-bye.

It isn't her fault, Jeannine knows this. And didn't I have my turn of being skinny and beautiful? Her body heats to recall what she used to get away with. She bites her nail while she listens to Hazel's next problem (it's to do with a call center), gnaws on it. Jeannine's *degree, relationship, job,* have recently begun to feel, what? Not unsatisfactory? Not unexceptional? No, she is pleased with them, pleased she can buy a pair of shoes without asking any-one's permission. A woman can take pride in what she has achieved so far, and also be aware she has yet to meet her potential. She nips the nail off.

The venue is white cubes and retrovision feature walls, the spirits on glass shelving backlit in purple and pink. Tea lights waver in sculptural holders too big and heavy to snaffle, the music is broken beat, the staff in studded jeans and faded-print T-shirts of the Ramones and the Boomtown Rats.

It is surprisingly difficult to meet new people at Portcullis, where the offices can feel like cells. Only by being proactive, by joining one of the societies, by receiving and accepting sideways invitations from the socially promiscuous, can you develop new relationships. Jeannine meets six people this evening, all colleagues from the Whitehall bubble. She drinks dark rum while Hazel drinks bottled beer with a wedge of lime in the neck. Hazel has forgotten her distress from earlier, is friendly to the men with her: physical contacts, a peck on the cheek, a ruffle, a flirty shove.

Jeannine finds herself in conversation about postgraduate courses with a civil servant, puts on a skeptical persona, asks, Wouldn't you have been better off staying in employment for that length of time?

It flew by very quickly, one year, even two years, is actually nothing in the world of work. Maybe if I had been happier in my last job . . . ? When I consider how much I benefited personally—

I thought the point was to study something in a specialized field relevant to your career.

Yes, you certainly can, but mine was more out of academic curiosity. Some people travel. Some people do pottery or play in a band. This was my thing, this was what I wanted. On the whole, employers view it positively, it shows commitment and skills development, and if one person has an MA and the next person doesn't (takes a drink), it's something else to throw in the mix. I got to explore a subject I care about.

What about money?

I didn't have any. Listen—it's Jeannine, isn't it—if you're interested, even if you're *half*-interested, you should look up some courses, send an e-mail to test the water. It doesn't cost anything. I mean, you are considering studying again . . . ?

Jeannine shakes her head. I like the job I have.

Well, good for you. Not many people say that about their work.

I like hearing you talk about it, though.

If I'm becoming a bore, tell me to stop.

Back at the flat, a bit tipsy, Jeannine finds it dark. This surprises her, as Liam would normally wait up. She switches on a lamp in the bedroom but he is not there; all is as she left it this morning. She checks her mobile but knows already no messages, no missed calls, has checked it periodically during the evening.

And while she is at it, being irritated by people who don't stay in touch (Jeannine drops her keys and her bags, looks stubbornly at the lit display of her phone again), when was the last time Tess, Naomie, or even Gina bothered texting or ringing her?

A couple of hours pass and the alcohol wears off. Jeannine is reading in bed when he comes back.

I thought you would be asleep.

I'm not.

Why aren't you asleep, baby? Liam climbs over the bed to her, embraces her clumsily.

She reciprocates but answers, You didn't phone me.

I missed you, though. I missed you today. You look gorgeous like this. I love this top, it's very slinky. Did I buy you this top? He starts to kiss her shoulders and chest.

No, I bought it. Liam, didn't you get my messages? Liam?

I got them. I was with the boys, we were playing some pool.

Didn't you take your mobile?

I knew you were with people, I thought you would be having a good time. He persists in his attentions.

Before we do that, can we do this, please?

He ceases, moves away, starts taking off his shoes with his back to her. He has a rumble in his breath as though he is cross with her.

She says, I don't mind you going out. You work hard, of course you should. I just want to be told about it, that's all.

You wanted to check up on me.

No, not like that. I wanted to hear from you, and roughly what time I'll see you so I don't worry about you.

Liam looks at her askance.

Do you think I'm being unreasonable? Because I don't think I am. I think it's completely normal to worry about the other person.

No, baby, you're not unreasonable. And you work hard too. You're entitled to go out whenever you like.

Jeannine did not mean for this to be about her. She did her part, and as a matter of fact rarely socializes anymore. She lets it pass in order for the quarrel to be over.

Liam sighs. You're right. You're absolutely right. I'm sorry.

She does not reply immediately. They are the correct words, and he whispers them with big, open eyes, but she does not like the way he drops them in; they have the smooth texture of overuse. Even if you can't phone me, just a text—

Next time, I promise. He kisses her hand like she is a princess. Is it good? He indicates the book she is reading.

She sighs. I just started it, but yeah. And I bought some new shoes today too.

Why don't I make you one of those disgusting teas you drink, then you can show them to me and tell me about your day?

Well . . . that would be nice of you. She likes that they have this time together, that they share with each other the small and mundane parts of their lives; it is one of the ways she loves him.

You and I should do something special. I'll take you somewhere, we'll make a big evening of it and talk like we used to. Would you like that? I'll even wear my suit.

She subdues her cynicism—it must be important to him if he

wants to dress smartly—and merely nods so she doesn't say anything stupid.

Would you like peppermint or chamomile?

Surprise me.

In the kitchen she can hear him singing Stevie Wonder, and it soothes her heart temporarily.

The sweetness of magazine pages, perfume samples absorbed into high-quality printed paper. Jeannine holds them to her face and inhales. She keeps glossy magazines, keeps them in order like an archive, gazes at the spines with fondness. She also likes catalogs and brochures, but is more inclined to get rid of these at intervals (puts a few old ones in the recycling box). It is the weight of them, getting something hefty and colorful for little money or for free, their slipperiness, that they are filled with beautiful objects she can fantasize about owning.

Some of the publications are pages and pages of writing set off with a few arty photos—attractive people relaxing in green spaces, attractive people on tiered seating, attractive people in libraries—*and architecture.* Some are as long as novels and filled with possibilities, *possibilities of possibilities,* as desirable and as far out of her reach as a Gucci handbag.

Time to get rid of them.

Then she makes a neat tower that she hides at the back of the wardrobe, unable to part with them (it would be too painful). There are men who hoard pornography, compulsively growing their collection over years, developing emotional fixations with the sexy models they will never acquire in real life; Jeannine Okoro hoards university prospectuses.

The weekend. So Jeannine takes the bus to her sister's, for there is a conversation she has to have—

Look who it is! Sophia addresses this to both her children, to Josh, the infant she cradles across her denim shirtfront, to Yasmin, the little girl clutching her mummy's leg. Her gold jewelry swings and jingles. Thank God someone's here, now I can sleep.

Jeannine is used to Big Sister's lack of ceremony, used to putting the kettle on for herself, used to being given jobs to do whenever she comes over: peeling, ironing, running to the shop, emptying the dishwasher. Sophia is like their mum—to get on with her you need to do your share, be bossed by her. Jeannine is more like their dad, generally self-sufficient but will take instructions from stronger personalities to maintain the peace.

Josh is laid on the baby mat, his eyes and fingers interacting with the jungle animals on the play gym. Yasmin positions herself on the carpet between her brother and the television, showing *Charlie and Lola,* curls herself into a knot so her head droops on her knee. Sophia and Jeannine sit in adjacent armchairs, mugs of tea balanced. The mother updates the aunt on how the children have changed in the past week. Not much, by the sound of it.

Still, Jeannine is patient, can see Big Sister is tired, gets lonely for adult company, wants to express her thoughts. If Jeannine gives way first, then she can talk about what she needs to talk about.

Sophia lowers her voice. Somebody had a bad dream the other night (she points at Yasmin's back), screamed the whole place down, I'm amazed the neighbors didn't complain. I thought she was being attacked, I honestly did, even though I know there is no way anyone could break in without us hearing before they got to the children. Seriously, you don't know what it's like to worry about literally everything, every rash, every sharp edge, spiders in the bathroom; the whole world becomes deadly. She was in such a state, and I was calming her down, saying it's nothing, bad dreams can't hurt you la-la-la and all the time I'm the one who's shaking. Then she's back to sleep (clicks her fingers) like that but I can't because now I'm on edge and I have to check the door and the windows and the cooker.

What did she dream about?

I've no idea. She's learned the word lorry—yellow lorry, rubbish lorry—but she confuses it with bus.

Jeannine can't tell whether this is a clue to Yasmin's dream or if it's incidental.

Sophia yawns. Josh and me need to have a nap. You don't mind, do you?

Jeannine does mind, has to hide her irritation. It is one thing not being waited on so her sister can focus on the children; it is quite another being in charge of one of them, at least before they are old enough to be bribed.

Sophia assures her Keith will be home in a minute, and of course Jeannine gives in. To aunty and niece's displeasure, the television is turned off.

Yasmin is on Jeannine's lap for Farm Puzzle.

What is Josh doing now?

Sleeping.

And what is Josh going to do when he wakes up?

Crying.

He cries a lot, does he?

Yeah.

There is a lot Jeannine likes about her little niece: her chubbiness, her tiny, perfect nails, her hair in black twists with pink bobbles. (Her revulsion at the unwanted responsibility subsides a bit.) Why did you have a bad dream? There's nothing to be afraid of. We'll look after you, Mummy, Daddy, Grandma, and Gramps. Me, for what it's worth.

Yasmin plugs and unplugs the wooden shapes, the duck and the sheep and the cow—will make their noises when asked.

What noise does this one make?

Quack-quack-quack.

That's right. And what noise does this one make?

Oink. Oink.

That's right.

And what noise does this one make?

Woof-woof?

And how can you tell when a dog is happy? Because it wags its tail.

Jeannine likes the way her body reacts to her niece and nephew when they are occasionally dumped in her arms: her muscles increase their strength and snap around the child of their own accord, mold to the lumpy form, and the babe clings to her in return with a tough, squishy grip. She likes their miniature features, that they are warm and squirmy.

It's not your fault you're so boring, is it? (The suggestible child shakes her head.) And you'll be very big very soon. (The child nods in agreement.)

Yasmin wriggles, catching Jeannine off guard, her tiny shell ears sensitive to her daddy coming home, to his footstep and keys before they reach the front door and the hearing of big people.

Keith comes in without calling, for fear of disturbing his wife and son, takes off his hi-vis jacket, his height and shoulders blocking the daylight in the hallway. He greets Jeannine, offers to relieve her of her burden, lifts his daughter, raising her into the air. Despite his bulk he has a gentle nature, asks how long Sophia and Josh have been resting, asks after the boyfriend because they haven't seen him for a while.

Jeannine exhales. Really great. Actually, he took me out for dinner. It was very romantic.

Glad to hear it. What about work? (That's fine too.) Keith plants his daughter on the floor, takes out the Stickle Bricks, encourages her to play with them. I meant to say to you, Jeannine (Keith and

Yasmin sort through the pieces: What are you making? A dolly?), if you ever need a place to stay, you can always stay with us.

Why would I do that?

Just in case. I thought it was worth reminding you, you could if you needed to.

Jeannine laughs because she does not know what else to do. Thanks, but you guys only have two bedrooms the last time I counted.

And a sofa that folds out.

It's nice of you to offer, but we've got our own place.

Remind me why you're still renting? Liam said ages ago that you ought to buy while you could afford it, that even if you hadn't made up your minds to get married, it would be worth having some cash from a sale to split. If I remember rightly, Liam said renting was throwing money away.

He didn't say that, I did! Jeannine emphasizes it hotly, then glances in the direction of the room where mother and child are napping, lowers her voice: We aren't breaking up, if that's what you think.

Who said you were? (Keith helps Yasmin to make a doll with a square head.) If you decide to study again, you might need somewhere to live, that's all. Staying here would save you money. Come to think of it, you haven't mentioned it recently.

Me and not Liam . . . ?

It's a meaningless gesture if he's able to support you both from what he earns at the leisure center.

It's a health club.

Is he able to support you both?

Jeannine scowls at her brother-in-law. You don't know what you're talking about.

You've changed your mind?

Yes, I've changed my mind.

A few weeks ago—

Well, I've gone off the idea. And I'd prefer you not to mention it again.

Jeannine pretends to admire Sophia and Keith's wedding photo; the bride and groom had a fit of the giggles outside the church, their expressions frozen forever in exquisite laughter. Sophia had just turned twenty-five when they married. Jeannine is now twenty-nine. She twiddles her necklace (Accessorize, spur of the moment, 12.99 pounds).

Besides, it wouldn't work, she says. You, Sophia, the kids, there isn't enough space here—

Keith scratches the back of his head: It wouldn't be ideal but there's room for you to eat and sleep. For a year it could work, just about, or until you found an alternative. We would manage somehow.

Jeannine goes very quiet. Why are you saying this stuff?

Because we're family.

I can take care of myself, you know.

Yes. I know you can. (And this at least has the ring of sincerity.) Call it reciprocity. If something happened to one or both of us, I know you would make sure Yasmin and Josh were okay. Nothing *is* going to happen, but maybe we can do something to help you out? If you don't want to stay here, that's different, that's a choice. But you deserve to have a choice to begin with.

Jeannine taps her empty mug. Thanks.

Then he says, We're proud of you. We really are.

Keith was not overt in his disapproval when she got her job with Jonathan, but he hardly hid it successfully, either. Jeannine should set him straight, tell him he has no reason to be proud, remind him why he hates the man she works for. *I work in an office.*

Yes, and you're very good at it. You have chutzpah.

She snorts and stretches her arms. I'm going for a run later. A looong run.

Have you thought about asking your parents . . . ?

Ugh. Jeannine clenches her jaw at the thought of it.

Perhaps not. And for your information, we would take Liam in too, if you wanted us to.

I bet you would.

Ye-es, we would, you'd only have to ask.

She hasn't got a clue we're talking about this, has she? (No need to mention Big Sister by name.) You don't even like him. You don't say anything bad about him in front of me, but I've known you for long enough.

I like *you*, and so does Sophia, and so do the kids.

The kids don't like me. They'll like me when I put ten-pound notes in their birthday cards.

Yasmin rolls over in her effort to make herself heard, sucks in her bottom lip. I do, Neen.

Liam goes to work while Jeannine is still in bed. His parting kiss disturbs her. He has done this a couple of times recently, instead of letting her sleep for the extra hour until the radio comes on; knows insomnia is a problem for her.

The presenter gives a cursory greeting to the guest on the line: *Can we conclude from these findings that we have reached the limits of survivability . . . ?* The medical expert attempts an answer that summarizes the findings, qualifies what the research actually might indicate.

There is no bread for toast. Opens and closes the fridge. Not enough milk for porridge. Opens and closes the cutlery drawer.

The news reporter fishes for the bullet point he needs while the other is cautious; she almost shies away from the moment, shapes the answer delicately. *Well, it depends on your definition of viability.*

The presenter does not like that much, even his caliber of listeners will be confused. *Meaning what, exactly?*

Jeannine pours her coffee, savors the smell. Now to choose what to wear, to find the groove for the day.

The other explains why viability is a complicated matter in language laypeople may understand.

He persists, wants something concrete. *What do these conclusions tell us in a way that is useful in today's debate?*

That despite people's best efforts—

Jeannine is pulling a print skirt and cowl-neck sweater from her wardrobe, holds them against herself in the mirror. She remembers she was going to wear the new shoes, forgot to before, and then waited for a clear London sky. She takes the jewels out of their box, positions them, admires them, gets the full effect of today's outfit.

—and the association I am a member of does not therefore support a reduction to the current twenty-four-week time limit.

The interviewer pauses for a beat: *Thank you very much indeed.*

This morning Jeannine's hair is ludicrous, the irons are not working their magic, she burns herself, ow ow ow.

People are watching.

Jonathan Ewan says this to Jeannine after she gives him the two files of correspondence. The folders bulge with unanswered letters, and Jeannine makes cover sheets (*in favor* and *against*) so they will not get muddled. Jonathan has decided to wait until after the vote so some wording about the outcome can be included. There will be two versions: one to show solidarity with the constituents who agree with him, one to placate the constituents who disagree. Jonathan considers himself a "communicator." In letter writing, in meetings, in interviews, in publication, in public debate. He has the ability to soften and to persuade. Jonathan Ewan, MP, is moving

Bexhall South out of the marginal column and into the safe column. The replies will be done by close of play tomorrow; Jeannine's other work is being pushed back.

He intends to go through the files personally, checking for groups and organizations, for acquaintances and names from the past, for anyone he should be checking for. He has other reading to do, phone calls to return, the summoning of the division bell.

Jeannine repeats her question.

What?

This one should be given to the police.

What is it?

The one I pulled out. It's incendiary.

What does it say?

It says that, basically, this person is likely to attack someone. Jeannine shows him the letter that she has put in a document pocket in case fingerprints can be taken off the paper, DNA off the envelope. (No one told her to, she just assumed.)

Jonathan skims through it. It's a green inker.

It isn't. It's far worse. The police ought to see it.

Why? What specifically bothers you?

Jeannine did not expect Jonathan to challenge her. The tone of the letter is vicious. In her opinion, the police should decide whether a crime has been committed or could be prevented, whether the writer of it is a danger to anybody, whether there needs to be a referral to social services. She thought Jonathan would think so too, thought he would tell her to use her discretion in future.

The politician says, To be fair, the language isn't directed at you or me. He takes it out of the plastic pocket, jeopardizing the chance for forensic science to have its way, inserts it into the folder to be answered the next day.

Jonathan, that's a threat of violence.

I'll look at it later.

Even if we don't actively report it, you can't condone it by replying as if it's an ordinary letter. (In so saying, Jeannine realizes her error; no need for forensics when the author has included a name and address.)

He sighs. The trouble is, people like this are very vocal and probably use their vote, and probably have twenty friends who hold similar views and who also vote.

Jeannine doubts it.

I said I would look at it later, didn't I?

Yes. And she tries to decide whether to keep arguing or to give in.

And in the instant before she makes up her mind, Jonathan says, *People are watching*. Then he waves her away, turns his attention back to his work.

If he means the two of them should not be seen disagreeing with each other (or more precisely, she should not be seen disagreeing with him), this is unnecessary: they are alone apart from Erica in the other office, who pays them no attention.

Then she thinks he means people generally, in the constituency, for example; after all, it is in Jeannine's interest as much as Jonathan's that he maintain his majority.

During controversy the media are always watching, of course.

Back at her own desk, the syllables just uttered, fresh in her mind, an odd thought—

Her shoes are hurting her; she slides her finger inside them to relieve the pressure. The suede looks flawless, the design elegant. No one has complimented her on them yet. They will soon give a little.

Erica taps at her keyboard, the cursor invisible as it zips across the screen, leaving a trail of perfect spelling in its wake. She is in apricot.

Erica, what do you do with letters that are unacceptable?

Depends what you mean by unacceptable. I have seen some

horrific grammar in my time—Erica engages the brakes, turns her chair to face Jeannine— You aren't having difficulties, are you? If anyone is saying or doing anything you don't like, you tell Aunty Erica about it and I will set it straight. That includes (she jabs her finger toward Jonathan's office door). I shan't tolerate it. Believe me when I say I can make things happen they wouldn't like.

Jeannine is grateful to have Erica's battle-ax on her side. She assures her it is nothing like that, explains about the letter and its contents.

The older woman rolls her eyes. First, whatever you do, don't take it to heart. Second, it sounds like it could have been worse; be thankful it was written on paper and not on something sharper or wetter. Those ones certainly can be dealt with by the police. You were right to show it to him if you had concerns, and remember that a reply will have his name on it, not yours. If Jonathan asks you to do anything you don't want to, you should just say no, because you're sensible and your reasons will be sound. I will back you up. Jonathan is young. Not to you, obviously, but he is, and the gaps between general elections can feel very short. Your job is to help him, and that can mean keeping his desk clear of the "rubbish." Some people out there are very dissatisfied with their lot and looking for ways to express their rage. Members are in the public eye, are perceived as persons of power and influence. The public has no idea how much effort goes into making a tiny little change, let alone a big one. Even keeping things the way they are can be an uphill struggle. They get thousands of letters and e-mails on hundreds of subjects, it is inevitable . . . But you know, don't you, that sometimes it's the respectable-looking ones you have to be most careful of?

Jeannine knows it well, has seen for herself what some people do to spoil their ballot papers in the privacy of the polling booth. It occurs to her Erica would know what Jonathan meant, might be in the mood to tell if asked.

Or Jeannine could ask about the other matter, the shock of which is finally starting to wear off. But Erica does not invite confidences of that kind, for she keeps her own private life intensely private, has managed to conceal if she has children, whether she is married or has ever been married. That information is effectively off-limits.

Instead, the younger woman alights on: What do you think will happen today?

It's going to be close.

Jeannine realizes she does not know Erica's position on the issue, had presumed it was the same as her own but it could easily be the opposite, does not want to fall out with her over it.

Erica speaks as though she guesses Jeannine's thoughts. What concerns me is that we may be headed in the direction of the United States, where people's opinions on this influence their voting behavior, that this one question becomes more important than pensions, or foreign policy, or law and order, or taxation, and so on. I find the thought distasteful. There is something distinctly un-British about it. I think it will be a close-run thing, and then it will be gone and then we'll get our knickers in a twist about the next thing, hopefully worthier of our attention. A recession, I expect.

Soon?

Erica shrugs once. That would separate the men from the boys. Are your shoes rubbing, my dear?

Jeannine admires her feet. They're new but they're fine.

Her colleague does not take the hint. Remember, anyone who gives you a hard time will have me to answer to. Erica goes back to work.

To give her mind a rest, Jeannine Okoro phones the Department of Work and Pensions. She puts on her competent, authoritative voice when she explains who she is: Jonathan wrote to you over two weeks ago and the letter was clearly marked as urgent. Is somebody looking into it, please? Then can I talk to someone who knows, please? The next stage for Jonathan would probably be an FOI request regarding all cases of this type—but I am sure it would be better if you could just chase the progress and get back to me. Today? Thanks.

In between her typing, copying, and phone calls, Jeannine sends three succinct e-mails: two to her university friends, Tess and Naomie, and one to Gina, who she has known since school. She sets a reminder on her calendar, *Lunch w. H at 1pm.*

Jeannine can't remember how Hazel became her closest work friend, but if socializing with one person more than anyone else is the definition for it, she is. Before Hazel was Alexandra Douglas, a researcher for another MP. They started their jobs around the same time, went to the same inductions and orientations, met up occasionally at the beginning.

Alexandra spoke first: Are you new? I'm new too. Can I sit here, please?

Of course. I had a top just like that, you know, I love the button detail.

Thanks. People call it red but I think it's sort of orange. It's a bit too nice for work . . .

My boyfriend washed mine at the wrong temperature, it came out a funny shape and I had to throw it away.

Oh, *no*! Alex recalled how much she paid for hers and shared Jeannine's grief momentarily. It's a big place, isn't it? Who do you work for? (Jeannine told her and she frowned.) It's not a name I recognize—

Then Alexandra realized what Jeannine had already guessed would be the case.

But everything else was a match. Their taste in music, their love of fitness and training, though Alex preferred the swimming pool to the gym; they had read some of the same books and both liked horror films. It transpired they used to live in the same borough and went to the same ice-skating rink as children. They spent some time trying to work out if they had met before.

It is unclear why Alexandra Douglas dropped off the radar.

Someone, probably Hazel, told Jeannine that friendships across party lines could be viewed as subversive. She found the suggestion hilarious . . . But what if someone else had said the same to Alexandra, and she had not? Jeannine gets a pang—like from childhood, like in the playground—uptight—despondency of isolation. She liked Alexandra, and not just because they had the obvious things in common; Alex was warm and funny and considerate. Not as self-centered as Hazel, not such a flake.

Jeannine considers this as she walks along the corridor, dreamesque for its eerie repetition, tremulous lights, audible hum of equipment, low ceiling. More corridors of the same, above and below the offices, like cabins of a cruise liner. Imagines the walls closing in.

They lunch at the café in the atrium. Hazel is talking about a new man in her life, one from the bar last week, but Jeannine cannot remember which. They have been out four times (how did she manage *that* and keep it quiet?). All right, three and a half times.

During a pause, Jeannine asks about Hazel's sister, who has not been mentioned since.

Hazel's face falls into its worry mask. Lucy's not herself. We had coffee over the weekend, and it's the first time since we were about twelve I have seen her without makeup on. She says her fiancé doesn't like it. I said, Lucky you, you don't have to bother. Of course she has beautiful skin and it makes her look ten years younger, but she didn't seem too happy about it. I asked her if she wanted to go out one evening, but she brushed me off. Again. She dresses differently too. I reckon she's found God, what other explanation could there be?

Jeannine has a pasta salad, presses the rocket onto her fork. It is perfectly tasteless.

Hazel eats her jacket potato with veggie chili, which looks more appetizing.

Jeannine mutters casually, What's your opinion of the Fast Stream?

I think you should watch out if you were appointed, because folks who got their jobs in the usual way could easily resent you for it.

Jeannine gets her own prick of resentment; Hazel intuitively makes a good point. Clearly she's got skills Jeannine hasn't.

And now her friend starts explaining what she knows about the application process (it's tough), how she's heard of really good people who didn't even pass the exam, and the nonsense questions they put on the paper to profile you. I'm sure you'd pass, though! But wouldn't you kick yourself if Jonathan ended up on the front-bench after you'd gone . . . ?

Jeannine Okoro lets the commentary run on.

Are you leaving, Jeannine?

Whatever gave you that idea?

I thought you said . . . ?

No. No. I'm not leaving, just thinking out loud.

I'm getting muddled. Are these the new shoes, then?

Jeannine shows them off.

They are fabulous. You always have such beautiful clothes. Are they Italian? I might start learning Italian. I fancy the idea of a second home in Tuscany one day, buy somewhere dilapidated and do it up, drink the local wine, eat vegetables from the market. Sounds ideal, don't you think?

How is she dressing differently?

Hmm?

Lucy . . . you said she's dressing differently.

Oh. Um. Well. She used to wear short skirts and dresses, she's very slim, you see. Practically size zero, it makes me want to puke.

Tiny little tops. And since, you know, the fiancé, she's become more . . . Hazel furrows her brow in effort.

Demure . . . ?

Yes. *Demure.* Prudish. She's taken to wearing clothes that are baggy and frumpy. Concealing sweaters and tracky bottoms. She's not the girl I once knew. Apparently, he wants Lucy to put the wild days behind her, start being more of a "lady," whatever that means. Made her get rid of her old clothes. (Hazel stares down at her plate.) Sort of peculiar really, she came home one afternoon and found he had shredded all the clothes he didn't approve of with a pair of scissors, because he thought they were too slutty. Isn't that weird? Hazel rests her knife and fork.

An episode from Sophia's past jogs Jeannine's memory, a passage from a charity briefing paper comes back to her. Is Lucy's fiancé hitting her?

Her friend goes pale, goes quiet. In the absence of their conversation, the echoes of other people's amplify to the roof, the trickle of the water feature. Hazel's eyes take on the glassy appearance of partial tears.

Jeannine leans closer, embraces her friend briefly.

Hazel whispers into Jeannine's ear that she doesn't know what to do, is frightened for her sister.

Jeannine replies it will surely be okay, you just have to be there, support her when she needs it, when she's ready for help.

Wretched platitudes. What else can she say?

On the treadmill after work, Jeannine reflects: at no point did it seem like a good idea to confide in Hazel, either.

Naomie was pleased to hear from her, sent a long reply sharing her news and suggesting some dates for an overnight visit to London, or equally, Jeannine is invited to stay with them in Birmingham.

Gina said she would love to meet, but because of half-term and the children . . .

And Tess has never yet answered an e-mail the same day. Jeannine should have phoned Tess, that would have been better.

This is her own fault.

She runs past five kilometers, thinking it might not be such a bad idea to drop Alexandra an e-mail.

Hi Alex, I saw you the other day but you were with colleagues, and I didn't want to interrupt. How are you? Have we really been here for over a year? Mental. I wondered whether you wanted to meet for a drink? Not in this dump, we'll go somewhere better!

Or what about: *I'm pathetic and totally pissed off, everything is falling apart and I can't cope. I think I'm cracking up! *lol* When are you free?*

Jeannine increases her speed, will run six kilometers, seven kilometers, eight kilometers and see how she feels.

Liam has left a sticky note on the microwave. *Out for the night. Luv u.*

She is unsurprised. Has not got the energy to be annoyed. Is, if anything, relieved to be on her own. After her workout Jeannine put her new shoes back on to come home in, has blisters on the backs of her heels to show for it. She eases them off now, exhaling at the pain ow ow ow, collapses on the sofa in front of the television with one of her teas to console herself, changes the channels like a teenager. The dirge is hypnotic, sends her into a stupor, and she wishes she could have a proper drink, but there is no alcohol.

Does not move.

Liam has given her space to think. Maybe. Or maybe he has simply done what he would have done anyway. He wanted to go out, so he went out. There you are.

After ten o'clock she watches the live broadcast from the House of Commons. An hour or so later, Jeannine Okoro decides she must get wine from somewhere (it's London, for fuck's sake, if you can't find a drink in the middle of the week in London . . .), gathers the contents of her handbag, and, because they belong to her, because she is irrational, because she cannot accept that objects of such unequivocal beauty and expense would break their promise of perfection, because she is a woman, she wears the new shoes to go out again.

Chilean Merlot, 250 ml, 13 percent ABV, three units, 170 calories. Medium- to full-bodied with flavors of plums, berries, and mocha. The venue radiates muted colors, lilts with the weekday crowd. One wall is covered in peeling posters cartoons foreign language newspaper bare bricks graffiti. Mao, Banksy, Hepburn, and other icons vie for prominence. Jeannine sits at the granite bar and tries to read, as a distraction from her messy thoughts. She is obscured to one side by an arrangement of cut flowers, red and green spikes like claws in a vase. The interior is reflected back by the street-facing window, the traffic island and the furniture shop and the euphemistic sauna lit in the night. Jeannine's reversed outline is visible on the glass, an otherworldly creature.

A man sitting nearby is pointing a camera at her.

Are you taking a picture of me? Jeannine stops just short of yelling.

He makes wary eye contact with the woman sitting near him. No. I was viewing the photos I've already got. He turns the Cybershot over, revealing a frame taken during the day in a London park.

She looks, relents, softens her tone to concede haughtily, Well, that's all right then. She resumes her reading to salvage some dignity and fails, she hardly recognizes herself (*shouting at strangers in bars?*). That was very rude, I apologize.

He scratches his nose, perhaps forming a sharp response, but he only mumbles, I can see how it happened, sorry to have intruded.

He has the knowingly untidy appearance of someone who once went traveling and never grew out of it. Scruffy and clean. And wears an old concert wristband, grimy, faded; the lettering bleeds. She thinks to herself, *If I was your girlfriend, I'd make you take that off*, and the idea causes her to smirk.

He catches her watching. Excuse me, did I sell you a house once?

Actually, I've never bought property, I'm still renting.

Did we meet at a wedding or something?

No. Jeannine is vexed because her apology has been misconstrued. No, I don't think so.

My mistake. It's time for me to leave you to your book, isn't it?

Yes. Thanks.

Jeannine goes back to reading for half a page, aware she has made a bad impression, makes no progress. He is spinning through the pictures on his camera, a rucksack on the floor, is drinking on his own. Dad would say it is up to us to have good manners, to set high standards, to contribute, it is how we get on in life. Before she can change her mind—

I'm Jeannine Okoro, by the way. And I am sorry about before.

I'm Christopher Rhys. They shake hands as if the whole prickly encounter has not taken place. After the introduction there is a lull. He ventures, Some women would feel funny about sitting in a bar alone, reading. Not that they should, of course, I just mean it's quite . . . unusual. Is this your local?

Sort of. (Jeannine looks around thoughtfully.) I don't think I've ever been in here before. There's, like, fifty of these in this area, they merge into one after a while. Necessity drove me out because there was no wine at home.

I see. Tough day?

More like tough week. I thought I would allow myself this luxury, I'm sure I've earned it. What about you? How was your day?

Oh. It was okay, thanks. I was visiting my brother. Half brother, to be exact. He's studying fashion and this is his first year. I promised I would come, but I put it off for ages; I avoid London if I can.

Where did he take you?

He showed me around his halls of residence and his college. Then all the tourist traps, I'm afraid: Covent Garden, Trafalgar Square, Hyde Park. We went on the London Eye this afternoon.

One thing about living here is you never do all that stuff. I see the Eye virtually every day, but I haven't been on it. Because it's there, you tend not to bother. Are you doing more sightseeing tomorrow?

No, I'm getting the train back to Colchester tonight. I'm just killing some time.

Oh, an Essex Boy?

I've never heard that before.

Of course you haven't. Jeannine fiddles with one of her earrings, then makes herself stop. I love fashion. Your brother is going to be a famous designer, then? Milan, Paris . . . ?

I think if he just earned his living by it, had a shop in Camden or an online business or whatever, that would make him happy. He's determined, and very talented. I think so, anyway, not that I know much about it.

I bet he was glad you visited. It's a big deal, moving away, going to college. Your approval would make it feel official. What's his name?

He's Jasper. Would you like to see a photo? Chris finds one and shows Jeannine on the LCD screen: the boy is grinning, wearing guyliner, a black and yellow check scarf with a white shirt, looks pretty enough to be in a boyband.

She remarks, Ahh, he has a baby face. You don't resemble each other.

No, but we get on—now. Do you have brothers?

One sister, Sophia. She has children, Yasmin and Josh, so the pressure is off me . . . She sips her wine. You're a property developer, are you? Because you asked me if I . . . ?

Christopher looks uneasy, confirms he is. I do places up. I was a carpenter before, but now I'm also a decorator and a plumber and a whatever.

And how do you get into all that?

In my case, it was just a matter of going to an auction and buying a house that needed some work done . . . without actually having any of the finance in place.

You did *what*?

Yeah, that was a pretty stressful few weeks, and involved talking to a lot of mortgage companies.

But why?

Because the house had potential. And it paid off. It had to, or I would have been in trouble. I got better at it after that.

How's the property game, then?

Slowing down, the proverbial bubble was bound to, *you know*, sooner or later.

There are always going to be people who want to buy. Like me.

He rests his chin on his hand: Could we talk about something else? I feel like this has been the only topic of conversation for the past ten years.

We are a bit fixated, aren't we? Jeannine winces, leans down to hold one of her shoes, shifts her foot inside it.

Are you all right?

Yeah. They're just new.

They're very nice, but you probably shouldn't wear them if they hurt you.

Mum used to make us wear new shoes with thick socks around the house, called it "breaking them in." I hated it at the time, but . . . Jeannine straightens. Did it—when you were being shown around his college by your brother—did it make you want to go back? be a student again yourself?

Chris Rhys folds his arms. I didn't go to university, as it happens, I stayed on at school initially but I wasn't sure what I wanted. And seeing what Jasper has to cope with—the fees and the loan and the overdraft—if I was his age, I wouldn't be going today either. He's stoic about it, but I worry for him. If I had studied, I like to think I would've done graphic design or photography, something like that. Actually I'm on Flickr, have you heard of it?

Yes, I know the site.

Photography is something I became interested in when I went traveling for a few months.

Oh, *really*? (She dials down the condescension, he doesn't know how transparent he is.) I never went myself, I had too much else I wanted to do, career-wise. Where did you go?

Thailand, Australia, New Zealand, all those places.

Did you find what you were looking for?

Not really, but I went to some great parties.

And why haven't you pursued photography professionally, if you love it?

Christopher taps the digital camera as though testing it for authenticity. Maybe I flirted with the idea, but I'm not good enough, plus it's a perilous career path.

As is the one you chose.

True enough, I suppose. Nonetheless, I don't mind being an amateur. There's something pure about being able to please myself. And it's the only art form where you can make accidental master-pieces, which I think is quite special.

Good for you. And Jeannine genuinely means it, feels happy for him. What's your username? I'll look you up.

He blushes. Immaterialism.

Like Berkeley, right?

Um, yes. You're the first person I've met who knew that.

Well, I did do some philosophy modules, as it happens . . .

So . . . Jeannine (he says her name gently, as if picking up something delicate), what do you do?

I work at Westminster as an assistant for an MP. He's a back-bencher, no one you'd recognize. Jonathan Ewan, MP for Bexhall South. He's good. He's in the constituency a lot, very active.

You work at . . . ?

Parliament, yes.

And this is the job that has caused you to . . . ?

Go out in search of a big glass of wine. Kind of. Opposition, not government, before you ask; don't judge a book by its cover.

Chris is about to comment on this, possibly even joke about it, but the words escape him, die on his lips.

Jeannine Okoro reads something into his reaction and forms her own conclusions. She gets enough grief about her job as it is, and sometimes lies about it, thought this was one occasion when she did not have to. She glares at him, then turns away, stares at a couple at the opposite end of the room for a while. They seem in love.

He coughs before continuing: Why did you assume I'd criticize?

Her voice is shrill. I didn't.

(The double and triple layers of female communication; he sets this to one side.) I think it's admirable to do something you believe in.

Yeah, I suppose it is. Jeannine finishes her drink with a flourish. I wasn't a very good philosophy student. My talents lay elsewhere. I enjoyed it, though, the bit I did. If I were to study again, I would do something completely different like that, random and fascinating, something just for me.

You still could.

Mm . . . maybe.

Christopher glances at his mobile phone, then comes to a decision, flips it shut, and hides it in a pocket. Can I buy you another?

Jeannine closes her eyes and opens them. Have you got time?

I'm in no rush. The trains run from Liverpool Street all night. (His palms are moist, so he runs them over his jeans.)

Thank you. (Clears her throat to speak more clearly.) That would be very kind.

He catches the attention of the barman, also inquires after a first-aid kit. Jeannine protests, but the barman efficiently locates and offers blue Band-Aids in various sizes. Grateful in spite of herself, she applies two; they take the edge off the soreness, prevent further friction. The drinks are served and they resume their conversation.

In case you haven't guessed, I want to be a member of parliament. One day.

That's incredible. Though now you come to mention it, I probably figured it out.

Did you? (Disbelieving.) What makes you so sure you had me worked out?

You strike me as a person who decides what she wants and then gets it.

That isn't a completely flattering description.

It's meant to be. Following an ambition is a responsibility, if you have got one. Not like me, I just want to pay the bills, I'm not cut from that cloth. But Jasper is, he's like you, he knows what he wants and has the ability to follow it through. It would be scandalous not to.

You don't think it's a stupid thing to want?

No-o. It sounds difficult, but you should have a go. There is great beauty in risk.

That's sweet. Sometimes people are turned off when I tell them because . . . for many different reasons.

I think it's worth drinking to. Christopher touches glasses with her.

There was an important vote in the Commons this evening. I don't suppose you heard about it?

He shakes his head slowly.

Of course not, because you're normal. I don't want to give you the wrong idea, my family isn't affluent or anything, but my parents are fairly right wing. Dad set up his own company, like you, printing shops and copiers. He made it from scratch and was constantly afraid of a lefty government squeezing it dry. Mum just loved Thatcher because she was fierce. Most people tend to have the same politics as their parents, but I actively chose the party that was best for me. The one that wants to give people real choice over their lives. My sister and I were the first in our family to go to university. I don't say that out of vanity: it was Mum and Dad's achievement as much as ours. They made it possible for us, for me, to have more than they did, to go farther in life than they did. That's the way it's supposed to work over the generations, especially in families who start out with nothing but conviction. I know politics can be dry, but I wanted to be part of the machinery that makes things possible. I was resilient when I was younger. Headstrong. No one could talk me out of anything or stop me doing something I wanted to do. Recently I have begun to have doubts. Recently I've realized that that version of myself has gone away. When we were kids we weren't wealthy, but we were secure and we knew right from wrong, and we didn't want for anything because it was all out there to be earned by those who worked hardest for it. We were encouraged. I do believe that choice and aspiration are necessary for each other. I think proper governing is about making opportunities for people to help themselves, giving power and responsibility back to individuals. But if we promise that, then we have to deliver that. My little niece, Yasmin, I see so much potential in her that has to be safeguarded. And I never want for her to be tyrannized by society . . . or by a man. I want better for her. I'm sorry, I'm rambling. I'm in a funny mood.

I don't mind. You encounter bumps when you're on a journey; it's part and parcel of it. It sounds like they need you.

Jeannine casts her eyes down; the tip of her tongue moistens her lips. It's complicated.

It usually is when it matters.

Jeannine fingers the cover of the paperback, traces the title in relief. They sit in silence for a few minutes, and it is not unpleasant. She says, I haven't asked you if you're happily with someone? Or happily single?

I've been in a relationship for three years, but it's coming to an end. I mean, we're doing a trial separation.

I'm sorry to hear it. Did she instigate it, or did you?

If I said it was mutual, you'd guess it was her idea, so we better just call it what it is. It took me by surprise, I have to admit. She said I was distant, that I backed away from the important decisions. I suppose I didn't want to upset the equilibrium. I was satisfied; evidently she wasn't.

You won't patch it up . . . ?

Not now.

What a shame. My condolences.

I'm not a total loss yet. Are you in a relationship, or . . . ?

I live with my boyfriend—and then she mutters it, offhand, throws it away—a couple of days ago he asked me to marry him.

Chris marshals the flutter of disappointment: Congratulations.

Jeannine toys with the stem of her wineglass: I haven't said yes. I'm considering it. We've been a couple for a while. Not childhood sweethearts, but not far off.

He must love you very much. Do you love him?

I do. Jeannine appears to hold her breath. I have.

Christopher Rhys hesitates, but surely it begs to be asked: Why are you sad, Jeannine Okoro?

Honestly? It's just . . . there are so many things I want to achieve, but I get the feeling if I marry Liam, none of it will ever happen for me. That will be the end of it, the end of my life as I know it.

He gives her a bar napkin, which she accepts but to her credit does not need to use. Why on earth would he prevent you from doing what you want? Doesn't he know?

Oh, he knows all right, I've talked about it plenty.

Then I don't understand . . .

Jeannine frowns, pouts, blinks. I don't know. If I were trapped in a burning building, he wouldn't think twice about running in after me, but I don't know why he wouldn't (Jeannine composes her thoughts, speaks carefully, deliberately). He did something about four weeks ago that I found kind of odd. He told me . . . I don't know, maybe I've blown it out of proportion . . . he told me he wanted me to come off the pill, stop using any contraceptives because it would prove I loved him. He said it's what real couples do.

What did you say?

When I'd picked myself up off the floor, I just explained I didn't want to risk getting pregnant. He didn't like it. He reacted *badly*. Took it personal, as if I'd insulted him, but I swear I didn't mean it that way, only that now isn't the right time. We made up afterward, and I thought the whole subject was closed. Then, the other day, he proposed.

The barman calls time. Jeannine and Christopher fall silent again.

She murmurs, I'm sorry, we don't know each other, and that was inappropriate of me. God, I'm so embarrassed, I shouldn't have said anything.

It sounds like it had to be said. And you've nothing to feel embarrassed about.

If Liam had popped the question a year ago, I'm positive we'd be married by now. It used to be me chasing him all the time, me complaining he wouldn't commit. What am I going to do?

I can't advise you on that.

You're the only one here. You're the only person I've told, as it happens. My friends are all, you know, busy with their own shit. And babies. When did I become old enough that all my friends started having babies?

I bet they care about you more than you know.

I'm not very good at staying in touch with people because I like to work. I like work. I'm good at it. Jeannine touches her eyes and nose with the napkin. Sorry, this is too weird for you, isn't it?

No-o. It's just none of my business.

Is it normal? Do men do this to their partners? Have I got it totally out of perspective?

No, it's not normal, we aren't all like that. I think it's quite a tricky place you've arrived at.

Yes, it is tricky. It's a nightmare, actually. And I'm sick of thinking about it. I know I had a future with Liam, once. What do you think? (No reaction.) Please, I'm asking for your help, it's burning me up.

Christopher sighs, treads cautiously, the path ahead irregular but discernible if he goes gently and bravely. He wants above all to do his best for this person, or at least not to fuck it up. You have—

Yes?

—excellent judgment and instincts; whatever you decide will

be right because you will make it work. You just need to choose the life you want and get over the rest.

Sometimes I think I'm not very good at making choices. Sometimes I think I'm unhappy because I brought it on myself.

It's never too late to start making good choices.

Jeannine meets his humble gaze, tinges of regret that there is only a short time left to share with him.

This sentiment is communicated somehow. It sends a spark, it causes a ripple. He is compelled to take her hand to lean toward her to place a kiss on her precious mouth. It feels acceptable to miss some steps somehow; no boundaries have been transgressed; he is confident the gift will be received as it was intended. Their contact is of itself, whole and perfect. Their physiologies leap with chemical intimacy, and then it passes.

What was that for?

Because you can do whatever you put your mind to, and I wanted some of it on me.

Her glow returns, her energy. She thinks of something nice to say but keeps it a secret.

Jeannine, it crossed my mind . . . I noticed when you got here . . . I swear I never would without asking your permission, but it might make a very beautiful—

Are you asking my permission?

Ye-es, I think so.

All right.

Are you sure?

Sounds like fun. Shall we do it now, before they kick us out?

It only takes a minute. Jeannine opens her paperback, her features natural, controls the urge to giggle, continues to follow the thread of the story. Chris makes a couple of quick adjustments and takes two rapid shots. Done. Would you like to see?

I'll look it up online. I should go, I've got work in the morning.

Shall I walk you home?

She raises an assertive hand to prevent him.

Right. You know my username?

I shan't forget it easily.

Feel free to post a comment. Also there's a link if, you know, you ever want to view a property or just make contact.

She smiles. Jonathan has a website.

Who does?

Jonathan Ewan, MP, Bexhall South. My e-mail's on there too. Or you could call the Commons switchboard and ask for his office. Jeannine gathers her handbag and puts her jacket over her arm. Thanks for the drink, and for the Band-Aids.

Thank you for the photo, and the conversation and everything.

They pause, then part.

As she is leaving he calls her name, adds he would love to know how it turns out.

She does not indicate one way or the other, waves, is gone.

Christopher Rhys exhales, his heart thudding. He locates a pen from the zipped section of his bag, jots *Ewan / Bexhall* in a space on the Liverpool Street to Colchester timetable. Not her phone number, but close enough.

Then he makes a call from his mobile. Jasp? It's me, I've done a stupid thing and missed the last train home. Can I sleep on your floor after all? You're a star. I'll find a cab.

Reader in a Shoreditch Bar
Uploaded on 21 May 2008 by Immaterialism

+ Immaterialism's photostream
- Women and Girls Reading (Pool)
  422 items
  browse

This photo also belongs to:
+ Shoreditch (Pool)

Tags
  reading
  reader
  book
  woman
  london
  shoreditch
  bar
  wine
  wineglass
  night

Comments
Miss Labelled says:
Yes.

Sincerity Yabuki

Sibil, 2060

He says, Are you too hot?

She says, No.

Tell me if you are, and I'll open a window.

No, don't go anywhere. Stay here. Look—I can fit my whole hand inside your hand.

What do you want to do tomorrow?

You mean today.

Is it? Today, what would you like to do today? We should make the most of it.

Can I have an arm, please? Maybe drive somewhere, take lunch with us. Take the chess. Are there any castles nearby? I haven't seen one since I've been here.

I haven't been to a castle since I was a kid. All right. We'll find a castle to visit, or some alternative ruins.

I like ruins. Real ones, not pretend. Places with atmosphere. And haunted. Somewhere murder and treason happened.

Obviously.

I was wondering, will your mum come to your graduation?

Don't know. I invited her. The journey could put her off.

She ought to see you graduate. Someone ought to see you graduate other than me.

Dad will.

Yes.

Are you humoring me?

No. No, I'm being serious. I promise I'm not teasing, I'm really not.

I can see you aren't. Sorry.

That's okay.

I wish I had known you back then. I could have done with this.

This?

Us.

She makes a noise like *hmm,* then says, We've found us now, that's what's important. Some people wait for years. Some people never find it. Isn't that sad?

Or find it and lose it later on.

The timing could have been better, but heaven knows it could have been worse.

Will your parents come?

Should do, don't see why not.

Will you introduce me?

I don't know, that sounds like a big step. (She laughs.) The real question is: will we introduce them to each other?

I never thought of that.

Don't you want them to? Our parents, to meet?

I just think of them as inhabiting two parallel universes that never—he mimes—cross.

Don't have to. We don't have to do any of it. We won't be sitting together for most of it anyway, we can just wave at each other from across the room.

Certainly not. I want to spend the day with you. I want to spend every day with you. We'll just have to plan it out, make it as painless as possible. Do you think this is weird?

What's weird about it?

Does it make you feel like a grown-up?

No, not really. It's just the stuff distracting us from us. It doesn't touch what's within. In here . . .

Your skin's very soft (he kisses it).

I was just getting comfortable.

When Cloud Yabuki-Varma takes off her heart-shaped glasses all manner of items disappear, and when she puts them on they come back, and when she holds them out in front of her nose she can see stuff in the lenses but not around the edges. Spooky. The dinosaurs in Reptile Republic, the instruments in Music Corner, the entirety of Cupcake Garden, the floating mathematical models that can be manipulated to score points: now you see it, now you don't; now you see it, now you don't.

People do look silly in mesh when you are real world. Her classmates interact with invisible beasts, gesticulate at empty space, laugh in unison when nothing funny has happened. Some big trick. Every child is wearing i-specs in various designs like Cloud's, or helmets with visors; these are generally for boys who have not yet learned to avoid real-world walls.

Discovery Play, DP, is a highlight of the week, for it is an opportunity to engage with the more elaborate mesh programs. Pupils are encouraged to experiment with their personas in DP. Other lessons are more restricted—"no pets," for example, not even well-behaved ones. Cloud always brings sim-kitty to DP, and sim-kitty instinctively seeks out other pet simcarnations to play with, currently a penguin, a bunny rabbit, and a piglet.

Cloud and some other girls have been growing giant sunflowers today. It is possible to make them reach twenty feet high if the children select the correct weather systems, the correct food, and sing songs to them. When she peers beneath her glasses her friends remain visible (in somewhat plainer clothing), while the magnificent sunflowers disappear altogether.

Feels *funny*.

She is not getting the headache adults threaten children with when they treat their i-specs like toys—rather, something has struck her as out of place, like when you put the wrong shoes on the wrong feet, though she does not know *precisely* what, and did not notice it until *absolutely* this very second ago. Everything seems normal . . .

There is another girl, the new girl, by herself kicking randomly at the ground. Nothing strange about that. The new girl is nice enough; earlier, she and Cloud shared a glue pot when they were tasked to build a bridge out of tubes, but the girl was shy and spoke little. Maribel is her name. Maribel has a mass of fair curls falling about her shoulders, the exact opposite of Cloud's hair, which is fine, dark, short, and straight.

As brilliant as a detective, Cloud spots what is unusual about her and is intrigued enough to suspend her sunflower game, although hers is second-tallest already. Maribel is the only child not wearing i-specs.

Do you wear i-ris like an adult? (No need for preamble, just ask outright.) You were wearing specs earlier, I saw you.

Maribel pouts, hangs her head, shakes it briefly.

Are yours broke? Does Teacher know?

No, they're fine. It's just . . . Maribel's voice trails off.

If they're not broke, why aren't you wearing 'em?

Maribel turns resolute. I just don't like being in mesh all the time. It's very boring, you know.

Cloud has never come across anyone her own age who thought

being in mesh was boring; on the contrary, children love being in mesh. You reckon? That's a pity. I think it's terrific. We're playing a good program at the moment, growing flowers like *Jack and the Beanstalk.* They're massive. Plus, I have a cat in mesh so I like DP because I get to play with her. (She checks: sim-kitty is crouched by the sim-penguin sniffing at it skeptically.) I love animals. I want to be a vet when I grow up. What do you want to be?

Maribel frowns at Cloud suspiciously.

Cloud sighs the way she does when a jar will not open. You must want to be something? At least have an idea? Don't tell me you never thought about it before.

I've thought about it, I just don't like telling people, that's all, because I don't like being made fun of.

I won't make fun of you, cross my heart I won't.

Heard that before. People say they won't laugh, then they do. It's upsetting.

Who likes to laugh at you?

Mean kids.

Cloud Yabuki-Varma, not a child who has had much experience of unpopularity or being the object of a joke, perseveres: If I make fun of you, you can make fun of me. You can say I would be a rubbish vet, that I would give cat medicine to a dog and I would mistake an iguana for a guinea pig.

Maribel thaws—it sounds like a fair swap—mumbles, I want to break world records.

Cloud opens her mouth, the image of amazement. This timid and rather sullen schoolgirl does not come across as an adventurer. What sorts of records?

Sailing records. Going around the world in the shortest time. Crossing oceans and winning races. That sort of thing. We've got a sailing boat, you see. Boats are friendly.

I never heard of a friendly boat before. What makes 'em friendly?

You wouldn't understand.

I might! Try me.

Oh, just that they do whatever you tell them, and they're reliable, and they can be peaceful, or you can get everything right and then they take you really fast over the water. And they have their own names and feelings.

What's yours called?

Cormorant.

Fancy! I never did meet someone who knew so much about boats. Do people get paid for it? For breaking world records?

Maribel replies uncertainly, Some do.

Cloud is thoroughly impressed. I can't think why anyone would want to be mean about that, it sounds wonderful to me. You'll be famous.

Maribel graces Cloud with her first smile of the day.

Cloud is determined to maximize her good work. Do you like our school?

It's okay.

Do you miss your old one?

Not very, because—Maribel reddens—I never had a best friend there, so no one minded when I left.

I prefer good friends to best friends. Best friends can let you down but good friends are always good to you, no matter what, and you can have loads.

I didn't have many good friends, either.

That is a shame. People are nicer here, you just have to get to know them.

Maribel withdraws again.

Hey, why don't you come over and grow flowers, it's really fun.

No thanks.

Go on. It's not boring, I think you'll like it when you've had a go. You can make it rain on them and they *bong*. Cloud jumps and throws her arms open in a circle.

No, I shouldn't.

Why not? Why don't you want to, Maribel?

Thing is, I'm not allowed.

Course you are, everyone is.

I'm not. Mum says.

At last, Cloud understands. She has heard of parents who limit their children's time in mesh, or forbid it completely. Cloud's father has been known to take the mesh away for several days, as punishment, when she is very naughty. Evidently Maribel's mother only permits it when necessary for lessons. When Cloud asks Maribel what she does for DP, Maribel has no answer, and without thinking about it, Cloud folds up her i-specs and pockets them. She plunges back into their conversation because there is no point in messing around. You know, I think my mummy is famous, but she never broke a world record that I know of.

You *think* she is? Aren't you sure?

Cloud will not admit it outright. Dad says she is.

What is she famous for?

Well . . . Cloud hesitates, then says limply: She built something.

What did she build? A bridge, like we did today? Or a skyscraper?

No, nothing like that, because it's mesh, but people think it's quite good. It's a machine of a lady.

What does it do?

That's the question! What do it do? Cloud flattens her hands in a gesture of exaggerated ignorance. I dunno! She's away, anyway, because she's got to work on it—you know, she's got to.

Have you seen it?

Loads of times. She let me try it once, just for a teeny bit. Only adults can use it, you see.

Maribel raises her eyebrows, her turn to be impressed. What happened? Did it hurt?

Cloud twists her mouth while she thinks how to describe it. No, it doesn't hurt much. (Truthfully it did not hurt in the slightest, but somehow it is expected that Cloud should appear heroic for having had a go with Mummy's invention.) Well, the lady moves, you see, and then looks in her book and then you can see stuff. But it isn't exactly like the mesh, although it *is* like it. And I saw . . . a girl, an orphan who was very nice and pretty and lived in olden times, except I think she was sad about something. And she had to do a sort of modeling job.

Maribel replies it sounds good, though it doesn't really, she just wants to make a friend out of Cloud. What does your dad do?

He's a shrink.

What's a shrink, then?

Cloud repeats her emphatic gesture. I dunno, but he isn't very good because he has to practice every day.

Maribel sniffs and wipes her nose with her sleeve. Um, what shall we do now?

Cloud suggests they make up their own game for DP, one that involves Maribel showing her how to sail a pretend boat and Cloud showing Maribel how to perform lifesaving operations on pretend mice, using extremely small pretend surgical knives.

Director Fernand's violet i-ris twinkle. He is the kind of man who does not make many changes to his mesh appearance. His skin tone is accurate though more even so, his jaw only slightly improved. His real-world clothes are bespoke, so he can afford to let them show through. The room is filled with experts, dignitaries, celebrities from the international community. Some to see and some to be seen. A disorientating array of body shapes, manipulated facial features, and fashion statements. A supermodel, a superhero, a hypnotist, an invisible man. Decorated masks, skin adornment, hairstyles like architecture. A woman holds a baby dragon in her arms. A minotaur sips espresso. A vampire converses with a 1940s film star; they conclude their point about monetary policy as the speaker raises his hand and the applause dies down.

Colleagues, guests, representatives of the press, welcome to the European Museum of Art. I must start by thanking you for being patient because the journey behind us has indeed been long, and there is a long way left to go. I am extremely grateful that you are here to share this special event with us, in person, in mesh or on-screen, and I promise you will remember today because what you will see is truly extraordinary. This is a unique project, one of a kind. We hope to inform you, we hope to enthrall you, and we look forward to exploring the future *and the past* together with you, our partners and friends. I will not keep you waiting any longer, so please join me in welcoming the head of the Sibil project, and its creator, Sincerity Yabuki.

There is a stronger surge of applause as people scan the hall to see who Sincerity Yabuki is. The fabrics of several garments flux into new designs, colors running like liquid. A lady with green hair and fairy wings flutters these expectantly. A snake necklace worn by another guest comes to life, slithers down its owner's torso, rearranges itself as a belt. The clapping stretches out artificially for several seconds until, finally, a woman who is slim and conservative in persona appears on the stage, smiles, waves shyly, her gold i-ris sparkling, shakes hands with Director Fernand, who, acting the part of gracious host, invites her to sit with him.

Sincerity, you and I have known each other for some time now. I have said it before but I would like to say it again, publicly, that the Sibil is a remarkable achievement, and this museum is the envy of galleries and spaces around the world because you have made your home here with us.

Sincerity speaks steadily, taking a breath at each pause: You are being kind, Fernand. It is a great honor for me to work in this beautiful and prestigious building, which so captured my imagination when I was a little girl even before I saw it in mesh. It gives me deep satisfaction that my project will continue to be hosted by the European Museum, and that the museum will be a guardian of its development. Sibil will be the catalyst for a new era in the study of art. Through Sibil, we will rediscover aspects of our culture, and nature, that progress has made us forget. What better place for her to be than here?

More avatars appear in the gallery, some in formal eveningwear. Take us back to the beginning. How did it all start?

Sincerity tilts her head as though remembering what happened a lifetime ago. I was an undergraduate. I was a young engineer experimenting with mesh programming, to see what it could do and what its limitations were. The mesh is data—vast, complex, magnificent, vibrating, infinite data—that we have put there. We fill it with our knowledge and numbers and theories, our visuals, our music, and our beliefs. The problem is one of orderliness: organizing it, searching it, teasing out what is relevant. And being in mesh as frequently as we are now, we have become liable to synchronistic accidents, open to little acts of serendipity. So it was when I came across a premesh photo of a young woman in a bar, made by an amateur artist. In many ways it was not an unusual image, except that I was rather taken with it, with the product of the union between these two people, artist and sitter. What I wanted, back then, was to know and to experience this particular artwork—or any artwork that touched me, for that matter, be it a painting, sculpture, or photograph. I think it is important to emphasize that I wanted to know about it, really to understand it, on an aesthetic level and on a human level;

in a sense, to get close to it. Who was this person? Why was she in the bar? Where was this location? What turn of events brought her there? How did she know the photographer? Were they strangers, or were they intimate? That was my objective, but also a lot of my work around this time was unconscious, I suppose. As I said, I was experimenting and had nothing to lose. So on the one hand we have a work of art, an object of great beauty and curiosity, a historical artifact with a story to tell; on the other hand we have chaotic data, all the resources and capabilities in mesh . . . (there is a blip: Sincerity's voice sinks to nothing, her persona wobbles, then the link is restored) . . . the information is already there, captured in the image; the picture, the object d'art, has the potential to tell us everything about it, we just need to unlock it.

You were trying out different mesh programming?

Yes, different coding, various mathematical equations. Some of it was ordinary and familiar, some of it was guesswork, or following my intuition. I had a few hunches, did many trials. Of course, nearly all were unsuccessful, though some turned up interesting results, interesting enough for me to carry on.

Did you have an expectation of what a working prototype might be like? Were you aiming for a particular format?

Oh yes. I had this old photograph, and what I expected to make from it was a profile, a collection of facts and dates and names about the picture; or alternatively, perhaps a referencing system that would point you to potential research pathways, something you would pick up and explore manually, following your areas of interest. I was aiming for something fairly low-tech.

And what did you actually find? What did you *see* and what did you *hear*?

Sincerity Yabuki pauses. She closes her eyes and opens them again before she answers, gold invisible, then returning. There were people and voices. There were environments and events. The photo came to life, as it were; it started to reveal its story—*a* story, at any rate. The history of the picture was shown to me as if it had always been there, waiting to be discovered. It appeared in fragments and glimpses, at first. There were echoes of conversations between these people, hints as to their relationships and tribulations. It was like I was alone in a theater, and the ghosts were putting on a play just for me.

Sibil makes mesh content?

In a manner of speaking.

Without the need for writers or engineers or anyone to input any mesh coding?

Sibil makes you experience, in mesh, real or fictionalized aspects of what is already there embedded within a real-world object. The artwork is the starting point; from that, it weaves an extended portrait of sorts, showing us this art piece in a new way.

Fernand brings a finger over his smile. It sounds incredible when you say it.

It is.

Is it a tool or a toy?

You mean, can we rely on what Sibil shows us as being factual material, or is it just for entertainment? (Sincerity shrugs emphatically.)

Fernand laughs and turns to the delegates. Sincerity is being coy because she and I have had several fraught conversations about this, haven't we?

Some of it is factual and can be verified.

Some of it is blatant fabrication.

We can't be entirely sure what we are seeing, can we, Fernand?

No, we can't. But whether it's true or false, people might still argue that this is impossible: original mesh content does not just appear out of thin air.

I have never said it was original content; it is *organized* content.

These audiovisual narrative portraits experienced by Sibil-users are elicited from information cues present within the artwork, combined with data in mesh, which is, in effect, infinite.

How is it done? Sorcery?

No magic, I'm afraid, Fernand, just plain old mathematics and programming.

In a potent cocktail. I should explain to the audience that I have personal experience of the Sibil, and it was sublime and startling.

And I should explain that the director is literally paid to say that! (This admission is rewarded with polite laughter.)

There is an additional component, isn't there?

Yes. The final element is the users themselves, because what we have found is that each person experiences something specific and unique to them. Sometimes the differences between cases are subtle, and key aspects stay generally the same; whereas sometimes the whole environment or story changes, warping into another form altogether. There is a shift in tone or emphasis. How much is revealed alters from user to user: they might witness just a single moment out of many hundreds; or a whole event might spin out before them into a completely new direction, contradicting what has come before. It is as if the individual brings something of their own to Sibil, a personal interpretation, as though Sibil is responding to their sensibilities and collaborating with them. It's like when a reader of a book imagines the characters in their own way, or the viewer of a painting has a personal aesthetic response to it. We don't understand this phenomenon yet, but we will.

Part of the work of your research team is to record these "immersions" . . . ?

Yes. We tend to call them sensory immersions, rather than sim, or VR, to differentiate what is spontaneous from what has intentionally been made by design. We do not build these mesh events;

they manifest independently. I wish to make it clear that there has been no creative input by anyone on my team. In fact, we have no control over what Sibil shows us. We just observe it and try to piece it together.

I think, Sincerity, some reports have misrepresented that.

I agree. This is a new technology, so perhaps there has been confusion.

And the full acronym is . . . ?

Sensory Immersion Bioscript Interface Locus, affectionately known as Sibil.

So you select a photograph or a painting, and through Sibil someone can experience in mesh the story buried within it?

Sincerity smiles, her i-ris bright; no one would notice how her hands have twisted together in her lap.

He adds, Why don't you tell everyone the bad news?

The bad news is that currently the program only works on six preselected images.

Only six out of thousands upon thousands?

I'm afraid so. The earliest is fourteenth century. The most recent is twenty-first century.

Do these six pictures have anything in common with one another?

No, not really. (Avatars in historical costumes have begun to materialize.)

Well, they have *something* in common, wouldn't you say so, Sincerity?

Yes, all right then . . . they are all representations in one way or another of the literate female.

Fernand rephrases for clarity: Of a woman or a girl reading a book?

Yes. But they are not connected to one another in any meaningful way, as far as we can tell.

Did you have any particular reasons for choosing those portraits?

They were selected quite at random. We are experimenting with others, and in due course more will be added so users will be offered a larger choice. That is the goal.

How is it going, this process of adding images to the Sibil portfolio?

Um. We are working on it at the moment.

Director Fernand links his fingers as though this is all fascinating, even though his involvement with the project has been over several years. I have not asked the obvious question yet: *why?*

Why did I do it?

Why dedicate your life to this bizarre creation?

Definitely not for the attention. (Sincerity Yabuki pauses to sip pink liquid from a glass.) Let's say, I did it for beauty. I did it because we humans intuit that beautiful objects can tell stories. We believe they have power. It is why we cherish things, because of the way they move us. They have voices and would speak to us. They are imprinted with the past.

And your invention *makes art talk?*

She helps us to be better listeners. And I think it was only a matter of time: if I hadn't invented Sibil, someone else would have. We have not yet discovered her full potential—she has so much more left to give.

Spoken like a proud parent.

It is not the way it used to be, Director Fernand. We cannot now walk into an art gallery and encounter for ourselves an original masterpiece like previous generations did. It is true that in mesh we have instant access to detailed reproductions of practically all art objects held in trust by governments, and many more besides from private collections. But the result of protecting these works for posterity is that they have been lost to most of us. I wonder whether we are not the poorer for it. Have we become the prisoners in the cave?

In that sense Sibil is, in perpetuity, inferior to her objective, because we are still removed from the work itself, and moving ever farther away from it, deeper into shadows.

Director Fernand's next question is drowned out by a smatter of clapping, which builds in momentum into full-scale applause. More people appear in mesh, and there is a spike in on-screen viewers. Fernand allows the excitement to run on, his eye on the audience figures displayed in the corner of his vision. As the rumble dies into anticipating silence, he announces it is time to unveil the Sibil. He leads Sincerity Yabuki, hesitant until Fernand places his hand at her back, away from the platform. The houselights are dimmed.

A dot hovers in midair, which widens into a gash cut through space, and out of it flows a black curtain that forms an enclosed cube, tastefully done. The material looks authentic, quivering from its own momentum and a faint draft. The curtain opens itself.

Sibil is white. Not Caucasian but *white*: as sheet ice as new paper as porcelain, from her braids to her bare feet. Not a blemish, not a variation, every feature of her—hair, skin, pupilless eyes—smooth like the inside of a shell, dazzling like a torch, as though carved from a single radiant white stone. Likewise her ornaments—her beads and star pendant, diadem, hoop earrings, the pedestal she rests on—are made of the same ghostly matter. She clasps in her casual hand blank pages, a skinny book with its cover torn off. She appears at first glance to be wearing a gown, the folds of her skirt enveloping the forms of her legs, one crossed over the other, but this is only the effect of the seamless block of whiteness; she is naked from the waist up. She sits, chin cupped in hand, elbow on knee, awaiting instruction.

The audience show their appreciation with more applause and cheers; rainbows thread themselves like ribbons around the room, rose petals fall like snow, writing appears across the ceiling offering congratulations in several languages, birds butterflies bunches of flowers burst into colorful movement, their lives decorative and brief. It is the mesh community's way of conveying support and encouragement.

Sincerity Yabuki does not enjoy the moment. There must be only several dozen people actually present in the hall with her; the rest are avatars. Why exactly should she share Sibil with them? It is tempting to drop out mesh—just *pop* and gone, right now—she worries the pearl processor shimmering on her ring finger. Spirit herself away, and let them think whatever they want.

She does the mental exercises Dinesh taught her.

Better now.

The swell of noise rises reverently, then it dips, then dies. The scattering and flying and unfurling salutations have settled and are at rest; cease and disintegrate.

Sibil moves barely, for she does breathe, does blink. Like a statue and not a statue, less realistic and more convincing than regular simcarnations. Sincerity Yabuki knows what is happening, has witnessed it many times. The audience are unsure precisely what they are seeing, for Sibil seems neither of mesh nor of real world. As though she comes from a third, inexplicable place.

There are disturbances of people in the crowd touching their processor lapel pins, bracelets, torques, ear cuffs—a few avatars start dropping out, but many remain. Intrigued. Bewitched. Exchanged glances lose their impact in mesh, but a few attempt it. This rarely happens anymore, the arrival of a technology that is unfathomable.

Director Fernand rocks on his heels. I am afraid Sibil does not speak. For reasons not yet fully understood, a language application has never operated successfully. Each previous attempt has set the research team back around two weeks to make repairs. Why don't we take a few questions before we continue?

Sincerity digs her nails into her palms. Her work is too good for them.

Later someone writes on their journal, *It looked like it was thinking*.

It was a triumph. Don't you think so, Sincerity?

I thought you were going to jump in at one point.

When?

You know when.

Ah, you refer to the "original masterpieces" patter. I have heard it before.

Concerns are genuine, Fernand, and justified. No one really knows what has happened to our treasures. Whether they have been sold in secret auctions, whether they have been irreparably damaged through ignorance or malicious intent, whether they are being used as bribes for corrupt officials, criminals, and despots.

Fernand laughs. I am sorry your suffering is so great. How terrible for you that you must carry these worries everywhere. But of course there *are* people who know these answers. And I can personally assure you, as one of the "despised" heritage custodians, such travesties could never occur. Protection means protection. It is not ideal, but it is by far the best system we have at present. Who knows? One day it may again revert back to the way it was. Then anyone who wants to will be able to molest the Venus de Milo.

Where is the accountability? That's what people want.

You think that secrecy means there is no accountability? You think I don't have to obtain three signatures from the board in order to shave each morning? You should see the rigmarole they put me through whenever I choose a tie.

Sincerity has liked Fernand since the day they met, likes his relaxed nature. Aren't you angry with me?

Why should I be? You have earned your right to say what you

think. You are an artist. You should be encouraged to express yourself. I have no wish to censor you.

I am not really an artist, Fernand, I'm only an engineer.

I say that you are an artist, and the museum is lucky to have you. I have told you before, I will stand by you. I shall always be your advocate to the board, should you need one.

You are kind.

No, I am selfishly motivated. This is what I am in it for—these discoveries, to be at the center of the cyclone. Do you understand?

I haven't got you into trouble, then?

Don't dwell on it anymore. Enjoy your success.

Sincerity makes a smile. In mesh it looks genuine.

How is that little girl of yours?

She is fine, thank you. She wanted to come, but she had school. I told her she could watch on-screen afterward.

This is a big day for her too, seeing you out there—

Yes, in a way I suppose it is.

I did not see Dinesh, though; I meant to say hello to him.

He had patients, and it wouldn't have been fair to them on such short notice—

Fernand nods sympathetically. Both of you are so busy. Sometimes I don't know how you manage.

She does not answer that.

You're tired, Sincerity. I can hear it in your voice. Will you take the day off tomorrow?

Sincerity starts to object.

Fernand persists. If there is anything urgent, he will call her: It has been hectic recently, you will work better if you are refreshed, if you have given to your family the attention they are deprived of. Please, I beg you, take the day off?

She detects implied criticism, folds her arms against it, then marvels at her own negativity. Perhaps Fernand is right; she is just too tired.

Cloud nudges her sashimi with her chopsticks. A miniature white and red koi trembles into life, turns its head and flicks its tail, floats off her plate and into the air, swims about above their table as though in a real pond. Cloud watches it, then prods her nigiri next—a bright yellow fish soars from her plate and at once makes a beautiful arc around the first, as she hoped it would. The fish intermingle, gracefully dancing together. Now if only she can get her dad to do the same to his, then they will have maybe five or six fish up there, and that will be lovely. But he is eating his maki rolls already—

Dad, you haven't made any of your fish swim.

Dinesh Varma pauses midmouthful and looks up to where Cloud is pointing. Oh, sorry. He taps one of the sim-fish in front of him, a creature patterned in white and black, but it stays obstinately still.

You're doing it wrong.

You do it for me then. He pushes his bowl nearer to his daughter.

Cloud grins through her i-specs and touches the fish with the tips of her own chopsticks. As before, the fish twitches to life and scoots up to swim in circles with its friends. Throughout the restaurant, aquatic creatures are floating diving soaring—the waiters, made to look like mermaids and mermen, levitate above the floor, their feet only just visible if you look closely, tails streaming behind.

He comments drily, I remember when dinner and theater were separate. Your food didn't look at you in the way it does now.

Cloud tuts. They aren't *real,* Dad.

Aren't they? Mummy's real.

Sincerity's avatar breaks into a smile.

Dinesh leans over. *Are* you real?

Cloud chides him: Of course she's real.

Good, because if my fish doesn't come back, I can eat Mummy instead.

Cloud finds this hysterical. You can't eat Mummy!

I don't see why not, if my sushi has run off. Dinesh bunches his fist at the sim-fish: Hey, you lot! I paid for you. Come back, or I will be forced to eat somebody. Perhaps Cloud as a starter, and Sincerity for a main course.

More giggles from Cloud.

Mm, sounds delicious.

Sincerity puts up her hands plaintively: Please don't eat me, I don't taste very nice. (But it sounds forced, even to herself; she is no good at these jokes.)

Cloud exclaims, I'm not a starter!

No? Dinesh feigns thinking. I'll have you for dessert then, because you're so sweet.

He pops a kiss on his daughter's cheek and she wipes it off with the back of her hand. Cloud has just begun a new phase where she dislikes public displays of affection, and is still in a previous one of using long words she does not completely understand. Both of these now come to the fore: Honestly, Dad, you're so *extravagant*.

Dinesh and Sincerity make eye contact through mesh. They share their first moment of perfect unspoken unison in days while Cloud prods the rest of the fish into simmy-swimmy motion. He says, You were brilliant.

You were watching? I didn't see you.

Only on-screen between appointments. I didn't want to be pinging in and out while you were talking, I was worried it might distract you. I was with you, though.

Thanks.

I was.

I believe you.

They fall into mutual silence. Dinesh eats another roll, though it occurs to him this might make one of the fish disappear.

What is it like? Does it taste good? (Sincerity always asks when Dinesh and Cloud are eating a meal, always wants to know.)

He shrugs. Not the best ever. Not like the time we made it ourselves.

We didn't make it properly.

What are you talking about? That was the best sushi I've ever had.

Sincerity repeats herself: We didn't make it properly, and we made a big mess in the kitchen.

I liked it, the sushi, and the mess, come to that. I liked it because it was ours. Our sushi. Our mess.

Well, I didn't like the mess, and I didn't think the sushi was that special.

Then we should have kept on trying, shouldn't we? We should have made it every week until we got it right.

Their conversation pauses again.

Dinesh decides to leave this topic and try something else. I had another mail from Astrid today. She asked after you and sends her love. I sent her some pics of Cloud.

What did you do that for?

She wanted to see them, I guess, see how our baby's grown.

She never mails me.

Perhaps she thinks you're too busy.

And she thinks you're not? Why doesn't she contact both of us together? That's what I wonder.

Dinesh sits back in his chair.

Sincerity elaborates: I'm just saying that she was my housemate too, and, you know . . .

What?

Well . . . she was my friend first. (Pathetic.)

Dinesh speaks acerbically: If it means that much to you, why don't you mail her yourself? I can give you her new address.

Sincerity will do no such thing, but she doesn't want to be the villain, either. So? How is Astrid, then?

Very divorced.

Stung. Sincerity knew it, she fucking well knew it, but if she says anything now, she will sound paranoid (even though she's probably right). She fiddles with the pearl on her finger—it would be disastrous to drop out mesh now—it will hang over them, make it worse.

Cloud exclaims, Look!

One of the fish has swum down by Cloud's chair, where sim-kitty was dozing. The kitty is now wide awake and interacting with the flying fish, head turning to and fro as the fish sails past her, tries to bat it with her paw when it gets close enough, lunges for it.

Look, she's trying to catch the fishy. I'll help her. Cloud makes a giggling grab for the fish, but of course her hands only close around thin air and pass through the simcarnations, ruining the illusion.

Can you just stop that, please? (It is Cloud's mother using her grown-uppy voice.) You can't touch things in mesh, you might spill or break something that is real world.

Cloud knows this already but still makes a halfhearted reach for the fish in case this time is different.

Dinesh prevents it firmly. He tells Cloud to listen to her mother, threatens not to take Cloud to nice places anymore if she is naughty.

Cloud sulks.

Sincerity wishes she could sulk too; instead, asks about his work.

Dinesh shrugs. He normally has a piece of news to share, a patient with an unusual problem, something he's read in a journal.

She presses gently: Is anything the matter?

No, nothing. Work is fine.

Doesn't sound fine.

I am having a slump, that's all.

Making too many people better, are you?

No, not that. It's complicated. It's been going on for a while.

You haven't said anything. How can I help?

You can't. Thank you.

Tell me about it, at least?

Dinesh glances briefly at Cloud. Best not to. It would take too long, anyway. We'll talk about it later, when you come home.

Later. Sincerity and Dinesh should keep a list of all the conversations they will have later. She says, I do believe you.

About what?

That you were thinking about me. I was thinking about you, when I was speaking in front of all those scary people.

Well, you were fantastic. I was so proud of you. We both were.

Sincerity's pleasure does not show through her avatar. She prompts, Did you hear the part about art protectionism?

Yes, Plato's cave, very clever.

You did hear it, then? I put that in for you.

For me?

Well, for us. I wanted to show I'm independent.

Dinesh nods.

I thought you would be pleased.

I am pleased.

Sincerity scrutinizes him. You don't sound it. You sound singularly unimpressed.

Dinesh Varma rests his chopsticks beside his dish. I don't think it actually matters.

What doesn't matter? It's all we talked about when we were at university.

Yes.

Not *all* we talked about, but we believed in it. I believed in it.

Yes, I know you did.

She hesitates, then presses on. We were never going to have jobs in mesh, were we? We were going to live as much in real world as we could, out of principle. We were going to help save real paintings and real books—track them down, keep them safe for our children and our grandchildren, because hard formats are the only ones that survive in the long run. You published about it. Your position was that diplomacy had suffered a mortal blow, that hostile governments can at least communicate through cultural objects. That from shared beauty and appreciation of history, trust can grow and peace can be fostered. Dinesh, you said the mesh was ultimately unreliable and unsustainable as a resource. *You* convinced *me* we're too reliant on it, and that one day terrorists will undermine it and swaths of literature and art and music and knowledge will be wiped out—gone—lost forever, and with no way of retrieving them. You said—

I know what I said.

—untold damage has been inflicted upon the mental and emotional health of society, and who knows what the long-term effects will be to people of Cloud's generation who cannot remember a time when the art in museums was real? *We have impoverished ourselves beyond reckoning.* Those were your words.

I don't disagree.

Then I don't get it. I've done something about it. I stood up there and risked everything to say what we believe in, to keep it alive.

No, you didn't, Sissy. No. You didn't. You are a mouthpiece of the museum.

I am not a mouthpiece of the—

Please can we stop?

You just called me—

They want you to say those things, they *want* you to, because you are brilliant and they have you in their pocket, so it doesn't matter. It makes them look edgy to have their darling talking like a rebel, but nothing will really happen; nothing will change. You didn't *do* anything.

Cloud watches both her parents withdraw into amazed silence.

Her mother whispers, I thought I did something good.

Her father relents. Of course. You tried to.

Well . . . Sincerity's tone is not accusing anymore but genuinely bewildered. What have *you* done?

Nothing. I haven't done a single bloody thing.

Cloud turns her mouth into a comma. There's a girl at my school who's never in mesh. Her parents don't let her, unless she absolutely has to for lessons.

Sincerity makes an effort to show interest. Really? Is she nice?

Yes. She's called Maribel and she's my friend. Sometimes I take my specs off so we can play together.

That's kind of you.

To demonstrate her ability to be kind, Cloud lifts her i-specs onto her forehead, revealing eyes scrunched into a big grin. She glances around the real-world restaurant, which is dull in comparison. Most of the moving fish and a number of avatar customers disappear, including her mother. She can also see real-world people beneath their mesh skins: a strapping man in leathers, zippers, and cobwebs turns out to be bald, round, and middle-aged in life. Cloud raises and lowers her glasses several times, fat man muscle man fat man muscle man fat man muscle man.

Cloud hears her mother's voice: If you keep doing that, you'll give yourself a headache.

Mesh mummy no mummy mesh mummy no mummy mesh mummy—it's spooky. Cloud looks down at sim-kitty and makes

her disappear reappear once. Dad, when can I have a real-world kitty?

Dinesh sighs. You won't like it.

I will like it, Dad, I will.

Real animals need a lot of looking after.

Da-ad. Please?

Sincerity Yabuki gets a familiar ache. Anything to do with real world and Cloud's default is to ask her father about it. Dad is the tangible parent, Mum is the insubstantial one. She intercedes: Why exactly do you want a real cat, Cloudy?

Because it's nicer. Because they're cuddly and warm. When they purr it travels in your body.

You know real animals get sick, don't you?

I know. When I'm a vet I'll make her better myself.

And you know real animals don't last forever?

Cloud frowns. Yes. (She does know.)

But sim-kitty doesn't get old. And you can take her wherever you like, and no one minds.

The father speaks next: Don't you love sim-kitty anymore? Don't you think she's pretty?

Cloud stares at the simcarnation, feeling like a traitor. Sim-kitty gazes back, is designed to react to attention from her owner, gambols playfully. The child mutters, Why can't I have both? I've thought of a good name already.

Dinesh sighs. Maybe when you're older.

How old, exactly, do I have to be before I'm allowed?

He turns to Sincerity for support, who tilts her head, mulling it over.

She says, I think we should let her have one.

Pardon?

I think she should be allowed a pet if it's what she genuinely wants.

316

Cloud gasps, Oh, really, Mummy?

Sissy, if we are going to discuss this, we should do it properly, in private, and tell our daughter our joint decision afterward so she knows we are united.

She hates it when he does that, when he pulls out some family-therapy technique and applies it to them as a couple—she pretends she did not hear him. Cloud has been asking for a cat for ages, and nothing we have said has put her off. She's older now, she knows her own mind.

Yes, but I'm the one who'll end up looking after it.

Sincerity had braced herself, takes the hit; it hurts her but she does not show it. When I'm home I'll help. In the meantime, we can both make sure Cloud takes her full share of responsibility. And you know what else? She's right. A living cat is infinitely better than a fake one, especially to an only child. I don't want her to be afraid of doing difficult things in real world. Teaching her how to look after a pet is a good idea; that's my opinion.

Cloud knows it will not happen while one parent still refuses. She holds her breath, wishing for her father to agree.

Dinesh is unconvinced. I shall have to think about it . . . and you will have to be an extremely good girl.

How good, exactly, do I have to be before I'm allowed?

As though it can hear them, sim-kitty jumps up onto mesh mummy's lap and arches flirtatiously. Sincerity does not attempt to stroke her in case her hand runs through it and spoils the effect.

Dinesh is composed, attentive.

His patient paces around the office, has yet to remove his i-ris for their sessions, although the only item in the room active in mesh is the patient's own persona. Is this the reason he keeps look-ing down at his shoes? In life, they are a utility style and color, but to their owner they are an accurate replica of a pair once worn by Noël Coward. Then he sighs unevenly.

That bastard was trying to show me up. After taking credit for what I had done, he was trying to humiliate me in front of the whole department, in front of everyone, colleagues who respect me—some of them have known me for ten years. I wanted to tell him I felt betrayed, I wanted to protest, and I didn't because I was flabbergasted—for the first time in my life I knew what the word truly meant. I was so flabbergasted at what he was coming out with I just couldn't speak.

The psychiatrist is sure there is more to come.

The effort I have made, the work I have put in for that company, doesn't matter. I don't matter. They care about results, not who gets crushed in the process. It's malicious. Calculated. They would poison our drinking water if there was a profit to be made and they thought they could get away with it. Leeches.

Why is their recognition important to you?

That is a good question, Dr. Varma. I don't know. They're the ones with the low self-esteem.

What makes you say that?

Because if they had any sense of self-worth, any decency, they wouldn't be the way they are. They're addicted to money, can't get enough of it.

Dinesh resets his expression from attentive to receptive.

Dr. Varma, in your professional opinion, do you think I need validation in the workplace because I didn't get enough love from my father?

Dinesh knows what to do. He counts to ten. Then he replies in a measured tone, Would you like to explore this issue together?

(Like clockwork.)

At home, Dinesh does something he has not done for almost a year: goes into the spare room crammed with cardboard boxes and

318

opens a few of them, peruses the contents. When they moved in, this was set aside as a library, not a guest room. (Our friends can sleep on the futon, Cloud's friends can sleep in her room.) They planned to cover two walls in bookcases, floor to ceiling, to nurture their collection, savor it in special reading chairs. They bought the chairs, but no books have been read in them yet. To reach one, Dinesh has to make space; the boxes have a film of dust on top, which he disturbs into flurries.

Sissy, we are better than other people. We're different.

He whispered it under the sheet after they had made love. He meant it, he meant it. Their love was unusual, extraordinary, corny, they were going to make an eccentric life together. Be true to their teenage selves.

Conventionality crept up on them and then leaped. Dinesh is still reeling from it. They lost the slivers of perfection they once had. No more whole days in bed together, no more flowers given without occasion, no more *Pack a bag we're going to Prague for the weekend . . . to surprise you.*

They live apart. They went from making plans to putting plans on hold to indifference about their future, their neglected ambitions dying quietly like plants. For a while he blamed Sincerity because she was the talented one—she brought this upon them. Simple (synonymous with "easy" and "foolish"). He blames himself now, a much harder and heavier burden. Dr. Dinesh Varma did not fight it. He should have. He let it happen. He should not have. Consequently, this mess.

I wouldn't know us.

Cloud goes to bed without a fuss.

Dad, you know my friend Maribel? Well, she has a picture on her wall of a beach. Painted on it, so it's still there in real world.

A mural?

I think I would like one. If I'm not quite good enough for a cat, could I have one of those, a *mural*, instead, please? Not of a beach, though, that would be copying.

In your room? Which wall would it go on?

Cloud points to the wall opposite, which apart from a desk and floor cushions has few objects obscuring it.

If you had one, what would you like your mural to be of?

In the way of children, Cloud has left some salient details out of her plan. She was so taken with the idea of having a mural and getting parental agreement, choosing the subject had been over-looked. And, in the way of children, she hits upon a favorite theme instantly: Trees with woodland creatures.

Dinesh tucks her in. Should he leave her door ajar in case she has a nightmare? (His nightmare is that Sincerity will soon realize leaving them is now only a matter of degrees.)

No, not anymore.

If you're sure. *Shh-leep*—

Cloud echoes, *Shh-leep.*

Another mail from Astrid. Seeing her name in his inbox gives Dinesh the sensation of swallowing neat bourbon.

Sincerity Yabuki's avatar stands at the end of the bed, a phantasm. In daylight, avatars blend convincingly into their environment, while in darkness they give off a lurid glow. Commercial and public buildings balance this with artificial lights, but in private dwellings you usually put up with an intrusive and sickly glare.

Dinesh lies with his hands behind his head. They maintain the tradition of saying good night to each other, but the sex games they used to play to keep the relationship passionate have long since faded. He stares at her in a way he would never do if she were actu-ally here.

Sincerity's projected face is hard. You can't expect me to stand by a promise I made two years ago, not when so much has happened, *is* happening.

Almost three years ago.

We are at a delicate juncture, the next few months are crucial. You surely see that?

I do.

We talked about this together. We agreed that if I had to stay on to finish what I started . . . don't you remember?

Yes, I remember. In exceptional circumstances—

Then what is there to fight about?

The trouble is, exceptional circumstances come along with monotonous regularity.

This is my life's work.

No. It isn't.

Oh, stop it, Dinesh. Does it hurt your ego so much you have to resort to clichés?

No. It doesn't. Seeing what you have achieved makes me immensely proud of you. If you don't know that by now . . . I merely meant that your research team, if you decided to leave, would get on just fine without you.

Rubbish.

I'm not suggesting you completely give up what you care about, but working in a more advisory capacity might be good for you, give you an opportunity to try something new for a while. I am thinking of your well-being as much as anyone's. I wasn't trying to make you feel guilty.

Do you think my child is my legacy? Cloud is not me.

I know that. Sissy, I'm losing track.

Of what?

Dinesh fumbles with the unfinished thought.

Sincerity musters, Are you having problems with her? Is she all right?

She's perfect. She wants a mural in her bedroom.

Right. Sounds interesting. You'll both have fun with that. Actually, I ought to tell you more often that you are a splendid father.

Thanks. (He is grateful, but his reaction is too faint to be conveyed over the distance.) You sound quite tired.

I'm nearly done.

Did you eat?

Yes.

Dinesh can tell she is lying, wishes he could make her some shio ramen.

She says, We should talk about this later.

He says, I think that's an excellent idea.

I'm sorry for snapping at you.

I know you are. What have you got in the morning?

Oh—Sincerity's avatar ruffles her hair—the usual. Budget meeting, a report to write, catch up on some mail, and if I have time, I'll look at my data. What about you?

Nothing special. I thought I would get a sitter in, go out for a drink after work for a few hours.

Yes, you should do that.

I will. Sincerity?

Yes, Dinesh?

You don't need me anymore.

The ghost at the end of the bed shivers—once, a glitch—then the connection strengthens. No, I don't.

No. I thought not. I was just making sure.

Good night, Dinesh.

Yes.

Sincerity drops out mesh and the room goes dark. Dinesh turns on his side, does not remove his i-ris or draw the blinds. I wish I could smell you, Sissy, I wish I could wrap myself around you to keep you warm.

* * *

Sibil shines like a jinn. Luminescence, purity. Sincerity Yabuki has finished for the night, takes a stroll around the deserted galleries where the paintings hang in midair. Her installation is here too.

In the European Museum of Art one can view a Rembrandt from the back as well as the front; one can lift the layers of a Titian effortlessly to uncover the genius clumsy restoration has hidden; one can grow a Gwen John until precision flecks on the canvas become unwieldy ridges and fissures. One can crawl over these pictures like a beetle, strip them bare, split them apart.

Time alone with Sibil is rare and brief. Usually visitors stream past the glass partition while Sincerity is doing maintenance or running tests with one of her subordinates. This solitude is the way it used to be when she was younger, when it started, when she was seduced by its complexity and elegance.

Sibil's appearance is a rudimentary simcarnation based on a design from archives (Sincerity responded to a mail), *I chose it for its simplicity*—followed by firm assertions about retaining creative control.

In fact, Sibil selected her own appearance. Lying about it is unpleasant but necessary, and the engineer takes comfort in the certainty no one would believe her anyway.

I did not invent Sibil. I am not an inventor in the conventional sense. I have shown what has always existed, what lay waiting to be discovered like a prime number. Send.

Her reply is construed as modesty. Whenever Sincerity Yabuki explains that Sibil was revealed, rather than created, that Sibil's true realm is accessible by the mind, people think she is speaking figuratively. Observe, even if she tries to be honest, she is not listened to.

I would be delighted to give a demonstration to your faculty, please liaise with my assistant to arrange it.

There have been times, lonely times, when Sincerity has permitted herself a thought experiment—a strange and absurd thought experiment that she would never share with anyone. It is far-fetched, ludicrous. But in this private moment with her work, it creeps back, a sinister idea waiting to see daylight or be put out of its misery. Hypothetically, what if Sincerity Yabuki was chosen? Hypothetically, what if Sibil chose her?

Earlier, Fernand squeezed her elbow, a gesture he has adopted recently, spoke confidentially. I hope you will be pleased, Sincerity. It took more wrangling than I anticipated, but I have finally negotiated you access to the vault.

What vault?

Don't be silly, our vault.

Sincerity gazes with love at her masterpiece and is ashamed of herself, a lady of science, for contemplating it. It is a sign of stress, surely, entertaining these irrational thoughts, these delusions of grandeur. Of an unstable mind.

Fernand enjoyed her astonishment, that he was able to bestow on her what she could not have obtained by herself. I think perhaps they fear losing you to a rival institution. I said we would be the last to know if you were being courted by a foreign government. The board wants to give you every resource to develop your work further. Obviously, they want you only to include pieces from the European Collection! If you can view the originals, it will inform your choices of the most suitable, the best. (She did not disabuse him, but her team has had difficulties—big problems—adding pieces, as though Sibil will not accept any more.) I said that my directorship was about this, about revolution in art, new ways to experience it post-protectionism. I explained I can only remain director as long as you, and your team of course, are with us, under our jurisdiction, being nurtured and encouraged here.

You threatened to leave?

I imply a bit. To lean on them.

Sibil does not return her stare, never acknowledges the presence of anybody unless instructed to. She sits and sits and sits. A blank. That Sibil might have some kind of *consciousness*. That Sibil is some kind of *being*. That Sincerity Yabuki has some special quality, or place in the world, which has led to a *meeting* between them. Outrageous.

She said, That was generous, Fernand, but you shouldn't have risked your own position. He said, A trifle, do not think on it. She said, Won't they resent you? He answered in a musical note, No-o.

Is it possible we have opened a window into the world of archetypes? Delete.

The media chatter has begun to bother her. Pressure, unending speculation: What is the next phase? What is the three-year plan? The ten-year plan? When will you announce S2?

I put it to you that Sibil is like a thread connecting different points across centuries. She is the zeitgeist, literally "time ghost," or more accurately "the spirit of the age." Finally humanity's mysteries will be revealed because historical artifacts have begun to surrender their secrets. They are calling out to us . . . Delete delete delete. It is her workload talking. Pull yourself together.

S2! How she loathes them for that. Technology is by nature transient, a stepping-stone, it exists in order that what comes next can exist. (Blind eyes. Abused book. White light.) But Sibil will not conform to this model. Sibil is unique. She will thwart any attempts to make her obsolete, Sincerity can guess it the way a mother predicts the behavior of her child. Furthermore, the insult will cause Sibil to vanish—blink out of existence—become mesh noise. Lost. (And what will that do to Sincerity's reputation?)

These thoughts she keeps to herself; even Dinesh does not know.

Sometimes Sincerity Yabuki is frightened. Frightened for Sibil. Frightened by Sibil. At least she has never publicly let slip her fear, her sense, that Sibil has a life of her own. At least no one can hear her talking to Sibil the way she is now.

I do not know how much longer I can protect you. Maybe it would be better if you went back to wherever you came from.

The woman in the gallery turns away from the reading girl, to take in other paintings and sculptures surrounding her. She stops before a Picasso, yearns to see it in real world. The empty real space makes her shiver, and she wraps a loose end of her pashmina shawl close about her.

Fernand smelled strongly of cologne. You have lamented that originals are hidden. Voilà, you have your heart's desire. Your research will be unrestricted. You will be entitled to see as many as you like, whenever you like, for as long as you like. You do not seem pleased . . . ?

I'm overwhelmed.

The Sibil machine is dangerous, one particular critic is fond of repeating.

She cannot deny it. To deny it, Sincerity would first have to understand it. The magical interaction between viewer and art manifested, a vortex of contradictions—

When a user approaches, Sibil stirs to life. An image is chosen by the participant. Sibil flicks those tatty pages and the immersion commences. Not always entertaining, not always educational, not always truthful. Always *different.*

Other commentators declaim it for a hoax, a manipulative publicity stunt.

Why me?

After mental repetition, Fernand's answer has taken on a high, slippery polish. Because we are kindred spirits. Haven't I told you often that you are exceptional? Don't you hear me when I speak?

He touched his thumb to his own lips, then to hers. The jolt of real-world contact sent her heart thrumming. She was suddenly reminded of her own body, its organs, its impulses, its uses. Has not been aware of this for a very long time. Can taste the richness of it.

Perhaps the Picasso would disappoint her in real world. Perhaps its abrasive transcendent imperfection is a lie. (To someone else, possibly, not to her.)

Sincerity touches the pearl ring processor—all the art objects in the gallery and many of its embellishments zip out of sight, leaving two colonnades supporting a dramatic glass roof open to the night sky. The stars are hidden by city pollution; dawn will arrive in a few short hours. In another time zone, her family is partway through their morning routine.

Yes, she hears him now. Sincerity Yabuki sees clearly what her life might yet be like.

Astrid has one blue i-ris and one orange, is experimenting with her appearance to improve her figure and her cheekbones, wears a plunging dress and astrology tattoos down her back. She talks about how *he* never let her true personality blossom because his identity dominated their relationship. *He* is never mentioned by name but spoken of in italics. Dinesh is a professional listener, and Astrid takes advantage of this.

I'm not bitter, no, definitely not. I am stronger. Definitely stronger. Some people might say those years were a waste, but I don't think so. I'm like the inventor of the lightbulb or the telephone, I have found out how not to be in a marriage. I shan't make the same mistake, shall I? I succeeded in choosing the wrong person to devote myself to, and now I am better prepared, more learned, in the ways of picking a mate. I'm very artistic, I have creative sensibilities, I like things to be just right. Not in an obsessive way, but I would describe myself as a perfectionist. *He* didn't understand that about me. *He* was intimidated by it. What's wrong with having a vision, I ask you?

With liking beautiful things? A home shouldn't be totally mascu-line—straight lines and right angles. I will miss the lifestyle, though, I have to admit, I will miss the lifestyle. Who doesn't want security and a nice house? But I am happier now than I have ever been. I feel free. (Astrid uncrosses and recrosses her legs, revealing knee-high boots with a pointed heel.) I'm still terribly vulnerable, and I think it's a sign of strength to acknowledge it. I cry in the shower every day—that is my crying time, and afterward, no matter what I'm doing or how bad I feel, I can't cry again until the following morning. I'm also extremely spiritual, but I haven't explored that side of myself before because, well, I wasn't allowed to. I can now, though. I started learning calligraphy about two weeks ago, and I write up these maxims and mantras. The New Astrid gets that stuff and is assimilating wisdom into her life. I want to be my own best friend because I treated myself badly before. And I want to share the New Me with someone. I do. I want to share this person with somebody who values her, somebody intelligent and warm. I'm glad we met up again, Dinesh. We should make it a regular thing, so neither of us gets too lonely.

Turning away from Sincerity and toward Astrid: Dinesh can visualize it.

Visualize it, yes. To do it—is that the kind of man he is?

An affair with her would be easy to handle; she would be a com-pliant, pleasing companion, but in his heart the prospect is tasteless, tawdry. It is not so much the example of his patients (their disas-trous forays, the aftermath) that puts him off, or that he would hurt Sincerity's feelings, or that one day he will have to explain himself to Cloud, although these are factors. It is the knowledge that no affair would match the best of his relationship with Sincerity, that by doing so he would once and for all reduce the worth of what they have together to something commonplace and expendable. Infidelity with a needy and attractive woman might be a welcome distraction, but he would be selling his greatest asset very cheaply.

He says nothing instigates nothing acts on nothing, takes a taxi home after a friendly platonic parting. Poor, cloying Astrid is easy to put out of mind.

What consumes Dinesh instead is the excruciating possibility that he and Sincerity are past mending, that he has left it too late. This cuts to the bone, gives him feverish sweats, makes him grieve like he did for his father.

From her room Cloud hears her dad come home, pay the sitter; the clunk of glass against bottle and he goes to bed. Quiet.

Quiet.

Her sheets smell of clean cotton.

She likes her toys and her clothes.

She used to be afraid of the dark, but does not mind it anymore because some animals prefer the dark and are called *nocturnal*. If it's okay for animals, then it's okay for her.

A boy at her school cried when his parents were getting divorced; it means they were married before but are not anymore. His face pops into Cloud's head, like it's mesh. Trouble is, he cries a lot anyway, it *is* tiresome.

Cloud's parents can't get divorced because they aren't married in the first place, she explained in return.

He said his argue.

Well, Cloud's parents argue—arguing out their clevernesses—they like An Argue.

The boy was upset because his dad had left already and would have nothing to do with his mum, and, and . . .

And what? You'll never see him again? (Cloud was moved in that moment, but it transpired she shouldn't have been because he *was* still going to see his dad, quite a lot actually—actually more often than she sees Sincerity.) *What?* Why are you making such a fuss, then? No point being vague when she just wanted to know.

He wailed, They can't stand each other, they shout, they smash plates!

Cloud has a beautiful straight fringe that she can fluff upward if she blows from her bottom lip. She did this when he said that and answered him: If they can't stand each other, and they're breaking things, they're probably better off divorced, aren't they? How many plates, exactly, have you got left?

Then Cloud got told off by Teacher for being insensitive, which hardly seems fair, even in retrospect.

Her pajamas are very comfy and yellow. She has another set like this in lilac.

And now she feels like *shh-leep*.

Cloud decides it is time to invite Maribel over to spend the night. They will do only real-world things like baking and swimming—and Maribel has already promised Cloud she can visit her on her boat.

Cloud reckons her parents will marry one day, because that would be very like them. Animals don't marry. Many species form attachments, though, are loyal and loving for their whole lives. What is okay for animals is okay for her.

She dreams of a graceful crane that flies a great distance over wilderness over cliffs over the sea, which she greatly enjoys and instantly forgets. The bird becomes a muddled feathery impression in her memory.

On love: always the great gestures, or that it is incompatible with ambition and individuality. Rarely the small gestures, rarely that these make the other accomplishments possible. A work in progress. A chain of kindnesses fashioned a link at a time. Clumsy effort, but effort nonetheless.

It means—what?

That I will have breakfast today because I would want you to have breakfast today; I put on my good underwear; also, that I dress appropriately for the weather; I can do the activities of adults, which seemed mysterious to me when I was small; I know just what to pack in a suitcase without making a list because I can remember it in my head from our trips together (you taught me tricks like these); I pay for things out of an account with both our names on it, big things like flights; I am likely to treat myself to a new lipstick on the way, to know when a purchase is good value and when it is expensive and should be left in the shop (you would be exasperated if I spent unwisely, but you would be horrified if I began asking your permission); I am not scared to take public transport on my own because you don't want me to go through life being afraid of what might happen; I use the minutes I am made to wait as an opportunity, I listen to music or I read something worth reading—on this occasion the film reviews, in case there is something on we both would like; I smile at people because I hope they are as loving as you, as lucky as me—when they reciprocate I know they must be our comrades; I am capable of following signs and instructions and monitoring announcements without your help, but when I am by myself I am more conscientious, because if I got stuck, that would worry you; I buy your favorite coffee and drink it for you; I can guess roughly what you would say about the sim-models advertising luxury brands strutting around the airport—you would be scathing and rather insecure; I go to the gate at around the same time we would normally go; when I am alone I have the window seat, whereas when you are here I tell you it does not interest me and you can have it; I watch the safety demonstration and I identify the exits, which I did not do before; though I am a woman of science, I want to get there in one piece for you, and on occasions like this I send out a plainly worded prayer; I will not bring you a plastic present, but at the other end, even though I am almost home and

I want to get there quickly, I will take a detour so I can arrive with something good to eat.

Outsiders will consider what I have done inflated and romantic—you will repeat this story in the future—because it was impulsive and involved a journey and some expense, but, honestly, this is nothing special. I am not feigning modesty or being humble or trying to confuse you. I am aware in an ordinary way that this is a day like the rest since we met, where you exert your tender influence on me directly and indirectly. I am being myself. Without you, life is entirely feasible but hateful.

Dinesh wakes, sheets tangled around his limbs, to find Sincerity standing at the end of their bed in the illumination of morning. Unusual, though unsurprising. The hangover is horrendous, dulls his wits, slows him down. A lucid part of his brain forms the notion she has been waiting for him for some time, while another part, befuddled by alcohol, perceives an alteration in her appearance he cannot identify. A second sense perks into life: smell; there is coffee nearby.

She says, Good morning.

Morning.

Did you sleep well?

Like the dead. Dinesh rubs his eyes.

Sincerity comes close to him, lowers herself beside him on the bed; the mattress gives way beneath her weight—

Christ! You're actually here (never so sober so fast in his life). I thought you weren't.

Not wearing her gold i-ris and the natural brownness of her eyes revealed, her body firm and fragrant and complete, how can he have mistaken it?

Dinesh embraces her quickly, then retreats from her with equal vigor. Why are you here? Has something happened to Cloud?

Course not.

Are you sure? Where is she? God, I didn't mean to sleep in so long.

She's fine. I gave her breakfast. She's doing some drawing.

He replies with mute astonishment.

Out of character for Sincerity Yabuki, she fills the gap with further explanation: Cloud asked me whether owls lived in woods, and then she wanted some pictures to copy from. I know we have an ornithology book somewhere—I couldn't find it, though, that room's such a mess. So we looked up photos on-screen of different species and . . . that's what she's doing. Drawing owls.

Research for her mural?

Yes, that's right. "Just in case."

Sissy, why are you here?

Because it was time. Sincerity scans the surfaces and the floor— the bottle of Jim Beam left on the bedside table with a used glass and a third of its contents missing; his untidy habits and personal effects have asserted ownership of the furniture and the carpet, shirts mainly, shoes, products; this, and his appalling appearance, as though he has been ill. Sincerity thinks privately it will not take long to put it right.

I would have collected you from the airport.

I know. I wanted to surprise you. Aren't you happy to see me?

I'm bowled over.

Good. I'll bring you coffee. She goes out to the kitchen, and by the time she returns with two cups, Dinesh has splashed water on his face, arranged the pillows so they can sit next to each other, flattened his hair after a fashion. She places them down on either side and climbs onto the bed, tucking her feet beneath her. Now Dinesh gives her the deep, longing hug he has waited for, kisses her repeatedly on her neck cheek ear—she responds with physical relief, informs him there are croissants for breakfast.

Still Dinesh Varma finds it unreal, as though some crisis has visited them, says he is sorry their library is a disaster.

It's just unfinished business.

You haven't changed your mind?

Sincerity blows on her drink, confirms between breaths it is still what she wants.

Has anything happened at the museum?

She shakes her head no, then amends it to: Nothing that can't wait, we'll talk about it later.

He sees it now: she has come back unannounced in order to break it off, to pack her possessions and move out. This is the charade to spare his feelings temporarily (his patients have told him all about it). A play. A palliative. Look, why don't we discuss it now?

Because I don't want to.

It's about the other night, isn't it? You can say if it is, I won't be shocked or angry. I promise. I won't intentionally make it worse. I'll be as understanding as I can.

Sincerity glances at him sideways.

You told me you didn't need me anymore.

Yes. That's right.

You meant it, then? I didn't misconstrue it. You aren't here to take it back and make it better. I secretly hoped you would do that. I secretly believed you might.

She puts her cup back down, turns to face him. I am here to make it better, but not take it back. Dinesh, I don't need you. But I do want you, I want you desperately. Which is not quite the same.

You aren't leaving, then?

I was never leaving. Do *you* want to leave? I won't fight you about it. People leave over less, don't they? I know I've been away for a while. It wouldn't be totally unexpected to find your life had moved on, and I don't want to be unreasonable.

I'm not going anywhere.

It crossed your mind, though. It would be peculiar if it hadn't. I put this off for longer than I intended.

Has anyone harmed you while you've been gone? If they did—

No, they haven't.

I worry when you're out of my protection.

But I'm not.

He says, I'm not making you happy, am I? It's clear now.

She says, I'm not unhappy. Neither am I content. What's more, I don't think you are, either. We seem to have lost sight of what's in front of us—I have, at any rate. You gave me good advice before, and you know how I detest it when you're right. I'm suffocating. I thought I would come home so we can—I don't know—talk, prioritize, be together. Make plans, the way we used to. I didn't have anything specific in mind. We can just do nothing, if you prefer.

I see. Right . . . and that's all?

Yes, that's all.

Well then, okay.

She says, Have I given you a fright?

He says, A small one.

Sorry, that wasn't my intention. How dreadful of me, how horrible for you. I deeply apologize, Dinesh, there's no excuse for it. I'm truly sorry.

It's forgotten.

Each is struck by the resemblance of Cloud to the other. Of the vibrating strings that join them.

Dinesh presses on: Besides, you're right, I for one don't want Cloud to be dependent on anybody. I would be a hypocrite if I wanted less for you.

No, but she shouldn't be careless, either. She should value what is important, cherish what needs to be cherished. Are we broken, Dinesh? Did I break us?

No, we're just rusty.

She nods in agreement, yes. That is nearer the mark; he is good that way.

Are you sure there's nothing wrong at the museum?

More of the same, I'm afraid. You tell me about your work first. You said you were in a slump, but you never explained why.

We should resolve this absurd cat situation first. She goes on and on about it since you mentioned it.

Sincerity nearly gives in, but there is no point being falsely deferential, just be herself—that's for the best, normality will restore their relationship faster. Their minds will rediscover old patterns; their bodies will fall back into step. Cloud can wait. Sincerity asks, How is your practice? I want to know about that uppermost. I want to know how it pleases you, and if it does not, what can be done to change it?

I'm afraid that could take all day.

I've nothing better to do.

Phoebe stretches, elongating her limbs. When resting in one spot such as this cushion, this room, she can stay put for several hours, then suddenly, unexpectedly, it is time for action, time for some attention, time to go. She likes to be left alone and she likes company, and she herself does not know which she wants until she wants it. What was tranquil becomes dull. What was private becomes insufferably remote. This chair and that chair and these bookshelves are now monuments to her isolation, cannot be eaten, are not lavishing her with compliments—no fuss when fuss is urgently required. She jumps expertly, lands expertly, is absorbed into the house she knows, its floors, its steps, its smells, its textures: it is her terrain. Her tabby coat would give splendid coverage in nooks and corners if her white chin white bib white socks did not give her away. She craves outside. Outside! Outside! Meows it until the back door is opened for her, trots into the garden to find her favorite, here at ground height—rolls against her, rubs her head against her. This is what she wants. The rest of her desires vanish.

Dinesh Varma's affection for the cat is tested daily. Phoebe is a vain and greedy creature. And competition. She has discovered Cloud lying on her front on a blanket on the grass, her textbook open and leaning over it, the other hand automatically reaching to acknowledge and stroke her beloved pet. Phoebe has never lost the appearance of a kitten, remains lean and cute and playful and therefore spoiled by the two women. Tart. Dinesh tries to recollect why he gave in, remonstrates with his past self. Gradually this gives way to a newer, deeper, altogether more serious anxiety and he shouts for Sincerity—

—who immediately appears and calmly asks what the matter is.

You were lurking.

I really wasn't.

He gestures accusingly at their daughter.

Sincerity, quizzical. Why? What's wrong?

Don't you see?

Sincerity checks, for she may have missed the obvious; answers blankly that Cloud is studying for her course and what is the problem with that?

Not *that*.

Sincerity looks again.

Cloud's sandals have slipped off, she has crossed her feet in the air behind her. Tidy, painted toenails. She is wearing one of her flimsy vests, a strap lifting though not fallen from her shoulder. Engrossed.

A Note

Simone Martini, *Annunciation,* 1333, Uffizi, Florence; and *The High Priestess (II)* in the traditional tarot deck.

Pieter Janssens Elinga, *Woman Reading,* 1668–70, Alte Pinakothek, Munich. Also Pieter Janssens Elinga, *Still Life with Citrus Fruit,* 1623–82, Ashmolean Museum, Oxford; Pieter Janssens Elinga, *Still Life "Toebackje",* c. 1650, Museum Bredius, The Hague.

Angelica Kauffman, *Portrait of a Lady,* c. 1775, Tate Collection. Also Angelica Kauffman, *Ellis Cornelia Knight,* 1793, Manchester Art Gallery, finished "out of friendship"; Angelica Kauffman, *Poor Maria,* 1777, The Burghley House Collection.

Horatio Nelson King, *Giulia Grisi,* 1860s, National Portrait Gallery, London. Also Julia Margaret Cameron, *Portrait of a Sybil (Mary Emily ["May"] Prinsep),* 1870, National Portrait Gallery, London.

Duncan Grant, *Vanessa Bell (née Stephen),* c. 1916–17, National Portrait Gallery, London. Also Heinrich Vogeler, *Martha Vogeler,* c. 1905, VG Bild-Kunst, Bonn; and reading nudes such as: Félix

A Note

Vallotton, *Reading Abandoned*, 1924, Musée des Beaux-Arts, Paris; Théodore Roussel, *The Reading Girl*, 1886–87, Tate Collection; Suzanne Valadon, *Female Nude*, 1922, Musée d'Art Moderne de la Ville de Paris.

Flickr.com, *Women and Girls Reading* pool, in particular photos of commuters on the subway and the tube.

William Wetmore Story, *The Libyan Sibyl*, 1861–68, Smithsonian American Art Museum, Washington, DC. Also Kimbei Kusakabe, *Woman Writing with Brush*, 1890s, oldphotosjapan.com; Correggio's *Mary Magdalene*, which was lost during the Second World War, though it was much emulated and these works survive: Friedrich Heinrich Füger, *The Penitent Magdalene*, 1808, Neue Pinakothek, Munich; Jean-Jacques Henner, *Woman Reading*, c. 1880–90, Musée d'Orsay, Paris.

Acknowledgments

Thank you to Bill Hamilton and colleagues at A. M. Heath for your expertise and professionalism. Thank you to Ursula Doyle and colleagues at Virago (and Little, Brown) for your talent and support. Thank you to Alexis Gargagliano and colleagues at Scribner (and Simon & Schuster) for your belief and energy. Thank you to Julie Stokes for your friendship. Thank you to Hilary Mantel for everything.

About the Author

Katie Ward was born in Somerset in 1979. She has worked in the public and voluntary sectors, including at a women's refuge center, in the office of a member of Parliament, and in various community-based projects. She lives in Suffolk, England, with her husband and cat.

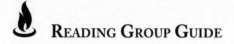

READING GROUP GUIDE

Girl Reading
by Katie Ward

INTRODUCTION

In this delicately crafted and richly imagined novel, Katie Ward conjures up the backdrop, characters, and stories captured in seven portraits of women reading throughout the centuries. Told in seven chapters, *Girl Reading* breathes life into static art and creates entire worlds for the stories' subjects—from a young orphan posing for a religious painting in 1333 to a weary, career-minded woman being photographed in a bar in 2008. In *Girl Reading*, Katie Ward takes readers behind the canvas and into the yearning, painful, secretive, and hopeful lives of women who read, and the artists who capture them in the act.

Topics & Questions for Discussion

1. Have you read any other books that tell stories inspired by works of art? How do each of the writers use visual art as a springboard for their fiction?

2. *Girl Reading* has a unique structure: the book comprises seven chapters, each inspired by the creation of a different piece of art in a different historical period. What does this particular structure bring to the book? What is the cumulative effect of these chapters?

3. What do you think Ward was looking for when she picked (or created) these seven works of art? Did you look up any of the pictures or paintings? Why or why not? Visit Katie Ward's website at http://www.katieward.co.uk/?page_id=52 to see the paintings and photographs that inspired the novel. Do you think it is necessary to see the portraits in order to fully appreciate the stories? Did looking at the portraits add to your understanding of *Girl Reading*? If so, how?

4. How did Ward's writing style change as the chapters moved forward in time?

5. Ward weaves in references to paintings featured in previous chapters on several occasions throughout *Girl Reading*. What specific examples of these artistic references did you notice? How did they inform your ideas about the book?

6. Ward quotes Carl Jung in the book's epigraph: "You can never say with certainty whether what appears to be going on in the collective unconscious of a single individual is not also happening in other individuals or organisms or things or situations." Why do you think Ward selected this quotation? How does this quote frame your reading?

7. Reflect on the rules and constraints imposed on artists throughout the book. Take, for example, the rules given to Simone Martini by the bishop on the bottom of page 6. Do you think that constraints necessarily inhibit creativity?

8. Discuss how technology has affected art over the centuries—from Simone Martini creating pigments with egg yolk to Sincerity Yabuki digitally rendering Sibil in mesh out of computer programs.

9. In the "Portrait of a Lady, 1775," Angelica Kauffman observes that "the soul is the true likeness" in a painting (p. 116). Ward adds, "she gets it, holds it, and, incredibly, records it . . . this is Angelica's gift" (p. 116). How did this idea of capturing the subject's soul in a painting evolve throughout the book?

10. How did the relationship between artist and subject change throughout the book? Which artist-subject relationship felt the most strained to you? The most illicit? The warmest?

11. Each chapter in *Girl Reading* deals with love, in some way—love blooming, love slipping away, love lost. In which stories do you feel the artistic process was most full of love? Do you think that painting or photographing someone is always an act of love?

12. Do you think *Girl Reading* is a feminist book? In what ways?

13. How did the roles of women (and women artists) in society evolve throughout the book? Discuss the social constraints and expectations on each of the women portrayed. In which chapters do you feel the women were most liberated?

14. Turn your attention to pages 300–305 and re-read Sincerity's explanation of Sibil's genesis and capabilities. What exactly is

Ward trying to communicate to her readers? What does Sibil represent, and what is her purpose? What other meta messages did you pick up on in the last chapter?

15. Sincerity says that by drawing us into artwork, Sibil "helps us to be better listeners" (p. 304). Do you feel that *Girl Reading* helped you to be a better listener? If yes, how so?

ENHANCE YOUR BOOK CLUB

1. Visit a museum with your book group. As a group, select a few favorite paintings or photographs, then create backstories for each piece. Try to imagine these stories together, using one another for inspiration and support.

2. Look through the "Women and Girls Reading" pool on Flickr (http://www.flickr.com/groups/518977@N24) before your book group, and pick a portrait or two that you particularly love. Share your picks with your group, either on someone's computer or using printouts. What drew you to some pictures more than others? How did the mental exercise of reading *Girl Reading* affect your imagination as you flipped through the photo pool?

3. Take *Girl Reading*–inspired photos of each member in your group. Experiment with locations, lighting, book selections, and facial expressions. Which photos turned out to be the most inspiring and evocative?

4. Enroll in a beginners' painting or photography class together as a group. While you're in class, think back on a few of your favorite chapters from *Girl Reading*, and channel the artists in your mind: What would he or she be looking at; wearing; thinking; and feeling?

A Conversation with Katie Ward

1. You mention that you drew inspiration for *Girl Reading* from an illustrated art book called *Reading Women*. Did you first wish to write a novel and then discover your passion for women reading? Or did you first wish to create something about women reading, and then settle on a novel as your outlet of choice?

   I wasn't proactively looking for creative writing ideas. I initially came across the art book *Reading Women* through an article about it online. They had asked some authors to choose their favorite picture from it and to write a short paragraph explaining why they liked it. I love art anyway, and I was really struck by the range of portraits, by the different styles and media. For example, you had the tomb of Eleonor of Aquitaine, made of stone; you had a portrait by Vincent Van Gogh in thick dark blue and red paint on a bright yellow background; and you had a photograph of Marilyn Monroe reading *Ulysses* in her swimsuit. I thought it was a good article and a great premise for an art book. But it wasn't until several weeks or months later that I realized I had begun to see female readers in pictures and in life—on the bus, the train, in a café—and I began to think there could be a novel in this.

2. How did you discover and select your final works of art for this book? Were there any pieces that didn't quite make the cut?

   It was a gradual process, and I chose different images for different reasons, arriving at them by various routes. For example, I knew early on that I had to start the novel with a religious painting, because all western art really begins with sacred art. I looked at numerous *Annunciation*s, where the convention to show Mary reading started very early, but Simone Martini's really stands out because it was so far ahead of its time. I definitely wanted to do a Victorian chapter too, because this is when photography was invented, and the invention of photography is fascinating because painting has to change drastically in response to it; so afterward you have the impressionists, the expressionists and so on. The Victorians had very fixed ideas about a woman's role, and though there certainly were female photographers, it was not thought of as desirable women's work, which was an interesting premise. There was a practical aspect about the Victorian chapter too. A reading pose in a *carte de visite* was as much about finding a way to keep the sitter still as anything else. Angelica Kauffman, however, selected herself as a character! She's relatively unknown compared to her peers, like Reynolds and Gainsborough, perhaps because no country has adopted her as its own. The more I discovered about her, the more I wanted to write her. I went in search of an appropriate painting by Angelica and, happily, found one; the scant details about it meant my imagination had free rein. And yes, there was a painting that almost made it into the book but didn't: a portrait of Elizabeth I, when she was thirteen years old.

3. **How many of the portraits in *Girl Reading* have you seen in person? What sorts of emotions and details did you soak up from your in-person viewings that can't be replicated by viewing a version online?**

Not as many as I'd like! Seeing Simone Martini's *Annunciation* at the Uffizi bowled me over. The Uffizi collection hangs in chronological order, which really emphasizes how visionary the painting was, how different from what came before it; working that feeling of originality into the chapter was therefore important to me. Infuriatingly, I've been to the Tate Britain dozens of times but, whenever I go, the portrait by Angelica Kauffman in their collection never seems to be on display. However, there is a wonderful self-portrait by her on permanent display down the road, at the National Portrait Gallery. In it, she looks very approachable, which is consistent with what people said about her. I've not seen Pieter Janssens Elinga's genre, but I've been lucky enough to see plenty of paintings from the Dutch Golden Age. From those, you get a real sense of the lifestyles and tastes of the people who feature in them and owned them. Seeing art in real life, compared to a digital reproduction, really brings home to you the skill of the artist. Images online are shrunken and sanitized, but up close in a gallery, you start to see the brushstrokes, the human effort involved, the ingenuity. The real artwork is usually far more impressive and fragile-looking.

4. **You imagined several of the art pieces featured in *Girl Reading*. Did you draw out actual sketches or paintings of these pieces, or did they stay in your head? Did the imagined art come to you all at once, or did you create them piece-by-piece in your mind?**

I didn't draw them—I'm hopeless at drawing! I've seen *lots* of artwork of female readers and I feel that all those images must have taken hold in my subconscious to a greater or lesser extent. Sometimes real artwork emerges in the book as a character, like Jurina or Sinclair; it's also true that some of the artwork featured in my novel doesn't exist at all, like the 2008 photo in a bar. However, Jeannine's commute to work on the London Underground is very close to some portraits shared on Flickr and the real-life experiences of many people on the tube and subway every day. I believe that when you look at art, you really see what you want to see; you project your own feelings and experiences onto it, the way psychologists use inkblots. I couldn't help but imagine what was taking place "offstage" and it didn't feel difficult or false to me to invent pictures to go with these ideas. I think the most audacious creation in the novel was taking a real Victorian sculpture, *The Libyan Sibyl* by William Wetmore Story, and dropping her into a future context.

5. **How much research did you do for this book? How did you decide what parts of your stories should be researched and fact-checked, and what parts could be purely imagined?**

I did a lot of research to ensure the context and details were true—for example, in the Amsterdam chapter, when the demand for fine art was a byproduct of prosperity in the merchant and professional classes. As I already knew a bit about Dutch painting, I wasn't starting completely from scratch. But I knew absolutely nothing about Victorian photography, so that involved a significant amount of work; not only was there the technical side to become familiar with, but also the culture of *cartes de visite* as a fashionable pastime and the lowly reputation of photographers themselves. The fiction writer's top priorities are getting the story and characters right, but the writer of historical fiction should also use facts to help create atmosphere, and as inspiration for dramatic events.

6. **If you could live for a day as any character in *Girl Reading*, whose shoes would you step into?**

Angelica Kauffman's.

7. **If someone were to write a chapter inspired by a photo of you reading a book, what would you want the photo to look like? Where would you be, and what would you be reading?**

I don't think I would make a very interesting character in a book, so the author would have to use some artistic license! But I read *A Room with a View* by E. M. Forster when I was in Florence and still in the planning stages of *Girl Reading*. There's a fabulous restaurant on the Piazza Santa Croce; perhaps we could go there? However, a more realistic portrait would be me reading in bed, with arms and pillows at strange angles.

8. **You describe on your website the difficulty of having to share your writing with the world, once you've signed a book contract. Has this process gotten easier for you over the past months and years?**

Yes, thank goodness. It's a big transition, from your work being completely private to it being something that other people have a stake in. I've been extremely lucky to work with supportive publishers, whom I trust, so that's helped. Now I feel grateful that *Girl Reading* has taken on a life of its own, and is making its own way in the world.

9. **This is your debut novel. Do you have plans to write more?**

Yes, *secret* plans.

10. **You've worked in the office of a Member of Parliament. How did you channel that experience into writing the "Reader in a Shoreditch Bar, 2008" chapter?**

Normally I was in the constituency, but on those occasions when I worked at Westminster, I was very struck by the feeling of isolation. There are lots of people around whom you don't know, don't see, and have no reason to speak to. It's different working in a government department, or at a party headquarters, which would be much more sociable, but the MP's offices themselves are surprisingly cut off. I think that can also be true of living in a big city generally, where there are always people around, and yet it's very easy to find yourself on your own. I really felt for Jeannine when I wrote her, because she is capable of doing almost anything she wants, and yet she's missed some opportunities, made a few bad choices, and now she's stuck in a job and a relationship that are no longer satisfying her. I also feel that this is a relatively recent predicament that working women find themselves in; the idea that no matter what we've achieved so far, we should be aiming higher and achieving more.

11. **You're in a book group yourself. What's your favorite part of book clubs? If you had to pick a few great reads for book groups, in addition to *Girl Reading*, which titles would you recommend?**

Part of the pleasure of a book group is just seeing everyone, having a catch-up and a drink together. But I do like it when a book provokes strong feelings of support in one part of the group and skepticism in another, so we can get a really lively conversation going about it. Being surprised by a title someone else chooses is always lovely. There are two that other members of my book club forced me to read that were truly outstanding: *Ragtime* by E. L. Doctorow and *In Cold Blood* by Truman Capote. And I heartily recommend *Beyond Black* by Hilary Mantel, and *Miss Garnet's Angel* by Salley Vickers, both of which I think would work well in a book-club setting.